DELPHIN HOMECOMING 1936 – 1949
BOOK ONE

DELPHIN HOMECOMING 1936 – 1949

Book One

BY

VICTOR SUNSTAR

Cover Art by: GARTH www.artbygarth.com

WWW.DELPHINHOMECOMING.COM

Published by Waldenbooks Publishing

ISBN 978-1-63498-212-2

Printed in the United States of America

Acknowledgement

With Respect, Awe, And Thanks For Their So Inspiring Me To

Visualize, Research, Write And Create… Jason Katims - Roswell Tv Series Donald P. Bellisario - J A G Tv Series Leslie Bohem - Taken Tv Series

Steven Spielberg For…

Et And Close Encounters Of The Third Kind And Taken

Tiare White - A Lovely Humane Being, Healer And Writer, Director, Prodcer

Who believed in me, encouraged, motivated and fully understood me And Also To My Planetarium Co-Producer and Amigo

JOHN YOUNG

Fleet Planetarium

And to an incredible military historian, creator and director of the US Army Camp Roberts - Military History Museum

Gary McMaster

And Especially To My Shipmate and Pao Joe Ciokon

USS Midway Aircraft Carrier Museum

List Of Characters: 1936 – 2016

Delphinians

- King Arthur – 1912–1986 (74) Queen Glinda – 1916–Princess Selena – 1932–
- Delphinoids – bio androids - 6 male and 6 female units or as many more can be incubated as needed
- Shiri – alien girlfriend to President Truman Karen – alien girlfriend to Howard Hughes
- Altair – alien husband to Sara – married – 1953–1986 Embry – alien husband to Amelia Earhart
- The Amadores – Creators Of The Universe

Earth People - Major And Minor Character

- President Harry Truman – lead Commander Sara Winchester USN – lead Howard Hughes – lead
- Amelia Earhart – Ailema - lead President Dwight Eisenhower – lead President Ronald Reagan – lead
- Ernest Hemingway
- Capt. Mike Nelson,USA – husband to Selena
- Capt. Davie Jones, USN – USS Starfish - submarine capt. – bad guy CPO Joe Ciokon, USN – USS Midway aircraft carrier
- Capt. Joe Stoner, USN – USS Midway aircraft carrier Commander Frank Stryker, USN – Executive Officer USS Midway aircraft carrier

- Capt. Peter Tamaryn, USN – Water Island, USVI – base Adjt William Randolph Hearst – bad guy
- Marion Davies
- President John F. Kennedy President William Clinton President Barrack Obama
- Gatita – Selena's six toed kitten – 1948-1964

Story Locations – 194 8– 2016

- Florida – Key West and Miami San Juan Puerto Rico
- Alien Starship – "Lifestar" USS Midway – aircraft carrier
- Water Island and St. Thomas, USVI, Caribbean Davis Monthan Air Force base, Tucson, Arizona Fort Huachuca, Arizona and Mustang Mountains AREA 51 – Nevada
- Washington DC and Camp David Hawaii
- Howland Island – western Pacific

California

- US Army, Camp Roberts – Bradley Hearst Castle -San Simeon Vandenberg Air Force Base - Lompoc Santa Barbara and Montecito
- Univ. Calif. St. Barbara – Isla Vista
- Westmont College – Carroll Observatory - Montecito Ojai – Villanova Prep and Thatcher School
- Ventura – and the Rincon for surfing and Brooks movie studios Los Angeles – Union Station and Chinatown and Olivera Street Los Angeles - Griffith Observatory and Mt. Wilson Observatory Hollywood – RKO and Paramount Studios
- Burbank – Walt Disney Studios and Vahalla Memorial Park and the Portal of Folded Wings – Memorial plaque of Amelia Earhart Disneyland – Anaheim – 1955 - present
- Marineland of the Pacific – Pacific Palisades – Alien Dolphin Research 1954 to 1987
- La Jolla – Scripts Inst. Oceanography
- Long Beach, Queen Mary Hotel - 1967 to present Long Beach Aquarium
- San Diego – Balboa Park and Fleet Planetarium and Seaworld
- San Jose – Winchester Mystery House and Rosicrucians Egyptian Museum Lick Observatory – Mt Hamilton – San Jose
- Monterey – Monterey Bay Aquarium and Cannery Row
- The MOON – farside alien base – Van de Graaff crater

Chile – South America

- Arica – Morro de Arica San Pedro de Atacama La Serena
- Santiago Valparaiso Quillota
- Concepcion and Lota - Chiflon de Diablo Coal Mine

- Breath of the Devil Coal Mine Frutillar – sacred spiritual energies
- Puerto Montt and Puerto Varas – Lake Llanquihue y Osorno Volcano Punta Arenas and Puerto Natales
- Patagonia - Tierra del Fuego
- Picada de Zancudo – Delph Starship secret base – Tierra del Fuego Chilean Antarctica

Argentina – South America

- Buenos Aires Bahia Blanca Bariloche Usuhauia
- PERU – SOUTH AMERICA
- LIMA and CALLIO MIRA FLORES
- CHORILLOS - OBSERVATORY and PLANETARIUM AREQUIPA -
- CHARACTERS FAMILY TREE
- King Arthur and Queen Glinda Princess Selena
- Selena and Mike Nelson marry 1956 Daughter – Jane (named after Jane Russell)
- Son – Howard (named after Howard Hughes)
- Amelia Earhart and Embry – Amelia joins pod 2 July 1937 childless
- Sara Winchester and Altair – marry 1953
- Daughter – Athole (named after Sara's mother) Son – Harry (named after Harry Truman)

Note To Readers

There are several notations of Latitude and Longitude in case you want to go to Google Earth or play with your GPS units. HAVE FUN !

The USS MIDWAY CV-41 is now an extraordinary NAVY Museum docked at 910 Harbor Dr x Broadway in San Diego California. The Frame and Bulkhead and Hatch Designators in this story are accurate for you to go visit their actual locations aboard the Midway. The Fantail Café has some awesome food - including the best hot dog on the 7 seas.

But, unfortunately, no hot dogs nor peanuts are available aboard the Lifestar starship galley - which is presently hidden in a 50,000 year old, false cliff side hanger at:

52* 12' 38.74" S

71* 39' 12.74" W

The Little White House is now a Historic Museum along with The Hemingway House and Museum in Key West Florida.

You can also go enjoy lunch at the actual Peppe's Café where Glinda, Selena and Sara celebrated Selena's 16th birthday in 1948

If you visit the still operating Miami Seaquarium you can see where Selena jumped in the giant tank and freed her earthly dolphin cousins. But, don't ask the management about that because they are still pissed off ever since 1948 at losing their 8 captive dolphins…

If you visit St. Thomas, Charlotte Amelie in the US Virgin Islands you can also take the launch over to Water Island and play on the beaches as did the Delphinians back in 1948.

In upcoming Book Two – Delphin California Dreaming – You must go to ARMY Camp Roberts to visit their Military History Museum. Its only open on Thursdays and Saturdays. Camp Roberts is where President Truman and Commander Sara Winchester took their Delphinans for their final social orientations and training - Dec 1948 until the start of the Korean war in 1951. Its located about 18 miles north of Paso Robles on California Hwy 101.

Also, don't miss Hearst Castle along Hwy 1 north of Morro Bay.

But, they absolutely will not let you see where Hearst hid the bodies…

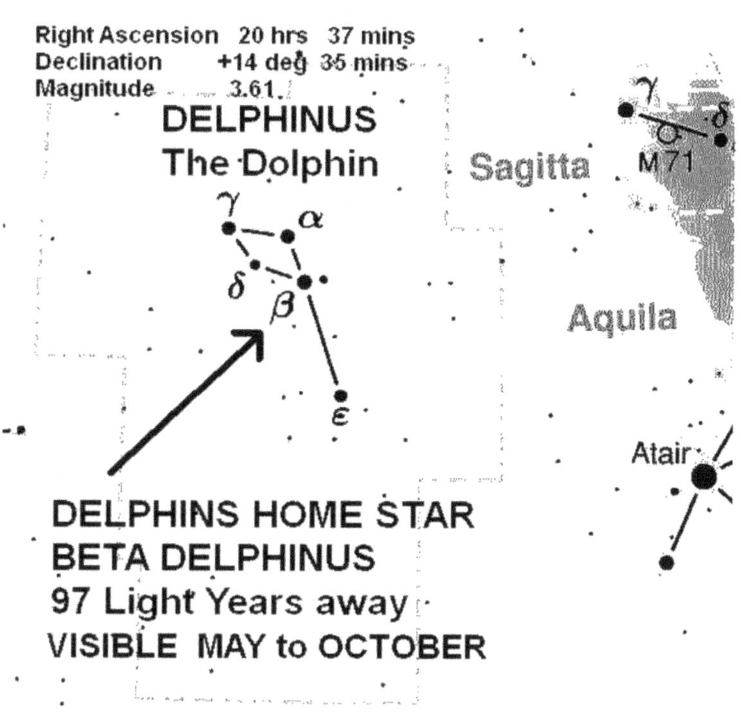

BETA DELPHINUS β DELPHINUS lies at a distance of 97 light years, 564 trillion miles away from EARTH. The speed of light is 186,000 miles per second. So, when we look at β Del we are seeing it as it was 97 years ago. The Delphinains traveled for 372 years at a speed of 5,813 miles per second - sacrificing five generations to reach Earth in 1936.. The actual star system of β Del is a spectroscopic binary with a pair of F stars which orbit each other with a period of 26.66 years. The system is about 1.8 billion years old. Our SUNstar is about 5 billion years old. In 1814 Italian Astronomer Niccolo Venator, as a star catalog joke, gave it the name of Rotanev which is his last name spelled backwards

Prologues

South Eastern Arizona

50,000 BC about 10pm with a first quarter moon.

The Mustang mountains 3.8 miles north east of what is now known as Elgin Arizona in the north end of the Mustang Mountains and Mt Bruce, at times called the Biscuit - its northern most 6,087 foot peak at 31* 43', 13.43" N x 110* 30' 05.13" W with its outsized southwest facing vertical 300 foot cliff face.

A small nameless prehistoric tribe, ancient ancestors of the Chiricahua and Mescalero Apaches was gathered around their mesquite campfire. They were frantically dancing, chanting, drumming and singing to keep away the gigantic evil black crow apparition that they were always in deep fear of. Now once again, they heard the thunder like rumbling of the mysterious cliff face nest that was again opening, sliding down to release the giant gaage (flying black crow). Many times over the last years, this band of hunters and gatherers of pine nuts had seen and felt the mind, heart and body thrumming of the giant starship as it exited and then days later, always at night, returned into its colossal magic mountain nest.

Aboard the ancient alien starcraft the cute, relaxed, smiling human form female commander, telepathed to her crew of 130, "We will hover here for a few moments to be sure to frighten that small band of humans who live down there at the tributary head of the little river south west of our cliff face base." (Later named the Babocomari river).

She also announced to the crew that they were going to the lovely and scenic three and a half by three mile lake at 37* 15' 53.39" N x 115* 47'

51.67 W to explore the mountain ranges along the lakeshores to the west with the idea of building another starship base. Seven of the remainder of her crew was still in their underground backside moon base located at the Van de Graaff crater.

She telepathed her navigator to set a course of 353.04 and to keep an altitude of 4000 feet. Almost at the same instant they accelerated, a large 164 foot (50 meter) 300,000 ton meteor entered the atmosphere above what was later known as northern Arizona.

They were still accelerating at 3562 miles per hour above what was later known as the Winslow Arizona area when in a 1 in 17 billion chance, the blazing meteor hit them at about 45,000 miles per hour. It instantly shattered their 300 foot starship to smithereens and then slammed into the plateau below creating a 30 megaton blast that made a major 1.2km (180 mile) deep meteor crater and obliterated all animals, plants, and any pre- historic humans within a 1,500 km (932 mile) radius.

Delphinian starship - Lifestar On the command bridge Velocity 3,348,000 miles per hour 10 light years away from Earth Earth date: March 21, 1903 Android, Delnoid 1, beamed telepathically to their fifth generation pod leader… "Excuse me, we have begun picking up some extremely powerful radio frequency bursts which are registering at an impossible electromotive force of sometimes up to 20 million volts! Whoever, somewhere in our target sol system, flashed these apparently directed energies out into space, must have somehow had to of been generating output voltages with at least an astounding 1,100 amperes of antenna current!"

The telepathic voiceless pod leader also on the starship's bridge squeaked sharply, clicked rapidly just like a dolphin and telepathically beamed back to Delnoid 1, "Very well, please keep me advised if there are any changes in this amazing signal. Continue on course for the yellow star system."

The Delphinian commander squeaked once, smiled, clicked softly and telepathically beamed to all 172 surviving now despondent crew aboard Lifestar, "This could be very encouraging."

He paused, clicked softly and thoughtfully for a few seconds and beamed, "Now, after sacrificing almost five generations, we know for sure that there are, at least, some technologically capable life forms on that water world planet."

Table of Contents

CHAPTER 1 AMELIA

The Place – The Pacific Ocean – just north of the equator Longitude 176 degrees 28 minutes 27.37seconds West Between Howland and Baker Islands

The depth: 13,526 ft.

The Date: 2 July 1937 – early evening

Aboard the submerged Delphinian starship, Life star

As she groggily awoke, Amelia Earhart slowly realized that she was in a bed, a very nice, soft, comfortable and perfectly supporting bed. But as she reached down to feel the sheet and its mattress, all she felt was air and she thought,

"How can this be?" As she tried to open her eyes and focus, she began to fuzzily see people standing around her, and in her head and body she felt very powerful, loving and healing energies. How nice she thought and just as she was peacefully dozing back to sleep, she thought she heard, "Squeak, squeak and then some strange rapid clicks. Echoing only in her mind she sensed, "Amelia certainly has had some impressive and adventurous life dreams…"

The next day, she once more returned from her serene sleep. She again felt for the comforting velvety sleep sack and her comfortable mattress but once more, she realized with a bit of a start that she was feeling only air under her and she sensed that there was a soft, warm, kind of sensual, fuzzy sack like blanket enveloping her nude body. As she slowly opened her eyes, she again felt very loving, healing, soothing energies. She could more clearly see the people around her bed. There was a lovely lady touching her fingertips to each side of her head and another woman was holding her right hand. She heard in her head, "Amelia, Amelia can you hear me, can you feel me? Can you see me?"

She groggily nodded her head, smiled slightly and whispered, "Oh yes…I can hear you…"

She opened her eyes more fully and realized that these people in silver and also some in gold flight suits were helping her. She struggled to return to more consciousness and awoke gasping and screamed, "Oh God! Oh no!" as she remembered that the last thing she saw was the ocean rushing up to her plane. She remembered hearing and feeling the terrifying impact and the loud wrenching and tearing of metal then the noise of cold rushing sea water. She then heard in her head, "Amelia, I am Glinda and you are now waking up in our, uh hospital after we rescued you from your plane crash.

Do you remember what happened, dear lady?"

Suddenly Amelia drew in and let out a loud quick breath and hoarsely said,

"Oh my God, Fred and I had to ditch after we ran out of fuel. Am I

aboard the Coast Guard cutter Itasca?"

Glinda, still beaming calming energies to her, flowed into her mind, "Yes, dear lady. You are remembering what happened, Amelia. We felt your terror as your plane crashed in the sea above us and we quickly surfaced to rescue you."

Amelia tried to sit up but Glinda gently pushed her back down as she echoed in Amelia's mind. "Amelia, where were you flying to?"

Amelia recalling more clearly said, "We were headed for Howland Island on the second from the last segment of my around the world flight and we had taken off over 22 hours before from Lae in Papua, New Guinea. We were really afraid because we were dangerously low on fuel and I could not hear any radio or understand the Morse code responses from Itasca. And, even at 1000 feet, we could not see tiny Howland Island through the persistent low marine layer clouds covering the sea." Again Amelia tried to sit up and again asked, "Are we aboard the USS Itasca?"

She felt Glinda saying in her head, "No Amelia, you are now aboard Lifestar, our, uh, our ship, and we will take care of you and when you are better, take you to Howland Island or anywhere in the world that you want to go. Now you must rest and absorb our healing energies and these nutritious medical fluids flowing into your blood stream. Please rest now dear earth woman, recuperate and when you are stronger, we will then fill you in on all that has happened." As Amelia again sank into the soothing healing energies, she mumbled, "What about Fred. What's happened to Fred, is he ok?" And just as she began to slip into a deeper sleep she winced as she grimly remembered hearing Fred screaming from his rear navigation compartment, "My God we're going to die Amelia. We're going to buy the farm!"

When Amelia awoke again she still remembered Fred's dreadful screams. She also felt soothing, loving, sympathetic energies as she realized that a lovely woman was holding her right hand and the woman who had talked to her, was sitting on the other side of her bed, gently holding her other hand. But again, she was anxious feeling only warm air under her nude body.

She opened her eyes fully, looked fearfully at the woman on her left and asked, "Where am I? Who in blazes are you?" While she asked these questions, she continued to feel down each side of her body, and frantically asked, "Why is there no mattress under me?" As she became more fully awake, she began to be really alarmed and wondered, "Is this a dream? Am I dead?" To her further astonishment she heard in her head, "No dear Amelia, you are not dead. You are ok and you will soon be completely well again. But you were also having some serious stomach problems, so, our medicos cured that for you. Are you feeling better now than before your crash?"

Amelia then noticed that her stomach felt fine and there wasn't any acid or burning feeling anymore. She smiled gratefully and said, "My gosh, you are quite right, my stomach is feeling just fine now."

The head medico holding her right hand beamed, "That's really great Amelia. I am sure that after some more balanced nutrition, you will feel totally fit soon. Please try and rest again now and tomorrow when you are stronger and healthier we will explain everything to you." Glinda clicked softly and soothingly and again beamed calming and deep sleep inducing energies into Amelia.

Glinda then heard in her head a worried telepathic question from her husband, Arthur, up on the starship's bridge. "How is our guest doing Glinda? Has she recovered consciousness yet? What in the name of Amador are we going to tell her?"

Glinda mentally beamed back to her husband, the co leader of their pod, "I think with this visitor, after she's adjusted to us, we will simply tell her the truth. Maybe she can somehow act as a connection for us to President Roosevelt or perhaps at least to their new League of Nations in San Francisco."

Arthur beamed, "Hummmm… maybe so, but remember, when we return her to earth, we must erase all of her memories about her contact with us. With the coming of the horrible second world war on earth, we just cannot yet risk any unplanned discovery of us by any of the earthers."

Glinda responded beaming, "I agree husband. When I mind probed Amelia, I found her to be very unique, special, and strong and really self-determined, I think she may make a very adept first contact for us. Amador knows we sure need a reliable, sane, trustworthy contact and human agent on earth. Also, even though she is married to a Mr. George Putnam, she is not at all happy or really strongly emotionally connected to him. Right after their marriage she took off her wedding ring and has not worn it since. He apparently is only a very handsome mask. He's a psychic vampire for energies from famous people and he has a horrible foul mouth and temper to boot! She is a very independent woman and I really feel and hope that she can be our initial vital connection to the government of the United States. I also discovered that she is very good friends with Eleanor Roosevelt, the President's wife. Apparently one time Amelia took Mrs. Roosevelt on a night time flight over the USA capital of Washington, DC and Eleanor was so enthralled that she soon got her student pilot license with hopes of having Amelia as her flight instructor. But, then her husband, the President, forbade her to take any flying lessons."

Arthur beamed to his wife; "Hummmm. How peculiar that a husband could forbid his wifemate anything. Well then, maybe President Roosevelt will think our Amelia Earhart to be a bad influence on Mrs. Roosevelt."

Glinda beamed to her husband, "Well Arthur, Amelia, and only through Mrs. Roosevelt, will have to somehow win the confidence of Mr. Roosevelt. Certainly after he begins to learn about us, our Amelia and Mrs. Roosevelt could hopefully certainly gain President Roosevelt's undivided attention and respect for our plea to live on earth and also respect our need for maximum secrecy."

Arthur gave a soft moan and beamed, "OK, whatever you think my clever queen. We shall see how sincerely open she might be to effectivly helping us while keeping our secret plans to land and live on earth."

Glinda beamed, "Oh Amadore I do hope so! We have reached the stress limit of our pods patience and frustrations over the six confining generations that we have traveled to find a new and safer water world home. Respect and honor always dear, that our previous five generations sacrificed their irreplaceable life dreams in this trusty old starship to get the last remaining,160 of us, to Earth."

Arthur moaned sadly thru his upper spinal blowhole, clicked lowly and sadly and slowly beamed, "My Queen, I will always and in all ways bless and honor our brave podcestors. So, I also hope that Amelia will ally with us and help us connect with the President. But with their coming world war, I truly wonder now if we made a good choice to come to their magnificent water world."

Glinda beamed, "Remember dear, that along with the catastrophic meta gravity un-stability, our sea levels fell beyond being able to sustain us any longer on our home world. Also, the alpha male egos, greed and endless war and destruction of life dreams are why 300 of us left our home world in this ancient star ship 372 years ago. And now, moan, squeak, click, click, click to come here, only to discover that the same fear, egos, greed and war insanity is raging on this beautiful blue water world."

Arthur beamed to his wife, "Well beloved queen of mine. This is for sure the end of our flight. Our, what… 50,000 year old creaking and stinking starship, from the ancients, desperately needs major and minor repairs that we can no longer accomplish now with our totally depleted spare parts, our inadequate equipment and materials onboard to design and make replacement parts."

The next ship's time morning Amelia awoke to find Glinda and several other people standing around her bed. She gradually noticed that she was now in a smaller room. She reached to feel for the mattress and was still anxious to again feel only air beneath her. She quickly sat up and looked down as she panicked and frantically felt for a mattress. She almost began to freak out as she looked uneasily at Glinda and demanded, "Ok sister, why is there no mattress?"

Glinda put her hand over Amelia's left hand, smiled and without moving her lips beamed into her head, "Amelia, you have no mattress because we don't use them. You have been sleeping in an antigravity bed and you are aboard our starship Lifestar and… we are now orbiting your planet."

Glinda waved her hand to a female crewmember standing by the curved wall. She touched a small red plate and the nanocrystaline metal wall section became transparent revealing the extraordinary view of Earth from 500 miles up.

Amelia sat there thunderstruck, gawking and totally mesmerized at her home world and its beautiful oceans that she had almost died in. But as plucky as Amelia was, she silently took all of this in and submissively said, "OK Glinda, please… please do tell me more."

Glinda gently clasped Amelia's forearm, smiled and beamed into Amelia's mind images of her crumpled plane on top of what she supposed was the top of the starship she now found herself in. Glinda then beamed, "I am so sorry dear lady that your navigator, Fred Noonan, did not survive the crash into the sea between Howland and Baker islands." " Our medicos tried for hours to try to save him, but he was too badly injured."

Amelia felt tears come to her eyes and she began to have the heebie- jeebies and really cry as the impossible enormity of all this truly settled into her mind and spirit. She cried, "Oh poor Fred. He was only 44 and he was going to use the publicity and profits from our flight to open his own flight school at the Grand Central Airport in Burbank. Now we will have to make a memorial plaque for him someday at the Portal of Folded Wings in the Valhalla cemetery which is across from the Burbank airport's west side rail road tracks."

Glinda reached out and took the now completely anguished crying aviatrix into her arms and sent caring, loving and soothing energies into Amelia. After about a minute, Amelia, wiping her tears with the back of her hand, sighed and said, "Dear Glinda, whoever you are, thank you. You have saved me and now, I have a million questions for you. Who are you? Where do you come from? How did you know I was crashing? How did…"

Glinda clicked softly and looked affectionately into her eyes and beamed, "Amelia, may I please touch my fingertips to you head?"

Amelia apprehensively nodded her head and with a resigned sigh said, "Well, Ok…"

After Glinda connected with Amelia's mind and spirit, she quickly let the entire story flow into Amelia's mind of how they had stolen this ancient starship from a military history museum and traveled 97.5 light years for six generations to come to try and resettle on earth. Glinda then clicked and smiled as she related, "Like the rest of the world, we were eagerly following your flight on our vhf and shortwave radio frequencies, when we heard your frantic KHAKK calling Itasca, and heard you say, 'We must be on you now, but cannot see you. Gas is running low." We then simply calculated where your plane was going to crash. We rapidly maneuvered our starship just 40 feet (12 meters) under water in that area between Howland and Baker Islands to stand by in case we were needed.

As your plane crashed and lost its inertia, we ascended to gently lift up your slowly sinking Lockheed 10E onto the flat area on the top hull of our ship. Then, four crew members exited the roof hatch and rescued you Amelia. Another crew member using an anti gravity cart, retrieved all of the loose salvageable items inside your plane."

Glinda gestured to the corner of the room and there, on a table and on the floor, were most of her and Fred's baggage, notes, maps, food, flashlights, water canteens – almost everything, even some of the damaged soaked stuff had been recovered from her plane. Glinda unfolded a piece of paper, clicked softly and beamed, "Dear Amelia, we know you are a woman of strong vision and true courage. I really loved reading your poem. She then handed the paper to Amelia.

Courage

Courage is the price which life exacts for granting peace. The soul that knows it not, knows no release

From little things;

Knows not the livid loneliness of fear Nor mountain heights, where bitter joy you can hear

The sound of wings.

How can life grant us boon of living, compensate, For dull gray ugliness and pregnant hate

Unless we dare

The soul's dominion? Each time we make a choice we pay with courage to behold resistless day

And count it fair.

Amelia Earhart

Amelia tearfully hugged Glinda and said, "Oh Glinda this is so special. I am very glad you retrieved this from my things." She hesitatingly asked, "So, what did you do with my airplane?"

Arthur, from the bridge, beamed to Amelia, "I am Glinda's pod mate and dear brave pilot lady. When we submerged, we had to let your aircraft sink to the bottom. It is important that for now, no one knows what happened to you. I am sorry but we must protect the secret of our presence on your planet."

Amelia, while at the same time understanding this, also began to feel anger and more trepidation as she realized she was abducted and was a captive of these kind and loving aliens.

Glinda sensing Amelia's concerns beamed, "Dear Amelia, you are not our prisoner. You may leave us anytime you want to and we mean you and all earthers no harm."

Then one of the women, wearing an all-white flight suit, brought a light blue hospital like bed tray to her and on it was apparently food. But Amelia, in open-mouthed astonishment recognized only the regular bottle of Coke a Cola sitting next to a traditional light green soda fountain Coke glass half filled with ice.

The woman smiled and beamed, "Dear Amelia, you must try to eat this solid food. It is very nutritious and tasty too. I programmed our food synthesizer to try to prepare this to your earthly tastes."

Amelia, seeing no fork or spoon, simply picked up an orange colored bit and chewed and remarked, "Why, this is quite tasty. What is it?"

The lovely alien woman smiled as she used an earthly bottle opener to open and pour Amelia's Coke and also handed her a hospital style accordion bent soda straw. She beamed, "I am glad it is to your liking Amelia. I am Mariana, our chief nutritionist. This is what you would call seaweed and those white bits are fish chunks and the caffeine and sugar in your Coke will also help replenish your blood sugars and normal human body energy levels."

As Amelia tentatively sipped her Coke she asked, "Coke? Oh jeepers!

Where on earth did you get it?"

Glinda grinned, made a joyful squeaking sound and beamed, "Amelia, since our arrival to earth back in 1936, we discovered Coke during our uh, exploratory walkabouts onshore - and we totally adore it! We almost all drink it every day now."

Arthur squeaked and clicked as he beamed, "Uh Uh, not for those on duty here on the bridge my Queen."

By then Amelia had begun to take a good look at these handsome beings. The three other lovely auburn haired women in her room were all dressed in silver flight suits but honey ginger haired Glinda had on a gold colored flight suit. As Amelia thought to herself, "In my life I had come to realize that when things were going very well indeed it was just the time to anticipate trouble. And, conversely, I learned from pleasant experience that at the most despairing crisis, when all looked sour beyond words, some delightful 'break' was apt to lurk just around the corner."

She then noticed a young girl with curly dark hair nearby, also wearing a gold flight suit. She was smiling and apparently beaming joyful and excited love energies to her. She seemed to be a very lovely, bright and exuberant child. Amelia reached out her hand to the lovely chestnut haired star child and said, "Oh you are so lovely, please come here."

The girl stepped over and took Amelia's left hand and beamed to her, "My adopted earth name is Selena after your lovely moon." Amelia

then clearly heard high squeals of delight and some rapid clicks coming from behind the excited young girl.

Amelia smiled and asked, "Oh ok dear little Selena" "How old are

you?"

Selena squeezed her hand and beamed proudly, "I am 5 of your earth years old now. I was born in space in your year of 1932."

Selena reached, put her arm under Amelia and laid her head on her chest as Amelia tentatively and lovingly fondled her curly golden walnut hair. Amelia then began to hear some low pitched but rapid clicks, almost like purring. And incredibly, she heard in her head from Selena, "In my life I had come to realize that when things were going very well indeed it was just the time to anticipate trouble. And, conversely, I learned from pleasant experience that at the most despairing crisis, when all looked sour beyond words, some delightful 'break' was apt to lurk just around the corner."

Amelia gasped in delight and said, "Oh my God! You actually can read and totally memorize my mind!" Amelia smiled lovingly, looked at Glinda and said, "Oh she is super bright and lovely and full of loving energies. I am really thankful to have encountered all of you and again my whole hearted thanks for rescuing me."

Glinda smiled as she put her hand on Selena's back and beamed, "Dear brave Amelia. We are so happy that you are ok now." Amelia smiled and said, "I realize now that none of you can talk. Is that true?" Glinda nodded her head, clicked softly and smiled as she beamed, "It's true Amelia. Since we evolved from dolphins on our home world, we are completely telepathic and sonic." The contented clicking and happy squeaks and squeals that you feel and hear from Selena are also part of our emotions and natural communicating."

Three days later Amelia was completely healed and reenergized. She sat at the amazing and magnificently decorated round table in the alien's main meeting room with Glinda, Arthur and Selena. After they finished off a delicious fish and processed seaweed dinner, they sipped their cokes, which the aliens seemed to get just a little bit mellow on. Amelia asked Glinda, "Uh your majesty, May I please thank those who went topside and rescued me?"

Glinda smiled and beamed, "Ok, I will summon them and they should be here in a few minutes. Why do you ask this?" Amelia who had been a dedicated pilot since her first flight lessons at Kenner

Airfield in Long Beach California when she was 23 said, "It is customary to always thank those who rescue us from crashes."

She then sadly thought back to the previous evening when they gathered in the small funeral chapel of the starship to return Fred Noonan's remains to the eternity of space and time. Glinda, Selena and Arthur holding her hands, stood on each side of her along with several crew members of Lifestar. Glinda recited the traditional blessing and farewell for the mortal starstuff remains and spirit of Fred to be returned to the creators - of this and other universes - the Amadores.

"Beloved Amadores, creators of space, time, and precious light, life and awareness, we bless and release the body our fellow being as all of his 44 Earth years of life dream mind recordings have now returned to you."

Arthur then pushed a red button and the airlock outer door slid open and Fred's silver shrouded body simply floated silently out to space and eternity. Amelia then heard all of the Delphinians singing. It was an emotional combination of soft moans and low and slow clicking that clearly demonstrated their sadness and respect for Fred.

As Glinda was holding Amelia's left arm, Selena tearfully clung to Amelia's right arm, Amelia asked, "Glinda what exactly are life dreams?" As the spiritual leader of her pod, Glinda smiled and beamed to Amelia, "Every living being and most higher animals in the universe, each night, when we are in stage four deep sleep, we transmit, through our universal delta brain waves, everything we have thought, seen, heard, felt and done, back to our creators so they too can enjoy the life dreams of their creations. Don't you do that on earth?"

Amelia became taken aback as she mouthed, "Oh sweet Jesus, Joseph and Mary! Creators of the Universe, oh my dear God in heaven…"

They walked hand in hand from the small chapel with its curious Madonna like sculptures and spiritual artwork on the walls. Selena beamed to Amelia, "We love our Amadores because they created us and gave us unconditional free choice to try to always respect each other and make good life dreams come true for all." Glinda beamed in, "Yes because anything thing we think can become true. Good, bad, sad, or happy - we are the response able creators of our own life dreams every moment of each day."

Amelia said, "Oh Glinda, that is so beautiful and wonderful for self and social responsibility. I wish we on earth could learn your spiritual ways. Will you please teach me?" Glinda, who began to feel more hopeful that Amelia would be their prime contact and crucial colleague, smiled and beamed, "Of course Amelia, I will be glad to share with you our spirituality."

Selena squealed and beamed, "Oh mother, pleaseeee, can Amelia come live in my cabin?"

Amelia, who now found herself crossing into a new, exciting and inconceivable life now far removed from her previous earthly flying adventures and connections, grinned as she said, "Oh Glinda I really am excited and totally glad to be welcome and needed here. We have wondered for centuries if we are alone in the galaxy and now of course, I alone know that we are not alone. I have so much to ask you and to learn from you and really, I do indeed want to stay with all of you!"

Glinda squeezed Amelia's hand as she thought to herself, "I thought so.

When I probed your mind I realized that while you are reluctantly

indulgent of your husband, you do not like at all what he has done by patronizing you for publicity and financial gain. So, understandably you despise his horrible foul mouthed tempers and his psychic vampire like super sponge ego supposedly all for your flying career. You do not have a real spiritual marriage with Gerald Putnam and you have finally now, thank Amador, become totally used up by his seemingly endless, cold abuse and exploitation of you.”

Glinda smiled as she beamed, “Amelia welcome to our pod, family as you call it. I hope you can stay for a long interval and learn from us. We have so much to share with you and frankly, we need your help in contacting your President Roosevelt.”

Amelia exclaimed, “Please know that I will do anything I can to help all of you. Do you know that I am actually good friends with the President’s wife, Eleanor?”

Glinda, already knew that but she just looked amazed and beamed, “Oh really! That would be so helpful Amelia. But with your frightening world war coming, we now feel that we must wait for more peaceful times to contact your government to ask for uh, refuge.”

Amelia looked frankly at her new alien friends and said, “Did you know that president Roosevelt asked me to try to spy on the Japanese ship placements as a part of my around the world flight? But when we could not find Howland Island and then crashed, well, dear lady, I am truthfully relieved to be free from such covert and dangerous espionage war games and worries. Oh Glinda, I agree that another horrible senseless world war is coming and I think that there is nothing you or I nor anyone else can do to stop it.”

Glinda beamed and moaned, “It was the same on our home world Amelia. The alpha male egos and their endless over reactive lymbic hormones eventually caused the political and social ruin on our beautiful home water world orbiting beta Delphinus in the constellation that you call Delphinus. This is truthfully why our pod pirated this ship and fled for six generations over these 372 light and life years with hopes of finding a new peaceful home water world like your magnificent Earth.”

Amelia held her new ally’s hand as she tearfully cried, “Oh dear Delphinians, welcome home, but now with the coming war with the Germans and soon the Japanese, I fear that our world would not be at all safe nor ready for you now…” Just then, Amelia noticed a really handsome curly dark haired Delphinian and that he was also wearing the round tortoise shell eye glasses that apparently all male Delphinians always wore. He was wearing a medium blue flight suit and the rather strange very wide black and silver trim shoes that all of the Delphinians wore. The other three were amazingly dressed in earth like khaki trousers and each wore turtlenecks; one in a light grey, one in blue and the last one, an attractive female dressed in an off white.

Glinda grinned and beamed, “Enough of this deep and onerous war talk for now. Amelia, I want you to meet your rescuers. This is Delnoid 4M, Delnoid 5M and Delnoid 6F. And finally here,” she mirthfully squeaked “In his, semi formal flight suit, is Embry, our chief pilot and one of our celestial and earthly navigators.” Amelia stood to shake their hands and as she did, each one, to her astoundment, kissed her on her cheek as she shook their hands. Then to her even further bewilderment, as she shook the hands of the three Delnoids. They each actually said aloud, “Hello

Miss Earhart, I am very thankful you are ok and well again." Amelia looked at Glinda in confusion and stammered, "Why… why… they can talk! How is this possible?"

Glinda looked at Arthur who gave her an affirmative nod and explained, "Amelia these Delnoid units are actually uh, what you would call,er, made from us, but they are especially designed biological androids. We call them Delphinoids. They are produced by us to help us and since we knew we would be coming to earth, we genetically modified them so that they can speak aloud. They each have been programmed to speak in English, Spanish, French, German, Italian, Japanese, Chinese and Russian. We too have been learning these languages ever since we came into AM radio range of your planet back in your year of 1899. On your Christmas eve in 1906, we heard what might have been your first radio show. We heard somebody playing Oh Holy Night on the violin and then someone recited a passage from your bible. I have since read it and its fascinating and some of its stories parallel some of our spiritual legends.

As Amelia again shook the hands of the Delphinoids, she looked admiringly at Embry and invited him to please sit next to her. She thanked Glinda and Arthur for saving her and again after looking directly into Embry's eyes, she very uncharacteristically hugged him and whispered, "Oh thank you so much Embry, I do hope we can spend some time talking about uh, flying."

Embry winked at Glinda and beamed, "That is exactly what I want to enjoy too dear Amelia."

Glinda grinned and beamed privately to Arthur, "OK good, she is hooked." Arthur just let out a descending relieved squeak from his blowhole as he grinned and squeezed his wife's hand under the table.

CHAPTER 2 ELEANOR

The Japanese sneak attack on Pearl Harbor occurred on 7 December 1941. On February 19, 1942, FDR signed the heartless and needless Japanese American internment executive order number 9066 to remove all Japanese from the West Coast inland to stark and freezing or baking hot concentration camps in California, Arizona, Utah and Idaho. All of it was done to supposedly to protect Americans. Eleanor Roosevelt was furious with her husband for caving in to the war hysteria and the anti Japanese racial prejudice. But, in spite of her pleadings, he ordered the internment of over 120,000 loyal Japanese Americans. Half of which were innocent infants, children and women!

After her visit by covered jeep to the central Arizona Gila River relocation camp on April 23, 1943, Eleanor, after eating dinner at the camp with the Japanese prisoners, returned late at 10pm to her modified twin tail C-87A / B-24 Liberator Express aircraft number 124159. It was blithely named, 'Guess Where II' which was waiting for her at Falcon Field which was the temporary war time British Air Corps training facility located 5 miles north east of Mesa, Arizona. She ordered the co-pilot and all of her staff, except for her pilot, to get their overnight bags and get out of the plane. Once she had them all lined up at the ladder of her plane, she said in her usual shrill voice, "I want all five of you to please wait for me here until I return hopefully by 10 pm day after tomorrow. The Falcon's Roost restaurant will stay open for you until midnight and re-open for breakfast, lunch, tea and dinner for all of you until I return." She continued, "I know it can be hotter than hell here in central Arizona during the day even now in early springtime but, the evaporative roof coolers here should keep everyone comfortable.

There is plenty of coffee, coke, beer and sandwiches and again - I should hopefully be back in about 72 hours. I have chosen to visit the Manzanar relocation camp in California alone in order for me to see what it is really like without any camp officers trying to cover up anyoutpoints. When I think of those poor unfairly interred Japanese Americans and especially the children and infants I am outraged! The barracks here are also ready for you. So please be sure to get a good night's rest. All of you should take advantage of this opportunity to meet and thank the brave young British pilots training here for the European theatre."

Her chief assistant, Malvina Thompson, sputtered, "But, but Mrs.

Roosevelt, aren't you going to need me and other staff to accompany you?

Eleanor grinned and said, "No, no thank you. I want to go alone and unannounced to see what it is really like in that camp. It was the first one built and opened in mid March of 1942. Now, all of you please listen up. This is top, top secret and your jobs depend on each of you keeping this, uh, little surprise side trip of mine completely confidential…"

After the take off, Eleanor sat in her seat, opened her briefcase and from a secret document compartment, she withdrew and opened a well worn plain manila envelope. She again, still in disbelief, unfolded and read again the handwritten letter on a strange, almost metallic like, very light blue paper which was folded in the well worn rectangular brown hardcover flight log of Amelia Earhart. She cried as she again read the last entry made by Amelia on July 2, 1937, after 20 hours in the air after she had taken off from Lae in Papua, New Guinea. The log book notes column said, "Oh God it will be so good to get back to California. I hope we make it."

Holding the flight log to her breast, almost like a prayer book, Eleanor recalled the Sunday on March 7th 1943, when her whole universe changed forever. She had been reading and relaxing in her living room next to the fireplace on that weekend. It was her separate residence, at her own Val-Kill Stone Cottage, about 2 miles east of her and FDR's home on their tremendous mile square 640 acre (259 hectare) Roosevelt estate in Hyde Park, New York.

Fala, the President's black Scottish Terrier, lying at her feet, scrambled to his legs and started barking furiously and even his somewhat short curly back hairs hackled. Eleanor was unsuccessfully trying to calm the freaking out pet, when her colored staff maid came into room and said, "Excuse me Mrs. Roosevelt, the secret service man says there is someone at the front door to see you."

Fala raced off, teeth barred, claws slipping nosily on the wooden floors, he was barking frantically and growling as he had never done before as he scrambled towards the entrance.

Eleanor wearily rose from her chair and followed the maid to the front door. When she got there she found agent Jim Grant standing next to a really nice looking dark haired man who was dressed in a proper grey and off white striped three piece suit and a brown tie. The stranger at the door smiled, looked directly at Fala and the frenzied little dog amazingly stopped barking and laid down in a submissive posture with his small tail wagging in acceptance of the stranger. Eleanor told her maid to please collar Fala and keep him away.

Jim turned to Mrs. Roosevelt and said, "Excuse me ma'am. This is Mr. uh, what did you say your name was sir?"

The man politely removed his brown Fedora hat, looked directly into Eleanor's eyes, smiled and said, "My name is Delnoid uh, Delbert that is."

The agent gruffly said, "Well, I checked his Federal ID and it id's him as Delbert Delphino from the Pentagon alien affairs office. So, he is ok Mrs. Roosevelt."

Eleanor had sensed the unusually good energies coming from this very handsome visitor. She held out her hand and as they clasped, she suddenly felt very strong caring and trusting energies between them. Eleanor, with admiring eyes only on Delbert, flicked her left hand dismissively as she said, "That will be all for now. Thank you Jim." She gently pulled on Delbert's hand and said, "Oh my, somehow I am so delighted that you came by dear sir."

Delnoid 7M smiled and said, "I am very relieved and glad to have found you at home Mrs. President, uh, that is, Mrs. Roosevelt." Eleanor smiled and said, "Oh please, do call me Eleanor."

They sat facing each other in front of the fireplace. They were in the living room near the study. She sat on the blue couch and he sat on the blue chair with wide white trimmed panels. Eleanor asked, "Would you like something cool to drink Mr. uh, Delbert is it?"

He nodded appreciatively, almost like a kid, grinned and said, "Coke please. Oh, I do love ice cold Coke Mrs. Roosevelt."

Eleanor dismissed her maid after receiving coke, ice in a glass and ice tea for her. As they sat there Delnoid 7M, smiled earnestly and said, "I have come to visit you to bring you a message from a dear, uh… mutual friend of ours."

Eleanor gave a half smile and asked, "And, who might that be? I don't believe I have ever met you before Mr. Delphino."

Delnoid looked very attentive as he stood and asked, "May I come sit next to you on the couch Eleanor?" As he sat next to the flattered First Lady he said, "This is so Mrs. er, Eleanor. We haven't met before, but I am sure you will welcome the news that I bring from your long lost friend, Amelia"

Stunned, Mrs. Roosevelt exclaimed, "What are you saying sir?" She was wide eyed with shock, she stiffened, dropped her ice tea glass on the floor and scowled, "Sir, my dear friend Amelia has been missing and presumed drowned for the last five years."

Delnoid 7 smiled and beamed soothing energies as he asked, "May I hold your hand Eleanor?"

She, surrendering to his loving alien energies said, "Very well Delbert, I trust that it will be all right - whoever you really are…"

As Delnoid 7 held her hand he said, "Please close your eyes now Eleanor." He then telepathically beamed into Eleanor's head the whole story of Amelia Earhart's crash and rescue by the Delphinians. As she grasped the incredible magnitude of what he was sharing with her, she stamped her feet rapidly on the floor and broke into tears of joy and disbelief.

At the end of his astounding story he reached into his inside coat pocket and withdrew a well worn 4 x 7 inch brown rectangular, leatherette pilot's log book and said to Eleanor. "This I bring to you as proof that it is from our Amelia along with her handwritten message to you." He beamed into her mind, "Of course only you alone can know that Amelia is alive, well, and happily and safely living with us." He withdrew his hand from hers, they both stood and she fell into his arms sobbing and smiling simultaneously, "Oh thank God she is alive. Thank God! We had given up all hope for her years ago. Thank you for this incredible and miraculous news dear Delbert..."

Delnoid 7M telepathically beamed to her, "When you read her note, it will tell you where to come to meet her." "She has much news and a vital plea for you Mrs. Roosevelt."

Then to the utter shock of Mrs. Roosevelt, she heard in her head, "Hello dear Mrs. Roosevelt. I am Glinda, queen of our pod uh, family. I am in our starship 500 miles above you right now. Thank you for receiving our and Amelia's messenger dear First Lady."

We love you and will explain our vital plea to you when we meet at the location listed in Amelia's note on the 24th of April, of this year. The meeting is set for the end of your upcoming Arizona trip. So, please plan accordingly."

Just as Mrs. Roosevelt had ordered from the coordinates on Amelia's note, her favorite pilot, Charles Alfred Anderson, flew northwesterly on a heading of two three niner niner one (239.91) degrees to latitude 36 degrees 44 minutes 12.88 seconds North and a Longitude of 118 degrees 08 minutes

40.74 seconds west. In approximately an hour and a half they covered the 427 miles from Falcon Field to a strangely out of place large Army airport.

The airport had a 4,800 foot runway, a small tower 7 miles south east of Independence, California, at highway 395 and the Manzanar Reward Mine Road where it crosses the California aqueduct. The south end of the runway was right across from the Manzanar camp. For the landing Eleanor, who still adored flying, went forward and plopped herself down in the right co-pilots seat.

Charles lowering the plane's nose, said, "Mrs. Roosevelt, according to the map, we're on a straight in final approach heading of 350 degrees to land on the longest runway here. Please fasten your seat belt now Eleanor uh, Ma'am"

Eleanor exclaimed in her shrill voice, "Charles, use your powerful landing lights and do the best you can chief!" Charles switched on the lights, smiles and said, "Well Eleanor, any landing we can walk away from is a good landing." Eleanor, hearing that, resolutely remarked, "I trust that we will be just fine but as soon as you can stop our trusty old Guess Where II from rolling, turn off the landing and all the other lights as quickly as you can!"

At 00:30 on the 24th, Charles stopped the plane and killed all the lights. Mrs. Roosevelt grabbed and flicked on a flashlight and said, "Well, so far so good. Fortunately we don't see any lights on around here at all in the tower nor in that lone hanger. Maybe they have gone over to the Manzanar camp or into Independence for the night. The only lights I can see are across that highway coming from the camp offices and barracks. Ok now chief pilot Anderson, this will be a top secret, super top secret mission for me. So, you must obey me and put the blackout window covers up now and promise to remain inside the plane until sunup, no matter what you may hear! I should be back - hopefully by 3pm day after tomorrow.

If I do not return, you must fly back to Mesa, pick up my staff and return directly back to Washington. You must report immediately – in person - to the President and tell him, "Gone with the Wind." Is that understood Captain Anderson?"

The fighter pilot ace 1 who had flown Mrs. Roosevelt everywhere since May, 1941, after she went for a flight with him during her visit to the Tuskegee Aviation Institute, reached out, took his First Lady's hand and said, "Oh dear Mrs. Roosevelt, Please do be extra careful dear lady."

Eleanor squeezed his hand, smiled and said, "Oh please don't worry. At sunup you can remove the window covers and walk about outside if you wish" There is plenty of grub in our galley.

Charles smiled and said, "Yes Ma'am! If anyone comes by I will tell them I am just waiting for parts and a repair crew."

Eleanor smiled and said, "But again Charles, be sure to remain inside the plane tomorrow night with all window covers back up. If I return at night. I will knock three times on the hull with this flashlight. Your career and possibly your very life depends on you keeping those covers up after dark tomorrow and staying inside this plane tonight no matter what! Ok?"

She impulsively bent over and reassuringly patted his right shoulder a couple of times.

CHAPTER 3 REUNION

Eleanor descended from her plane and Charles pulled the lanyard to close the bottom hinged ladder hatch behind her. She waited quietly to let her eyes adapt to the moonlit darkness and to be sure that no one was around. As she stood there, under the bright, now just 3 days past full moon, she was thinking. "Well, at least this 16 day old moon was just bright enough in the east to help us land…"

As she was admiring the bright moon filling the clear California sky, she noticed a bright shooting star to the left of it. But wait! It wasn't a shooting star. It was moving and it was rapidly approaching her. The blue light from the object winked out and she soon began to hear a smooth low pitched hum like vibration. Bathed in the moonlight, about 100 yards away, she saw a flying saucer approaching behind the plane and angling to the left from where she stood in utter astonishment at the east side of the main runway. She then heard a male voice in her head, "Eleanor, come walk over to just this side of the aqueduct bridge and we will meet you."

As she breathed, "Oh Jesus, Joseph and Mary" she heard in her head, "Fear not Mrs. Roosevelt, we will land in just a few seconds. Please stand just where you are right now." The 30 feet (10 meter) saucer stopped and hovered at 20 inches (half a meter), a hatch swung open and an amazing blue light beam walkway served as a ramp. As Mrs. Roosevelt stood with her mouth agape, she saw a trim female form dressed in a sky blue flight suit running down the glimmering ramp towards her with her arms outstretched and she heard tearful cries of, "Eleanor, Eleanor its meeee, Amelia. Oh it's so good to see you again my dear, dear flying friend."

Eleanor took Amelia in her arms and after they had both hugged they looked at each other tearfully. Eleanor, looking at Amelia's now long auburn hair said, "Oh dear God! It's really you! It's really you Amelia. I have missed you so, so much my beloved dear, brave friend." Five foot nine Amelia, standing tip toe to hold her elderly five foot eleven friend, grinned, looked up with her blue eyes and said, "Yes it's really me Eleanor and I have so much to tell you and show you. But, we only have about 22 hours before you must be back here to make your surprise inspection of that horrid internment camp day after tomorrow. After the inspection, you fly back to Mesa, Arizona to pick up your entourage and fly back to Washington."

Eleanor smiled and asked, "Back here Amelia? Why, what on Earth do you mean, back here?"

Amelia took her hand and towed Mrs. Roosevelt towards the waiting silver flighter with dark blue trim. She grinned mischievously and said, "Eleanor, remember the night flight I took you on over Washington back in April 1933 while I was still wearing my white evening gown? Well my dear First Lady friend, you ain't seen nothing yet!"

After they entered the saucer, a very handsome latino looking curly haired man, curiously wearing old school round horned rim glasses, stood and held out his hand. Eleanor shook his hand, Amelia took his other arm and said, "Dearest Eleanor, I want you to meet my husband Embry." Embry and Amelia embraced Mrs. Roosevelt as she shed tears of joy because she knew only too well the loveless marriage, just a partnership really, that Amelia had endured for seven years with greedy promoter, George Putnam. Proudly looking at them in their sky blue flight suits, she said, "Oh I am so very happy for both of you. This is splendid and truly exceptional. I am overjoyed for both of you!" Embry led Eleanor to a semi sunken human form fitted seat just behind Amelia and beamed, "OK Mrs. Roosevelt, I am now going to activate your seat's force field to secure you during our short flight back up to our starship." Eleanor looked apprehensively up at the handsome Delphinian pilot and nodded uneasily. She reached forward and tapped Amelia on her left shoulder saying, "Oh Amelia, please pinch me. I simply cannot believe this is happening." Amelia reached back, patted Eleanor's hand, and said, "OK my dear wanna be aviatrix, I'm going to take off as soon as my husband gets seated."

After Embry sat down and activated the flighter's force field, he beamed to Amelia, "OK my darling earthling pilot lady, let's go home!"

As Eleanor sat there waiting for the acceleration of takeoff, she said, "Amelia, when will we take off?"

Amelia grinned as she touched a red button with her left index finger to neutralize the colloidal crystals of their nanocrystaline hull and the solid flighter hull turned completely transparent.

Eleanor gasped and shouted, "Oh my stars! Oh sweet Jesus, Joseph and Mary. Look at all of the stars! And look! There's the moon too!" Amelia was laughing and said, "Look down now Eleanor. Look at your magnificent home world dear first, First Lady in space"

Eleanor reached again to hold Amelia's shoulder and cried, "Oh Amelia! It's beautiful. I never imagined how inspiring our blue water world could be."

Amelia smiled proudly and said, "My dear First Lady, I only wish everyone on Earth could see our home planet like this. If all people could see our magnificent blue marble from space like this, they would all understand how small and fragile our world is and perhaps we would choose to respect each other better. And see our planet as the united harmonious and response able humankind should be."

Eleanor asked, "Oh my goodness Amelia. How high up are we?"

Amelia who was now mentally plugged into her flighter paused and said, "Since we can now see the whole receding sphere of earth, we are 1,119 miles high Eleanor."

Eleanor sat there speechlessly and she saw that Embry had swiveled his co- pilot seat leftward around 60 degrees to face her. He grinned, pointed upwards with his left index finger and beamed, "Eleanor look up overhead now." As Eleanor looked up, she gasped as she saw the approaching dark underside of the 300 ft starship. She caught her breath again and managed to ask, "Oh my God Amelia, is that really your ship?"

Amelia grinned and said, "Yep! Home sweet Lifestar! It's been my unbelievable home since the second of July 1937. I have so much to tell you and share with you dear Eleanor." Amelia then concentrated, using her mind and hand controls to gently guide the thirty foot flighter in its underside berthing port along with the five other docked flighters. The flighter was securely docked.

Embry touched his first and index fingers on a small yellow plate at his control console and as he did so, their seating platform began to slowly rise as overhead, the roof of the flighter and the dock port covers slid smoothly and noiselessly open. Once they had risen from their seats, wide eyed Eleanor placed both hands over her mouth and nose as she shrilled, "Oh, Oh Amelia. I simply cannot believe this. Am I really alive now? Are you sure Charles did not crash our B-24?"

She then noticed four majestic human like beings coming up to her and as they reached the now thoroughly flabbergasted first lady, they hugged her. As they did so, she felt powerful loving and caring energies but much much stronger than she had felt when Delnoid 7M had briefly held her back in March. Smiling, Amelia, who had also joined the hug, said, "Mrs. Roosevelt, I want you to please meet Delphinian King Arthur, his Queen Glinda and this lovely young lady, age 11, is princess Selena." Selena again hugged Mrs. Roosevelt and as she did, Eleanor clearly heard some low rapid clicks and what seemed to be joyful squeals coming from behind the excited young princess. Glinda, still holding astounded Mrs. Roosevelt's hand smiled and beamed, "I am so glad that you were able to come dear First Lady of the United States." Arthur took her other hand and beamed, "Welcome indeed to our Lifestar ship Mrs. Roosevelt."

Glinda beamed again, "We know you must be amazed at our ship and presence above your planet and soon, after we enjoy breakfast, we shall enlighten you."

Arthur beamed, "Please have no fears Mrs. Roosevelt, we have only good intentions and mean no one on Earth any harm. We seek only some, um, relocation assistance from the United States and your husband, President Roosevelt." He made some low thoughtful clicking sounds just like his daughter had just made.

Eleanor, by then regaining her composure, looked Arthur right in the eyes through his old school style, horned rim, Persol Italian style eyeglasses and said, "So, King Arthur are you telling me that you wish to relocate to Earth? Well then my dear, uh, majesty, I can assure you, because of my years of friendship with my dear friend Amelia, the president and I, even if I have to drag FDR kicking and screaming in his wheelchair or hold a pistol to his head, he and I will certainly do all that we can to assist you. After all, as I have always believed, what one has to do usually can be done, especially if we follow our true heart conscience!"

Amelia smiled, hugged Eleanor and said, "These are peaceful, loving and totally communicating beings Eleanor, just as all of us children of the universe should also be on Earth - where instead, we seem to have alpha male egos, endless conflicts, abuse in families and society as well as endless wars among nations."

CHAPTER 4 TOP SECRET

Eleanor Roosevelt met with her husband, President Roosevelt, back in April of 1943. It was right after her amazing Amelia encounter during her Japanese relocation camps visits to Arizona and California trip. But as usual, FDR choose to ignore her preposterous Amelia Earhart and her absurd and bizarre aliens story. Even though he had been thoroughly briefed and was in on the Roswell crash and investigations loop. He commanded her, on threats of divorce and imprisonment or worse… to say nothing about her meeting with Earhart and her flight of fancy aliens because if she talked, it would most certainly cost him his re-election in 1944. After President Roosevelt was re-inaugurated in January of 1945, Eleanor, in March, again went to her now seriously ailing husband and threatened to divorce him if he again refused to meet with Amelia and her people. Again FDR refused and before Eleanor could try again to persuade him, he died in Warm Springs, Georgia in the arms of his mistress on April 12th, 1945. So then,Eleanor, Amelia and her aliens agreed to wisely gave time for the new presidential transition dust to fully settle.

In October, 1945, the Delphinians and Amelia decided to secretly try to initiate contact and try to negotiate a homecoming treaty with Eleanor and the now ascended President, Harry Truman. After the 1947 Roswell crash and the endless years and layers of cover-ups, the US government, with President Truman, along with their top level top secret alien investigation groups, such as majestic-12, knew for sure - with the Roswell crash and even earlier encounters and evidence, that aliens were indeed visiting earth. The big question was what to do about it. Keep the cover-ups going and growing or let the world know that we are not alone in the galaxy.

To make this alien threat official US government business after the Roswell crash, President Harry Truman, presented this official but cryptic presidential order at the initial meeting of the National Security Resources Board at the White House, 13 November 1947:

TO P S E CRE T – EY ES ONLY

The White House – Washington DC

Memorandum – COPY – for the Secretary of Defense 24 September 1947

Dear Secretary Forrestal:

As per our recent conversation on this matter, you are hereby authorized to proceed with all due speed and caution upon your undertaking. Hereafter this matter shall be referred to, only as Operation majestic - 12.

It continues to be my opinion that any future considerations relative to the ultimate disposition of this matter should rest solely with the Office of the President following appropriate discussions with you, Dr. Bush and the Director of Central Intelligence.

Harry Truman

President of the United States

CHAPTER 5 AMELIA, ELEANOR AND HARRY

As often as he could during his two terms, Harry Truman, loved to retreat to the little White House on the navy base in tropical Key West, Florida. On February 20, 1948, President Truman, with two of his top secret staff, flew from the Key West navy base, approximately 900 miles, to Puerto Rico.

As they flew, President Truman sat gazing out the window in deep thought. He profoundly recalled Monday, January 5th. It was after the 1948 New year's weekend celebration that went from Thursday through Sunday. That Monday his life changed forever at 10am when he received an urgent private phone call from the unmistakable shrill voice of Eleanor Roosevelt. "Why, hello Harry. How are you doing? Did you and Bess have a nice New Years?"

Harry felt down cast as he replied, "Well, as usual Eleanor, my Bess at home with her mother in Missouri did not want to be with me here in Washington. So, I passed a relaxing weekend – just catching up on some of my reading and planning my rest and recuperation trip down to Key West, Florida next month." Until my phone rang…

The former first lady said, "Listen Harry, is this line secure?" Harry glanced at his desk and saw he was talking on the black phone. He cleared his throat and said, "Well, Eleanor, please give me your private number and in a moment and I will have my receptionist call and transfer this call to my yellow phone." As he picked up the yellow handset, he realized that this must be something rather important if Eleanor Roosevelt needed to converse with him securely. Maybe it had something to do with her work at the UN.

He cleared his throat and said, "Well hello again Eleanor. So tell me, what can I do for you dear First Lady?"

Eleanor in her familiar shrill said, "Harry, a dear old friend of mine and I must meet with you as soon as possible about… well… let's just say for now, it's a really crucial, uh…a super secret matter. When can we come see you in private?"

Harry again cleared this throat and said, "Well just a moment Eleanor, while I check my agenda, ok, would uh, Friday, March 12th, work for you?"

Eleanor raised her shrill voice, "Harry, this is of uh, vital national importance and we must meet with you immediately - please! I am right now up in my Val-Kill cottage estate here in Hyde Park, New York. We can fly down to Washington as soon as possible."

Harry said, "Well Eleanor, let me recheck my calendar…ah here we go, how about Wednesday, January 14th?"

Eleanor then implored, "Oh Harry can't you meet us any sooner?"

Harry, by then was getting really curious said, "Well my dear lady, if it's really that important… But I must tell you that the only date I have available where we can meet for a couple of hours in total privacy would be, let me see here, on the 8th, Thursday the 8th."

Eleanor smiled her toothy grin, looked over at her companion, Amelia, and said to the president, "Oh splendid Harry. The 8th will just have to do."

Harry, with his pen poised over his yellow notepad inquired, "Ok, so Eleanor, besides yourself, who will be coming with you?" Harry thought he heard some muffled feminine giggles as Eleanor then said, "Her name is, uh Ailema, er…Riddle. Yes, that's right Harry, her name is Ailema Riddle. That's A-I-L-E-M-A Harry, she is dear old flying friend of mine."

CHAPTER 6 DAVIE JONES GRUDGE

After the 6 hour flight from Key West naval air station, President Truman and his staff touched down on the 5000 foot runway 82 of the Isla Grande Navy air strip at San Juan in his Air Force One, a modified C-118 Lift master he had named 'Independence.'

There was a day of deliberate and well publicized press coverage of the Puerto Rican meetings, touring and a banquet. On the eve of February 21th, 1948, President Truman and his small party of official Puerto Rican guests were seen by the press and other local Puerto Rican dignitaries and Navy officers and sailors boarding his presidential yacht, The USS Williamsburg. As far as local official, party, press and public knew, they were to cruise from Puerto Rico to make an official Presidential visit to the lovely Virgin Island city of Charlotte Amalie. This typical Danish city with its red tiled roofs was purchased from Denmark during WW I to thwart the risk of German takeover because it was too close to the USA's strategic islands which are now the USA owned Virgin Islands.

At 4 am on February 22nd, 1948, the Presidential yacht sailed away from the San Juan harbor. The real President Truman stood on the moon lit dockside of the US Navy submarine base at Isla Grande watching the lights of his yacht sail away. He ardently hoped that his lookalike aboard the yacht would not screw up by blabbing too much. Mr. Truman did not want his actor double exposed as an imposter and jeopardize his secret meeting with the Delphinian leader, Arthur. The meeting was indispensable to the future of the planet.

Standing on each side of the President were 26-year-old Navy Lt. Commander, Sara Winchester, who was also an anthropological PhD from UCLA. Also, 33-year-old Maj. Phillip Corso representing General Nathan Twining from Truman's UFO alien investigations – the Majestic 12 group.

They quickly boarded the USS Sea Cat, SS 399 submarine and within 10 minutes it got underway mostly unnoticed, and cruised out of the calm moonlit early morning shimmering waters of San Juan harbor. After the sub cleared the island, President Truman went up to the conning tower where he and the captain were alone top side. Truman looked upward apprehensively for awhile at the stars which were mostly washed out by the moonlight in the Caribbean sky. He informed the captain who was sworn to secrecy, of the importance of this critical to all mankind, mission. Ironically, they were almost in the south east corner of the infamous Bermuda Triangle.

The President told the captain that as soon as the sub was at the meeting location, all crew except for himself, his two advisors and the captain, were to remain sequestered below. One main reason that a sub had been chosen for this extraordinary alien meeting mission was that it had no portholes for curious crew to see out of. Normally a submarine like Sea Cat has a crew of 80 men. But, strategic for this mission, the Navy was ordered to carefully determine the minimum skeleton crew that would be needed to safely operate the sub. So, aside from the president and the two members of his staff, there was only Captain Davie Jones and 12 crew members aboard.

Truman looked at Captain Jones grinned and asked, "Davie Jones, is that your real name Captain?"

Captain Jones scowled and mumbled, "Yep, uh, yes sir it is. My father was a fine merchant marine second officer and then a rancher - that he was sir…" Truman then clearly sensing the uptightness and glibness of the captain tried to make pleasant small talk and asked, "So, where to you hale from Captain uh, Jones?"

The captain scowled and smirked as he said, "Well sir, I hale from cowboy country up there in Montana."

Truman nodded his head and said, "Well then sir, you are a long way from your ranch while you are at sea."

Jones frowned and grumbled, "Well, yeah, I reckon maybe so Mr. President. But, I lost my ranch back just before this dang war started when my pa died and the property was taken back by the damn greedy, heartless bank."

Truman realized he had a very disgruntled and resentment filled hombre in front of him just said, "Well captain, I am sorry that you lost your inheritance. The lack of work and the dang war sure have affected far too many lives with hardship Captain." Jones just kept scowling, avoided eye contact with the President and remained overtly silent.

As the presidential yacht, USS Williamsburg, cruised on its diversionary course heading of 87.25 degrees towards the US Virgin Islands. The USS Sea Cat was cruising on the surface at flank speed of 37mph (59 kph) on a set course of due north running along the Puerto Rico to Bermuda line of the Bermuda Triangle. Their exact course of 03.869 degrees would cover the distance of 108.76 miles in only 2 hours 55 minutes. It would bring them to their rendezvous point just after sunrise - as requested by the aliens.

They were to wait at the exact alien rendezvous point of latitude 20 degrees 00 minutes 18.02 seconds north and longitude 66 degrees 00 minutes 12.78 seconds west. This open water spot was over one of the deepest areas of the Puerto Rican trench with a depth of 24,700 feet (15,000 meters). The hand- written note handed to President Truman by Amelia Earhart told the President to submerge at the rendezvous point at sunset - 18:28 (6:28pm) on February 22nd, 1948, and to wait there at a depth of 200 feet until contacted… Since they had about eleven and a half hours to kill at this station before submerging President Truman asked Captain Jones, "Say Captain do you have any fishing tackle aboard?" The normally hard faced Jones brightened a bit, grinned and said, "Oh, are you an angler too Mr. President? Certainly, uh, sir, I will get my gear and some extra tackle then we can at least enjoy some fishing before full moonrise. Maybe we will get lucky and catch us a few tuna for dinner at 19:00."

Harry thought to himself, "Well, I doubt we will still be aboard for dinner."

On the way to the deck ladder, Harry stopped and rapped on the steel door frame for Sara Winchester, his anthropological assistant, and said, "Sara, do you like fishing?" She exclaimed from behind her drawn blue canvas curtain. "I am putting on my swim suit. I thought I would get some sun and maybe a swim while we wait at our station. And, oh yes sir, Mr. Truman, my dad used to take me fishing off of the Santa Barbara Stern's Wharf. Many times while I was an under grad student, I would also take a break between classes and go swimming or fishing at the Goleta Beach pier which was just a 10 minute bicycle ride from my University of California, Goleta campus."

Harry paused, grinned and said, "Oh the Goleta beach pier. Isn't that near Ellwood where that shore side refinery was shelled back in February of 1942?"

Sara giggled as she responded, "Why, that's exactly right Mr. President. You have a terrific memory. But, I bet you didn't know the reason the Japanese submarine captain shelled Ellwood. It was because before the war he was a tanker captain and one time when he came ashore he slipped and fell off a sand dune and got a butt full of prickly pear thorns."

Harry laughed and said, "Well, that wasn't in the official Navy reports we got back then. Ok Sara, come on topside whenever you are ready."

The captain and President Truman were sitting with their feet and fishing poles dangling over the side. Harry cast his line into the sea and thought, "Gads, my dear friend, Ernest Hemingway, back in Key West, would love this both for the fishing off of a sub and this mind-boggling historic story that will unfold tonight." Sara appeared and even the president did a double take at his beautiful 26 year old assistant wearing her government issue Rayex sun glasses and clad in her tight fitting, one piece, white swim suit. Harry regained his composure and while trying to avoid staring at her asked, "Where is Phillip? Isn't he coming topside too?"

Sara grinned impishly as she began tucking her hair into her white Playtex swim cap. "Nope, unfortunately Col. Corso is feeling a little green under the gills Mr. President."

The captain stood and walked directly in front of Sara, he looked her up and down almost wolfishly behind his very dark Rayex glasses. He tipped his cap and said, "Excuse me Miss Sara, while it's a lovely and perfect calm day for a swim, there are sharks in these waters." He pointed off the portside and sure enough there were scores of fins and splashes. But neither he nor Sara could tell for sure if they were sharks or dolphins.

Sara reached and asked, "Oh Captain, may I please borrow your binoculars?" He removed them from around his neck and self-importantly said, "OK… but be sure to use the neck strap cause they are like a shooting off of a horse, miss." Sara, putting the strap around her neck asked, "Oh, how so captain?" He grinned, chuckled a bit and said, "Well you can only drop them once, just like you can only shoot a rifle astride an untrained horse only once before he bucks you off."

Sara thought, "Gosh, this drug store cowboy has been at sea way too long or away from his horse for way too long." Just a few moments after she raised the binoculars to her eyes, adjusted the two tubes to make a bright round circle of vision and focused them, she let out a long oooohhhh. "They are dolphins and there must be hundreds of them leaping and playing out there. I don't think I have ever seen pods of that many dolphins all together. I wonder what is below to excite all of them like this?" Sara took off the binoculars and handed them back to the captain as she smiled and thought to herself, "Oh captain, don't forget to put the strap around your red neck... sir."

Sara's grimaced because her hair was pulled as she tugged off her tight Playtex swim cap. After shaking out and running her fingers through her lovely auburn hair, she said, "Gosh darn it! I was really hoping to enjoy a swim. I get so little vacation or swimming time these days." She then laid out her small dark blue USN issue towel and gorgeously laid down on her back to be a sun goddess for awhile as the captain fished and stole lured, if not yearning, glances through his Rayex glasses at Truman's really sexy assistant.

After about 10 minutes relishing basking under the Bermuda Triangle sun star shine, Sara suddenly heard a shot ring out and as she jumped to her feet another shot rang out. She looked up to the lookout on the con mast and saw a man shooting his rifle at the dolphins. She screamed, "Sailor! What the hell are doing? Those are dolphins. Stop, stop! Don't you shoot them!"

By then, the President and the captain had leapt up and as Harry stood at Sara's side, the captain hurried towards the fore deck under the con. He glanced mortified at the president and then shouted up, "Seaman Wilson, what in blazes are you doing? You are standing watch and not on a hunting trip. Stow your piece, get below and send, uh, yeoman Topolsky to stand watch." The seaman grudgingly stowed the special watch rifle in its water tight compartment and grumbled, "Jeeeeze F. Christ captain! You always let us shoot at dolphins and sharks. So, what the hell is wrong with you today?"

Sara turned towards where the dolphins had been and there was nary a dolphin to be seen. Then she noticed that one of them was floating and flopping helplessly in the water about 100 yards (91 meters) off. She ran over to the captain and tearfully pleaded, "Oh please sir, can we go see how badly injured that poor dolphin is?" The captain, not knowing that Sara was a Navy Lt. Commander, glared at her and grumbled, "Yeah, ok miss, but dang it, it's just a big fish fer Christ's sake!"

The president, a farm boy and sportsman who was very pro animal and upright, looked sharply at the old sea dog and said, "You go see to it Captain! And that, sir, is a Presidential order. And I never want to hear about your men ever shooting at any marine life again unless it is at the sharks! And you sir will never be disrespectful and insubordinate to any of my Navy officers or staff ever again! Do you clearly understand that Captain?"

The sub slowly pulled abeam the mortally wounded dolphin, the captain nodded to the new watchman who then aimed a bead at the dying dolphin's head and fired. The now lifeless dolphin just floated and within seconds, several other dolphins gathered and were squeaking, squealing, moaning and clicking furiously as they quickly as possible maneuvered the carcass of their pod member away from the dreaded sub and its murderous humans.

Sara was sobbing as the president hesitantly reached out and put his arm around her. She placed her head on his shoulder and wailed, "Oh Mr. President, they are an equally, if not a more intelligent, species that we share our water world with…"

The now pent-up President Truman held his lovely, crying, swim suited assistant, and tentatively softly patted her trembling bare back as he thought, "Well, this will be a big black mark in that seaman's record. Also there will be an executive write up for condoning such shooting by this drug store cowboy of a Captain."

As the now disgruntled captain stood there he thought, "Ok mister Missouri farm boy, goody two shoes democrat president, I was entirely right to vote republican and not vote for the likes of Roosevelt nor you sir, and now you have made an enemy. And you, Mr. Truman, will regret this day!"

CHAPTER 7 SURFACE THE SUB

As the moon rose in the east at about 17:30 (5:30pm) the sub's sonar operator called for the captain to come to the sonar shack ASAP. When he arrived, the sonar man was now completely alarmed and said, "Captain, I am getting an object echo with a return time of 5.2 seconds from something really gigantic at a depth of 24,000 feet and it's now ascending very rapidly up towards us. The captain apprehensively asked, "What kind of an echo are you getting chief?" The chief replied, "Captain, since the velocity of sound in salt water is about 4,800 feet per second. This is the biggest deepest return echo from 4,000 fathoms that I have ever analyzed. I have never seen or heard a big approaching signature like this in my 15 years in Navy subs, sir." The captain turned to President Truman and scowled, "Well Mr.

President, it looks like whatever is coming to meet us is really big and ascending very rapidly from the abyss of the Puerto Rican Trench."

President Truman earlier had been worriedly gazing skyward for alien craft atop the conning tower, thought to himself, "Well boys, I never really could imagine that our new friends would be coming to us - not in an UFO that can crash on land but in a USO (Unidentified Submerged Object)."

Suddenly the sonar operator clasped both hands to his headset and said, "Quiet please! I am hearing a voice in English even though our sonar isn't supposed to be capable of receiving voices." After a few seconds the sonar man picked up his pencil and wrote what he was hearing. He quickly finished after about 10 seconds and then he dutifully handed his transcription to his commander in chief, President Truman. As the president quickly and anxiously read the note, he got a matter of fact look on his face and resignedly told the captain, "Please surface the sub."

CHAPTER 8 CLOSE ENCOUNTERS OF THE DELPHIN KIND

As the Sea Cat was breaking surface, a tremendous dark blue disk also broke surface about 60 feet (30 meters) from the president's comparatively puny submarine. The alien craft was so big that the president, his two staff and the captain standing crowded together on the conning tower could barely see it from end to end. The President said to the captain, "How big do you reckon their craft is?"

The flabbergasted Captain Jones said, "Mr. President, I reckon it's at least about 300 feet (91 meters) in diameter."

The awe-inspiring half submerged alien craft slowly approached the Sea Cat to pull alongside her. There was only about 20 feet (6 meters) between the gigantic starship and the sub. The alien craft stopped and remained exactly in position alongside the president's sub.

In his head, President Truman heard a pleasant female voice… "Please come down to your vessels foredeck and wait." As the president and his two amazed assistants descended inside the conning tower to go below and then forward to the first foredeck access ladder and hatch an extraordinary, ribbon like, wide blue beam flashed from the alien craft and remained steady and level just 1 inch (2.5cm) from the foredeck's bobbing deck level.

As the president and his brave party stood on the fore deck gawking at the strange blue light ribbon, It was glimmering slightly as it rose, lowered, grew and shortened in length to compensate exactly for the distance and exact height between the sub's deck level and the alien craft as the slight sea swell barely rocked the two crafts. The incredible walkway beam was about 6 feet (2 meters) wide and about 3 inches (16cm) thick. President Truman on deck and the astonished captain, still topside the conning tower, next saw a rectangular yellow backlit opening appear about 2 meters above sea level where the space craft's strange blue light ribbon gangway originated from.

Truman then heard a merry squeak and a pleasant melodic female voice in his head. She said, "Please walk over and enter our ship President Truman."

The president and his cadre exchanged apprehensive glances and the President said aloud, "Do you mean that we can actually walk on this light beam?"

The lovely female voice in his head said, "Yes, of course. It is perfectly safe to walk on." As the president walked towards the edge of the sub to where the blue walkway was beamed, he crooked his left arm to signal everyone to follow him and he stepped onto the blue light beam. As he did so, Sara and Phillip, who had not heard the telepathic invitation, shouted, "Mr. President, don't! You'll fall into the sea." By the time they yelled, the always indomitable President Truman was standing with both feet wide apart and flexing his knees to test the incredible light beam. He turned back towards his staff with both hands on his hips and said, "Come on you two. It's safe and… that's a Presidential order."

As Sara and Phillip hesitatingly stepped on the shimmering blue beam, the president gave all of them a big grin and said, "Come on and follow me into history. You're about to participate in an extraordinary exopolitics." Then he thought to himself, "Hummmm, this incredible story can go two ways. Historically it's going to be the first official diplomatic contact between the USA and an alien race and hopefully extraordinarily successful. Maybe, we will be abducted or worse…If our talks fail, this advanced race could attack us. Gosh darn it… If only this breakthrough could be made public."

The president then quipped to himself that his staff certainly deserved, to say the least, the US Alien Medal of Incredibility… "Perhaps I ought to commission a new alien affairs cabinet position with full honors and medals accordingly." As he was approaching the soft yellow lit entrance way to the enormous mind boggling craft, he thought, "OK Harry! Back to Earth with your thoughts." He then stepped onto the 1 meter deep, 3 meter x 6 meter rectangular gangway entrance threshold of the mind-boggling undersea space craft.

As soon as the president and his two awed staff were standing inside the ship, the port they had just entered through squeaked, clanked and rattled down and as they each turned to see the port closing, they looked panicky at each other. They all heard in their heads, "Please don't be fearful, we are peaceful beings."

As the President and his now really apprehensive cadre turned, they saw several humanlike beings clad in silver flight suits and three beings clad in gold flight suits. The beings were, to say the least, beautiful. Perfect almost. There were four absolutely gorgeous females and four statuesque males who astonishingly were all wearing round horn rim glasses. There was also a male and female wearing kakhi slacks and turtle necks.

The President grinned and held out his right hand and said, "I am not sure if I should say welcome to planet Earth because Eleanor told me that you all have been here for what, 10 or 12 years now? But, nonetheless, welcome friends from the stars."

The aliens smiled at the President and then looked briefly at Sara and Phillip and the male leader beamed into all their heads, "We thank you Mr. President. This is the first formal meeting of this era for your present national culture and our species and we have much to discuss, plan and agree upon…"

The alien king extended his hand to the President and as Truman clasped the alien's normal looking five fingered hand, he beamed into the president's head, "I am Arthur uh, King Arthur as you in your social hierarchy might categorize me. Our former home world orbits the star you call beta Delphinus" As Arthur shook his hand, Truman thought to himself that he feels quite human and as the President and the alien King looked into each other's eyes, they could clearly see and feel the kindred intelligent beingness between them.

Arthur then cordially greeted the two others in the President's party. To the utter astonishment of the President and his anthropological specialist, Sara Winchester, Arthur leaned towards her and gently and respectfully kissed her right cheek. Sara was overwhelmed but also obviously quite flattered and pleased. Accordingly, after the Delphinians each shook the hands of the President and the other male of his party, the other male aliens in turn also kissed Sara's cheek.

The president and Phillip looked kind of desperately at each other and wondered if they were supposed to also kiss the cheeks of the lovely female alien's as they shook their hands. The president and his group saw that all of the aliens were grinning and making a low level rapid clicking noise as they heard in their heads, "Yes, Mr. President, you fellows should always respectfully kiss the cheeks of all female beings that you meet."

The president then thought he heard some very subtle squeaks and also heard something like a chuckle in this head. "Mr. President I wish to introduce you to some of our pod. This is my, uh what you might call my Ambassador to Earth, Delnoid 1. He 15 others like him have been modified so that he can speak aloud for us. This lovely lady beside me is Glinda, my wife and my Queen, and this exuberant girl is my lovely daughter, Princess Selena." Glinda extended her hand to President Truman and as he took her hand and kissed her cheek, he felt powerful caring, love energies flowing from her into his mind and spirit.

He then took Selena's hand and as he bent slightly from his waist and kissed her cheek he felt again calming, caring, charming energies from her. He swore that he also heard two mirthful short squeaks and a squeal coming from somewhere behind the princess. Sara heard it too and saw Arthur and Glinda looking exasperatedly and beseechingly at their now irrepressibly grinning squeaking, squealing and soft rapid clicking exuberant15 year old teenage daughter.

President Truman looked at the royals and said, "I would like you to meet my chief cultural anthropologist, Navy Lt. Commander, Miss Sara Winchester and my, uh Army alien research specialist Col. Phillip Corsa."

Arthur turned to his right and beamed, "Mr. President, I would like you to meet, uh, Ailema and her life mate Embry. Embry is our chief flight master and Amel... uh Ailema is our uh, cultural affairs officer and our earth exploration flight coordinator and pilot."

Embry dutifully kissed Sara's cheek and then shook hands with the President and Phillip.

While the president and Amelia were locking - shrewd to see you again eyes with each other, Embry quickly and forcefully beamed to Mr. Truman, "For now Mr. President, please sir, it's really best that we maintain uh, rigid formality and secrecy about Amelia during our first meetings."

Harry who was again delighted to see Amelia again especially in the context of this incredible alien starship, smiled, nodded his head and said, "But of course Embry, of course, whatever you say."

Arthur then invited them to accompany him for refreshments and snacks. And as they began walking down a curved inner hallway, one of the female aliens beamed, "I hope that you will like our seafood."

The president and his still flabbergasted staff just looked at each other resignedly, but now they felt a bit more confident as they walked with the aliens to partake of the alien cuisine and possibly discover the destiny of planet earth. As they walked with the aliens, Sara who had once visited Egyptian and many Mayan and a large number of Inca ruins, whispered to Phillip, "It really smells terrible, damp and really moldy in here. Some of these walls seem to have slimy yucky and smelly green moisture dripping down."

Philip nodded his head in agreement and whispered, "It really smells like a fish factory in here. This star craft must be exceedingly and incredibly old."

Sara, then recalled the Pacific Fish Co cannery that she had visited during her studies at the Naval Post Graduate School in Monterey, California, pinched her nose, looked over at Phillip and just rapidly nodded her head in agreement. Sara then pulled Mr. Truman's arm and made him slow down and once they had fallen a bit behind the aliens, she looked wide eyed at the president and whispered, "Mr. Truman, did you look ,at uh, that Ailema? Gosh, she sure looks a lot like Amelia Earhart!"

Harry grinned enigmatically and paused as he pondered and said, "You know Sara, you are quite right. She certainly does look like an older but not as gaunt, and somehow a happier Amelia Earhart. Except now, her hair is walnut brown and quite long and lovely."

The still baffled Sara said, "Well now, this has sure got me speculating. Did you notice that she has the same buck like two front teeth with the same gap between them that Amelia had?"

The wily president looked stealthily at Sara and whispered, "Gosh, you are right Sara. And she has the same girlish laugh that Amelia had. Uh, I seem to remember that from the Pathe newsreels." Harry made a poker face as he recalled her teeth and girlish laughter during his astounding meeting with Eleanor and Amelia, risen from the dead, just six weeks ago in his oval office when his life changed forever… Truman, to divert the rocketing curiosity of Sara, harrumphed and whispered, "But Sara, come on… this just could not be. Remember Amelia perished before the war along with her navigator, Fred Noonan, back in July of 1937." He thought to himself, "Sara is no dummy and I am distressed that for now we apparently must keep Amelia's being alive very hush hush!"

He then heard in his head alone. "Mr. President, this is Embry, Amelia's husband and as you must please respect, we must always and forever keep Amelia's secret to ourselves. Because she now has a new fulfilling and happy life with us Delphinians and this is the way she wants it…"

Harry, looking around for Embry, silently and wisely thought, "You are quite right uh, Mr. Riddle, and we will at all costs preserve and keep your wife's secret from humankind, sir!" Embry, who was up ahead with Arthur and Col. Corso, beamed to his wife, "Dear, why in Amador's name did the president call me, Mr. Riddle?"

Amelia squeezed his hand and giggled girlishly as she whispered mischievously, "Because my dear alien husband, it's a secret. A deep and dark secret, but nevertheless, a jolly good alien riddle!"

Harry recalled one brief skeptical comment from his wife Bess, back in early 1946, when she confided in him that her friend, Eleanor Roosevelt, once told her that there were aliens trying to connect with us to land here on earth. Now Harry really knew that such rumors were completely true. Because he, Phillip Corso, and few others in Majestic-12, knew the truth about the Roswell crash in July, of last year. And now, four small grey alien bodies, were being kept in cyro tanks at Wright Patterson AFB in Ohio. But, they sure did not look at all like any of these aristocratic, spiritual aliens.

Shortly, they all turned right and entered a large softly lit room with some kind of strange, but sweet melodic and smooth squeaking, squealing, trilling and occasional soft clicking. There was soothing music playing softly and unobtrusively in the background. As the soft waving musical notes played, some of the pale different colored light along the wall tops occasionally glowed, dimmed and sequenced in tune with the relaxing musical notes.

There were four large 10 x 16 foot (3 meter x 4.8 meter) image screens just above eye level on each wall of the rectangular banquette hall. The screens were depicting amazing images of what must have been the alien's ancient home world as seen from space. There were also scenes of three magnificent domed cities on a cluster of smaller islands all surrounded by tremendous beautiful blue oceans. One screen also showed many exquisitely dressed beings who looked just like their hosts.

Sara pointed and exclaimed, "Look! Oh look...there are dolphins swimming in that bay."

They were led to an astounding round banquet table with twelve seats around it. Phillip noted with relief that all of the seats were all apparently designed for humanoids.

As the president and his party were seated across from Arthur and his kinsmen, Arthur beamed, "After we have drinks, relax, and taste some of our seafood that we trust that you will like, I have a few remarks to make. Then we can get down to our issues, mutual concerns and expectations…"

When he finished beaming, a side panel whisked open and two lovely young, apparently teenaged, alien girls appeared each pushed what at first glance appeared to be a normal restaurant serving cart. But as Phillip looked more closely he exclaimed. "Oh, my gosh! Look at the serving carts. They, they have no wheels! They're floating about 2 inches (5cm) above the floor!" The two charming girls, dressed in white black trimmed flight suits, started putting down plates of food and drinks at each setting. As the waitresses arrived at each setting, the President and his two associates' jaws dropped open and they gasped as they saw Coke in apparently authentic earth bottles.

There was also, along with coffee, something that seemed to be plain water with ice in glasses. The glasses were cleverly made from cut off, rim polished empty Coke bottles.

President Truman turned to Arthur in open-mouthed amazement and asked, "Oh my gosh, do you always drink Coke on your ship?"

Arthur grinned as he waited while his girl poured fizzing Coke from its bottle into a glass that had ice in it. He picked up his glass admiringly and beamed, "Oh we treasure your coke, we just can't get enough of it. Apparently it's the sugar and caffeine in it that we are all crazy about. We each drink at least a bottle or two of it every day. So, what will you have to drink my dear Mr. President?"

Truman, always the diplomat, said, without missing a beat, "Uh, Coke of course amigo. We shall all have aCoke. Where on Earth do you get this?" He quipped. "At the Safeway?"

The alien Arthur frowned and asked, "The Safeway? What on Earth is a Safeway Mr. President?"

Glinda beamed privately to her husband, "Arthur, it's a USA supermarket chain…"

Arthur, not missing a beat, quipped back to the president, "Oh course Mr. President, where else on earth would we go for our Coca Cola sir?"

Arthur was of course perfectly aware that the earthlings rightly suspected that the humanoid looking aliens had probably visited many earth side places to explore. By then the cute waitresses had used their perfectly normal earth size bottle openers and filled everyone's glass with nice cold Coke.

Arthur stood, smiled majestically and mentally proclaimed. "A toast with our favorite earth beverage to our two cultures and may we long enjoy peace and this delicious Coke between us!" Delnoid stood, raised his Coke and exclaimed aloud, "Salud to our friendship and homecoming!" Sara sipped, giggled and thought to herself, "Hummmm Coke seems to be giving them a bit of a high."

Glinda, easily reading Sara's mind, cocked her eyebrow and looked over at Ailema and winked and looked admiringly at Sara. She relished sipping her Coke while Selena, sitting excitedly next to Sara, was nosily gulping down her Coke and clicking contentedly like a kitten purring. The toasts finally started to break the ice between the earthlings and their alien hosts, as all raised their glasses and drank their cokes.

The smiling Arthur beamed, "Please try some of our alien snacks. We have what you call seaweed, as vegetables, and sea food made from your earthly fish." Sara saw an orange red, curly, crispy thing on her plate and she searched around for a fork to eat it with.

The breathtakingly lovely alien woman sitting next to her noticed her apparent confusion and mentally asked Sara, "What do you need my dear earthling?"

By then, Sara noticed that all of the aliens were picking up the variety of the strange looking goodies and the small fish pieces on their plates with their fingers and were popping them whole, one by one, between copious swigs of Coke, into their mouths.

They all easily carried on mental conversations with the President and his now more relaxed colleagues who were feeling as if they were dreaming or hallucinating all of this, unbelievable encounter of the alien banquette and Coke.

 Sara asked Glinda, "Your Majesty, I am pleasantly surprised at your earth sounding names. Arthur and this incredibly beautiful round table we are sitting at are certainly not from any alien culture or world. And Glinda is, as I recall, the good queen of the south from our Wonderful Wizard of Oz stories."

Glinda squeezed her hand and beamed… "Sara, you are the anthropologist! I would have thought that you would have realized we are all totally telepathic. It's our Delphin rooted language and because of it and our sonic abilities, preclude any need for actual names. We normally easily identify each other by sonics – like wavelengths." Glinda looked Sara directly in her face, smiled lovingly, clicked softly and beamed, "Oh Sara, Arthur became fascinated - as we all did with King Arthur and the Knights of the Roundtable. So he, like the overgrown child that he is at heart, decided to call himself Arthur after your great fictional king. By the way, you are absolutely right Sara; this is exactly why our banquette table is round and designed like an image of the round table we saw in the book. Also, during our small excursions into many places in Latin American and once in the lovely Italian port of Portofino, we, loved the peoples' Latin energies or ondas as they call them. We decided that since we were going to need names here on earth, we listened to the radio and learned some names by just carefully listening to people in all of the puertos that we visited."

Sara nodded in understanding as she asked, "Well then, what about Delnoid?"

Glinda smiled, clicked in surprise and she replied, "Delnoid, well, it's just what we call our super high level bionic android helpers. But he keeps telling me he wants to be called Tic-Toc after one of the Wizard of Oz mechanical man characters."

Sara noticed that Ailema, across the table from her, was occasionally staring almost hopefully and little forlornly directly at her as her mate, husband Embry, held her arm and seemed to be smiling while beaming loving and reassuring waves to her. Sara also noticed that he kept holding on to Ailema's arm.

When the square and triangular plates were empty and each had seemingly non-ending Coke being poured, Arthur said, "Now, before we can get down to business, would anyone like some Colombian coffee? I think a human in South America by the name of Juan Valdez makes it. We sometimes drink it in the morning amigos. Our metabolism is different and Coke and sugared coffee act to make us feel, uh, happy and at the same time, calm us down and centers us so we can focus and concentrate better." (classic ADD.)

The visiting earthlings all smiled but declined the coffee. Arthur, talking through Delnoid, told President Truman that earth, because of its abundant oceans, diverse climate and quite a few still uninhabited coastal areas, earth was ideal for them. They wanted to try to make a formal alliance with President Truman as a first step towards living on Earth and developing future technological, economic, social and cultural cooperation and exchanges.

But, the president could not help thinking, "Bullshit amigo!" He demanded, "Why then are you abducting humans and performing medical and sexual experiments on them?" As he thought bullshit, he became alarmed as he remembered these aliens could read their minds.

Arthur immediately interjected with an overwhelming beam, "We are a superior and very advanced race and we are only trying to understand and improve on our alien human hybrid conceptions that are vitally needed to continue our race."

The President angrily said, "What about the lives, human rights and life dreams of those you take away, huh?"

Arthur became righteously irritated as he strongly beamed, "Mr. President! Since we are the superior and advanced race, truthfully there is nothing you can do about our investigations amigo. And besides, sir, what about those uh, grays that you hold at your secret base in Dulce, New Mexico?

President Truman exclaimed, "Well amigo, obviously as you wanted, we sure have gotten straight to the point of your inhumane interference issues between our species."

Politically tough old Harry voiced, "OK your highness… amigo, where do we go from here? Are you planning to invade and enslave all of us?"

Thankfully at this brinkman point Queen Glinda grasped Arthur's arm and all heard in their heads her melodic but firm voice saying, "Please gentlemen, we are all children of this universe and you two alpha males need to quit butting heads together like two ancient Delphinian and Viking warriors. Remember dear, the purpose of this vital first meeting is to try to form peaceful understanding, cooperation and co-existence between all of us!"

The president and equally alarmed Sara and Phillip rightly concluded that Glinda was fortunately, one way or another, wearing the pants, uh the gold jumpsuit of the family.

Sara noticed that Ailema seemed to be quite upset and alarmed. She tried to stand up but Embry looked sharply at her and quickly made her sit back down.

Arthur looking abashed at his queen beamed, "Glinda, you are quite right my dear lady. Mr. President and friends, I do apologize for my regressive tribal alpha male overreactions. Let us try to resume our negotiations peacefully. Let us not let our ancient limbic fears, tribal alpha male egos and destructive over reactions trash our so important to all, initial talks and negotiations."

The President thought, knowing perfectly well that the aliens would read his mind, "Well, at least you are civilized and advanced enough to respect who you and we are." He smiled diplomatically as, in turn did King Arthur, his wife, Delnoid and their other associates.

Sara, who was President Truman's advisor for extraordinary cultural anthropological issues, was awed at this extraordinary backing down towards pacification, away from the destructive and escalatory alpha male posturing. She was indeed impressed and grateful. Such alpha male ego based over reactions had throughout human history and probably throughout the Delphinians own history, been the prime causes of excessive fear based arrogance, greed and ego motivated abuse in families which escalated up through society, politics and to all out wars.

As Sara was thinking that, Selena, the beautiful young brunette princess sitting next to Arthur and Glinda, was grinning excitedly and reading her mind. She smiled at Sara and thought to her, "Sara, come with me. We have much to talk about while these bully boys are sorting out their agendas."

As the cute alien princess stood, Sara tapped the president on his shoulder and said, "Mr. President, the princess wants to talk with me in private. May I please be excused?"

President Truman looked up at Sara and gave a half smile and whispered, "Of course you may, Sara. I do hope that you two young women can add more insight, understanding, flexibility and peace to this present damn exasperating Mexican alien standoff." Sara stood and walked around the table to join Selena and as she turned to Arthur and Glinda, she smiled and asked for their indulgence. Arthur nodded his head in approval, smiled back and beamed to the two women, "Indeed girls, please see what light you two young female spirits can share with each other.

It seems that the need that all women have is the ability to talk about everything in the universe which is indeed truly… universal…"

Selena, towing Sara by the hand, started to leave the banquette table. Harry Truman saw Ailema start to stand up, but again, her mate quickly pulled her back down to her seat and she looked really furiously at Embry… Harry also noticed that Glinda looked at Ailema with alarm and as she did, the

Amelia Earhart look alike quickly calmed down, looked at Glinda, smiled and tenderly and apologetically kissed her husband's cheek.

CHAPTER 9 GIRL TALK

Selena led Sara out of the meeting chamber and down the hallway into a surprisingly large library with almost all the shelves filled with books. Sara noticed that a few Delphinians were sitting reading and also a crew of two males and two females were installing more book shelves. Sara seeing the books asked, "Are all of these books from your planet?"

Just then she also noticed that Selena was looking semi indulgently at all of the Delphinians who then began leaving the library but with mirthful smiles, curious looks, clicks, squeals and squeaks at the princess and the remarkable earth woman.

Selena squeaked, smiled and beamed, "Oh no Sara, back on our world and in our starship we didn't have any books. Everything that we read and reference, are in our artificial intelligence and data storage systems, as you might call them. These systems can beam directly into our brains from in here or from little uh, portable electronic notepad storage devices we read from."

Sara was amazed as she realized that Selena was describing an electronic display, TV like kind of a small book devise.

"These are earth books that we have uh, purchased here and there and I dearly love all of them. I especially love the children's picture story books…"

Sara wide eyed asked, "Selena do you mean to tell me that you have read all of these books?"

Selena squealed in joy and beamed, "Oh yes Sara, we each try to read one or more each day to practice reading and understanding your culture and history.

I dearly love reading your stories. We also now have them all uh, scanned and recorded on our individual electronic pads as well as in the ships main memories. But, most of us find that we really prefer and enjoy just handling and turning the pages to the next exciting or emotion filled part of the story and we also relish smelling these books. Additionally we enjoy just sitting quietly or in our cabin beds reading before we sleep at night. Do you want me to tell you one of the fairy tales?

Selena then blithered nonstop and beaming, "Sara, I also read and really enjoyed all these wonderful children's picture storybooks; Abraham Lincoln by Ingri & Edgar Parin d'Aulaire, They Were Strong and Good, by Robert Lawson, Make Way for Ducklings by Robert McCloskey, The Little House by Virginia Lee Burton, Many Moons, which was illustrated by Louis Slobodkin and written by James Thurber."

Then she squeaked, clicked contentedly and beamed, "I cried about Prayer for a Child, illustrated by Elizabeth Orton Jones with that so moving text by Rachel Field; The Rooster Crows by Maude & Miska Petersham; The Little Island, illustrated by Leonard Weisgard and text by Golden MacDonald. The books excite me about our upcoming landing and new lives on earth."

Selena squealed, as if taking a deep breath and continued, "I also love to draw. And someday I want to make illustrated children's stories all about our Delphinian culture and our epic six generation journey to earth. Later I'd like to write and draw all about our earth cross breeding and earth born children. Also Sara, I so loved this book, White Snow, Bright Snow, illustrated by Roger Duvoisin and written by Alvin Tresselt but I have never actually felt or walked on snow yet."

Sara cocked up her eyebrows, smiled in astonishment as she said, "Well Selena, I am truly envious of your reading and memory abilities. I just wish that I had time to read as much as you do. How long does it take you to read a book in English?"

Selena grinned proudly, made another funny squealing sound and beamed, "Sara, I can read through a book in about an hour. I can also read in seven earth languages; English, French, German, Italian, Japanese, Chinese and of course, Spanish too. How long does it take you?"

Sara was really amazed at Selena, stammered, "Uh, well, it usually takes me three or four days and most times even longer to read a book. I only have time to read while I am in bed just before I fall asleep."

She, then forgetting her new alien friend's telepathic abilities, thought to herself, "Golly, your intellectual abilities must be thousands of years ahead of us!"

Selena grinned, clicked rapidly and proudly beamed, "Sara, we are actually only about 1,000 years ahead of your culture."

There were 24 tabletop viewing screens in the library and two chairs at each station. Selena invited Sara to sit at one of the tables and Selena beamed to go on and explain, "Our race long ago evolved with our innate dolphin telepathy heritage that had millennia ago become our only way to communicate between ourselves and now with you humans. But we can also hear sounds with our super keen sense of hearing.

Sara remarked aloud, "So, can you still vocalize?"

Selena became kind of downhearted and beamed, "No Sara, we can't talk aloud."

Sara touched her arm and tenderly asked, "Selena, why are you sad?"

Selena looked dispirited and beamed, "Well, even though we can telepathically and emotionally sing and share our hearts, spirits and vision about our loves and losses, and our personal and pod life dreams in our minds and hearts Sara, I kind of always wanted to be able to sing aloud, especially since I have been listening to your wonderful music on our ship's radios. Just recently on our AM radios we started picking up a new program you call the Grand Ole Opery. The Delmore Brothers and Arthur Smith are my favorite Boogie Woogie players. And that Bing Crosby on NBC is simply dreamy Sara…"

Selena then reached out, touched the screen and the irresistible toe tapping sound of the Boogie Woogie Stomp by Albert Ammons blared out into the starship library. Sara looked down and saw that Selena was tapping her left foot with her strange wide black trimmed golden boot.

Sara, who also could not help tapping her foot, grinned and said, "Selena do you know that our President Truman, besides being an almost nonstop reader, is one heck of a good piano player? I heard him play the boogie woogie once and he is really good with that beat."

Selena squealed and beamed, "Oh Sara I would love to hear him. I so love your earth music, especially your boogie woogies. I just love to dance to that flipper flapping tapping music."

Sara grinned and exclaimed to Selena, "OK, stand up and take my right hand with your left hand and move like this…"

Within seconds Selena who had a genius photographic memory, was dancing the boogie woogie exactly as Sara was gyrating and laughing. As the soul thumping music ended both girls hugged and laughed as they sat down next to each other. Selena beamed, "Oh Sara, I just love to bunny with you."

Sara couldn't help grinning yet again as she realized that Selena had memorized most all of the 1940's slang and said, "Oh me too Selena, I just love chatting with you like this!"

Selena exuberantly beamed, "Oh Sara. I now have a great collection of music and songs from 1940 right up till yesterday. Would you like to hear some of my songs?" She touched her blouse and as the upper right breast pocket slit opened, she pulled out an incredibly small white hexagonal gadget with a white neck lanyard with two wires with ear buds dangling from it. "I record all of them on this digital player and I use my tiny little earphones to listen."

Before Sara could ask Selena anymore questions, Selena rattled off part of her memorized list of many popular 1940's songs; "All Things You Are by Tommy Dorsey, Tuxedo Junction by Glenn Miller, White Christmas by Bing Crosby, Chattanooga Choo Choo by Glenn Miller, Coming In On A Wing and a Prayer by The Song Spinners, Swinging on a Star by Bing Crosby, Doctor Lawyer Indian Chief by Betty Hutton, Rum and Coca Cola and that jiving boogie woogie Bugle Boy by the Andrews Sisters is one of my favorites to dance to."

Selena beamed excitedly, "And last year I was curious about, Smoke Smoke That Cigarette by Tex Williams. Sara, why do people smoke cigarettes?"

Sara replied, Selena it's a horrible addictive habit, it makes me sick and it also causes serious diseases in humans like bronchitis, emphysema and we now suspect that it also causes lung cancer."

Selena became very concerned and frowned as she touched her friend's arm and beamed, "Do you smoke Sara?" Sara feeling totally ashamed said, "I smoked when I was 16 and it kept making me hack, so I finally kicked the habit when I was 19 and I have never smoked since."

Selena tenderly held her new earth amiga's arm and just for a few precious quiet moments, beamed healing and loving energies into Sara.

Selena opened her eyes, moaned and beamed, "Oh Sara, someday, hopefully soon, mom and I will give you a complete healing for your body and lungs."

Sara hugged her alien and said, "Oh my goodness Luna… I actually feel, uh, more energized right now. Thank you dear princess, I am looking forward to experiencing and learning all about your healing arts."

Selena squeaked and clicked rapidly and beamed, "We will be happy to heal you and others Sara. How is President Truman's health by the way?"

Sara smiled and said, "Well, someday, hopefully soon you and your mother can ask him to allow you to examine and rejuvenate him. Although, for a man of his age at 64 now, he seems to always have as much energies as I do and he seems to also usually be in good spirits too."

Selena squeaked, clicked worriedly, then looked alarmed as she reached for the touch screen and squeeked even more rapidly, she beamed, "Oh Sara, wait a minute.

I have to look up rejuvenate. I know you can explain that word for me.

But, I want to quickly read all about it in our dictionary databases."

Sara relaxed as she marveled at her alien's response ability towards accurate understanding.

Selena continued, "Sara when you are reading, do you ever get to the end of a sentence or a paragraph and realize that you have no idea what you just read?"

Sara grinned as she said, "Oh my gosh, I do that all of the time."

Selena clicked rapidly while at the same time she read all of the definitions of rejuvenate and beamed to Sara, "Well my earth friend. Did you know that there is an exact reason for such confusion after reading. It's because you went past a word that you did not understand or misunderstood. And, as we read and study, we build up a stack of misunderstood or not understood words that would stretch from the earth to the moon! It is so important that whenever you are reading that you realize these symptoms of confusion then be sure to use your finger to point at each previous word until you come to the word that you just misunderstood and then go to a dictionary to fully define that misunderstood word. This is why I am now taking time to clear up my not full understanding of the rejuvenate word."

Sara was amazed, "So there was a reason for confusion while reading." She looked excitedly at Selena and said, "Please teach me later all about your really great reading and understanding techniques – ok?"

Selena then clicked in satisfaction and beamed, "Ok here is the definition:

Verb rejuvenate (third-person singular simple present rejuvenates, present participle rejuvenating, simple past and past participle rejuvenated) 1. To render young again.

Selena squealed in delight and beamed, "I will be super glad to teach you our reading and study techniques. Before earth we didn't have any books, we Just had data bases on display screens. But as soon as we started reading, we realized that our vocabularies were really almost nonexistent from only hearing and not reading actual words. So our education department came up with this wonderful study method to help us realize when we encountered a misunderstood or not understood word. It's amazing what trouble just one little misunderstood or not understood word can cause. I remember while I was studying and drilling this procedure, I found I was totally stuck and really frustrated that I simply could not get through one particular activity.

My course instructor realized I was having trouble and asked me to carefully re-read the activity's instructions. As I followed her instruction, my frustration and stress were still evident. At that point, my wise instructor asked me what the word stress meant. I fumed, squealed and clicked like this in pure frustration and exasperation and I beamed to her, "Just like I feel so totally frustrated right now".

Mt instructor squeaked in anger, "Selena, for oceans sake! Remember and respect that we are all telepathic and now I and this whole course room full of students are feeling and reacting to your distracting frustrations. Just then everyone squealed and clicked loudly in irritated agreement and then all of them beamed at me. "Selena get the dictionary and clear up that word." So as I looked up stress, I found it had another definition besides feeling stressful, it also means emphasis. "So Sara, right then and there, my discovering the meaning of that word in context with my exercise instructions, enabled me to get through the drill and then I and everyone in the course room felt better and calm.

Sara was amazed that such a simple thing as a not understood or a misunderstood word was the root cause of failed understanding in reading and studies. She reached out and gently touched her alien's arm and said, "Oh goodness Selena, you must write a book all about this wonderful break through study method. It can revolutionize reading and study."

Selena grinned, clicked happily, squealed and beamed, "Ok Sara, I shall do that right after I write my book about our homecoming to our new magnificent water world home!

But first and foremost we need to keep Mr. Truman as healthy as possible so he can win the November, 1948 election in order for him to continue to help and officially support us in our vital homecoming." She squeaked again, smiled and beamed, "Anyway, I really love your earth music and songs Sara." Selena rattled on, "This year so far, I really grooved on Saber Dance by Woody Herman and Manana by Peggy Lee but another of my favorites is Buttons and Bows by Doris Day."

Sara reached out and gently held Selena's arm and said, "Whoa whoa little eager beaver star sister, once we get you to earth, we will get you your own jukebox."

Selena smiled and with a curious look on her face beamed, "Sara that would be the cat's meow! Uh, what's a jukebox? Is it a box you keep juke in? I shall look it up in our ships dictionaries." In a moment she turned to Sara, frowned and clicked in impatience as she beamed, "Well gosh Sara, it's not in our system, so please tell me what a juke box is!"

Sara laughed, regained her composure and said, "Oh my ever inquisitive Selena, it's a coin operated music box like your mind-boggling miniature music playing devise around your neck, except unfortunately, it's about 400 times bigger."

By now, most all of the ice between the two young women had been broken and melted and they both smiled and laughed. Sara said to Selena, "I have so many questions to ask you that I and humanity have would like to know almost ever since we first looked up at the stars from around our ancient campfires."

Selena, still tapping her foot to the rocking beat, grinned and beamed, "What? Wait a minute Sara, I need to turn down the radio." Selena then beamed, "We've been asking the same too Sara. We are curious just like you but as I said, we are only about a thousand years ahead of you."

Sara was also well versed in Astronomy and cosmology, said, "Wow Selena then it's all exquisitely true, we are all children of the light and life giving stars in this magnificent galaxy."

Selena then went on to explain, "The creators have forever used their successful bi lateral symmetry design matrix for all human like bodies for intelligent species who walk on all other worlds and also amphibians who swim in the seas. Because this design succeeded so well throughout time to work for the prime law of the universe, which is to morph to survive."

So, as we both must respect. Every living thing on all worlds has to obey the prime axiom of survival. To do this we must always adapt and evolve. So we Delphinians are simply from almost the same sea born matrix as you, but again, we are just some 1000 years ahead of you."

Sara excitedly asked, "Tell me again, what star does your home world orbit?"

Selena beamed, "The star you call Rotanev. It's the star you designate beta Delphinus at a distance of 97 light years. It's ironically in the constellation that you call the Dolphin. From your star maps, it's the second brightest star. It's the one that connects the dolphin's body to its tail."

She suddenly became quite downcast and sad. She began to cry, squeak and click as she beamed to Sara, "We have been living out our lives, hopes and dreams in this too damp and stinky old starship for just over six generations now Sara."

Sara exclaimed, "Do you mean that you don't have a home world anymore dear amiga?"

Selena realizing that she might have shared too much placed her index finger over her lips and made the apparently universal shhhh sign. She stood up, took Sara's hand and gestured with her other hand for Sara to get up and follow her. She held Sara's hand as she pulled her human blessing of a new girlfriend out of the library, just like one school girl would tow another. She turned left down the main hall until they turned right and went down another hallway to walk for a few meters until Selena turned right again and towed Sara to the narrower dead end of that hallway.

Sara became a little bit concerned about why and to where her new alien friend might be towing her.

Selena placed her open palm of her left hand on a beige door in front of them and it glowed briefly with a very faint blue colored handprint and slid open. Selena led Sara inside and the door slid shut.

Selena echoed in Sara's mind, "This is my cabin dear new confidant. Privacy is still cherished and respected. Each crew member's apartment was built by the originators of this starship with electronic and physical telepathy blocking barriers that cannot be switched off and only overridden by pod leaders!

Sara realized her new amiga needed to share with her in private, sat down on the very comfortable earth toned fabric couch. Selena joined her and broke into more tears and made strange moaning, squealing and clicking sounds.

Sara reached out and held her new star friend until her sobs finally diminished and said, "Selena, why don't you all just land somewhere and make a homecoming here on earth? We will help you of course."

Selena beamed, "Some of the few remaining alpha males aboard this six generations old controlled and closed society on our life ship insanely want us to force you earthers to give us a place. Absolutely dear Sara, I can beyond any doubt, assure you that the peaceful and sane majority of us aboard Lifestar, cherish and hold our precious long evolved, hard won standards of ethics, morality and peace. We will never let such an insane attack and absurd impossible doomed to tragic failure seizure of your world be attempted!"

Anthropologist Sara understood that she had encountered a small and completely cloistered society. In spite of its advanced technologies and medical sciences, had really only its racial Delphinian memories, traditions, life agreements and images, all trapped bubble-likefor 372 ardous years in their Lifestar ship. Just like the anguished ancient Mayflower with its pilgrims had been Just like a slave ship in some ways.. But this remaining crew of discouraged and despairing souls had been trapped aboard with their comprehensive unbroken racial memories for six seemingly endless generations.

She told Selena, "I will never tell anyone any of this dear Selena. This I promise to you." Then as an afterthought, she asked, "How many of you are aboard this gigantic life boat?"

Selena looked kind of scared as she hoarsely tried to whisper with her useless unformed voice box… "160…" Selena was really irked by her useless vocalization efforts stamped her feet, squealed in frustration and gave up on trying to speak. She reverted to telepathy and beamed, "Just 160 of us remain now dear Sara."

Emotional Selena teared up again and beamed, "In the last six generations, in spite of our so called advanced society's minds and evolution. Almost a third of the too supersensitive us - about one hundred Delphins over the last 372 of your Earth years in deep space - have chosen to step outside for a final walk through the airlocks of this interstellar brig without a spacesuit into the perpetual peace and freedom of eternity…We are all supersensitive and are all totally telepathically and emotionally connected Sara. So once a Delphinian decides to end it, others, usually their mates and their children would sometimes follow…" Just like your earthside dolphins will also do."

Sara quickly calculated in her mind and realized, "Oh my God that was almost three or four of you each year."

Selena then reading her new confidants mind quickly thought. "No Sara it was actually more than that each year since the deadly despair and hopelessness inside this damn brig of a smelly starship did not really set deeply and psychologically into our pods until during the middle of the third generation."

Sara bearing in mind the contagion of suicides in groups, sighed as she said, "Oh my God! So there were at least over a third of you during your last three generations who suisided in hopelessness.

As Sara again held her distraught new alien friend she cried, "Oh dear princess I am so sorry…" She asked, "Couldn't your medicos or psychologists help them and try to prevent such suicides?"

Selena squeaked and moaned as she beamed, "No Sara we don't have any, what do you call them?" Sara replied, "Psychologists Selena, psychiatrists and psychologists." Doctors for troubled and out of balance minds.

Selena sniffed, squeaked, moaned and continued, "Because usually, as a soul connected pod, we just beam group healing and deep loving energies to restore each other. But here, we've been forever away from our now destroyed beautiful home world's oceans. We've been trapped inside this horrible, artificially illuminated, giant, smelly, nano-crystalline and titanium canister voyaging between the endless stars, generation after generation. We all feel sad helplessness, trapped and frustrated. So the main losses came from those who so valiantly knew that their generation would never live to see Earth. Anyway, it's the ultimate courageous price they sacrificed for, til now, after 372 of your years, to endow our homecoming to me, my family and pod who hope to live, walk and cherish our precious life dreams here on your magnificent planet. We especially want to swim, squeak, squeal and play in your oceans under your light and life giving Sunstar."

Selena's eyes again brightened as she beamed, "Sara, the times over the last 12 years since we landed or surfaced our ship has been cherished. It allowed us to let in fresh air, to swim, play and frolic with your beautiful dolphins, our earthly cousins." Selena let out a long moan and then a semi happy squeal as she beamed all of her mixed yet happier feelings to her Sara. Sara asked, "Ok Selena, why then did you all wait so long to contact

President Truman?

Selena beamed, "We were super wary about contacting you earthers directly until we could listen and learn your earth society ways and intentions. But, as we listened, mainly to your radio, our anthropologists and sociologists sadly realized how tribal and warlike your alpha male earthers still are. During and even after your insane and horrifying second world war, we decided to occasionally, carefully and secretly visit your world to research and explore followed with short as possible stays at our underground base on the back side of your moon." Selena looking very hesitant beamed, "But Sara, some years ago, we met a human who actually knew President Roosevelt's wife. Back then, after Mrs. Roosevelt spoke to her husband, he chose not to believe her about our contact here. And, fearing loss of re-election - he forbade his wife to ever again talk about us. Nevertheless, back in 1945, in March, Mrs. Roosevelt again planned to talk to her really sickly husband, but in April, he passed away."

Selena not wanting to compromise Amelia's and Mrs. Roosevelt's secret meeting with President Truman, grimaced, gave a sharp squeak and lied as she beamed, "So you see Sara, we recently contacted your President Truman through that Tesla experimental alien research antenna at your Ft. Huachuca Army base down in south eastern Arizona. And so dear Sara, here we are and I am so glad, relieved and happy being here tonight with my new earth amiga!"

Selena stood, wiped her eyes and walked over to a large view screen on her wall, picked up a small candy bar shaped box, clicked, and softly pushed a button on the amazing wireless remote control of some sort and beamed, "Sara please look at this. It is the first view we saw of your earth and moon as we approached our hopeful new home world in 1936. I was only four."

As Sara looked and walked over to Selena, she put her arm around her waist and cried… "Oh Selena, it's so beautiful. It's magnificent and so spiritual looking. I feel so small and humbled seeing an image of our planet and our moon like this…"

Selena clicked softly, squeaked softly and beamed, "I took this image myself Sara and someday I will make a print and give it to you.." Still hugging her friend's waist, beamed, "Yes Sara and as soon as I saw your beautiful water world, I knew, I just knew that we had at last, after six frustrating and distressing generations, finally reached our homecoming."

Sara just stood there mesmerized for a moment and asked, "Exactly where was that image taken from?"

Selena smiled and beamed, "It was taken inbound - after we passed your planet Mars on our way to Earth. I have another one of the earth and moon that one of our scout flighters imaged from Mercury while it was scouting that way too hot sunward dwarf planet.." Sara remembering her astronomy class at Westmont College Observatory at Santa Barbara asked, " Isn't Mercury a planet?"

Selena squeaked and beamed, "Nope, it's really just like Pluto. it's a small moon size asteroid captured into orbit by your star." Then hugging, the two females bonded more and Sara irrepressibly grinned in joy while Selena cried, squealed, clicked super rapidly and moaned, "I still cannot believe I am finally going to freely walk and swim on earth."

Sara asked, "How long do you usually live?"

Selena looked resignedly at her new amiga, squeaked softly and beamed, "Well, usually we live until medical science can do no more and our life dreams and spirits return to our creators, the Amadores – which is about 100 to 125 of your years."

Sara stammered, "Is that all? Gosh, with your medical sciences I would think you could live a quality life for at least, what? Two hundred years."

Selena beamed, "That is very true Sara. We have the technologies, medicines and therapies to extend life to almost 160 years. But, long ago, it was decided - there was no point in living so long in this gigantic tin can. So, the medicos have always, except for curing pain and diseases like cancers and heart and other physiological breakdowns, just let us live out our normal gift of a life span of about 125 of your years. It's just like your still developing earthlings will eventually be able to also do."

Sara asked Selena, "So tell me, what really happened to your home world dearest star child? Was your home world destroyed by the supernova of your star?"

Selena sadly shook her head and beamed, "No dear Sara. Our pod history shows us that our equally beautiful home, an 80% water world, was destroyed by a rare catastrophe which happens only on water worlds with large oceans like earth has and my home world had. Sometimes the sea levels fall rapidly which causes the pressures on the ocean bottoms to lessen and all of the trapped methane and calthrate compounds are released which cause the destruction of most life forms on the surface and in most of the oceans too. But, I am always really skeptical of that story because I have, from birth, heard non ending legends about how our persecuted peace loving pod of 300 actually had to resolve to escape the never ending and ever escalating fighting on Delphenia." Selena beamed, "Oh Sara, I have so much to share with you but look at the time, we must soon be getting back to the others."

Sara sitting there mesmerized thought, "Your alien histories and cultures are amazingly so parallel to ours with our legends and ancient warfare and endless fear, ego, greed and betrayal sagas."

Sara just held Selena's waist as the lovely Delphin girl telepathically wailed, "Oh Sara, I so want to walk on your magnificent world with you and swim together with your dolphins in your splendid seas! To swim in beach coves and bays without constant fear of discovery of our ship is the one thing we all really want. We have on board a very small saltwater exercise pool, but it's just not the freedom and ecstasy we enjoy when swimming in the open seas." Selena then grinned and made a strange high pitched screeching almost painful squeal.

Sara, a bit taken off guard asked, "What was that for?"

Selena squeaked, clicked merrily and beamed, "Oh that was the siren voice of sound of a mermaid Sara!"

Sara quite stupefied exclaimed, "A mermaid? Are,are there really mermaids?"

Selena again squealed and clicked in mirth and beamed. "Nope, I was just joking with you Sara."

Sara vocalized, "Look Selena, there is so much we can do to help you. Have you ever thought about just outright asking for the help and relocation assistance that we can give you?" Sara realized that as advanced as the Delphinians were, they still have similar, but much less, social egos, reactions and problems all trapped and festering for six generations aboard their lonely, depressing, ancient starship.

Selena whistled and squeaked happily as she beamed, "Sara the formal asking is what we are bravely starting tonight. And from our mind and spirit readings of your President Truman, we truly sense he is the perfect, kind, humane and trustworthy human to begin real negotiations with for our homecoming."

Sara hugging her new alien confidant smiled and said, "Oh Selena, please tell your parents I agree with you about our President Truman and I will do all that I can to help him help you get landed in your new home world.

But, I have one main question I still need to ask you." Selena smiled and beamed, "I will try to answer it Sara."

Sara screwed up her face and asked, "How did you do it? How did you grow past your limbic cultural adolescent fears, egos, rages and angers to survive for how many years now? Billions?"

Selena squeaked, grinned and beamed, "Sara, we all can not be any older than the universe. We think this universe, since it was created, is only about 14 or 15 billion years old and yet, it's just a tiny part of countless other universes and dimensions in endless space and time."

Sara grinned and said again, "But Selena, how did you manage to not self destruct yourselves?"

Selena beamed, "Well, since we abandoned our home world with all the fighting, maybe by now they have self destructed. That's a question that I hope we, in future, can enjoy spending the time it would take to theorize about. But for now since our time is short, do you mind if I touch your head?"

Sara looking kind of apprehensive and said, "Well... ok..."

Selena softly warned Sara, "You alone, among all your other humanoids, will, as I mind meld with you, know our true history, hopes, dreams and Delphinian weaknesses. So you must for now and always promise to keep this to yourself dear new sister."

Selena gently placed both of her finger tips on each side of Sara's head and as she touched, they became totally mentally connected. It was way beyond the telepathic communication they experienced earlier. This was like Selena's whole mind, heart, soul and pod history flowed into Sara's mind, heart and soul, understanding and knowingness - as Sara's total life dream memories also flowed completely over into her new alien sister. After about only three minutes of this powerful soul melding contact, Selena squeaked and clicked softly, sighed in exhaustion, dropped her hands into her lap and beamed, "Sara, now do you understand?"

Sara breathlessly stammered, "Oh Selena we are so alike and I now understand and respect that we humans have so much left to accomplish in our growth, understanding and choices for the future. I actually now thank God that you fantastic loving beings have come here."

Selena smiled and beamed, "I agree Sara and I pray that you earthlings will eventually grow to share with us noble, mutually created and manifested life dreams of peace and harmony on earth."

Sara smiled for a second but her smile then turned into a concerned frown as she sternly looked Selena straight in her eyes and asked, "Dear new star sister, how is it with your vast knowledge, social, spiritual and technological skills that you must occasionally kidnap living human beings to experiment and interbreed with?"

Selena squeaked, clicked softly, raised her eyebrows and just earnestly beamed, "My dear new sister from Earth, it is only for our pod survival to learn how to change our physiology so we can quickly physiologically adapt to survive comfortably in your atmosphere."

Sara, looking very apathetic and saddened said, Well, I hope someday you can help me understand such disrespect and cruelty dear alien."

Selena looked very sad, contrite and resigned, whistled softly from high to low and beamed, "Oh dear Sara you must try to realize that if we don't land here and acclimate and be able to inbreed. It will be the end of our pod and the whole six generations will have squandered their lives for an impossible and barren dead end life dream."

Sara nodded her head in agreement as Selena beamed, "Oh my dear new earth friend, please, please know and please trust that we have never harmed any of the ten or so humans that we have only examined. We always fully erase their memories of us and all that they ever experience is missing time from their lives and sometimes a headache and sometimes a few weird and inexplicable dreams."

Both women now accepting, compromising and tolerating their mutual realities, smiled and hugged each other. Sara had heard about the inhumaine tactics of the , CIA and Wright Patterson in Ohio Air Force Base and also their dreaded and usually fatal white rooms at their Dulce New Mexico secret alien medical base, shuddered deeply within herself.

Selena sensing her friend's deep foreboding, reached and rummaged around in a center drawer in her incredibly cluttered desk and handed her a small black oval amulet with a silver galaxy symbol on it and assured Sara, "If you ever need my help, like if you are in danger from your dreadful military or fanatical religious minorities or others, just press this pendant to the center of your forehead like this, right here where what you call your third eye is and which we call melon and I will know that it's you.." Selena beamed as she passed her hand over the top front of her golden jump suit, it split apart as she pulled the exact same galaxy pendant from between her breasts. "We will come rescue you!"

Sara smiled gratefully and asked her new mentor, "But if I am being tortured inside a white room, will you have to kill all of my captors?"

Selena smiled and beamed, "Well hopefully not! But if we have to use aggression and our psychic powers or even laser weapons… we will! Just always be sure to keep this pendant and anytime you feel in danger or if you need me, use it and I will know where you are and I or my mother or any of us will connect telepathically with you dear Sara.

Also, my mother is a super telepath and if you lose your pendant or have it taken away from you, just scream beam for help and she will immediately find you no matter where you are." Selena went on, "Most all of us want to treaty with you, but so far our three surviving fifth generation older alpha male ministers and one stubborn doctor, keeps hoping that they can, with abducted human DNA just force you to allow us to adapt our species to comfortably survive on your world or another with the same atmosphere and oceans. "We have come too far and for too many generations to give up hope about living on your world."

Sara said, "Oceans, Selena do you need seas to survive?"

Selena beamed, "Appropriately you, me and all children of the universe and our ancient creators too, all come from the endless seas of space and time. On our ancient home world there was not enough moisture in our atmosphere and so, for millions of years, we evolved as an intelligent underwater mammalian air breathing species - just like your dolphins and whales did. Our ancestors lived out their lives under water in our world. It's kind of like always being in the womb. Since we could not of course talk underwater, we have telepathy and so do our old home world dolphins. But they also – like us - use their built in natural sonar with high pitched squeals and clicks too."

Sara was overwhelmed as she said, "Do you have built in sonar?"

Selena threw back her head and squeaked mischievously and, just for fun, she let out a short series of high to low pitched squeaks and squeals just like her dolphin cousins on earth. She then turned to the small shrine in her room with a beautiful female figurine hanging on her wall and concentrated and in a split second, the whole beautiful icon gently swayed back and forth. Selena grinned as she beamed, "That was from my melon sonar earthling." When your sub sonar man heard our sonar woman telling him to surface. She was using her sonar."

"Go on", Sara appealed as Selena's sonar absorption subsided.

"Well, just like all of you evolved, our sea born species evolved, and that coupled with our great natural curiosity, sense of humor and spirit of play - just like alot of you humans luckily seem to have. As you may know Sara, with the universal law of attraction, what we think and need, we can create and once we firmly develop whatever, Mother Nature as you call her, gives that to all future generations mentally, physiologically and genetically. Thoughts always become things don't you know."

Sara, then sadly recalled her poor mother, Athol, who was bi polar said, "Yes it's so true that everything physiological and mental – good, bad, sad or glad and happy – seems to run forever in our genes and chromosomes. Sara nodded and said, "So I believe that too Selena, whatever we think becomes true - good, bad, happy or sad."

Selena clicked softly, smiled knowingly and continued, "We slowly over millions of years evolved to become full amphibians with legs and eventually all of the human characteristics that we now have. The gas mix in our atmosphere was quite similar to yours with 70% Hydrogen, 20% oxygen and 10 % inert gasses. But the relative humidity on our home world was higher - always at about 70% or preferably more my dear anthropologist. Your dolphins can not be out of the ocean for more than a day at most and that is only if they are in the shade. If they are out of water under bright sun they will die after an hour or two. You know how you all feel when it's hot and the humidity in Key West Florida is like 98% right?"

Sara nodded wide eyed and said, "Oh yes, been there - done that."

Selena continued beaming, "We need at least an average moisture content of 75%. The problem now is that we have about 60% less sweat glands than you do. This is why as genetically evolved amphibians, we cannot just land and say 'take us to your understanding and kindhearted leader and by the way… can we have millions of sponges and endless buckets of sea water'…"

Sara exclaimed, "75%, why then are we both not suffering now?"

Selena grinned apathetically and beamed to Sara, "We have altered the moisture and temperature in the air in this part of our starship to only 45% for your visit this evening. Also, we all have on a skin lotion which keeps our skin moisturized and we are all wearing special super moisturizer plugs in our noses. The moisturizing lotion is being continually developed by our dermatologists as you would call them. As soon as we got actual samples of your planet's atmosphere. So far, the experimental lotion is good for about only seven days. But, by using it every day, even here aboard our starship, we have found that because it is made up of progenitor human stem cells, it has been actually stimulating the growth of more eccrine sweat glands for us. We expect now that within three to six months we will be able to remain indefinitely and safely in your atmosphere. My mother says that when we first land we must go to an island surrounded by ocean for at least a month or two, maybe longer to acclimate and slather on our moisturizing sweat gland growing lotion to let our sweat glands really continue to regenerate naturally just like yours do."

Sara contemplatively thought, "Hummmm just like we evolved from the sea too after millions of years to become land beings."

As Selena looked in slight panic at the now blinking red digital symbols on her wall, she beamed, "Oh Amador! Mother is calling us and we must get back to the others Sara. The, uh the time limit for our nose moisturizers is almost up."

As the two, now bonded, women stood Sara noticed again the small shrine in Selena's room. As she held Selena's hand she asked, "Selena who is that fantastically beautiful woman in your… what is that? Is it a shrine?"

Selena smiled and with loving energies to her new earth sister beamed,"Oh Sara that's a statue of one of the creators of the Universe, an Amador."

Sara said, "One of the creators of the Universe! Oh my God Selena!!!"

Selena continued smiling and beamed, "Oh yes we always connect with their universal energies as we honor ourselves and all of the Amadorian dimensional creators and their creator who you call God."

Sara smiled, squeezed her aliens hand and thought, "Oh my gosh, she looks just like many of our virgin statues and shrines I've seen in Mexico, in

South America, in Italy, in France and even occasionally along some roadsides in southern California."

Selena, reading Sara's thoughts, squeaked, clicked happily and beamed, "Of course Sara, the universal love energies and nurturing creative spirit of us women are always everywhere. And Amador means, one who loves."

CHAPTER 10 ALIEN MEXICAN STAND OFF

As Selena and Sara, hand in hand re-entered the banquette hall, they could sense that both sides, while now respecting and tolerating each other, were clearly still at a rather ill at ease Mexican Alien standoff.

As President Truman saw Sara re-enter, he could clearly see that she and Selena had developed good rapport and compatibility and hopefully, worthwhile talks. Truman, trying to keep his mind empty, said, "Well, I guess this is all that we can realistically accomplish for now your majesty. I do hope we can meet again soon to iron out all of our differences and bury the hatchet."

Arthur grinned a bit as he beamed, "Hatchet, Mr. President? Why on earth would we want to dig a hole in your planet's ground and put a hatchet in it?"

Truman laughed heartily and said, "Oh Arthur, uh, your majesty, that's just an American slang expression that we say to mean stop fighting and make peace."

Arthur clicked, smiled and beamed, "I sincerely hope so Mr. President.

We sincerely want to avoid any hostilities."

While Selena and Sara had been exchanging their realities, cultures, hopes and dreams, the Delphins leaders, with their technological supremacy, had bluffed and negotiated an initial spoken accord with President Truman that they would not attack and would continue to operate in secret to prevent any worldwide panics. They also agreed and promised to not abduct any more humans for medical examinations. The aliens definitely held the stronger fear factors and also, if needed, presumed advanced military space weapons capability. They also insisted that the US government continue and expand their alien cover-up and disinformation tactics.

Truman, Sara and Phillip stood as did Arthur, Glinda, Selena, Delnoid One along with Ailema and Embry. Arthur placed his hand on the President's left shoulder and beamed, "Dear Mr. Truman, before you all leave, I would like to show you our command bridge. Will you please join me?"

Truman quickly looked left to right at Sara and Phillip and while seeing the slight nod of their heads, he said, "But of course your uh Majes, uh, Arthur. We would love to tour your bridge."

The humans and aliens walked down a fairly wide corridor towards the center of the ship and came to a remarkable 12 foot (3.6meter) large, clear blue tinted tube which rose directly upwards in the ship. When they all reached the tube, Selena let out a happy squeal and beamed, "OK everyone, please enter our zero gravity lift." She gently pressed her left palm on the tube wall and as if by magic, the tube formed an adequate vertical rectangular opening. Arthur, Glinda, Delnoid, Ailema and Embry all nonchalantly stepped in the tube and to the total astonishment of the president and his party, the aliens just floated there at deck level with apparently nothing under them.

Glinda clicked merrily, grinned and beamed, "Oh come on, it's completely safe, just like our blue light ramp. It's just a zero gravity lift. Please don't be afraid!" After Truman, Sara and Phillip entered, the transparent door deformed and before they knew it they had risen almost 48 feet up to the top deck of the awe-inspiring starship. When they reached the level of the main flight deck, the earthly visitor's jaws dropped when they saw a fairly large room with grand panoramic windows that were underlined and flanked with control consoles and several very comfortable chairs with headrests. In each chair sat male and female Delphinians who stood, smiled, squeaked and clicked softly among themselves as they greeted the President and his party. As each male kissed Sara's right cheek, Phillip and the President enjoyed kissing the Delphinian female's cheeks. Phillip was amazed as he looked around at all of the control displays and even a large screen display showing clearly the sea bottom 24,700 ft (15,000 meters) below them. Sara smirked as she saw that Phillip was easily charmed by the incredibly lovely Delphin female crewmembers and their human like, big wide beautiful blue eyes.

The Delphins and their amazed Earth visitors were standing gazing out at the sea and the moonlit submarine. Arthur beamed, "OK, we're rotating the control center to face more towards your sub." Just as the rotation stopped, all gave a quick gasp with oh oh's and excited, alarmed squeaks and rapid clicks as a small bright white flash came from the conning tower of the sub. Arthur clicked rapidly as he immediately placed the fight deck crew on full alert, apprehensively turned to the president he beamed, "Mr. Truman sir, is your sub firing at us?"

Harry Truman who by then had recovered said, "Oh no your Majesty, I can't imagine what that was. But we will investigate just as soon as we can return to our submarine."

Glinda, had been resolutely quiet for a moment as she read the mind of the human on the sub's conning tower. She gently pulled the president to her side and beamed, "Mr. President, that flash is associated with someone over there who is intent on betraying us to the newspapers and radio, uh, the press as you call it. Whoever he is, he really holds a lot of animosity towards you."

Harry grimaced, looked beseechingly at Sara and Phillip and said, "Gol dang it! It's that treacherous two faced captain Jones. I just knew he could not be trusted."

A Delnoid standing looking at a display screen said aloud for everybody's benefit, "I have analyzed that flash from our sensors data and it was from the rapid low voltage electrification of very thin aluminum filaments in a small, vacuum - probably glass or some kind of plastic bulb."

Phillip gasped and scowled as he said, "Why that dirty sea dog took a flash picture of this starship.

Harry, who was an avid photographer, said, "Well, it probably won't do him any good in view of the fact that most amateur photographers do not realize that such a small camera flashbulb is effective only out to about 6 to 8 feet (3 meters) from any Kodak Brownie flash camera."

Arthur touched the President's shoulder and beamed, "Mr. Truman look at this vu-screen." As Harry looked he saw an amazing, lit like daylight, live telephoto color image of Capt. Jones with a sailor standing beside him. Harry exclaimed, "Why that SOB, he knows that no ratings are allowed topside during our uh, encounter, uh, meeting here."

Sara gasped as she said, "Oh look Mr. Truman! It's that sailor who was shooting at the dolphins." Everyone now looked very concerned as they saw the captain loading another flashbulb into the Brownie. And then, just as the smirking captain was aiming the camera, a narrow green laser beam hit the exact center of the flash bulb and the whole camera shattered into countless small pieces.

 Harry agape, laughed, "Well, that'll teach that traitor to try to compromise our meeting."

Phillip grinned as he said, "Oh my stars. That was incredible Arthur!

What was that?"

Arthur grinned as he beamed, "Well, Colonel, from what we have read in a couple of your theoretical physics and engineering books, such a theoretical devise in your texts is called a laser - for Light Amplification by Stimulated Emission of Radiation." He then grinned, clicked merrily and sounded, "Zzzzzaaap!" thru his blowhole and beamed, "We call it just that and we have several such small, medium, large and extra large weapons on our star craft." He bluffed about the extra large laser weapons.

Glinda looked seriously at President Truman and beamed, "Mr. President I will accompany you back to your sub and I will erase all memories from your treacherous captain and any crew that may have seen us or our ship."

Harry impulsively took the queen's hand and said, "Oh your Majesty, that will be just what the doctor ordered. I was beginning to worry what we could do about this double-crossing captain and that crew man. Because…unfortunately…we do need them to take us on to Guantanamo."

Arthur squealed a loud laugh, clicked rapidly and beamed, "Well Mr. President, if you want to ditch your submarine ride to Guantanamo, we could take you back to your Key West White House or even to the main White House south lawn in DC in less than 12 minutes !".

Truman was simply totally in awe as he grinned and said, "Oh my, you really have done your homework about us haven't you?"

Arthur grinned, clicked gleefully and smugly nodded his head.

Selena smirked and thought to herself, "Our mind reading abilities sure helps us do our earth people's homework as you call it Mr. President!"

Glinda moaned as she beamed, "Of course I have to be able to touch his head to effectively erase his memories."

Selena squealed and beamed, "Mother, we do have hundreds of typical earth clothes in our costume department that you can change into."

Sara looked incredulous as she said, "You are quite right Selena. Because, if after erasing that scoundrels memories he would still see your mother in her gold flight suit and he'd surely remember that."

CHAPTER 11 MIND SWEEP

Glinda had changed her clothes and was now dressed in khaki slacks, a dark blue turtleneck sweater and she wore the curious high top wide black shoes with silver trim. She and the Delphinians accompanied the earthlings to the reopened hatch of their floating starship where again the Presidential party saw that the amazing shimmering blue walkway beam was back on and reached unerringly out to their moonlit and waiting sub's foredeck.

They all shook hands and the males exchanged cheek kisses with the females all around. The Presidential alien and UFO investigator Phillip said, "This cheek kissing sure is a splendid idea. I wonder how they got that wonderful and so friendly cheek kissing custom."

Not letting on that she was reading his mind, Glinda smiled and thought to herself and Selena, "Hummmm, Colonel, you must visit South America someday. They, next to the Italians, are the best cheek kissers in the universe!"

As President Truman kissed Amelia's left cheek, he whispered, "Are you really all right and happy here Amelia?"

She nodded her head, smiled and whispered back, "Yes, I really and truly am Mr. Truman. I am finally happily fulfilled and Embry really loves me - quite unlike my, abusive widower, George"

President Truman, Glinda and Phillip were standing on the blue walkway. Selena and Sara, still in the entrance to the huge spacecraft, hugged and cried that they hoped to see each other soon. Selena extracted her galaxy amulet from her gold flight suit and Sara extracted her galaxy pendant from her blouse and the two young women smiled and winked meaningfully at each other. Sara then reluctantly joined her associates on the blue beam and the earthlings and Glinda all walked back towards the sub.

Arthur held the waist of his tearful, softly moaning, clicking daughter and beamed, "Well sweetheart, do you think that Sara really understood us?"

Selena who was, as naturally gifted and expected, becoming a supersensitive spiritual extrasensory like her mother, beamed, "I know she did and she is now our main and vital link to being able to soon find a safe new home here on this beautiful water world." We are soul and mind bonded sisters now and I trust Sara completely and unconditionally."

Arthur just thought, "Hummmm. I do hope so. I pray to Amador that this new home world landing will happen. Because I find that I do love this magnificent water world and… our old faithful clunker of a 50,000 year old starship is just about at the end of its six generations. It has worn out its reliability from our seemingly endless plight and flight over the last 372 light years."

Once they were aboard the sub's deck, Arthur had the blue light beam gangway switched off so as to not let any more of the sub's crew see it.

President Truman was relieved to see that the captain was already on the deck and looking about as glad to see him as a mad wet cat. Truman made his sternest commander in chief face and said, "Capt. Jones, please summon that crewman who was shooting at the dolphins and your sonar man topside immediately."

The uncouth captain just stood there leering at the extraordinarily beautiful woman now accompanying the President gritted his teeth and grumbled, "Yes sir Mr. President, sir…" Captain Jones then saluted, turned to get Wilson and the sonar man. After some rather ill at ease minutes, seaman Wilson, the scowling muttering captain and the bewildered sonar man appeared and Truman commanded, "Captain and seamen, you will stand at attention, close your eyes and do not move, no matter what happens." Truman, glaring at the captain, curtly said, "Is that clearly understood mister?" The pigheaded captain, snappily griped, "Very well Mr. President."

Glinda stood facing the captain and as soon as she placed both of her palms on each side of his head, he immediately entered a world of nothingness. After about only a minute, she lowered her hands and beamed into his mind, "You will now walk over to the starboard side of your sub and look up at the lovely egg shaped 10 day old moon there above the western horizon." She turned to the now terrified ill-tempered seaman Wilson and placed her open palms on the sides of his head.

She immediately, as she had done with the captain, easity scanned his mind and erased all alien segments of anything he had seen and done. Now Glinda turned to the now wide eyed and anxious sonar man. She lovingly beamed, "Be not afraid Jimmy, I will not hurt you." She gently erased all of his memories of the alien encounter as well. President Truman, Sara and Phillip just stood there in awed astonishment of her incredible alien mind powers after she finished with Jimmy.

Glinda turned to the earthers and beamed, "Oh my dearest Amador! Mr. President, if those two are examples of typical males in your armed services, you must, in future, have us scan your captains and crew that we will be interacting with. These two are completely rotten in their very twisted, sociopathic minds, agendas and greedy treacherous actions. Your kind sonar man is indeed a compassionate and humane life respecting exception to his loathsome captain and that sociopathic, heartless, dolphin murdering shipmate."

Truman turned to Phillip and said, "I want this sonar man transferred to a good sub commander as soon as we reach Guantanamo. See that he disembarks this disgraced sub with us in Cuba. Take him with you to Washington for reassignment with a higher Master CPO level sonar rating at a new command center post or aboard a new sub in Norfolk."

Col. Corso proudly grinned, saluted and said, "Aye aye sir, uh Mr. President." Hen then ordered the captain, seaman Wilson and the now smiling, but clueless sonar man, to go below.

Glinda turned to the President, Sara and Phillip and as she embraced them, she clicked softly and beamed, "Well, we have overcome our first treacherous encounters with the likes of those two. I am concerned and sure there will be many more like them with hidden agendas and betrayals as we put down roots here on Earth."

President Truman, as he felt the alien Queen's powerful loving and pragmatic energies, looked her in her eyes and said, "My dear Majesty, uh, Glinda, we will always do all that we can to make your transition as safe and secure as we possibly can. There will always be troubled and disturbed people here with fear, intolerance and hidden agendas. But I assure you that Sara and others will guide and coach you as best they can to understand and cope with unspoken agendas and mind games here on our war torn and still too unsettled planet."

Glinda, returning the president 's gaze, beamed, "Dear Mr. Truman, in spite of our mind reading abilities, we will definitely need all of your kind assistance and earthly practicality in telling us how it really is, and guidance to make our six generation quest for a homecoming finally come true as safely as possible." She held her earthly trio and after again beaming loving and trustful energies, she turned and walked back across the now on again blue beam gangway to her starship.

As Sara waved tearfully, the president and Phillip turned and saluted the aliens still standing in the open port of their seagoing spacecraft. The aliens each raised their left hands and made the apparently universal middle and index finger V peace sign back to the humans.

As the President's party stood there on the now moderatly pitching deck of the Sea Cat after the blue beam gangway switched off and the hatch of the alien craft had closed. They then felt a penetrating vibration and heard a muted droning as the gigantic space craft slowly lifted off from the Caribbean Sea to slowly ascend up about 30 meters (100ft) and then, almost as fast as a shooting star, it flashed upwards and into space. Phillip followed it, totally open-mouthed and pointing with his finger he shouted, "Look! Oh Jeeeessssus… Just look at it go!"

After the aliens had soared away, President Truman and his party went below and the president told the now clueless but still scowling Captain Jones to set course for Guantanamo Bay, Cuba. The course was dutifully set to 270 degrees 54 minutes and… 16 hours later they would dock at the US Navy Guantanamo, Cuba facilities.

They were all sitting at the wardroom table, which was now put off limits to Captain and all crew by commander in chief Truman. He said to Sara and Phillip, "Well, our 1948 Puerto Rican verbal treaty with these aliens seems too one sided, ludicrous and mocking. These and probably other aliens have been visiting and possibly even staying on earth, apparently ever since ancient times. And they've been abducting, medically examining, breeding with and probably also genetically tinkering with humans ever since man and woman crawled out of the sea and began to walk upright and look like true humans!

But who the heck knows, maybe those other ancient aliens created all of us. We sure, except for those weird and creepy little grays, look and apparently think in very similar ways!”

Sara frowned and said, “Yes, this interference with us, is so like what my film director father always says; that the so called noble and idealistic non interference rule of visiting with other developing worlds and their societies, as written by that young science fiction screenplay writer, Gene L. Coon ‘is just a lot of idealistic wishful science fiction thinking and book and script writing crap. ” Sara looked directly at the president said, “But, Mr. Truman, I am now convinced and I don’t think the Delphinians are the same, or even related to the aliens who have previously visited and interfered on Earth. I also strongly suspect that they are a completely different group of, uh, truly kind visitors than the grey egg headed aliens who crashed near Roswell last July. I think Arthur knows about other past alien visitors and I think his saying that the Delphinians are also powerful intruders is just not true. I think he just said all of that to appear to be more convincing.”

Phillip added, I agree Mr. Prersident, “Did you get a look at how decrepit their ship was and how thin green and black slime covered some of the inside walls of that stinky old floating barge? I think the Delphinians are quite desperate to land and walk away from their six generations of imprisonment aboard their giant old tramp space scow.”

Sara, hearing this, just nodded in agreement as she remembered the six generations of Delphin history that Selena had mind linked to her about her amphibious ancestors. She already missed Selena muchoooo…

Shortly after the sub docked at the Guantanamo pier, four SP’s and two commanders boarded and arrested Captain Jones and seaman Wilson. As they were led off the sub in complete bewilderment, Captain Jones turned and scowled to the President, “Damn you Truman, what the hell am I being arrested for?” Truman, a former Army colonel, looked the treacherous hate filled captain directly in the eye and said, “High Treason Mister. You are being arrested for high treason and disobeying the direct orders of your supreme commander. And, accordingly, under the power of my memorandum of 24 September 1947, you and seaman Wilson will be totally isolated for quite some time.

There were two aircraft waiting for the President and his party at the Guantanamo Navy base. The president and Sara entered his “Independence - Air Force One – and Phillip and the rather perplexed sonar man and one of the commanders from Guantanamo entered the next plane to fly directly back to Washington, DC.

Sara asked the president where they were going and he smiled his irrepressible toothy grin and said, “Back to my beloved Key West Conch Republic so we can relax, really talk and plan in private my dear Lt. Commander alien expert!”

CHAPTER 12 KEY WEST

Three days later as Sara sat at a trusty Royal KMM magic margin typewriter in President Truman's southern little White House office at the Key West US Navy base. She had written up all, except her and Selena's secrets that had transpired between her and the alien princess along with her anthropological ideas and conclusions about the aliens.

After President Truman had spent half a day carefully studying her reports, he called her to join him in his office. When they were seated, he asked, "Do you think that we really can become friends and allies with the Delphinians Sara?"

She asserted, "Oh yes sir Mr. President! The time that I spent with Selena was so extraordinary, we really shared openly and we and the Delphinians are so incredibly similar. I think we can somehow help the aliens adapt to live in our atmosphere. While I am convinced that the Delphinians are actually not abducting and experimenting on humans, I trust now that they will keep their promise to stop experimenting with humans. From my sharing with Selena I also know that they genuinely want to become mutually beneficial allies and friends too." Sara looked sad and commented, "Please remember sir, we hunt dolphins and experiment on them. We have abused their trusting natures by heartlessly training them with mines strapped to their backs to blow up enemy ships. Now I realize and better respect how they, as a more intelligent species, must feel about us Mr. President."

Truman agreed as he said, "I will look into seeing what I can do to have the Navy Department eliminate such cruelties. Especially in view of the fact that I now realize it would be judiciously prudent of us not to offend our new dolphin heritage allies.

Sara said, "Well, Mr. President, if we analyze the history of abductions as far as we know, these or other aliens have not killed any people. But such encounters and reports of abductions by those Roswell grays and other aliens like the Nordics have always drastically changed the lives and dreams for most all of those who have been abducted. But, again sir, I am totally convinced that our Delphinians are not really abducting nor experimenting on anyone. Apparently from what we have been able to gather from a few purported abduction victim interviews - the aliens all seem to have powerful mind control abilities to place powerful hypnotic blocks in the sub conscious memories of their abduction victims, anyway that's my guess."

Truman sighed and said, "So Sara, what do you think we can do to help our new aliens peacefully settle here and progress to having their leaders trust us as we grow to trust them? "I, as well as Arthur, have to lead or have no business in earthly or exopolitics."

Sara said, "Mr. Truman remember that Selena told me that Arthur, Glinda and the majority of the aliens would never allow an attack on earth. She also told me that Arthur and Glinda vowed that they would take their star craft back into the depths of space before they would ever allow such insanity to come about. So, I suggest that we have another meeting very soon to try to show them and give them a realistic understanding and reliable hope for a home here on earth. That would better enable Arthur and Glinda to make their now small minority of old fifth generation alpha males stop any ROB irrational war plans in exchange for our conditional but maximum assistance."

President Truman said, "Hummmm… ROB ? That's a new one on me

Sara."

Sara grined and chiuckled as she explained, It means Reactive Olde

Baseturds, er, sir." That's what my dad used to call some of the old studio owners and project financial managers."

Truman chuckled and grinned as he wipped his glasses. "I think that another visit from our Delphin Royals and that amazing Delnoid 1M is a good idea Sara. Maybe we can barter with them for a place to live in exchange for their agreement to not attack and again, if it turns out that after then if this particular group of aliens does any more abducting… No more homecoming! I must maintain Sara that coming from a farm in Missouri, I never, even in a million years, dreamt that I would become president nor that I would ever be so involved in any such alien affairs which is still beyond belief. But, like the sign on my desk in Washington says, the buck stops here."

Sara nodded her head in agreement and said, "Selena told me about their total need and desire to make a homecoming on Earth. So, I too I hope we can have a meeting. Where we could invite them to join us incognito, touring and seeing one of our cities, its people and attractions."

"Great Idea Sara." said the President. "Where do you suggest?"

"Well, Selena wanted to be able to walk in a small town with me and on our Florida beaches and also to swim in our ocean. So, what about our meeting right here in Key West Mr. President? The whole logistics, secrecy and their safety would be vastly easier right here on this small navy base than in any bigger community or city sir. This can be accomplished if they are comfortable and if they can extend the time their sweat gland ointment and nose humidifiers give them in our atmosphere. We could also take them up to Miami. And since its still technically a Navy facility from being a convalescent hospital during the war, we could even have them safely stay a night or two at the exquisite Biltmore hotel in Coral Gables. Maybe I could also take Selena over to the wonderful Miami Sea aquarium. I know she would love to see her dolphin cousins there. We could spend the rest of the day at the beach and maybe even enjoy a picnic, with Coke of course!"

The President, tenting his finger tips said, "Well, we would have to meet them somewhere secretly at sea again in the USS Sea Cat since it's based right here at our Key West Naval Station and bring them ashore from there. How long did you say their nostril air humidifiers lasted?" "Hummmm, let me think Mr. President, we were aboard their ship for about nine hours when Selena became alarmed that her humidifier was running out." Sara continued, "So, when we contact them, we will have to ask how long they could visit with their amazing sweat gland growing moisturizing lotion and if they could bring along extra humidifiers?"

The next day the President called the top secret, alien radio communication facility at the giant U.S. Army Electronics Warfare testing base in Ft. Huachuca, Arizona. He later, at lunch, told Sara, "Ok, your message has been sent to the Delphinians asking for another meeting and they have agreed to send a small delegation. So you, my dear alien expert, will go again in the Sea Cat on March 13th to meet them at sea and bring them ashore here at Key West."

Sara worriedly asked, "Was Selena specifically invited?" The president smiled and said, "Sara we would never overlook inviting your best alien friend." She then queried, "But, Sir, don't you want to come too to greet them?"

Harry Truman who had always disciplined himself to do what was needed and right said, "Nope Lt. Commander, you are now in charge of this extraordinary project and besides, I must attend to just some matters of state during between now and your short voyage in order to be totally free for our reunion and negotiations with our aliens. Sara… I need to continue accomplishing my re-election strategy preparations which are now doubly vital for me to stay on board as President. That is the only way we can, if truth be told, follow through in getting our aliens securely landed here on Earth. God only knows what would happen to them if that arrogant jerk republican Dewey was elected in my place!"

Sara totally agreed, knowing very well that if President Truman was not re- elected, it would probably mean a catastrophe for the Delphinians, especially if a ROB Dewey got elected instead. She asked, "Do you suppose that they have earth clothes to wear? Mr. President, maybe you better radio again and ask if they have sufficient earth clothes for everyone and if not, please get me their sizes."

"OK, aye, aye Sara". He reached again for his yellow phone on his desk which could be patched directly into the powerful Huachuca alien radio antenna for his exclusive encrypted communication with the aliens. "I will do that right now."

CHAPTER 13 BRAS, PANTIES AND LASER CUTTERS

Two weeks later on 13 March 1948 at 18:00 (6pm) a gray Navy van pulled up to the docks at the Key West Navy base. A woman dressed in her Navy khaki uniform got out of the van and a rather large steamer trunk was unloaded from the van. She walked to the waiting submarine as the seamen hand trucked the steamer trunk and passed it to the waiting sailors on the sub's deck. Once aboard, Lt. Commander Winchester greeted the sub's new captain and returned his smart salute. Sara asked, "Captain Trost is it?"

"Capt. Carlisle Trost – Annapolis class of 1938, at your service ma-am."

Sara said, "So captain, I assume that we have a minimal crew aboard?" The captain smiled and said, "Yes ma-am, just 12 sailors and myself.

We have already plotted our course to the rendezvous spot in the Caribbean at 24:04 N and 82:15 W over the strange 2,600 feet deep coral reefs between the Pourtales escarpment and the Mitchell escarpment. That spot is just 43 miles from our base here in Key West. We have planned our sailing times so that we will meet your refugees well after dark, at 10 pm and we will arrive back here in Key West still under the cover of pre dawn darkness at about 5am tomorrow."

Sara grinned in anticipation and said, "Very well then captain, let's get underway."

After clearing the small Key West Navy base harbor, Trost submerged Sea Cat and shortly afterward they met in the officer's mess. Sara turned to the captain and asked, "Have you prepared the guest cabins captain?"

He replied, "Yes ma'am and these four cabins are apart from where any crew will be and near the forward boarding hatchway just as you requested." Sara smiled as she began to relax and dare feel glad that soon she would be with her star sister Selena again. Sara asked the captain, "Did the sailors put the steamer trunk in the large storage alcove between those guest cabins?"

Again the captain smiled and said, "Indeed ma'am, just as you asked." Sara excused herself and said, I must now go unpack for our, uh, guests captain."

Captain Trost gave a smile, saluted her and said, "Carry on then Lt. Commander, carry on with laying out your guest's wardrobes."

Before Sara left, she turned to the new Sea Cat captain and said, "OK sir, again, do you understand for purposes of national security, all of your sailors are to go to the aft torpedo room and wait until I authorize you to knock on that hatchway? Remember sir no matter what happens; your crew is to remain inside that aft torpedo room until I summon you to return us to Key West. This is for you and your crew's protection for vital national security purposes." Captain Trost looked solemnly at Sara and said, "Yes Lt. Commander, glad to be at your service, ma-am."

Sara stood and said, "Thanks for your cooperation in this vital matter captain." She grinned and thought with relief to herself. "And… just before we disembark back in Key West, Glinda will erase his memories about this incredible rendezvous."

Sara was unpacking the aliens clothing and smiled as she felt Glinda's presence and then in her head, Glinda beamed, "Hello Sara. How are you doing with all of the preparations for our visit? Did you tell the captain to be sure to have his crew stay out of sight in the aft torpedo room?"

Sara again smiled and simply thought, "Yes indeed your majesty. I was very firm about it and I do hope to God and er, Amadore that this captain will not get overly curious as did that sea dog, Captain Jones."

Glinda clicked rapidly as she beamed, "Well if he does, it doesn't matter because I plan to wipe his memories – just like the last time."

Sara smiled as she kept unpacking clothes and said, "Oh God! It will be so wonderful to see you and Arthur and Selena again, uh, your majesty."

Glinda beamed loving energies to Sara and thought to her, "Please Sara, just call me Glinda. We have been missing you mucho beloved Sara and we are excited to come visit with you and President Truman again!"

Sara still smiling said, "Ok then Glinda, I will see you aboard in I about four hours." Sara went into the storage alcove and after a brief struggle with the heavy steamer trunk; she got it opened. The first clothing that she sorted were the shorts, slacks, dresses, blouses, the one piece swim suits and Playtex bathing caps with colorful plastic flowers on the sides that she had picked out for Selena and her mother. She had also bought eight white bra's of what she thought might be the alien's approximate size, and also a dozen white and colored panties for each of them. As she was laying the women's cloths out on the first guest cabin's upper bunk, she wondered if Selena had ever worn underwear. As far as she could tell, all of the aliens seemed to only wear their silver, light blue or matte white, one piece jumpsuits. Although, the more formal gold one piece costumes the Delphinians had worn at their first meeting were to say the least, exquisite and really out of this world.

She went outside of the cabin and into the head where she had to stand as she peed, she pondered and hoped that aliens could use the tiny and inconvenient submarine bathroom. She wondered, "Why do they call them heads of all things?"

She was really glad that the reply from the aliens said that they could visit for up to 14 days by bringing extra nostril humidifiers. Part of the President's queries to the aliens asked if the earthly food would be alright for all of them. Peculiarly, the reply said that any food with the exception of peanuts and alcohol would be fine.

Sara hoped that because she and Selena were both petit women, that the clothes she had chosen would be ok. Selena's mother, Glinda, was about as big as her own mother. So she hoped also that the wardrobe and the underwear that she had picked out for Queen Glinda would fit. If not, she would have to make their first stop in Miami at Macy's to get better fitting clothes for Glinda.

Arthur and his almost too perfect, know it all, so called prime minister, Delnoid, would also be in the alien party. Sara had to kidnap one of the President's navy scribes who seemed to be about the same size as Arthur and Delnoid to take him to Macy's in Miami to get clothes for them. She, all during these last hectic days of preparing for the Delphinians visit thought, "Wow, I am becoming an alien visitors, tour guide and couturier Nazi. So now it was nice to relax a bit and enjoy preparing each of the alien visitor's cabins and laying out their earthly clothes aboard the sub.

Sara and the president had agreed on a cover story that none of their visitors could speak because of an unusual genetic family birth defect. In the president's messages to the aliens, he had emphasized that they should never transmit telepathically to any of the other earth people. The reply had been, to his and Sara's amusement… "Mum's the word Mr. Truman, mum's the word. And as you know, we can tele privately between ourselves or selectively to each of you. Please not to worry." As President Truman read the communication he wondered, "So, where on earth did they learn those British colloquialisms?"

After the enormous Delphinian craft surfaced alongside the Sea Cat the hatches were opened on both crafts. As Sara waited breathlessly on the deck, the beyond belief blue light walkway flashed out to stay exactly level with the sub's deck. As the three Delphinians and Delnoid 1M crossed over the beamed boarding ramp, Sara resignedly thought, "President Truman will be licking his chops thinking about all of the fantastic technologies he hopes the USA can learn about from the aliens who now nonchalantly walked across to the sub on their.

So hard to believe blue beam boarding ramp. Sara recalled that Truman had told her in his briefing; that the US Army researchers at Wright Patterson were even now investigating and trying to understand and retro construct all of the mind-boggling, not yet understood equipment, parts and technologies that had been recovered from the Roswell spacecraft which crashed on July 4th 1947. He had been informed that the little grays were probably not the actual aliens, but only bio engineered UFO drone pilots. They had been designed to link mentally and physically with their amazing stop in midair and turn on a dime exploration and reconnaissance crafts.

Sara, returning from her somber recollections, saw that Selena, Glinda, Arthur and Delnoid 1M were each wearing their normal light blue one piece jumpsuits and that they each had on what looked like medium size white with dark blue trim backpacks.

As soon as Selena stepped aboard the sub, she flew into Sara's arms and tearfully and ecstatically began squealing excitedly. Glinda gave her exuberant daughter a severe frown and Selena's excited and happy squealing just suddenly stopped. Sara grinned because she knew that Glinda had beamed a "Stop that. Settle down Selena" to her princess.

Arthur, according to the Delphinian and more likely their adopted south American custom, took Sara's right hand, drew her to him a bit and kissed her right cheek. Arthur shrugged his shoulders, squealed in delight, shoved his eye glasses atop his head and beamed, "OK… group hug!" Sara and her three aliens fervently embraced as she, like a dry Key West sponge, ecstatically soaked up their wonderful loving and nurturing energies which she had missed for about three long and very busy, hectic weeks now. After all of the loving greetings were finished, Sara dried her eyes and said, "Welcome aboard our small undersea ship, Sea Cat. Shall we go below now?"

Up on the sub's flying bridge, the lone Captain Trost watching all of this thought… "I sure wish I was not sworn to secrecy about this incredible alien meeting. It would almost be worth my Navy pension to break this story to the Miami Herald except then, the Navy NCIS would hunt me down and eliminate me and maybe my crew and probably my family too."

As Captain Trost re entered the officers mess, Sara looked sharply at him and said, "Well Captain, they are here. So now sir, could you please go to the aft torpedo room and get your conning crew so we can get underway to Key West. But remember sir, none of your crew should come forward into this cabins area nor anywhere near our uh, visitors cabins. Is that clear sir?"

The now abashed captain gave a half smile and simply said, "Aye Aye Lt. Commander. We will get underway shortly."

Sara then realized that she had been kind of curt and too starched, stood, walked over to the forsaken looking captain, took his arm, smiled and said… "Thank You Captain. Your excellent responsibility to duty and the unique top secret orders for this mission is really greatly appreciated."

Glinda joined them and simply hugged the captain and flowed grateful and loving energies into his mind and spirit.

The bewildered Captain smirked like a schoolboy smitten by his first kiss stammered, "Oh, it's ok. I am just glad to be included in this uh, incredible mission."

Glinda, smiling and still holding his arm thought to herself; "Well enjoy it while you can mister before I have to erase your memories when we dock back in Key West." She then gave him an extra energy filled hug and a kiss on his cheek."

Once the aliens had put their back packs into their small sub cabins, they all met to sit around the captain's rectangular California oak table. After the exchange of more pleasantries and cold cokes all around, Sara took 6 pocket size spiral reporters notebooks and 12 scripto mechanical pencils out of her bag. As she passed two notebooks and 4 pencils to each alien she said, "I know that you have fantastic photographic memories, but please keep these small notebooks and pencils with you at all times. They are part of our cover story for you that supposedly you can't speak because of, a, um, your, uh, a family genetic speech defect. So now, with these notebooks, if we are anywhere in public or near White House staff, you can just pretend that you are writing answers to our questions or you own questions and comments. Just scribble on and tear off a sheet once in awhile and hand it to me or the President so we can all just pretend that we are reading your questions or comments to us. I am so sorry for this inconvenience. But we could not think of another way to protect your inability to speak cover story."

Delnoid 1M, who could speak, looked very self-satisfied at Sara and said, "Actually, Sara, I think that this is indeed a very clever way to protect their speechlessness."

Glinda looked rather amused, clicked rapidly and beamed, "Well, though I really do not write a lot in English very often; I will try to, as you say, scribble occasionally in my notepad."

Selena who was also a really good artist said, "It's ok Sara, this will also give me some great chances to make some small sketches."

Arthur reached into his breast pocket and pulled out a small rectangular device, beamed, "I plan to use my digital electronic camera to record our meetings, travels and new friends."

Sara, an avid and accomplished photographer, reached for the camera and said, "That's amazing! May I look at it?" As Arthur showed Sara the camera, she gasped and said, "Wow, it's got a little viewing screen on the back of it just like a marvelous tiny color TV screen." She asked Arthur what kind of film it used.

Arthur gloated as he thought about how far advanced they were and beamed, "Film, Sara? It does not use film. It makes what you would call digital er, electronic color images and sound recordings like a miniature movie camera. But, it's like one of your gigantic black and white TV cameras that are set up at TV news conferences except that, as you can see, it's a thousand times smaller."

Sara, feeling a bit foolish but curious asked, "Digital, uh, please tell me, what is digital?"

Arthur grinned and beamed, "Well, dear earthling, it's well… uh… kind of an electronic image like television, except, the camera uses what you earthlings might someday call HD LCD with torus interconnects and zeta flops to work. But for us telepathic Delphs, I can also place it, like this, to my melon, uh, forehead, to transmit into my brain to store images, scenes, conversations, activities and events that I have seen and heard."

As soon as Arthur said that, dumbfounded Sara recalled the briefing that President Truman had recently received from the Army alien technology department at the Pentagon about the incredible small electronic and computer circuits that had been recovered from the Roswell crash back in July, 1947. Sara was sore tempted to ask Arthur what if anything he knew about the crash. But, she also knew that they were still playing an undefined high stakes Mexican alien cat standoff verses a mostly maybe defenseless earthling mouse game upon which the whole future of America and the planet may now depend on them befriending, trusting and cooperating with each other.

Arthur easily reading Sara's mind thought to himself, "I am so glad that you did not ask me now about the Roswell crash by those stupid, hot shot, bio engineered gray pilots flying through that giant summer monsoon electrical thunderstorm in their Tauri surveillance ship."

Arthur and Glinda and all of their generation's of 160 remaining crew had bravely escaped from beta Delphinus 372 earth years or six generations ago. They only wanted a new and safer home place far away from the minority of military industrial hawks and warring factions on their former home world which was probably destroyed by wars since they escaped.

It seems that it's almost a universal law that throughout time and space that persecuted philosophies, religions and minorities have always had to escape to find safety and peace away from the never ending escalation of greed and egos by the alpha males of the universe. Arthur had often prayed asking the creators why they made 20% of their children so fearful, greedy, ego filled, bi-polar,heartless, uncompassionate and warlike.

Glinda smiled time and time again knowingly, as she always had, beamed to her husband, "The answer would have been; you must live fully and you must use your universal life gift of total unconditional free choice and love to grow past all fear, ego and greed to eventually become like our Amadores."

After the ward room meeting with her aliens, Sara took them to their three small cabins. As Sara and Selena were hugging in her cabin, Selena squealed in delight and beamed, "I am so glad to see you again. And I am so excited about our being able to spend some time together and you're taking us on a tour of Key West. Then to Miami where you and I can enjoy swimming with our dolphin friends at your Miami's south beach. As you know, I have spent so far a tenth of my life aboard our Lifestar and this will be the first time I have really been able to safely visit any larger earth cities. It will be so nice - especially with you as our guide Sara!"

Sara said, "Selena I have never been happier to share like this with anyone." The two women joyfully hugged again. Sara looked at her friend and asked, "Would you like to try on the earth clothes that I got for you?

I hope that you like them and that they will fit you ok."

Selena stepped back and eagerly passed her hand down the front of her blue one piece jumpsuit. Then the invisible chest seam on the suit all of the way down to her ankles on both legs opened and fell to the floor and Selena simply stepped out of it.

Sara at first glance saw that Selena was indeed a very human, perfectly formed female. But she gasped as she said, "Oh gosh Selena! You do not have a navel!"

Selena looked down to her smooth belly squeaked, smiled and beamed, "That's right Sara, we Delphinians don't have what you earthlings call a belly button!"

Astounded Sara exclaimed, "How are you nourished while you are inside your mother?"

Selena turned around and in between her shoulder blades just to the left of her backbone was a small vertical half inch inch (1cm) slit. She then let out a variety of whistles, squeaks, moans and squeals from the fleshy slit. "This is our residual blowhole and while we are in our mother's womb, the umbilical cord is attached here; that way, just like when you humans are born, our system changes to air breathing through our lungs and along with those amazing actual physiological changes. Our umbilical cord attaching place also changes to become a residual closeable blowhole and through it, we can make a tremendous variety of fun and emotional sounds." She again repeated her repertoire of dolphin like whistles, squeaks, squeals and moans…

Sara also saw that Selena had no body hair and told Selena, "You are lovely. Maybe we can find for you an earth man husband." Sara giggled as Selena squeaked and clicked in delight. Sara then looked at Selena's feet and was stupefied to see that Selena didn't really didn't have toes. Her feet were small but with a wide at the front kind of rectangular triangularish shape, like small slightly tapered at the ankles flippers. Sara told Selena, "Hummmm, we may have a problem finding you some shoes. Here, try on these pumps that I got for you." The women's pumps of course would not even begin to go on Selena's wide vestigial flipper amphibian feet. Sara smiled reassuringly and said, "Well, no problema amiga, once we get to Key West, the President can have a Navy cobbler come in and outfit all of you with some good foot, uh, flipper uh, foot coverings." Sara then handed Selena her bra and panties.

Selena looked puzzled as she handled and examined the underwear. "What on Earth are these for Sara?"

Sara said, "I will show you." Sara kicked off her shoes and unbuttoned her Navy blouse and unzipped and dropped her denim Navy trousers and she stood there in her bra and panties.

Selena beamed, "Oh, I see and understand. Is this what all earth women wear?"

Sara said, "Yes Selena, the bra is to support our breasts and hide our nipples."

Selena contorted her questioning eyebrows, clicked, moaned and asked, "Why must you do that?"

Sara said matter of factually, "Well, most human females are still very conservative and modest and if a man sees us in the nude or looks at our breasts and nipples he gets sexually excited and will want to make love with us. So we try not to show our, breasts and private parts or our panties to men and usually we only undress in front of men that we are married to or when we want to make love."

Selena, imitating the human phrase she had heard, beamed, "Hummmm… Sara, we Delphinians just wear our jumpsuits and at night when we are in bed alone or together we females sometimes wear a light nightie or nice comfy gown but, usually we just sleep nude."

Sara smirked and said, "Well, sometimes we do that too. Uh, Selena tell me, do you make babies like we do?"

"What do you mean Sara?"

Sara pointed to her Venus mound, "You know, the male puts his penis inside us to plant sperm to make us pregnant."

Selena clicked excitedly, squealed a lovable laugh and beamed, "Oh that! We do that also for pleasure of course, but our eggs and sperm are collected by our ship's doctors so that only perfect genetic matches can be made and then the fertilized egg is re-implanted in our uterus."

Sara said, "Oh… I guess that someday that might be the way we will, uh, produce select babies here on earth. Do you ever have babies born with severe illnesses and physiological like what we call Bi-Polar or other birth defects?"

Selena smiled majestically and beamed, "Nope, never."

Sara looked astounded as she said, "That's fantastic Selena. Here on earth it takes us women nine months from conception to birth a baby. How long do you Delphinians females take?"

Selena looked curiously at Sara and beamed, "Oh, well, that's a three month difference. It takes us about 12 months from conception to birth."

Sara sighed and said, "Oh really! 12 months is the same length of time it takes our earthly dolphins to give birth. In southern California, where I am from, along the coast there, the dolphin birthing usually takes place in our fall season during the months we call September, October and November."

Selena meanwhile had been struggling to figure out how to put on the bra. Sara said, "Here Selena, turn around. Please let me help you hook that around your back." Anthropologist Sara was still amazed and fascinated by Selena's blowhole. She lightly touched Selena,s back as she asked, "Do you also use it to communicate?"

Selena grinned and again let out another short series of high to low squeaks and squeals in merriment. "No, but remember Sara, it's just a residual, like your appendix. But we use it for fun and sometimes for expressing emotions. Like when we are happy, playing, swimming, angry and always while we are having sex." Selena mischievously challenged Sara as she beamed, "What noises do you make when you are having sex?"

Sara realized that her new alien friend was almost completely uninhibited and she blushed as she said… "Well, I have had only a couple of serious boyfriends…"

Selena interjected, "Just life dream mates Sara? Not playmates?"

Sara said, "Well, for now, just for friendship, companionship and I guess for sex too. I have never been married Selena. My last Navy boyfriend from three years ago had been lying and cheating on me and he had a relationship with civilian woman while he was with me and he did not tell me." Looking kind of disgusted Sara frowned and continued, "So, when I found out, I broke up with him."

Selena's mouth opened, her eyes became enormous as she squeaked and beamed, "Sara! Did, did you really break him apart?"

Sara laughed and said, "Oh noooo Selena, that's the expression we use for choosing not to be together anymore."

Selena smiled and beamed… "Hummmm sometimes we Delphinians have several of the opposite sex we share friendship and sometimes pleasure with. Because as you must know dear amiga; we cannot be all things to another Delphin."

Sara agreed as she told Selena, "Well, in our society such widespread and open friendships between the sexes are tried sometimes. But emotionally and sexually or socially, we are just not able to avoid being jealous."

"Jealous, what is that Sara?"

"Well, it's an emotion with feelings of resentment of being betrayed and lied to, feeling hurt and rejected and sometimes angry because someone we trust, love and care a great deal about, also likes or loves being with another person."

Selena just let out a low pitched squeak as if she was saying, "Geeeeze, that's really backwards Sara." She beamed, "Because we, for the most part we really don't have such fears and insecurities in our species. I guess it's because we are completely and selectively telepathic and it's our norm to try to never have overts and withholds on each other. It's like your Earth dolphins except your alpha male dolphins here are sometimes way too aggressive and possessive. One time we were delighting in swimming with a small pod of dolphins in the Mediterranean, just off of the coast of Portofino, Italy. One horny alpha male bully tried to keep me isolated from my friends and finally… we had to sonic bomb him to chase him away."

Sara hearing that said, "Oh gosh Selena, well then, we humans and our earthly dolphins seem to have a long way to go on our evolutionary, social, sexual and spiritual scales. I want to ask though, do you ever breath through your blowhole?"

Selena smiled, made a small squeak and told Sara, "Not any longer. As I said, long ago as we evolved and slowly transited from sea to land, our lesser oxygenation and red corpuscles needs changed to supplying air to our lungs through our mouths and noses just like you do." Selena let out a proud descending squeal as she beamed, "I can hold my breath to stay underwater for 16 minutes Sara."

Sara was wide eyed as her appreciation of the differences in physiology of the Delphins settled into her reality. She looked amazed at Selena and said, "That is awesome Selena, I hope we can go diving together someday. I took SCUBA lessons from a navy seal commander. He is also a film consultant that my movie director father sometimes uses in his film making."

Selena smiled, squealed and beamed, "Oh Sara that would be wonderful. Can you stay down 16 minutes too?"

Sara grinned and said, "Oh no! We humans have to use an air tank."

Selena squeaked and beamed, "Oh we also have nostril plugs we can use that function like gills. Depending on the water temperature, we can stay underwater for about 2 hours as deep as 160 feet (48 meters) if we have to."

Sara hugged her alien amiga and said, "Oh yes Selena, it will be grand for us to dive together as soon as we get you to California!"

Selena squealed in delight and beamed, "Oh Sara that will be fantastic and maybe you and I can find lovers and husbands to dive with too!"

Sara, becoming serious said, "Look here Delphin girlfriend, I want to warn you. When you settle here on earth and if and when you get into relationships, there are things you need to know. I will teach you much about our conservative and also crazy social customs, like how not to cause jealousies and particularly how not be too trusting of any earthers. I especially do not want you to trust the men until you really get to know them really well. Because here on Earth, if I were to have several lovers and open relationships at the same time, I would be hated and shunned by others… Because Selena, we are still, just under our super thin veneer of so called civilization, we're still really tribal. Many of our more primitive and medieval cultures and tribes still kill the women if they are even only thought to have been unfaithful to their males. Especially the brutal radical Muslims and some Hindus also are the most bigoted about such so called honor killings." So, I hope when you come to stay here on our water world that you and I can live together so that I can guide and teach you how to be safe and not taken advantage of, ok?"

Selena squealed softly and had tears in her eyes. She hugged Sara and as she cried, Sara could hear some very very soft, like crying or moaning noises coming from Selena's blowhole. "Sara you are my best earth friend and guide for the rest of my life." And, I will share and teach all Delphs about this so confusing and ever changing social mores and rules of your people."

Sara was crying a bit too as she held her alien friend and said, "Don't you worry. I'll stand beside you always and in all ways dear amiga." After Sara adjusted and hooked Selena's bra strap, Selena frowned and commented, "Isn't it uncomfortable to feel this thing around your chest all of the time?"

Sara smiled as she remembered how long it had taken her to get used to her first bra strap at age 12 when she had proudly started wearing her first bra. "Honest, you will get used to it very quickly."

Selena turned and asked Sara to turn around and she felt Selena's fingers feeling her back and over and under her bra strap. "What are you doing?"

"I am," she squeaked, "feeling and recording your female back and seeing if you have a residual blowhole."

Sara then asked her alien to try some of the other clothes on that she had picked out for her. When Selena was dressed in a nice flowery summer skirt and white peasant blouse, she turned to Sara and beamed, "Well, how do I look?"

Sara said, "Absolutely gorgeous!" She then began looking around the small cabin, found a locker door and opened it. There luckily was an a 8 x 24 inch mirror on the inside of the door. "Here, look at you Selena."

Selena smiled, squeaked and beamed, "I sure look different and I love these clothes Sara."

The two good friends hugged again and Sara said, "If only each one of you from Lifestar could spend quality time like this with mentors in other good earth families and become trusting friends like we have. You all could easily and safely learn to live here on earth. Have your doctors and scientists made any more progress on modifying your skin moisturizing needs?"

Selena became kind of sad as she beamed, "No, not yet Sara. The very conservative minority is still resisting change. They are dragging their flippers about more quickly bioengineering a way for us to live in your dryer atmosphere so that we won't have to guard against what you call heat exhaustion and also hopefully not always be bothered with our super moisturizing skin cream. But for now, it seems that we will all have to use the sweat gland and super moisturizing cream until we can hopefully, the sooner the better, grow sufficient sweat glands."

Sara smiled and agreed, "It's always the same absurd and destructive alpha male politics and leadership that are resistant to change here on earth too." She frowned and asked hesitantly, "Is your father Arthur in that minority?"

Selena beamed to her Sara, "No, now he and mom are the leaders for very, as you would call it, liberal policies and peaceful change. So we can make a strong - sealed in fidelity stones - treaty with President Truman for us to hopefully come home to this world we have never lived on before."

Selena squeaked and clickety clicked, broke into tears as she beamed, "Oh Sara, I so want to come stay with you here on your beautiful water world. Being here with you now,I feel like I am homesick for a place I've never been before…"

Just then Glinda stepped into the small cabin with tears in her eyes and she looked lovingly at Selena and Sara. She made a soft sighing moan from her blowhole and hugged them and their emotional waves settled.

Glinda beamed, "Girls I am so glad and happy that you are able to relate to each other in such wonderful, bonding, love and friendship. I now know and hope that most of our people will really be able to learn your earth ways and social and love customs. That way they will all be able to safely make new life dreams here walking, talking, playing, swimming, laughing and loving under your light and life giving sun star that shines so blessedly on your so magnificent water world." "Dear earth woman, please always trust that we are your friends and you now are our dearest earth connection and supporter. This meeting for all of us aboard your submarine and in the days to come in south Florida, will be a needed and wonderful discovery process and I hope you trust us because we now know that we love and can also trust you Sara."

Sara smiled and then tried just thinking instead of speaking. She visualized all of her questions and fears for the aliens once they came to live on earth.

Glinda clicked reassuringly and just hugged Sara again and beamed, "Sara, dear Sara, be tranquil now. One thing at a time and one day at a time, I know that we are centuries and light years apart in advancement of knowledge but now that we are together we clearly feel and see how much love, expectations and growing trust as children of the Universe that we really do have in common."

Sara thought to both of her new alien friends, "I know and this is really the happiest and most important episode in my life."

Sara and Selena then noticed that Glinda was carrying her bra in her hand and was wearing one of the dresses that Sara had bought for her. Sara said, "Oh you look beautiful Glinda! Does it fit you ok?"

Glinda twirled and let out a happy squeak and beamed to her daughter and Sara, "Do you really like it? It's beautiful and fits me perfectly dear Sara. Thank you!"

Selena beamed to her mother, "How did that bra feel? Did it not comfortably fit your breasts ?"

Glinda frowned and beamed back… " As you can see Sara. I'm not wearing it. I gave up on trying to figure out how to put it on…" She unbuttoned and lowered her dress top, beamed to Sara… "Sara, could you please help me figure out this bra thing?" All three women broke into laughter with Sara laughing aloud in earth style and the two aliens joyfully squeaking and clicking Delphin style. After Glinda's bra was adjusted, Selena beamed to Sara, "Do you have a sharp knife?" Sara, taken a bit aback said, "Uh, sure, I can get one from the galley."

Glinda picked up her daughters crumpled flightsuit and beamed, "I have a better idea. Wait here while I go to my cabin to getinto my pack." In about thirty seconds Glinda returned with her small travel kit. She reached in it and pulled out a small yellow tube with a small black button on it. She picked up the flightsuit at the junction of the leg and its shoe part, As she touched the button on the tube immediately a small fairly bright, 3 centimeter long, red beam came out of it. She then carefully cut the shoe part away from the pant leg of her daughter's flight suit. When both shoes were free, Glinda handed the improvised shoes to Selena and beamed, "Here, princess, try these lovely flipper covers on." Sara then saw that Glinda had already figured out how to cut the shoes from her flight suit. The three women laughed as Selena paraded about a bit in her modified silver and black trim space shoes.

Sara said, "Still, once we get back to Key West, I can make an outline drawing of each of your feet and have a Navy base cobbler fashion some nicer wider earth shoes for all of you. We can also use these uh, flight shoes as patterns."

"That will be fine." beamed Glinda, "Come on, I think we better find your father and Delnoid because by now they will have discovered their shoe problems too."

As Glinda, Sara and Selena re-entered their cabin, Arthur was sitting on the bunk wearing his newly cut off alien shoes and Delnoid, who was holding his yellow beam cutter, was smiling proudly at his handiwork. When Selena and Glinda saw them, all three clicked happily and chorused a nice sounding harmonious mid pitched squeak…

Sara thought to Selena "I guess that means they are pleased with their new shoes, tee hee…"

Selena having received Sara's thoughts, beamed back to her amiga, "I think that with you and me practicing, you may be able to re-develop your innate ancient human telepathy sooner that anyone can imagine."

Sara impulsively thought back, "Me too." and commented, "You know, it is thought that a lot of the ancient Polynesian, Inca and other cultures had natural telepathic abilities over long distances. So maybe we present-day humans, as you said, uh, beamed, maybe we have only forgotten our natural telepathic skills. Selena, I am now curious. How far can your people beam thoughts and feelings?"

Selena smiled knowingly, clicked slowly and astounded Sara by beaming, "Just like you can Sara. Aross the whole universe if we need to Sara."

Sara just threw up her hands and said, "Goodness… Well my dear mind-boggling aliens, that is just more totally overwhelming revelations than I can absorb for tonight. But, I sure am looking forward to learning all about you and our ancient connections as children of the universe !"

Since by then it was 1am Sara yawned and announced, "Well my dear aliens, I am going to try to get some shut eye before our 5 am arrival back at our Key West Navy base."

Selena clicked and beamed, "What is shut eye Sara?"

Sara grinned and plopped herself down on the cabin bunk and closed her eyes and pretended to be asleep.

Glinda clicked and beamed, "That is an excellent idea Sara. Yes, let us all get some rest now. Tomorrow will be a big and special day for all of us."

Just then, the love struck and still grinning from ear to ear Captain, knocked at the door frame and said, "Uh, hi. I hope that all of you are getting settled in ok for our short voyage back to Key West."

He then realized that all of the aliens were wearing their earth cloths and he said, "Oh my! You all look swell, just like, uh, regular, normal, uh, that is to say, humans."

All of the Delphinians turned to the captain and beamed in unison, "Why, thank you Captain Trots." Then they all squeaked and clicked as they smirked in obvious laughter.

It was dawning when the Sea Cat finished tying up at the Key West Navy base wharf. Glinda, in her new earth clothes stood at the wardroom table, smiled her best come hither smile and beconed for Captain Trots to come closer.

As she reached out to put both hands on each side of head, he grinned, raised his arms and puckered up thinking that the lovely alien lady was going to kiss him. Instead, an instant after Glinda's hands touched his each side of his head, he just went totally blank for the flat out thirty seconds that it took Glinda to scan and erase his memories of them as aliens with a big old starship. The captain blinked, yawned and looked startled for a moment as if he was just wakening from a weird dream and said, "Well, uh, a'hem… "Well, er, here we are, safe and sound back in Key West. I hope you fishermen and your wives we rescued, had a pleasant little voyage in our submarine…"

A gray Navy van quickly pulled up next to the sub's boarding ramp and soon, the forward deck hatch opened and two men and three women emerged, crossed the gangway and quickly entered the van. The van drove off to go directly to the rear entrance of the nearby Key West White House.

CHAPTER 14 SPLISH SPLASH - GETTING TO KNOW YOU

After the President and Sara had shown all of their special visitors to their upstairs rooms, Harry poked his head in each room and said, "If you are not too tired, I invite you to come down to brunch at 11am after you have settled in and slept a bit." By then Mr. Truman had seen their modified alien flightsuit shoes and he said, "Well folks, nothing surprises me anymore. I guess that we better take all of you to a Key West shoe store on Monday."

All of the aliens grinned, squeaked in merriment, clicked and Sara began giggling as Selena kicked off her right modified shoe and gleefully showed the astounded president her elfin waving flipper foot.

Sara laughed again and said, "Well everyone, try to rest and we will see you in a few hours. Sleep tight." She took the astounded President's arm and towed him out into the second floor hallway as she told him about their toeless feet. He realized, "Well of course Sara, they would have, must of course have, those small sort of, webbed feet since they evolved from dolphins."

Sara frowned and said, "Mr. Truman, they don't have webbed feet, just uh, well… as you can see, they have uh, toeless, er, flipperish feet."

Harry, knowing never to be inexact with a woman just smiled and said, "I will call tomorrow and try to find or enlist a Navy cobbler with a high security clearance."

Sara became alarmed and said, "Careful please Mr. President. Others must never know about nor see their, uh, feet you know. I think that I can make some outline drawings of their flippers, and put some really short toe shapes in the outline so that the base cobbler can hopefully make or modify some shoes for them. Or at least make some kind of extra wide sandals that cover their toe areas for them."

Truman said hopefully, "I will look in me and my wife's closet to see if we have any kind of uh, wide slippers Sara."

Sara then remembered that the president did have a wife, although, she was almost never seen in public with Mr. Truman. She hesitatingly asked, "Mr. Truman, will Bess be coming to visit us at the Key West White House?"

Harry became downhearted as he sighed and replied, "Sara to be honest with you, Bess and my daughter Margaret, have accompanied me here to this tropical paradise White House only three times so far. Bess mostly stays at her spiteful mother's house in Independence, Missouri and truthfully, Bess really abhors being first lady. Sometimes I feel that she resents and, uh, can't stand me too. Yet, I've been nothing but devoted to her since we were six. I remember one time when she was christening two navy ambulance planes and the wrapped champagne bottle would not break. She, on camera, appeared to be the unflappable first lady with the unbreakable bottle. Later when I saw her in person, she was angry and told me that during her embarrassing attempts to break the bottle; that, well, she wanted to hit me with the bottle for ever putting her in such an embarrassing situation." The President removed his glasses and Sara saw that there were small tears in his eyes. She wanted to just hug and hold the so mistreated Harry, but instead, she softly stammered, "Oh Mr. Truman, I am so sorry about that, sir."

Meanwhile, Glinda had been reading their conversation and she thought to herself, "What a heartbreak it is that a nice, brave, honest and deeply caring human like Mr. Truman is stuck in such absurd, needless and heartbreaking co–dependency with such a selfish, fearful, heartless and unrelenting small minded country matron like Bess. Maybe I can fix him up with my unmarried sister Shiri!"

Selena, reading Glinda beamed, "I think that would be wonderful to have Mr. Truman join our pod mom!"

Glinda smiled and beamed back to her impetuous daughter, "Selena, who asked you?" Glinda then gave a few taunting whistles through her blowhole.

As she and Selena were sitting in her bedroom, Sara said, "We normally have quite a few white house staff and navy stewards. But, for your security during this visit, the President, I, and four secret service security officers, and a Navy cook will be the only ones here in the White House to take care of you to better minimize discovery during your visit here on earth.

They have all been told that you are elite mute refugees from South America here for top secret conferences."

Selena beamed to Sara, "What is a brunch? I don't think I have ever eaten a brunch."

Sara laughed and explained, "Brunch is not a thing but a word for combining breakfast and lunch."

"This is all so wonderful Sara, thank-you dear earth guide."

Sara then asked Selena to beam to her family to always be careful to never transmit telepathically to any others and to never let anyone see their feet. Selena beamed as Sara was talking and smiled as she went, squeak squeak...

Sara giggled and said, "Oh… and never squeak again either."

Selena immediately looked crushed from her merriment and Sara seeing that hugged her and said, "Oh Selena, it's alright, I was only teasing you…"

Glinda beamed into both girls from her room next door, "Ok you two get some rest now. Tomorrow is going to probably be one of the grandest days of our lives."

Sara looked bleary eyed at her alien friend and said, "OK, I am going to my room now and try to get in a cat nap before we meet for brunch and begin your first day here actually enjoying walking around in Key West."

Selena clicked softly, looked curiously at Sara and beamed, "What is a cat nap?" Sara smiled and explained that a nap was a short sleep. She asked Selena, "So, how many hours do you sleep each night?" Selena smiled and explained that on their starship the day night cycles had been set to their base circadian rhythms and that their eyes closed sleep periods were usually about seven to eight earth hours. Selena looked kind of uncertain as she beamed, "Sara, There are two beds here, please stay with me."

Sara smiled and said, "Alright amiga, I will be right back after I get some things from my room, ok?" Selena began to undress as she said. "Ok, I'll see you in a little while."

When Sara got to her own room, she opened her dresser drawer and pulled out the special present she had made for Selena. She then undressed and put on her cotton nightgown and padded in her scuffies back down the hall to Selena's room. When she got there, she was astounded to see that Selena was already sound asleep, completely nude on her bed. Sara then

noticed that Selena had one eye wide open and she drew near to her new alien amiga. Selena then kind of cleared her blowhole with a soft sleepy squeal and soft clicks and then beamed, "Oh good, there you are Sara." Sara not sure what to do or say simply stammered and asked, "Selena, one of your eyes was wide open. Aren't you going to sleep?"

Selena clicked happily and beamed, "Oh Sara, remember that we come from a dolphin heritage and sometimes, just like our dolphin cousins always must do in order to breathe and stay alert, we also occasionally use unihemispheric sleep. We rest one half of our brain in deep sleep while the side opposite our open eye is mostly awake to watch out for alien predators like you…" She then grinned, sat up, became almost scarily wide eyed and made claws out of her fingers and swanked, clicked and squealed in merriment.

The White House window air conditioners were fairly effective but also somewhat noisy in the south Florida tropical climate. Sara took the bedspread and gently covered her new companion. She set the wind up alarm clock on the bed side table for 10am and wearily crawled into her bed and as she relaxed, she felt very comfortable soothing energies coming to her from Selena. She smiled and as she dozed off she thought, "Gosh, we have so much to learn from each other…" She then heard echoing in her sleepy brain… "You sure do Sara." click click click… Sara turned her head towards Selena and saw that Selena had become a true normal sleeping beauty with both eyes closed now as she softly breathed in and out thru her mouth and nose.

Sara, as she groggily heard the incessant clanging of the alarm clock, tried to return from her delightful REM sleep… She drowsily became aware of splashing and squeaking coming from the guestroom's bathroom. She stumbled out of bed and rushed into the bathroom and there she saw nude Selena merrily splashing in the tub like a little girl, she broke into peals of feminine laughter. Selena saw her, splashed some more and let out even more joyful and excited squeaks. Selena beamed to her playmate, "This is wonderful Sara. On our ship we only have showers. Do come join me!"

Sara was embarrassed; she blushed nervously and said, "Selena… I… I have never bathed with another woman before…"

Selena clicked downward, became downcast and beamed, "On our ship we always share the showers and a very small swim tank together."

Sara, reluctantly taking off her nightgown said, "Well, ok." As she stepped into the tub Selena stood up to make room for her and began to wash Sara's arms. She squealed in delight, beamed Sara to turn and wash her back. Sara then hesitatingly accepted the wash cloth and began to gently wash Selena's back… After a few minutes of giggling and washing each other, Sara nervously said, "Well, it's time to get out of the tub and dry off and get ready to go to brunch with the president." Sara wrapped a nice fluffy beach towel around Selena and then grabbed the other towel for herself. Selena took her towel and began to dry Sara off and asked Sara to dry her off.

Sara by now was totally frustrated and felt very uncomfortable with all of this intimate bathing and drying. So she quickly dabbed Selena with the towel and as she picked up her now soggy nightgown and wrapped herself in a big beach towel she said, "Ok amiga, you finish and get dressed. I have to go to my room, and get dressed too!"

A frustrated Sara hurried down the hallway back to her room. The secret service agent on duty at the end of the hall whistled ever so softly and said to himself, "Oh Jeeeeze! There is that able grable looker Sara and wow! She's wearing only a sexy towel."

Once Sara was in her room she unwrapped her big fluffy towel and finished drying herself off in her own private bathroom. She found herself thinking, "Gosh was that a lesbian experience of the alien kind or just a normal, super playful friendly and a naturally totally uninhibited Delphinian alien girl?" Sara realized that if she and Selena were going to live together in future; they would have to slow down and establish some privacy, bathing and cultural ground rules… She also made a mental note to rent at least a two bedroom house with a separate bathroom for each bedroom. Or preferably, stay together in her parents big beach side six bed room house in Montecito near Santa Barbara California.

After Sara quickly dressed and did her makeup, she headed back down the hall to Selena's room and as she entered she saw Selena sitting on her bed, fully dressed but looking really sad and cheerless. Sara went up to her alien, put her arm around her shoulders and asked, "Oh Selena what's wrong? Are you ok?"

Selena squeaked and clicked slowly and beamed, "Oh Sara, did I offend you somehow? I was just feeling so happy and playful when we were bathing together and as you left, I felt your powerful uncomfortable energies." Sara realized that her Selena was just being her normal playful Delphinian self.

"No, no amiga. It's my problem. You see here in earth societies, friends do not usually bathe together unless they are lovers… ok? Remember, if I was visiting aboard your home ship, you would be guiding me and teaching me about your cultural customs."

Selena looked at Sara and beamed, "Oh Sara, I have so much to learn. Please forgive me if I made you feel uncomfortable and please always in future be sure to always tell me and show me how to behave here on your world…"

Sara, said, "I am here for you no matter what dear Selena, and don't feel bad or worry because I will shepherd you and we will have a wonderful time together on this our first day walking together on Earth dear little sister. Hey look at this. I made this especially for you." Sara handed Selena a rectangular gift wrapped in white paper present and as Selena was hugging her again and profusely squeaking and clicking to thank her…

Sara asked, "Well, aren't you going to open it?"

Selena stepped back and questioned, "Open it? What do you mean Sara?"

Sara said, "See, you have to unwrap it silly." Sara helped Selena tear open the gift wrap. As the gift wrap came off, Selena saw that it was a lovely color photo of Sara in her formal Navy uniform in a nice dark walnut 5x7 frame. Selena broke into tears and loud squeals as she again hugged her friend. She finally settled down and beamed tearfully to Sara, "No one has ever given me such a precious thing before Sara." Sara held her alien friend as Selena started to recover her emotions.

The two young women, so apart in space and time and their cultures, but now bonded in true loving friendship, walked hand in hand down the hall to the elevator which would take them to the first floor and to the Presidential breakfast. Selena suddenly stopped and turned and began to tow Sara back towards their room. Sara anxiously asked, "What's wrong?"

Selena excitedly beamed, "I almost forgot to change my humidifier

Sara."

As soon as they got back into the room Selena went to her light blue backpack on her bed and passed her hand over it and as it opened, Sara could see there were some clothes and other things that she had no idea what they were in Selena's pack and said, "I hope you can show me tonight some of your amazing treasures and things."

Selena beamed as she put a new humidifier into her right nostril and beamed, "I would love to!" She went over to Sara's bed and picked up the photo frame and said, "But, before we go, I have to put this, now my most precious possession, into my pack for safekeeping." After she closed the pack, she monetarily pressed her left hand on the lid and a faint blue hand print appeared, just as had appeared when Selena had used her hand print to open her cabin door on the Lifestar during Sara's first visit.

Sara and Selena walked into the dining room and saw that Arthur, Glinda, Delnoid 1, and the President were all seated and had already started enjoying some morning coffee.

Selena looking very amazed and pleased beamed to Sara, Glinda and Arthur, "Oh look at the colorful flower print shirt the President is wearing!"

Glinda happily grinning, squeaked, clicked and beamed back, "Yes, I really like his choice of shirt! Does he wear such attractive shirts often Sara?"

Sara smirked and looked openly at her aliens and nodded her head and then said to them, "We have no idea what you all can or should eat or drink. Except, of course we know no peanuts and alcohol. Please tell us if any of our beverages or food is not safe or inappropriate for you…"

Delnoid grinned enthusiastically, gulped his coffee and said to Sara and the others… "It's ok, we have studied most all of your food and drinks and as we previously radioed to you via your Fort Huachuca antenna, and so as far we know for sure- that the only things we absolutely must not consume is alcohol or peanuts. This, er, coffee is really amazing. I feel drinking it just as I do drinking your wonderful Coca Cola."

The president said, "Of course Delnoid, just as you radioed me. But no peanuts? Why no peanuts?"

Delnoid, now gulping his orange juice, explained, "Well, like some of you humans who have rare fatal reaction to peanuts; we Delphinians cannot ever tolerate your peanuts. But for now our immunologists are testing to learn how to inoculate the related immunoglobulin E in us and also in you by the way, against this deadly allergy."

Glinda squealed in delight, smiled and beamed, "OK then, let's eat! I cannot wait to taste your earth breakfast as you call it!"

Sara jiggled the little silver tinkle bell and two black government servants in white uniforms entered with two silver trays loaded down with a traditional American breakfast of bacon, ham, grits, eggs, hash browns and toasted breads and jams… Sara then gasped as she saw that there was also a jar of Peter Pan creamy peanut butter and as soon as she saw it, she grabbed the arm of the server and said, "Dwayne, please take that away! Our, uh, South American guests are all allergic to peanuts…"

Glinda seeing Sara's brusque action, beamed to her, "What was that Sara?"

Sara explained, "It was peanut butter that can be spread on bread or toast…" Glinda smiled and beamed a thank you to Sara as she privately thought to herself, "Sara is indeed a true friend and ally. She is determined to protect us and make our visit and relocation to earth safe and secure." Glinda beamed privately to her husband, "Arthur I now know that Sara is the one we need and seek and I hope she will agree to our plans."

Arthur, with a quick low squeak and some slow and low clicks, took a swig of his Coke and beamed back to his wife, "I agree." Glinda then noticed that Selena was looking very alarmed at her and Arthur. She beamed privately and emphatically to her daughter, "Selena, you know what we must try to do but we would never force Sara to breed for us."

Selena avoided her mother's eyes and tried to re-focus on enjoying her breakfast as she sat next to her dear Sara who she knew she probably would have to eventually ask her to be with her in their white OBGYN insemination clinic aboard their starship.

As soon as each plate had been served the president said, "OK, I now need all servers to leave the breakfast room please. Don't worry about or do any of the dishes and please tell cook that you all may have the rest of the day off until uh, 6:30 this evening. Please be sure that all of you leave the White House and go into town and enjoy yourselves. He then stood and pulled a wad of money from his pants pocket and handed each worker some $100. bills. He then grinned and said, OK be sure you give the others their money and be double sure that I do not catch any of you in this little White House til 18:30!

After they exited, Harry asked, "May I give a blessing to our first earthly meal together?" Arthur and Delnoid smiled and Glinda nodded her head as the President prayed, "Dear father, please bless our new friends and allies from the stars and this food that universally nourishes all of us in body and spirit, amen."

Sara then grinned almost uncontrollably as she recalled the silly breakfast prayer that her uncle Jim Petersen had sometimes said when he visited them when he came down to Montecito from Santa Barbara California. "Bless the biscuit. Praise the hen. Throw back yer head and shovel it in!"

Holding Sara's hand, Selena started squealing and clicking rapidly looked at her Sara and beamed privately to her, "That was a funny prayer Sara."

Selena then again tried to conceal her growing trepidation as she thought to herself, "I will never let them inseminate you unwillingly Sara - no matter what!"

Glinda scowled a bit, looked matter of factly at her daughter and privately beamed, "Selena. Please don't think so negatively. You know we would never force any human to breed for us!"

Arthur, to divert the growing upset in Selena beamed, "What is that wonderful smell? It smells just like the roasted animal we tried while we were visiting Hawaii in 1940."

The President picked up a piece of his bacon and asked, "This?" Arthur beamed, "Yes, it sure smells wonderful!"

Truman still munching on his piece of bacon said, "Oh, it's what we call bacon. It comes from a pig."

Arthur crunching his piece of bacon beamed, "Oh, well then, we have enjoyed pork in many earth places. I remember us eating delicious pork at a luau with Ailema and Embry while we were all at the Mona Hotel at lovely Waikiki Beach on the Oahu Island in Hawaii."

Glinda then began clicking rapidly in alarm as she sent Arthur a stern private telepathic warning… "Be careful! Be quiet about Ailema! Remember that Sara was way too curious and concerned that Ailema looks just like Amelia Earhart. Yes, she looks quite different now with her husband Emery. But we dare not let that flying cat out of the bag, at least not just yet!"

Embry, aboard Lifestar was tuned into the conversation and beamed to Glinda and Arthur, "Ailema says that she will be so glad when it becomes safe for her secret life with us to be revealed to the so wonderful Sara. She also says that she misses and really wants to enjoy meeting with and flying with Eleanor Roosevelt again."

The President asked Arthur, "So, exactly how long have you been on earth? It seems that you have visited almost every country on our planet?"

Arthur smiled and beamed, "We have probably visited more places on your world than any of you ever have."

"Well then," quipped President Truman as he chuckled, "It's always true that tourists always visit and see more places and events than us busy locals ever do."

Delnoid said to everyone, "We in have been here for about 12 of your earth years Mr. President."

Truman, looking at Glinda asked, " So, how old are you now your maj… er Glinda ?

Glinda then eager to change the subject away from Ailema, smiled clicked and quipped, "Mr. President, you know on earth, that it's not polite to ask a female her age." as she ticked in mock indignation again in a tsk, tsk, tsk manner.

Selena was grinning from ear to ear. She squealed and beamed to all of them, "Yeah, it's not polite, but I can tell you that I am about twenty eight percent of my mother's age."

Sara then realized that she was not really sure of exactly how old Selena was so she turned to her amazing young friend and asked, "So, ok Selena, how old are you?"

Selena squeaked, smirked and beamed, "I am, as of today, going to be 16 of your earth years."

Sara nodded in agreement and grinned as she realized that what Selena had told her about their life spans was correct and that it made sense that Selena was 15 and that her mother was now about 32.

The president then asked, "So, does that mean that you are among the first of your 6th generation of your ancestors who left beta Delphinus so long ago to find an appropriate home world? After what was it you told me? That your planet became un-inhabitable because of a geologic cataclysm." Arthur and Glinda half smiled and nodded. But they of course knew that the President knew what he did about them only from the semi true information they had asked Selena to share with Sara.

Sara smiled and said aloud, "Selena, since today your 16th earth year birthday, we will have to go enjoy a special birthday dinner for you."

Glinda smiled at Sara and beamed, "Why that's quite right. We will have to prepare some special earth food for my budding princess. What do you suggest Sara?"

Sara smiled happily as she said, "Well, on our walk about in Key West this afternoon. I am sure that we can find a special restaurant and have a special birthday luncheon for our Selena"

Selena by then was grinning ear to ear and beamed, "Does everyone on earth celebrate their birthdays?"

Sara looked kind of amazed and said, "Why of course, don't you?"

As Glinda looked rather somber, Selena moaned and beamed, "Noooo Sara, we just let the onboard computer system keep track of our passing years. After just two generations in deep and empty space, we all opted to forget about birthdays on board Lifestar by us being trapped, generation after seemingly endless generation in our big sub light speed life raft. Birthdays ceased to have any real happy or spiritual meaning for us. Especially not for all the 5 generations before us who, except for just a few elders who are still with us, they could never dare hope to live to see earth."

Sara receiving this revelation said, "Well, from now on we will always celebrate all of your birthdays. For me, when I start a new orbit around our light and life giving sun star, I go out and try to find a star shining from as many light years away that is as old as I am. I call them birthday stars. On my birthday last January 26th, I went out and enjoyed looking at alpha Lyra. It's a fine bright star we call Vega and it's 26 light years away from Earth."

Arthur clicked and grinned as he beamed, "How unique! Maybe we can all begin do that too Sara."

Sara grinned and continued, "Well Selena. I just happen to know which star is your 16th birthday star shining in the small constellation of the Eagle which is at the south apex of what we call the great summer triangle. Its Altair and its 16 light years away."

Delnoid then grinned proudly and said, " OK I have just calculated an entire catalog of human birthday stars for each human age in years. Shall I recite it ? You see the first birthday star is one you call alpha Centauri. Its four light years away and since it's the closest star there are no birthday stars for ages 1,2,3… The… All three aliens then glared at Delnoid as Arthur beamed, "Del, for catfish sake. Not now – ok?"

Selena squealed and clicked rapidly in delight and beamed, "Oh how funtastic. Can we go out tonight night and see Altair?"

Sara paused, looked at the President and said, "Well of course. That flat Navy dock area is just nearby and if it's clear we could probably see it from there. "You know what? We could make it a small dockside birthday and home star party with a small picnic, birthday cake and Coke !"

President Truman said, "Wow! Birthday Stars. How educational. I will make an order to base security to have those dock lights switched off tonight for our picnic."

All three aliens then looked lovingly at Sara and beamed in unison, "Oh Sara. Thank you for such compassion and a Navy dockside birthday star, party would be wonderful !"

Sara's jaw dropped as she asked, Oh my gosh ! How do you do that unison answering ? Its delightful and amazing !"

Glinda smiled, squealed and clicked as she beamed, "Oh Sara its just a telepathic alien thing - just for you Earthers. Then everybody broke into laughing, squealing clicking and laughing.

Delnoid, then interjected," Say, since are talking about the star you call alpha Aquila. The constellation you call Delphinus lies just north eastish of the Eagle and that is where the star you call beta Delphini or Rotanev is and that's our former home star at 97 light years or sigh… 6 generations away.

"But tomorrow, March 15th, Sara, Altair rises at 2:06 am and sets at 2:07pm. So unluckily it will be daylight and you won't be able to see it…"

Sara looked with amazement at Del, sighed and said, Oh my gosh you are undoubtedly right. My birthday star catalog is still at my parents house in California." Sara then reached over and took Selena's hand and said, Its ok sweetie… We can enjoy your birthday luncheon tomorrow and then when Altair becomes visible at night time. We will look at your 16th birthday star light…"

Delnoid being the walking, talking star catalog he was announced, "Well Altair is visible at night from July 2nd until January 9th and it transits on October 7th… Assuming that all three astrometric Altair observing times at at, er, about 7pm… So, from about this latitude…" Irrepressible Delnoid then continued, "By the way our Rotanev star is a joke name given by an 1800's Italian astronomer, Niccolo Cacciatore. It was his Latinized family name Venator spelled backwards."

The three Delphinians, Delnoid and the president all raised their eyebrows and looked knowingly at each other as the Delphs let out a descending soft squeal as they remembered how they all agreed to spell Amelia's name backwards to Ailema. Sara not yet in on the Amelia secret just slightly raised her eyebrows as she wondered what these presidential and alien so knowing looks were all about.

The still grinning president harrumphed and said, "Well, I am sure even without actually observing, what was it Alter? We shall all enjoy celebrating Selena's birthday tomorrow."

Delnoid being ever correct said, Uh, Mr. President sir, its Altair, A-L-T-A-I-R, uh sir…" Which is strangely the adopted earth name of our ships second officer."

Sara grinned and said, "Yes, tomorrow we shall have to get a nice sweet sixteen birthday gift for our Selena."

Selena beamed, "But, I already got a wonderful birthday present from my Sara."

Glinda and Arthur beamed as Delnoid asked aloud, "A what?"

Selena squealed and excitedly beamed to her family, Sara and Delnoid images of the beautiful framed photo Sara had just given her.

All four smiled approvingly as Glinda beamed, "Oh Sara how truly sweet of you." She then thought to herself, "We will have to calculate and convert all of our pods' ship time birthdays and memorize everybody's birthdays as we orbit this new star."

President Truman, with a million questions still on his mind, then cautiously asked Glinda, "Do you Delphinians believe in God?"

Glinda smiled and reverently beamed, "Mr. Truman, we are all children of the universe and each day we thank our and your creators, the Amadores for the gift and blessings of life and spirit no matter where we are in this universe."

Sara was quite moved by Glinda's universal vision and spiritual and soul filling ideas that she said, "I hope you can teach me more about your Amador and your spirituality soon."

Glinda smiled, clicked softly and continued, "We all must share light and life in all ways that we can."

Selena looking with love and spirit at her Sara, beamed, "Its true Sara and Mr. President. We are all children of the creators of this and other universes and I hope we can all learn to share and live in peace, respect and harmony together on earth."

Sara sat there taking in all of the profound peace wishes and spirituality of her now alien little sister. She smiled as she recalled the very wonderful, youthful and playful spirit in Selena; was for the moment very profound, spiritual and diplomatic.

Now totally inspired and mind melded with Selena. Sara emotionally cleared her throat and said to everyone, "We are here this morning, not by accident but by choice and as we talk, share and learn from each other, we will see that even though we have been separated by light years, we have so much in common that will help our mutual development, security, well being and spirituality too."

Arthur and Glinda smiled as Arthur beamed to all, "My Earthly friends and hopeful allies. I too wish for us to learn to live and share together in understanding, trust and peace. Please know that we Delphinian's really do need and appreciate your kind and open hospitality and growing trust. Together we must unfailingly try to understand and solve our differences, respect each other and quickly learn how we can adapt physiologically and socially to live in a balanced and beneficial trust on earth together."

The President having finished his breakfast said, "I agree with you Arthur and again I will do all that is in my power as president of these United States to assure your safe and secure homecoming to our world." After a few quiet moments, Truman cleared his throat and asked, "So, Arthur can you please tell us more about your star and home world?"

Arthur clicked softly, nodded his head to Delnoid 1 and then, like an endless walking, talking encyclopedia, the android proceeded to declare, "Mr. President, our water world orbits the star your astronomers have labeled beta β Delphinus in your constellation of Delphinus, the dolphin. And as I mentioned earlier. In 1814, Niccolo Venator Cassiatore strangely named it Rotanev which is Venator spelled backwards. Why such a eccentric jest I can never imagine. "Anyway," he continued, "It is what you designate as an F5.1v star. So its spectral class is brighter than your yellow G-5 light and life giving sun star. This is why male Delphs, because of the way our super light sensitive eyes have evolved, have to wear variable sun glasses. You can actually see β Del with your eyes, since its visual magnitude is medium bright at 3.617. It's the star that connects the tail of the dolphin in your so noteworthy dolphin like small constellation of Delphinus. As you may know Mr. President, the angular distance between the two pointer stars of your Big Dipper, Dubhe and Merak is 5 degrees.

Well sir, Delphinus, which lies to the east side of the great summer triangle of Vega Deneb and Altair is also 5 degrees. Delphinus is directly overhead on August 1st of each year and can be seen from April 22nd until 7 months later, when it settles down in the west on November 9th. Our planet's orbital period is, uh, was 993 earth days or about 2.7 of your earth years. It lies 97.508 light years from Earth and as you now know, it took us 6 generations or 372 of your earth years to make our seemingly never-ending sub light speed journey at 5,812 miles per second (9,299 kilometers per hour) or 23,083,200 million miles per hour (36,933,120 kilometers per hour) to come here after we departed in August of your year of 1612." Sara, who had enjoyed a few astronomy classes at her Montecito, Westmont College Carroll Observatory with its big 16 inch Newtonian and Cassegrain telescope thought for a minute, scribbled on her yellow notepad beside her plate and said, "Hummmm, that means that you were able to travel at about 3 per cent of the speed of light. Oh my gosh! That's incredible! What a courageous quest your saga was." "But, Del the Altair visibility times and dates you just gave is different from your, uh, data for Altair as a birthday star."

Delnoid looked amazed as he said, "Why Sara. Those birthday star dates and time were for observing at 7pm and the data I just gave you was for a midnight transit parameter." Arthur squeaked and smiled approvingly as Delnoid 1 continued… "But, we are not able to surpass the 669,600,000 million miles per hour (1,071,360,000 km) universal light speed limit yet!"

Arthur sighed, let out some hopeless clicks and privately beamed to Selena and Glinda "And for sure, our trusty old star ship is never again going to be able to obtain velocities anywhere near to only three percent of light speed ever again! More likely, only under 100,000 miles per hour or so, if we are lucky and our deuterium helium fusion drive holds up."

After their amiable breakfast, the president and Sara picked up the serving trays on the sideboard and started collecting the breakfast dishes and silverware from the large oak table. Glinda, Selena, Arthur and Delnoid immediately joined in helping clear the table. The new breakfast partners entered the kitchen. Glinda stopped open mouthed as she looked around the large kitchen of the Key West White House, squealed in delight and exclaimed, "Is this where you prepare your food?"

The president replied, "Yes your Majesty, er, Glinda this is where my White House staff of cooks and servers make all the food for me and my wife on the far too rare occasions when she is here and also for all visiting officials and dignitaries."

Selena clicked rapidly and beamed to Sara, "What is a dignitary?"

Sara grinned and said so that all could hear, "Dignitaries are very important dignified people like you dear little sister who are honoring us with your visit here in Key West."

President Truman looked at Glinda and asked, "So, how do you prepare the food for the 160 people aboard your Lifestar?" As soon as the President said that, Arthur glared at Selena and clicked agitatedly because he really had not wanted Selena to have told Sara about how few of them were left aboard Lifestar.

Glinda, sensing her husband's apprehension, beamed to everyone. "We all need to be as open and truthful as we can with each other and it's true that there are only 160 of us left aboard Lifestar. So I personally hope that we Delphinians can soon make a good agreement with you so that we can get invited to stay here as refugees from our planetary cataclysm."

Arthur screwed up his face and beamed to everyone, "I agree and I am so glad that we have been invited here to meet informally like this. I can see that we are opening up to each other more and more and from these informal conversations. I now know and trust that we can better understand each other and come to a mutually beneficial agreement to live together Mr. President."

As he was taking dishes from to soap sink and rinsing and racking, wiley poker playing politician, Truman, saw this was his moment to lay a few more draw cards on their alien negotiating table, and said, "Your Majesty, I too am so glad that you accepted my invitation to meet informally here at my lovely south Florida tropical base. Because, only by talking openly and frankly can we actually come to a realistic agreement for you, all of you, to come to your new home here on Earth. So maybe you, Delnoid 1 and I can parley here today while Glinda, Selena and Sara enjoy Key West and birthday shopping for Selena."

Arthur smiled, clicked softly and beamed, "Mr. President, I think this will be an excellent opportunity for us to, as you just thought, to now lay all of… as you say – lay our cards on the negotiating table. What do you think?" Delnoid 1 nodded his head in agreement and said, "President Truman, we do need your help to succeed and right now fortunately, Arthur and the other leaders sincerely want peace and a viable treaty with you. There is, just like war hawks you now have in your now growing cold war, a small and older but fortunately very small fifth generation minority of confrontation bent conservatives aboard our ship. But Mr. President, we assure you that the majority of our Delphinians only want peace and an opportunity to share with you some of our advanced technologies in exchange for security and a small oceanside community somewhere on your so magnificent and so appropriate for us, water world."

Selena hearing Delnoid then beamed to her mother, "Why didn't my father just beam this to the president?"

Glinda winked and beamed privately to her daughter, "It is better most times for now if these humans hear most remarks aloud as it impacts better on their understanding of what is being communicated."

President Truman dried his right hand on the dish towel, stepped forward and extended his hand to Arthur as he said, "I too am glad we are able to talk unofficially together like this. After we finish these dishes and have refreshed ourselves, let's meet in my small oval office."

As the two leaders shook hands and looked directly into each other's eyes, each was thinking, "Indeed we now begin to understand and trust each other."

"Sara…"

"Yes Mr. President?"

"Sara, would you mind preparing coffee, tea and of course cold cokes, some sandwiches, I saw a couple of prepared bowls of tuna salad and ham salad and sliced Velveeta cheese in the walk-in and please also bowl some potato chips for us before you lead these two lovely ladies around our picturesque Key West village?"

Sara smiled and said, "Certainly Mr. President." Sara turned to Glinda and Selena and simply thought, "Ok girls, let's make some sandwiches and coffee and also get some cokes for your husband, Delnoid 1 and the president. Then we can go back up to our rooms and get ready to enjoy some shopping and leisurely sightseeing."

Sara, who now knew that the Delphinian society was a totally equal society thought to Glinda, "Don't you want to participate in these vital meetings queen Glinda "

Glinda grinned, winked, clocked and touched the side of her head and beamed to Sara, Selena and her husband, "Don't worry, I'll be there telepathically as I also enjoy being your delighted tourist in charming Key West."

Selena, sniffing and sonic beaming around, quickly discovered the one pound round yellow tin of Red Dot Potato Chips and she excitedly beamed to Sara, "This must be the potato chips you wanted Sara. Look at this yellow can. There is a cute and funny little man drawn on it."

Sara chuckled as she picked up and opened the tin and said, "That is a drawing of a circus clown and inside are what we call potato chips." She offered the open tin to Selena who sniffed at it and tentatively reached in and took a chip. Sara laughed and said, "Its ok little sister. I'll bet that you can't eat just one chip, try a handful, you'll like them."

Selena started nosily chewing the thin crispy chips and let out a very loud whistle as she beamed, "These are really terrific and nice and salty too."

Just then they heard three chimes sound. Bing Bong Bing... Selena and Glinda with their extraordinary keen hearing both looked over at the set to low volume radio someone had left on. Sara giggled and said, "Oh don't worry, that is the NBC Radio chimes and its probably sounding to mark the top of the hour. Right now is when the Don McNeill's Breakfast Club show is on. Many, many people in USA listen to it for news, music and comedy every morning. It's kind of an American tradition."

 Selena squeaked and then perfectly imitated the NBC chime as she beamed, "Oh we have heard those tones many times on our ship's radios. We listened to NBC constantly during your WWII for news and also to learn more about your culture." She smiled proudly and sounded the NBC chime musical notes of G E C perfectly again, "Bing Bong Bing..."

After preparing, tuna salad, ham salad and cheese sandwiches and potato chips, the girls placed the lunches in the walk-in refrigerator. Selena spotted a box full of Hostess Twinkies. She picked one up and beamed to

Sara, "What are these?" Sara smiled as she took one for herself and one for Glinda and said, "These are really nice little cream filled sponge cakes. Try one, you'll like it."

Glinda, taking dainty bites from her Twinkie smiled, licked her lips and beamed, "Well really, none of us know how to cook and we, moan, click click click, don't have any marvelous and well equipped kitchens like yours aboard our ship."

Sara looked astounded and asked, "So, how do you prepare your food?"

Selena beamed, "We have an onboard fish farm, automatic food synthesizers and processors. We also now for the last 12 years since we landed in your Pacific Ocean, use our automated fish catching equipment which is a vital food and protein source for us since we have been here and also undersea on earth." " Our Earthly dolphin cousins always chase a large school of fish to out fishing equipment and electromagnetic capture field… er, kinda like your fishing nets work. We always give them half of the catch."

Selena continued, "I cannot tell you how wonderful it was after five and a quarter generations when we landed on your Pacific Ocean and were able to enjoy fresh fish after the bland synthesizer food from our stinky old fish farm and our uh, waste products." Sara thought, "Ah ha…" as she realized that the aliens almost totally depended on the Earth's oceans for the major part of their protein needs.

Glinda, now also enjoying munching her Twinkie with Selena beamed to Sara, "I would so love to learn to cook Sara. Will you please teach me sometime?"

Sara grinned as she thought back to her two alien amigas, "I would love to do just that once we get you all securely settled somewhere." She winked in fun as she thought to Selena and Glinda, "You can read English, right?" Both females moaned somewhat indignantly and beamed back, "Yes we can speak, read and understand so far, six Earth languages."

"Well" said Sara, "There is a great cook book by Betty Crocker and I will try to get you a copy when we are in Miami day after tomorrow." Sara asked Glinda, "So, have you given any thoughts about where on our world, along which seacoast you would like to settle in?"

Glinda beamed, "As you know, over the last 12 years we have occasionally gotten off of the ship and using our humidifiers, we have enjoyed visiting and discovering a few small coastal towns here and there on earth. But, we could not dare go to any big cities and quite frankly Sara, I am a bit concerned about our upcoming visit to Miami."

Sara smiled and assured both aliens that there would be four secret service officers with them and with their two-way radios they could summon aid, vehicles, a They got dressed for their walk about and prepared to leave the White House.

Sara, not really knowing for sure if she should call the Delphinians a fast Navy boat or even a helicopter if needed. Glinda just smiled and beamed thankful energies to Sara as she thought to herself, "We also will have a scout flighter saucer from our mother ship hovering at the edge of space 100 miles (160km) above Miami if needed."

Selena wanting to divert the pressing travel worries from getting any more tense, made a short attention getting squeal and said, "One of my favorite places was Portofino on the north western Italian Riviera. It was such a quaint and picturesque little seaside village. I would like to enjoy spending some time there sketching and painting. I think the amazing pastel artist Maxwell Parrish must have been there to get his inspiration. So, squeak, squeak, maybe you and I can go visit there someday Sara."

Sara smiled and said, "That would be wonderful Selena, but only when I get my short two week vacation times. Remember that I am a US Government employee."

Glinda then beamed, "Well, as you can imagine. We have visited and explored many areas on your beautiful water world and since we do need as much moisture as possible for our skin. We have been thinking about finding a place, maybe in the Caribbean, or possibly somewhere further to the south along the western Atlantic; or perhaps somewhere along the tropical coastal areas of Central America or Brazil or maybe north or south of Florianopolis in Brazil. Or possibly even further south, near Aguas Dulces, Argentina where there are endless white sand beaches. We have also been seriously considering Punta del Este, Uruguay where the Atlantic begins to become Mar de la Plata 196 miles east of Buenos Aires, Argentina. Punta del Este is only 71 miles east of Montevideo, Uruguay near where the German pocket battleship Graf Spee was finally scuttled after the battle of the River Plate (Rio de la Plata) in December of 1939.

We also love scenic Chile and the magnificent spirit filling Pacific Ocean, but that Humboldt Current, north flowing unswimable freezing water, even in relatively hot northern Chile and southern Peru is just way too cold for us."

Sara nodded her head in agreement and even shivered as she recalled, "Oh yes, I remember how cold the Pacific is from Chile on up to northern Peru along the west coast of South America. While my UCSB Anthropology class was staying in lovely Mira Flores near ugly Lima, Peru; we went down to the beach for a swim and some surfing on rented boards at La Rosa Nautica. And we sure, as frozen wet cats, straight-a-way scrambled out of that freezing water at that beach. Even though it is only 12 degrees south of the equator, that Humboldt current keeps the climate along the Lima coast just like it is at equally chilly, foggy and cloudy as San Francisco's cold water California!"

Arthur, just getting dressed for his meeting with Truman beamed in, "Oh yes, I remember that Mira Flores area. Embry, Ailema and I hovered there one late afternoon back in 1944 in one of our flighters. Because we discovered that there was an observatory and a planetarium on a hill top and a bit south of the planetarium was an Amador, uh, I mean what you call a lovely Virgin Mary statue on that same hilltop just about 3 miles south of Mira Flores. But the observatory and planetarium seemed to be abandoned."

Sara again amazed at the travels of her aliens and now also relative to her own travels remarked, "Oh my gosh! I remember seeing that observatory and statue of Mary on top of the Morro Solar above that horrible shanty town of Chorrillos just south of Mira Flores. Did you have such poverty and differences between rich and poor on your home world?"

Glinda clicked deeply and beamed, "Well, since we never used money as an exchange we never had such disparities between our pods."

Arthur clicked slowly and sadly and thought to his wife and princess, "Yeah, we had only society destroying alpha male egos and absurd fighting."

 Sara continued, "You really have been checking out many areas on our planet."

Selena teared up and beamed, "Yes, but now we are like kids trapped in our smelly old spacecraft looking longingly out of our portholes and view screens at a glorious water world fish and fresh air store. We so want, after five and a half generations, to get out of our oversize metal city and breath fresh air and feel sunshine on our shoulders and especially be able to swim in the ocean and also enjoy playing with our dolphin friends."

Sara, was beginning to find that not too much surprised her anymore questioned, "Friends… dolphin friends?"

Selena beamed, "Yes, like mom said, they help us gather fish and also many times since we have been on Earth we have surfaced near dolphins and as we swam and romped with them we telepathed a lot with them."

Sara grinned knowingly as she said, "Hummmm, oh that must be why there were so many dolphins frolicking above you before you surfaced to meet us back on February 23rd."

Selena teared up as she squeaked, moaned and beamed, "Oh that poor female dolphin that heartless sailor shot, her pod so misses her!"

Sara teared up too, hugged Selena and said, "I wish I could communicate with our dolphins and other sea mammals. I am sure they have much they could tell and teach us about living together in harmony and also about the damage we are doing to our own world's oceans."

Selena squealed, clicked excitedly and grinned as she beamed, "Oh Sara, I can be your dolphin cultural ambassador and translator!"

Sara nodded her head in an ah ha moment of understanding and total agreement and said, "I think that would be perfect Selena, especially since you can incredibly communicate fully with our earth dolphins! But for now, shall we head out to enjoy some sightseeing, shopping and your special birthday lunch?" Sara continued, "I thought we could walk about downtown and then enjoy a seafood lunch at Sloppy Joe's for Selena's birthday. After our lunch, there is a quaint modest aquarium here which was started back in 1926. Would you like to visit it?"

Glinda frowned, clicked and interjected, "I can see fish anytime. I just want to look at some earth clothes shops. Would that be ok Sara?"

Sara smiled and as she opened her purse she pulled out a big wad of money that the president had given her for the alien's shopping. She grinned and said, "Of course, remember you are uh, visiting South Americans and since you can't talk, be sure to use your notepads and pencils – ok? Which reminds me, we have to buy you each a nice purse!"

Glinda and Selena squeaked affirmatively, grinned as they dug in their only two purses that Sara had given them and brought out their notepads and with each holding up a Scripto mechanical pencil. They both beamed to Sara, "OK, we are ready teddies oh fearless leader. "Let's go shopping!"

CHAPTER 15 SHOP TIL WE SQUEAK

Sara picked up the porch wall telephone and said, "OK, we are leaving now." Almost immediately two men wearing sunglasses, in Hawaiian shirts, shorts and off white Panama hats appeared as Sara explained, "These are our White House Secret Service agents who will follow us to protect us..."

Selena and Glinda who read the minds of the two agents beamed privately to Arthur and Delnoid 1, "It's ok, they seem to accept as true that we are mute South American visitors."

Glinda thought, "I know that they are, of course, specially trained Secret Service agents, but they are only fallible humans and not at all like our bio - engineered guardian Delnoids."

Glinda then received from Delnoid 1 "Ah, thank you your majesty. Beam to us if you need us." All of the 12 male and female android Delnoid units were always completely connected and they could also all act, apart or together as one or more when needed.

Selena smirked as she beamed, "Yeah and those agents also think that we are really attractive. One of them was looking at you mom and he thought, "Wow that older dame is a real babe."

Glinda squeaked and clicked rapidly in annoyance as she beamed to Selena and Sara, "Why how can I be a baby? Selena, you are my baby girl, so why on earth is that man calling me a baby?"

Sara was almost in stitches as she thought to her two perplexed alien companions, "Oh Glinda, a babe means a really good looking woman."

The three women with their now sweating, trailing, aloha shirted secret service agents walked about town and looked around in the few curio shops. Glinda beamed to Sara, "This is just fascinating. I see so many things and I have no idea at all what they are." As they entered another tourist shop, Sara said, "Well, these tourist shops do have a wonderful collection of souvenirs, clothing, arts and curios. So, if you see anything you particularly like, I will help you purchase it."

Glinda beamed, "But if we buy so much, how can we carry all of our purchases Sara?"

Sara turned and showed her tan backpack saying, "If we get more, one of those guys in the Hawaiian shirts following us can carry some things too." Selena squealed and beamed, "Oh look at these little blue green glass dolphins. Aren't they beautiful?" Glinda clicked happily as Sara agreed.

Selena beamed, "I want this one."

Sara took the glass sculpture to the clerk, paid for it and asked the clerk to please wrap it very well considering that Selena would need to pack it for her flight home next week.

In the next shop there were a lot of colorful Cuban blouses, skirts, shoes and artwork. Glinda clicked in awe and beamed to Selena and Sara, "I feel so thrilled at being here. I have never seen such brightly colored clothes like these before. I think I would like to get this dress."

Sara said, "You can go into that small room behind the colorful curtain to try it on." Sara handed the dress to Glinda and asked, "Do you want me to help you?"

Glinda clicked softly and beamed back, "That would be so nice Sara."

Wide eyed Selena continued to browse around the shop. Sara accompanied Glinda into the small changing room with a mirror - where the flower print curtain door hung down only to about knee height. Glinda kicked off her silver alien flipper shoes and began taking off her dress to try on the dress she had picked out. Unbeknownst to Sara and Glinda, the clerk in the store was staring opened mouthed at Glinda's toeless flipper feet. The clerk called to her amiga clerk in spanish and pointed to Glinda's feet said, "Oh Dios mio Maria. Que pasa al pies de este pobre Senora?" (Oh my God Maria what happened to the toes of this poor woman). Maria looked at Penelope and said, "Aiiiii Santo, she must have some kind of birth defect."

Of course Selena was receiving their thoughts, so she took out her note pad and pencil and rapidly wrote as best she could on it in Spanish. "Si, mi mamma tiene un, tragic birth defect on her feet. This is why she wears those special shoes."

The concerned clerk read the note and asked, "Can you not talk senorita?"

Selena now enjoying getting into practicing notepad communication wrote, "No, all of my family have funny feet and cannot speak because of birth defects."

Maria looked down at Selena's alien shod feet and said. Oh, tu tambien amiga? (Oh, you too, amiga).

Selena did not miss a beat as she suppressed a squeal, grinned and wrote, "Si, me too…" Selena then beamed to her mom in the dressing room, "The clerks are concerned about your feet, but I handled them." As soon as Glinda received her daughters beamed warning, she immediately sat down on the bench and put her alien shoes back on. Sara quickly realized what must have happened and was about to hurry out onto the display floor to explain. Selena beamed to her, "Relax Sara, I've got everything under control out here."

Sara thought back, "OK, if you're sure it's ok. We will be out in a minute after your mother has put her own dress back on."

After Sara paid for the new dress. Selena, Glinda and Sara continued walking along the few remaining store fronts. Glinda squeaked, clicked and then beamed, "Well, that was sure a lesson in watching out for our feet."

Sara had by now become pleasantly used to just thinking instead of speaking so she simply thought, "That was great practice for you in using notepads to communicate with us earthlings. As soon as we get you settled on Water Island, I want to have many classes for all of you to especially teach you all about money, how to use it, spend it, save it and how banks work and most importantly, invest it for your futures. We have a good bank in California. It's the Wells Fargo Bank and we will open checking, savings and investment accounts there for all of you once we get you based in Camp Roberts."

Glinda beamed, "Sara we have so much to learn, especially since we have never really used money except for some cash Delnoid got for us now and then at some banks in some of the different countries and small towns we visited. So I, by all means, want to learn all about finances as soon as I can."

Selena, aware of all the sunken spanish treasures they had gathered, squeaked and beamed, "Me toooo… so I can buy everything!"

Sara giggled as Glinda squeaked sharply once and clicked rapidly in exasperated rebuke.

Arthur sitting at the conference table with Truman and Delnoid 1 clicked merrily and beamed to Glinda and Selena, "Yeah, with all the treasure we gathered from at least 20 sunken old Spanish galleon wrecks will surely let you shop until we all drop !"

Glinda then clicked, squeaked sharply as she beamed only to Arthur, Delnoid 1 and Selena, "Even in this short time on Earth. I clearly see the main god here is money - right above fear, ego and greed!"

Delnoid then chipped in, "But money is only a tool of exchanges and an idea based on mutual confidence and trust. We have the same values but in our minds and spirits for exchanging true heart emotional units for happiness, trust and satisfaction."

Glinda clicked in resignation and beamed," Well all we can do is try to preserve our values and use our money to purchase only the material things we need and not try to buy happiness!"

To change the subject. Selena moaned softly and resignedly beamed, "I guess though, we probably will have to be mechanical pencils and note pad toting mutes for the rest of our lives here on earth. We also must remember to never openly beam to anyone else for the rest of our refugee lives."

Glinda, with her total Delphinians' racial and cultural memories available to her, beamed to Selena and Sara, "It's now fortunate and lucky that we are the sixth generation homecoming from the ship because really, other than our pod memories, we have no actual home world to miss. So my young pouting princess, we will do what we must to continue living as inconspicuously as we can here on this lovely planet."

Sara said, "Let's stop here in Mallory Square and sit at this umbrella picnic table and I will get us some cokes." Sara returned with the nice cold refreshing glass bottles of Coke with straws in them. She asked, "What about Delnoid 1? Why is it he can speak?"

Glinda explained that all of the Delnoids, as bio engineered life forms, had been designed with the capability of speech.

Sara was a bit apprehensive as she asked, "Do you mean that Delnoid is not like you?"

Glinda decided to be open and honest with her new human daughter of her heart beamed, "Yes Sara, remember Delnoid is like a bio robot, like what you would probably call a biological automaton."

Sara with her Coke straw in her lips just nodded her head grinned and thought, "Oh like an android. I read about them in the Captain Future science fiction pulp books. The story had two of them. One was named Grag and the other, who was a shape shifter, was named Otho."

Selena then whistled, clicked excitedly and beamed, "Oh Sara, where can we get those books? Those stories sound great!"

Sara noticed that she and Selena were interrupting Glinda's train of thought said, "Ok kiddo, we'll stop at a newsstand on our way back to the white house, but for now I need to ask, "Why can't your researchers and doctors bio engineer your future children so they can speak too?"

Glinda and Selena looked somberly at Sara as Glinda explained, "Such modifications have been tried Sara. But without real human DNA through egg and sperm donations from humans, we find that such genetic modifications have so far proved to be by and large just unviable."

What Glinda did not share with Sara was that Ailema and Embry had been trying to make an alien human hybrid baby since 1938, but so far, in spite of the advanced Delphinian gynecological medical capabilities, they had no success.

Sara was beginning to get the drift of their situation. She was quiet for awhile as she sipped her Coke and thought, "But, gosh Glinda, you Delphinians are really medically advanced. I recall reading something about DNA in the Scientific American." She looked directly into Glinda's eyes, and resolutely said, "Well, since you say that you have the medical technology to take donated eggs, I will be glad to donate some of my DNA and eggs to you if that would help…"

Glinda knew very well that, in the past, such donations, without a truly willing and devoted human female to carry the embryo to full term, had not been at all vailable. For some reason as not yet fully understood; maybe metaphysical or spiritual love energy reasons, the natural genetic and biological modifications in embryos without mothers to carry them, just did not survive. Glinda's second sister Mamani, had devoted her entire life to such genetic research. She had discovered, with her great spirituality, that the mother of such bio engineered alien human babies had to actually have true devoted love energies in her mind, spirit and nervous systems as she carried and gave birth to the hybrid baby.

 Glinda thought to herself and Selena, "Well, maybe it's now or never…" She then beamed to Sara, "Sara, we are truthfully looking for a volunteer human woman to become inseminated with her Delphin husband's cultivated and controlled sperm to, Amador willing, hopefully carry the first Delphinian baby who can cry and talk for us."

Sara was quiet and looked thoughtfully her soda straw on the picnic table…

Selena moaned clicked softly and beamed, "We are also seeking an appropriate human male to impregnate me so I can give birth to the first Delphinian baby girl who can cry and talk and talk and talk…"

Stupefied, Sara who had always been very liberal, progressive and open in her California and Hollywood ideals and spirit, stammered… "So then, are you asking me to help you produce a child for you who can talk?" Glinda and Selena both squeaked,clicked and beamed with all of the love energies they had in their true hearts and spirits for Sara.

Glinda beamed, "Only if you are completely willing to help us Sara. We have never inseminated any unwilling females before and we would of course understand if you refuse. We had, referring to Amelia, "one human, uh, person, visitor aboard and she wanted to carry a Delphin baby. But unfortunately she was unable to get pregnant no matter what we tried."

Sara still stupefied said, "Oh, my gosh, you had another human woman aboard. Uh… So, what happened to her?"

Glinda who was never a good liar made a descending whistle and beamed, "Well, Sara she, uh decided to leave us, uh, just when world war two began so we erased her memories and returned her home to uh, Italy uh, Portofino, Italy." Glinda then tried to change the subject in an attempt to decrease Sara's curiosity, beamed, "Sara please let me explain some things about our Delphin language. We operate mainly on feelings, emotions and love energies and their profound effects on all of us and particularly on our embryos, fetuses and babies. Our highly emotional telepathic language is a significant part of our culture and our vital love energies that we all live and share with. So, it's quite unlike the way you humans relate to each other in your world. The Delphin language uses only our internal states of being and feeling as its emotional and physiological basis. All human languages use external sensory references like a rock, table, person, lemon – all nouns - together with their descriptors [adjectives], interrelationships, sequence, actions, etc. Humans refer only slightly, and too briefly at best, to their subjective internal states, to the extent that you humans often fool yourselves into thinking that you are talking about something else when you're only talking about yourselves. Like, I love you, I hate you, this food tastes lousy, or what a stupid piece of music. So Sara, always try not to take anything personally because, nothing others say and do is because of you. Others say and do what is a projection of their own life dream."

"So you see, for us and for your earth dolphins to use an object as external references in a language, would at best, be something of an extreme insult by assuming severe sensory impairment of the Delphin or dolphin being spoken to. It would thus imply his untrustworthiness and danger to the pod or our whole, in this present situation, our whole starship community. So in summary dear Sara, we communicate and live by feelings and love energies and the fact that you humans are not yet telepathic is probably why you have to communicate and live by things and not very direct love energies like we do. This is why genetically, the host mother, of our hoped for crying and talking hybrid child, must have her vital emotional and love energies constantly flowing in her nervous system and into her embryo as well as in her true spirit and heart."

Sara, open mouth now, said, "Oh my gosh Glinda, I now really better understand your culture and powerful love energies because I always feel them so deeply whenever any of you communicate to me. It's not like just talking or just hearing in my head, but also feeling and almost exactly duplicating your emotions, intentions, feelings and experiences too."

Glinda nodded earnestly and continued, "Ever since we Delphinians arrived on Earth, there have been raging debates onboard Lifestar between the aggressive alpha male minority and our more humane majority about how they should ethically and morally conduct such genetic researches, inseminations and bio engineering. So far, our respect for humans has chiefly prevailed. We also know about the cruel occasional abduction activities of other small gray alien visitors or their masters from the star system you call Tau Ceti. They also tried to establish themselves on Earth while operating from their lunar far side base. But so far, probably without any true cultural and physiological love energies, they too apparently have, as yet, failed to successfully birth any true human alien crossbreeds - especially since they are using terrified and unwilling abduction victims.

So you see Sara, both of us are very desperate refugee alien races seeking a home on Earth. We need a 100% true genetically balanced alien human hybrid being to successfully carry on our races. We Delphinians, above all else, know that if we do not succeed soon in producing the precise crossbreed that we need, Glinda moaned sadly, clicked softly and continued, "Our epic six generation pilgrimage will end with us and will prove tragically futile with the end of all of our precious life dreams."

Sara held Glinda's hand, nodded solemnly in accord and said, "Dear Glinda and all Delphinians, please know that the President and I will always and in all ways possible, do all that we can to help you land on Earth and continue to exist. She then asked, "Do you ever have contact with those grey aliens?"

Glinda looked horror-struck, squeaked sharply and beamed, "Oh dear Amadore no! They are heartless, cold-blooded, evil reptilian heritage creatures and apparently the way they abuse and medically examine their human and animal captives is dreadful and we avoid them at all possible costs. Fortunately our Lifestar armaments and force shields are stronger than theirs. We had a brief encounter with them when we first came to our backside moon base and we were able to shoot down two of their flighters. They, thank Amadore, for the most part, have left us alone since then."

The breeding and alien baby conversations were then laid to rest as each woman contemplated the enormity of their perceptions. For about three minutes, Sara, Selena and Glinda sat quietly sipping their cokes under the white umbrella covered picnic table at the small square café.

Sara finally said, "You have given me so much to think about. I of course now am totally devoted to help you my dear alien family from the stars. But remember, I also work for the United States government. And I know about some of the alien investigative bases and I have heard some frightening rumors about what they are doing at remote, top secret, deep underground facilities at Wright Patterson Air Force Base in Ohio. And also at Dulce, New Mexico and Edwards in California and now more recently in Nevada, at a new remote top secret place northwest of Las Vegas that they call area 51. So I know that if I choose to become pregnant for you. I would probably be taken and secreted away at one of those alien examination bases. I would not want to ever put myself, nor my child in any such danger. Also, unless you abducted me, I would not be allowed to ever see any of you again…" Sara broke down in tears and Selena and Glinda quickly stood up, walked around the table and held her and beamed only loving and bolstering energies to her.

Glinda beamed to Sara, "My dearest Earth daughter, we will never put you in such an impossible situation. But, you are quite right Sara. If you should choose to help us with finally creating a hybrid baby capable of talking, we would have to take you to live with us. But then, your, so far, very kind, president would of course probably view your willing kidnapping as an act of treason with the result being that we would never be allowed to stay on Earth."

Selena, now softly crying and holding her Sara, squealed and beamed, "Sara we will never betray your trust, friendship and love now or ever."

Sara recovering from her introversion brightened up, grinned and supposed, "But what if I fall in love with one of you Delphinians, get an official California marriage license, get openly married in an earth church and then have the baby?"

Selena's eyes widened as she squeaked in delight and beamed, "Sure, I could also fall in love with an Earthman and marry him and have his baby girl."

Sara kind of scrunched up her forehead and asked, "Say, how do you know it would be a baby girl?"

Glinda clicked in a deep tone, made an amazing diabolical Dr Frankenstein face and beamed, "Vee have our vays in our own white room my darkling earth woman." She then clicked merrily, winked and soon all three women were smiling with Sara giggling and the Delphins trilling, clicking and squealing gleefully again.

Arthur still sitting and talking with President Truman, beamed privately into the baby making conversations and concluded, "Glinda, you are the wisest and loveliest Frankenstein in the Universe. I suggest we play this day by day and if Sara and Selena, but only in their true hearts, meet someone to love and marry. I think that then we can indeed make an enduring and viable baby making transitions in an earth home certainly happen. I can determine now that even with our more powerful weapons, we still could not overcome or survive a direct hit from one of the newly developed atomic bombs that the USA has developed. So thank Amador that they do not as yet have any ballistic guided missiles that could reach us in space. Besides, the whole purpose of our epic saga has been, for the last six generations, to come peacefully and permanently home to this water world planet." He clicked softly as he beamed, "We come in peace to survive and not to be pigheaded."

Delnoid, who was recording all of this, beamed, "I agree, one step at a time…" He then thought to himself, "Dang, I sure wish I had been bioengineered to feel romantic and make love. I really like Sara."

Glinda, who could overcome any telepathy barriers, beamed sternly, "Del 1! You are an excellent assistant, protector and ambassador, but always remember that you are NOT programmed or built to procreate – OK! And please remember and try to respect what happened to us in Portofino, Italy, just after the humans ended their world war."

"Yes your majesty," was meekly beamed back by Delnoid 1. But then he excitedly beamed… "OK Glinda, so who can we introduce Sara to aboard our ship?"

Arthur beamed in, "Good question you two match makers, but can we please wait to beam about all of this until later when you get back home to this White House or even better, back to our ship in seven days?"

Glinda beamed, "Of course my king, how are the talks going?"

Arthur beamed back, "We are making good progress because Truman is almost like an overgrown political kid in a candy store when it comes to acquiring our technologies. But, it's going to take some exact talking yet to decide who gets what and only after we are assured of a safe seaside home place. And what will become of our ship Lifestar for escape plan B, if we are eventually forced to turn Lifestar over to their US Army and Air Force investigators. No matter what our kind and so well intentioned President Truman agrees to, we would of course never see our ship again."

Delnoid agreed beaming, "I would never want us to be stranded here if the natives became politically two faced and tried to grab our technologies or begin to fear us and try to uh, eradicate us."

Arthur, poker faced, beamed, "Well, it's a darn good thing we found that other smaller amazing ancient star craft under the next crater on our lunar backside base."

Glinda beamed to her husband, "This is all kind of scary Arthur, but it sure beats sitting and wasting our lives floating between the stars in our giant aging and almost worn out space lifeboat."

Arthur agreed and beamed, "I agree. Ships are safe in a harbor, but that's not what they are made for. What are you girls going do now?"

Glinda looked at Sara questioningly and Sara sensing what Glinda wanted said, "Well, I think we should all go enjoy a nice birthday lunch at Sloppy Joe's."

Arthur took a sip of his Coke and beamed, "The cheese and ham salad sandwiches were good and those potato chips were really tasty Sara. Thank you for that nice lunch. I have never had ham and cheese together before. And that yellow sauce and the white sauce were quite tasty."

Sara smiled and thought back, "Oh, that's the Sauer's mustard and mayonnaise"

President Truman, an avid poker player, was very shrewd with his facial expressions, had guessed that Arthur had been beaming to his wife, Selena and Sara. He looked Arthur straight in the eye and asked him, "So, how are our ladies doing?"

Arthur was taken a bit aback for an instant, thinking that somehow the President had read his mind… beamed, "Why Harry, they have been shopping till they dropped and talking about babies!" Arthur gave a purposeful blowhole whistle, winked and made a leering grin.

Truman exclaimed, "Babies! Babies? Are they going to have babies Arthur?"

Arthur, did not want the President to get too interested in the prospect of alien babies, just parried by beaming, "Talk about babies and children must be universal among females, er, women Mr. President."

Harry sat there dearly wishing he could read minds as he recalled experiments the CIA had done with telepathy by using subjects in their labs to try to communicate with other telepaths that were submerged in submarines deep in the Atlantic. Maybe he should invite one of those CIA test subjects to join Sara's staff.

Arthur easily mind reading this, just cocked up his eyebrows at the president as Truman remembered that he must not think so openly around these alien mind readers.

Arthur beamed to Truman, "Right on Mr. President. But, you should learn to keep most of your thoughts to yourself. But now, I sure would like to meet some of your gifted earthly CIA or other psychics to see if we can telepath together.

Glinda beamed in, "Oh yes, then maybe we could learn more about the lost telepathic abilities of ancient humans. It really saddens me deeply because it's so unlike our pod. You are not connected mentally, emotionally and spiritually, you are each frighteningly alone and unable to fully communicate; therefore you are too fearful because you do not have total knowledge and have become over reactive and self destructive. It must be terrifying to never be able to be selectively aware of all of the emotions of others. When others, like those poor troubled souls afflicted with what you call bi polar disorder, are unrelentingly paranoid, angry and hateful. While we Delphinians can always tune out, you humans can never tune in, except now, but only when we beam to you as a selected group or just individually."

Truman was thinking deeply about all of the lack of really open communications between politicians and diplomats. And also about failed and betrayed agreements and endless arguments between husbands and wives and their children - as far as that goes. He sighed and said, "Your natural gifts of mind reading and sharing openly or selectively and truthfully sure makes for a more truthful and trusting and loving society."

Sara holding Glinda and Selena's hands as they slowly strolled, sighed a bit tearfully as she thought, "Amen. We have so much to learn from each other for trust, peace and also for your security dear visitors."

Then, Truman decided to not hide his thoughts or feelings said, "Arthur, we are really having an alien cat, earth mouse game here and I hope we can, at least always talk frankly with each other because we both have something vital that the other wants. We can offer you your choice of any USA seaside home place or even negotiate or twist an international arm or two for a place for you outside of the USA, along foreign shores if you wish."

Arthur grinned and beamed, "So are you twisting my flipper and dangling a fresh earth home fish in front of me to get our technological secrets Mr. President?" That managed to break the growing tension for awhile between the two parleying leaders.

Arthur became serious and said, "Mr. Truman, leader of the USA, I am truthfully so glad that we are meeting here one on one, face to face, in informal secrecy as we try to come to a mutually beneficial understanding and agreement that will give 160 of us a home after - without a planet and afloat between the endless stars for the last six generations. Harry, I can't even begin to tell you how wonderful it feels for us to be able to walk under your SUNstar and frolic in your oceans here in your radiant south Florida."

Arthur then became solemn and beamed, "But, Mr. President, the thing that truly deeply worries me is, if or after we give you some of our centuries of advanced technologies and medical sciences, what use will be made of them in the future by your military, your greedy industrialists and their bought and paid for political hawks? Some of the equipment, processes, DNA and other advanced capabilities we have developed over thousands of years – even before we departed our dying home world. Harry, I just want to be assured that we will not be giving a child a loaded gun; and miraculous life healing and extension drugs that he has no understanding of nor social response ability to exploit responsibly sir."

Harry cocked up his eyebrow and said, "Arthur, I noticed that you broke the word responsibility into two parts."

Arthur smiled, clicked softly and beamed, "That word and concept of being able to respond to life; to be response able was thought of many years ago by one of our home world's early singer philosophers."

Mr. Truman advanced to Arthur. "So, you are saying and feeling that to give us your technologies would possibly make us a danger to ourselves?"

"That Mr. President is exactly what I am afraid of and that's what makes me in good conscience, now very reluctant to share with you earthlings any of the very advanced medical and other hardware and technologies and weapons that we have. Believe me when I say Harry, that I have the utmost trust that your intentions as president and as the wonderful humane being that you are, would be to response ably disperse and use the technologies only for the good and safety of all. You humans are so unlike our linked in common agreement by mind and spirit generations who respect past mistakes and historical hard won lessons and good life dreams. So, yes indeed my dear Mr. Truman, I really do worry that now, when you are up for re-election soon and we all, yourself included, have no idea what your potential successor would do with our powerful society and planet altering technologies. In both of our histories dating back almost since the creation of this universe by the Amadores, fear and ego driven greed and treachery, fighting and wars have sadly always prevailed."

"Now just wait a durn minute," interrupted President Truman, "Are you saying that this universe and we were, uh, created… by someone called Amador?"

Arthur raised his eyebrows upward in petty exasperation, and beamed, "You see, right there is an astounding planet wide, cultural shaking

revelation and a really significant spiritual emotional jolt. You can clearly see the turmoil such a statement issued by you or others would cause in your world societies and to agitate all of your astounding and absurd polytheistic myth based…Like what Delnoid 1?"

Delnoid then enumerated, "They have akin to 37 major different religions all more or less devoted to one creator. I think of all of your religions from the Zoroastrians to the Jews, Christians and Islam are the only ones who have gotten it right about the faithful idea of just one creator.

But, they also with their ego driven reactive minds, just like all of the other religions, have been arguing and fighting and killing each other ever since, as you say, since the get go! I have read, recorded and memorized the Torah, the Bible and the Quran if you need any specific data."

Arthur beamed, "I think now Mr. President, you can see why we are sore afraid to release any of our philosophies, technologies or advanced medical capabilities nor even much of our spirituality to you."

Delnoid solemnly nodded his head in agreement as he beamed to Glinda and Selena, "Are you getting all of this your majesty?"

Glinda beamed back, "Yes, we are and it's apparent that if and when we share with earthlings it could lead to major social upheavals, more fighting and war for ego, power and greed on this lovely but so un-evolved socially and spiritually magnificent water world."

She continued beaming to Arthur, Selena, Sara, Delnoid and to all of her fellow Delphinians above aboard their Lifestar, "We have pondered for generations now about this exact crossroads moment and this dammed if we do and dammed if we don't dilemma. We have grown beyond fighting over ego, power and religions. This, right now, seems to be a true divine test of our integrity not to interfere in other worlds; especially ones that are thousands of years behind us, if they have not yet fully self destructed that is…"

President Truman astutely saw and felt that they had come to an impasse because of their incredible commendable social integrity and response ability that the aliens now felt perhaps it was best for them to depart Earth and go seek another hopefully non populated water world."

Arthur and all of the aliens reading Mr. Truman's thoughts became really sad and began to enter emotionally into apathy and hopelessness if all their six generations long flight for a new home was to end like this.

Arthur could read some of the older but small number of alpha male minority already moaning and beaming, along with their leader Natrix, "See Arthur, we told you so. And now, we should fight them to make them share their water world home. These earthlings are after all… really inferior beings and far, far behind us technologically. They are not even close to us in spirituality"

Arthur then read Glinda beaming strongly to overpower all of the now commenting and hairsplitting Delphinians as she reminded everyone that, "Thousands of our years ago these earthlings were just like us and by that we can and should try to be guides and models for them to learn to trust and live in peace. After all, we all now know fear. The two post world war superpowers, the USA and Russia on this planet are now choosing to be in an absurd, overactive, fear based ego and greed driven vastly different democratic verses communist political, moral and social philosophic choices in a dangerous struggle. And accordingly, they are preparing and posturing to blow each other off the face of the Earth with their atomic weapons to stoke and establish their limbic alpha male egos and reactive fears."

It's bad especially now, with the growing paranoiac cold war foisted by the evil Russian dictator, Stalin. Accordingly, maybe it's moral that we are here now to try to act as teachers and mediators but also as their old President, Theodore Roosevelt has said, "Speak softly and carry a big advanced social, spiritual and technological stick."

Arthur solemnly nodded his head as he beamed to all… "OK everyone… vote now. Do we stay in peace or leave now? Remember there is no way we can ever fight or even think of conquering all of the earthlings!" After about three minutes of unimaginable mixed thoughts telepathically ricocheting between the aliens, Arthur clicked softly, squeaked happily once and then looked relieved at President Truman and beamed, "Mr. President, we have a majority and have mostly all have agreed to stay."

He then bluffed, "While we do not want war. As you know, we do hold the upper hand and if we have to defend ourselves, we can and will. We now offer to join earth society as teachers, not as invaders, but only as new co-members of your human race which all of creation holds and nurtures for our life dreams and your life dreams back to the creators. You earthlings have just finished a dreadful worldwide war between your fellow beings which needlessly destroyed millions of lives, life dreams and cities. The gift of life from our creators is precious and if you let us, we can begin to teach and help each and all choose to learn and practice how to grow from fear, ego and greed to reach for the highest, best and happy life dreams like we and all other societies in the universe have had to do or die. Some societies on countless other worlds have tried for thousands of years to achieve peace and harmony but they have failed because of endless limbic fear, anger, ego and also selfish greed."

Arthur continued to expound, "We, in spite of our telepathic spiritual agreements in our now peaceful society, in our distant past, have unfortunately suffered three major wars and hopelessness. About 2,000 years ago an Amador, a creator, appeared to a select few Delphinians and taught them how to be, do and have self and social respect and response ability and lasting peace. This, along with our present medical knowledge, skills, abilities and also our now six generations old technologies, is what we can offer you. Mr. President as you now know; we are not alone in the stars of space and time and we are all children of the universe."

Truman actually felt tears coming into his eyes and spirit because what the peaceful leader of the Delphinians beamed to him was so similar to the visit of Jesus to earth amazingly also about 2000 years ago also.

Truman said, "Arthur, I am really moved and thankful by your choice and offer. Nevertheless, we must indeed fly as low key as we can. Because, in our religions, tragically, the majority of ignorant, fearful ego reactive and uneducated people nailed our, I guess, Amadorian visitor and teacher to a cross 1,948 years ago. This is why most of our Christian churches now have crosses on their roofs."

Glinda, the prime spiritual leader of her people, picked up on the President's thoughts and words and thought to herself, "Hummmm, with all of those execution crosses on the roofs of your Christian churches, no wonder that another Amador has not yet dared to return to this world!"

She then beamed to Arthur and all the other Delphinians, "Bear in mind, we must come here in inconspicuous peace and not as evangelists dear husband and we must humbly integrate into their societies here on our new home world. If we start being outspoken, sanctimonious preachers or try to be saviors, they will nail our flippers to their tribal crosses and would probably use their too rapidly evolving atomic, and soon, nuclear weapons and eventually missiles against our starship. Also, I certainly do not want us to have to live at our small underground base on the backside of their moon!"

At that moment all of the Delphinians aboard Lifestar clicked rapidly and beamed to Glinda, Arthur, Selena and Delnoid 1, "We would rather die than return to space or permanently to their moon. We have traveled for six generations and we must not fail to make the best of whatever worthy good or adversities that we find on this world. So, give us our homecoming or give us death!" Arthur had mentally relayed the Delphinians' vote to President Truman, he then stood and warmly hugged the President and then telepathically embraced his family and Sara.

President Truman said, "Arthur and all Delphinians, I personally welcome you to come home to our water world for the vital homecoming that you seek. I also know, as do you, that your arrival and coming ashore must be top, top secret as possible as we search for a seaside rural place or village for you. I suggest that you invite Sara and her choice of other trust worthy social teachers to water island and then later, Camp Roberts in California so that they can, as soon as possible, teach and train you in our monetary, social customs and especially about our endless, unspoken, ever changing, two faced, frustrating social values and hidden agendas."

Arthur beamed to the President and revealed to him that they had anticipated the fundamental needed education and preparations for re- socialization and that they had, some years ago, for this generation's landing, begun comprehensive study and training in earth languages and customs.

Truman asked, "Arthur, where did you obtain the needed initial cultural and social information for such training?"

Arthur smiled and beamed, "As we came within radio range, about 31 light years out, your radio signals which originated in your year of 1905 were all recorded. We studied and memorized everything; including soap operas, quiz shows, children's hours, mystery stories, fine drama, comedy and sports transmissions and have compiled all of that into our direct mind beaming learning systems." " Works kinda like what you humans call sleep learning."

Harry harrumphed and said, "Arthur, those old and even current radio programs and more recently our TV signals, since about 1940, are just radio and now TV shows, they are idealized over dramatizations. They simply for the most part do not truly realistically exemplify how we humans really think, react, over react, overtly and covertly behave towards each other. They are just, well, dramas!" "I really hope you will agree to work with Sara on Water Island as you acclimatize for at least 3 months. She can share with you, model and teach and show you how to really understand and practice the realities and nuances and the endless and ever changing unwritten and unspoken rules and agendas of our society.

I'm sure Sara can also get all of you a basic contemporary and classical library with encyclopedias and dictionaries as well as films from our Water Island Navy base and whatever else you need to read learn and most importantly practice and apply in social and unspoken rule situations.

Delnoid 1 said, "Say, that's right, we can scan everything into our digital databases." Del then became more earnest as he asked, "Mr. President, just as a matter of, er, uh, scientific radio signals curiosity, what, if anything, can you please tell us about a Mr. Nikola Tesla? You see sir, when we were 43 light years out and then on until we were closer at 37 light years out from Earth, we got really excited for awhile when we picked up - over those six years - intermittent but so incredibly exceptionally powerful radio bursts which registered at an impossible electromotive force of sometimes up to 20 million volts! Why, it was beyond belief that whoever flashed those apparently directed energies out into space must have somehow had to of been generating such output voltages with at least an astonishing 1,100 amperes of antenna current!

We think whoever it was had ingeniously devised an incredibly super powerful magnifying transmitter of some sort. After that last burst that we picked up, we were fortunately then just close enough to your planet to be able to analyze and get at least a hemispheric idea of where the location of that incredible transmitter was. We later, in 1940, further analyzed our data and pinpointed the north latitude of 38* 47' 54.80 and west longitude of 104* 46' 48.60 of that place to be on a low 88 feet high hill, 3.3 miles (5.34km) south east of historic downtown Colorado Springs and 12 miles west of your 14,110 feet (4,286 meter) Pikes Peak.

Belatedly, in 1941, late one dark moonless night, we landed a flighter team on that hilltop. What we imaged from the air and found on the ground with our night vision cameras was an old rundown, large barn like building with a rusting metal 145 foot (44 meter) antenna mast with a 39.5 inch (1 meter) metal ball still on top of it. Inside we found some abandoned antiquated - but clearly very well thought out, designed and constructed, DC electric generators and also an amazing tremendous, what we have since discovered that you call a Tesla coil. But only after the war in the fall of 1945, were we able to begin to try to find Dr. Tesla. Lamentably, by then we had discovered that he had passed away on January 7, 1943, in room number 3327 at the New Yorker Hotel. Your FBI had apparently immediately broken into his suite and confiscated all of his papers." So, I need to ask you about this Mr. President, because we conducted our investigations and researches through the New York Times back editions at their uh, newspaper morgue.

We managed to get some leads and clues that some of Dr. Tesla's research and technical papers that had been seized by the FBI were later supposedly turned over to your present day Office of Foreign Technologies and Properties on the third floor outer ring of your Pentagon."

Truman knew very well about the Tesla matter, sighed exasperatedly and said, "Arthur and Delnoid, this is all very true, but my arch enemy, my own director of the FBI, J. Edgar Hoover, has still - by intimidating Colonel Corso and his boss, General Trudeau, thwarted all my attempts to get those incredible papers and documents released. That FBI s.o.b. thinks nothing of defying my direct Presidential orders!"

Arthur beamed, "Yes Harry this is why we are truthfully now so interested in him. Tesla was an incredible genius, along with his amazing so far ahead of his time technological developments; he was also researching into temporal displacements and multiverses. All these multiverses, by the way sir, are what we might call heaven too."

Harry sighed, took off and wiped his glasses, nodded his head in agreement and expounded, "I remember shortly after becoming president, I was briefed by my Navy secret R&D department about the incredible Project Rainbow which is now called the Philadelphia Experiment. In October of 1943, the USS Eldridge destroyer was apparently made to disappear for several hours from the Philadelphia Naval yards. It then astoundingly re-materialized 200 miles (320km) south at the Norfolk Naval Yards and then disappeared again only to re-materialize back in Philadelphia. There were horrifying reports of crew being imbedded wholly and partially in the steel decks and bulkheads and I also read reports that many of the crew completely vanished. God only knows where to and when. Other crew members went totally insane from that unimaginable experiment."

Arthur responded beaming, "Yes, we have gathered all the reports about Tesla and also that experiment, because understandably, we are totally interested in concepts about temporal displacement. If we knew more about that we would not have had to travel, sacrificing five of our generations in order to come to Earth. We think that Tesla possibly might have been some kind of a disoriented Amador or a time traveler from the far future from this space and time or Amador only knows where or when he might have come from." Truman now, almost not believing this conversation thought, "Your majesty, I am indeed awed and now beholden by your insights. In the future, after you re-settle in California, Sara will open any information channels you may need to expand on your incredible temporal transference researches." We can also put our alien communication technologies facilities down in Fort Huachuca Arizona at your disposal."

Arthur nodded his head in thanks, clicked rapidly, grinned and thought to Glinda and Del, "Yeah Harry, and I'll bet you would also love to learn how to time and space travel too."

Arthur, changing the subject, asked, "So tell us more about why you call J. Edgar Hoover, what is it you said? a S.O.B.?"

Delnoid with his total data retrieval mind began to expound. "Well you see Arthur, whenever a woman has an illegitimate child and she is really, bossy, disagreeable and bad tempered…"

Arthur looked sharply at Delnoid, clicked in severe annoyance and waved his hand to cut Del off and beamed, "Well now Harry, I have to tell you that we are keenly aware of your two faced, egomaniac FBI director's non-ending prying, treacheries and blackmailing.

Harry grinned and somberly said, "Arthur, I also shudder to think what, if anything, Hoover's damn agents and spies are doing to have investigations and surveillance on us as we try to get you safely and secretly landed on earth!"

Arthur, along with some of his telepathic crew, on several occasions, had picked up the thoughts of the FBI agents and others, including some nosey reporters of Mr. William Randolph Hearst and other publishers and radio reporters as they also snooped around. At times they had tried to follow the Delphinians when they were on short walk abouts." And also now, as they were working with President Truman and Sara, towards their homecoming, the reporters were still snooping.

Arthur beamed to the president, "Well Harry, I agree that the FBI and some others are of course snooping, but so far, we have managed to confront them and erase and re-program the minds of those investigators and reporters." Our security section aboard Lifestar constantly telepathically monitors and we send down a mind clearing crew on one of the flighters to er… handle such snoopers."

Harry sighed in relief and said, "Arthur, I am very gratified that you are on top of this interference and digging into our vital and top secret homecoming project. He then looked a bit distressed as he asked, "Say, do you suppose that damn Captain Jones somehow got word out from the Navy brig to the FBI?"

Glinda clicked and beamed, "Remember Mr. Truman, I totally wiped his memories of us completely out of his depraved and treacherous mind."

Delnoid nodded his head and said, "My guess Mr. President is that the FBI somehow compromised the security of your top secret National Security Agency alien antenna project signals in Ft. Huachuca. So, as you may know sir, after the war, the Army was trying to reconstruct Dr. Tesla's extraterrestrial antenna system experiments and on Jan 5th 1948, we picked up some of their initial powerful narrow beam experimental transmissions. You of course respect that anytime you have any beings; curiosities, egos and secrets always get spilt and bought and paid for or what you call blackmailed for - one way or another."

Harry heaved a deep sigh and said, "Well then, this now makes it totally imperative that I get re-elected this fall."

Arthur slid his eyeglasses atop his head, rubbed his eyes lightly, winked, squeaked and clicked as he beamed, "Well my dear earthling President, you are who we need and prefer. So, vee have our helpful political campaigns ways you know…"

Harry Truman was just that, a very true man. So, he then thought… "Hummmm, well am I that desperate to get re-elected? Now with needing to not fail in helping our peace loving Delphinians land safely, I guess I just might have to take Arthur up on his uh, helpful ways. "And besides, those Replusivicans and that yellow journalism magnate, Hearst, and his other newspaper cronies will try any dirty dog trick that they can to unseat me."

Arthur squeaked and looked the President straight in the eye and beamed, "Yep Harry, apparently all seems to be fair in love, war and elections here with in the egos of your spiritually isolated non-telepathic people here on your so politically ego and money driven planet."

The ever too verbose and know it all – tell it all - Delnoid said, "Yeah, I clearly remember when I was at the Carnegie library at H Street and Cypress Avenue in rural Lompoc, California, nine miles (14.5km) inland near a little place called Surf at the coastal Southern Pacific whistle stop at the dead end of Ocean Boulevard and the coast road of La Salle Canyon Rd. It's right next to the 94,000 acre Vandenberg Air Force Base and developing missal launching complexes of your now growing Air Force Space Command. I mind read and discovered an FBI agent in the next bookrack over. As I peeked between the books at him, he lowered his eyes as if he was only looking for a book. I then parted and shoved the books aside, grabbed him with my right hand and held my left hand to the side of his head, erased his memories and re-programmed him to think that a California earthquake had dislodged the books. I then even asked him, "Say, that was quite a quake, huh? Are you alright fella? I can give you the exact latitude and longitude of Surf California: it's 34degrees 41minutes 00.29 seconds North and it's 120degrees 36minutes…."

Arthur squeaked, clicked in agitation and cut Delnoid off by saying.. "Ok Ok Del, that's enough for now!" Del trying to stop his outflow meekly said, "But, it has an elevation of 46.7 feet above sea level…"

Glindasqueaked and clicked in exasperation, sonic beamed the Delnoid unit to stop and he amazingly just shut down like someone had switched him off.

CHAPTER 16 WAY OVERDUE FINES

Glinda, taking up on Del's Lompoc Library details and to change the FBI and re-election subject, squeaked and beamed, "Del we sure thank you for getting all those wonderful books for us. You know, I have read many current USA books and magazines. My eyes were opened wider by Shirley Jackson who wrote in the most recent The New Yorker magazine 'The Lottery', to demonstrate how perfectly normal, otherwise nice people, can with senseless tribal like violence, allow murderous horror like the Holocaust. We Delphinians still cannot fathom how any blessed with life beings could ever slaughter countless innocent men, women, children and babies too!" Glinda continued, "In The Human Comedy, William Saroyan really does tackle the question of prejudice against the setting of World War II."

Arthur joined in and beamed, "Richard Wright completed Native Son in 1940 and Black Boy in 1945, earned my admiration. But, I could not understand the government persecution over his communist affiliation which sent him fleeing from the USA to Paris in 1945." Harry, a vehement communist fighter, frowned and said, "Well Arthur, those commies are now seeking to take over the free world just as the Nazis and the equally evil Japanese militarists we just defeated almost succeeded in destroying democracy!"

Arthur sighed a low squeal and beamed, "Yes… I know. It seems the warring over ideologies, egos, power and greed is tragically endless and universal. But the Amadores assure us always that we have all been created with free choice without needing any divine intervention or intimidation. It's up to us to choose full truthful communication with no overt withholding and mutual understanding, respect and lasting peace anytime we want."

Truman listening reverently agreed, "Yes, it is completely up to us. But like General Eisenhower always warns and I agree with him, 'Beware the ego, greed and money which now rule our world.' We're to be especially aware of the ruthless corporate, political and military egos. In fact, that's about the only thing that my former commander in chief and I seem to be able to, if truth be told, agree upon. Arthur, all of my life I have fought against such prejudice and intolerance"

Glinda beamed in, "Well… we totally communicative Delphinians sure can't be too sanctimonious because long ago, before the appearances of the Amadores, the same selfish greedy egos nearly destroyed our society and beautiful home world."

Glinda clicked, moaned sternly and beamed, "But one thing that really infuriates me is that your former President Roosevelt signed that executive order number 9066 back in February of 1942. That order imprisoned at Manzinar California and other dreadful western USA prison camps over 120,000 loyal Japanese American citizens. Their homes, properties and businesses were stolen, and those good people's spirits and dear life dreams were destroyed. Why I can tell you for sure that Eleanor Roosevelt was totally outraged by her husband signing that cruel anti-democratic order. She even went to court about it! It's just too bad that she lost her case."

Truman looked aghast at Glinda and said, "Oh my God dear lady, that will be an atrocious, disgraceful black mark on our country until the end of history."

Selena squeaked once to try to break the too deep and morose growing energies beamed, "I think that the first edition of Dr. Benjamin Spock's, Common Sense Book of Baby and Child Care is considered by some to be re- shaping human child rearing. Maybe his advice can lead to better child nurturing choices beyond selfish materialism and greed."

Glinda smiled lovingly, squeaked and clicked as she added, "Princess, maybe you can write Dr. Selena's Definitive Delphinian Human Hybrid Child Rearing Book."

Selena, after scowling and clicking rapidly at her mother, beamed. "I was also really moved by, World War II as seen through children's literature such as, Rabbit Hill by Robert Lawson, Strawberry Girl by Lois Lenski, Miss Hickory by Carolyn Sherwin Bailey and just this year, The Twenty-One Balloons by William Pène du Bois"

Delnoid, dutifully standing by and as always, was recording all of this. He grimaced and said, "Remember again your Majesties, it was I who went to several east and west coast libraries. With my speech ability and with my false ID, I got several library cards to get all these great books for us. I need now to remind you that most of these books are at least now ten years overdue and the fines are going to be astronomical!"

With that announcement, everyone broke into squeals and laughter as Truman grinned and said, "Hummmm, I will have my agents go pay for all of those books and we will soon get you all of the books, films, taped radio and TV shows that you want. Uh, what name did you have on your library cards Delnoid?"

Delnoid grinned and said, "Oh that was easy Mr. Truman, I named myself Delano Roosevelt of course!"

Truman chuckled and said, "Why, that's logical Delnoid. Please get me a list of all of the libraries you went to and I will get my agents started on paying for the fines and books."

Glinda beamed, "Thank you again dear Mr. Truman. I am so glad that we are with you at this point in time and space with your realistic, really sensible, practical and peaceful mindset."

Harry restated one of his favorite sayings, "Well, a leader has to lead, or otherwise he has no business in politics. I choose to try to lead towards world peace instead of blood money like the military industrialists and their bought and paid for greedy politicians do."

Arthur beamed privately to Selena, Delnoid and Glinda, "But, remember this is also the man who signed the order for the USA to drop two of their atomic weapons on Japan."

Glinda beamed, "Yes, but he is a man who does have high integrity and courage to always try to do what he feels is right for the greater safety and good of all and to sustain and protect the ideals that they call democracy." Arthur clicked slowly and beamed. "Evil must be stopped and if the body has cancer. It must be cut out to save the whole, even if non cancerous cells are destroyed in the process...

CHAPTER 17 SPONGE BATH

The really profound telepathic exchanges with Sara, Glinda and Selena when they were sitting at their Mallory Square table were shared with Arthur, Delnoid and the President back at the Little White House. Sara, Glinda and Selena then slowly strolled on Green St. towards Sloppy Joe's when Glinda stopped. She picked up a golden yellow sponge sitting atop a pile in a display bin in front of the Sponge Market and beamed, "Oh this feels so nice and soft! What is it Sara?"

Sara smiled and picked up a medium size sponge and explained, "Well, if you put this in water it will soak up the water. We also put soap on it and use it when we are taking a bath or showering to sponge off and clean our bodies."

Selena picked up four of them and as she was clicking merrily and playfully juggling them, she squeaked and beamed, "Oh mother, let's get one for everyone on Lifestar. These will be so jolly for us to shower and play with!"

Delnoid 1, back at the White House with Arthur and the President, reading this beamed, "Selena, we will get a load of them later. I am now looking forward to a sponge bath from Delnoid 2F - my female counterpart."

Glinda clicked in merriment and grinned as she beamed, "Oh Del, you are fruitless and you always want to be a real romantic Delphin."

Del smiled at President Truman and Arthur as he spoke and beamed, "Oh how I long to be like that Pinocchio and become a real boy"

Glinda grimaced as she beamed privately to Arthur. "Husband we need to check his DNA cyborg "fairy tale" circuits soon!"

Arthur glared at Delnoid 1 and beamed, "Yeah… we certainly must do that as soon as we get him back to our ship!"

Delnoid 1 reading over both of them smiled and said, "Well Majesties, I am only following with my heart the learning and cultural programs you created me with."

Sara grabbed a dozen nice sponges and added them to the growing number of shopping bags. The two secret service agents were beginning to struggle and resent hauling the bags for the ladies. Sara said, "OK ladies, these will get you started with enjoying sponge baths."

Glinda beamed gratitude energies, "Oh Sara that's so thoughtful of you." Then she hugged Sara, squeaked and beamed, "Thanks." She gave a momentary stern look at Selena and beamed, "Princess! Stop juggling those sponges and put them in my bag!"

Selena squeaked loudly as she then pointed up to a tall wooden tower on top of a big old wooden warehouse. She beamed to Sara, "What is that tower for Sara?"

Sara paused for a moment. She was still getting back into present time from the absorbing baby talk and she slowly looked up to where Selena was pointing. She shook her head to clear her mind and said, "Oh! That is the shipwreck lookout tower. In the old days someone would be up there to see if any ships had wrecked on the shoals around here. If he saw a new wreck, he would ring the bell and everyone would rush out to the wreck to rescue whoever they could and grab anything of value that they could. In those days when a ship wrecked, anything aboard her was up for grabs for salvage and profit." There is a wonderful full size bronze sculpture all about this right near by. We can go see it after lunch. But, right now I am famished !"

Selena nodded her head and beamed, "Up for grabs? Kind of like shark eat shark, huh Sara?" Sara grinned, chuckled and said, "You got it kiddo! It's finders keepers and losers weepers."

CHAPTER 18 NO PEANUTS

Sara, Selena and Glinda were sitting at a rectangular table at Sloppy Joe's restaurant with a view through the open double doors of Duvall Street. Their two secret service protectors were sitting at a smaller two person table nearby.

Glinda beamed to Sara and Selena, "Well aces! It seems that now we are getting down to the social, practical day to day, nitty-gritty of our finally being able to land on Earth. I so hope that you will find some more excellent social teachers for us that are as kind and humane as you are, Sara."

Sara grinned and said, "Glinda you are getting so hep. Where did you learn the aces slang word?"

Glinda smiled as she beamed, "Oh, I read it in a detective story."

Selena squeaked and beamed, "Well you ain't a just flapping yer lips mom! You are so cool."

Glinda smiled confusedly, clicked, squeaked and beamed, "Well actually, it's rather too hot in here. I am getting nauseated by the smell of all the beer, liquors and all the cigarette smoke in here."

Selena scrunched up her nose and beamed to her mother and Sara, "I too am beginning to feel quite dizzy."

Sara stood, glanced severely at the two secret service men and said, "Ok, you are right. Let's get out of here. We can go right across the street to Peppe's Café which is not a noisy, smelly, rowdy booze bar."

The trio were seated on the pleasant little fresh air wooden fenced patio behind Peppe's. Sara reached out and touched Glinda's arm and asked, Your maj.. er Glinda, are you feeling better now?

Glinda smiled, squeezed Sara's arm and beamed, "Oh my yes, I can see that we are more sensitive to alcohol and cigarette smoke than we perhaps previously realized."

Sara looked at Selena and asked, "How are you feeling?"

Selena looked around to see if any other diners were nearby then gave an ascending whistle and rapid clicks as she beamed, " I am ok now and I am starving to death Sara."

Sara chuckled and said, "Ok you two; one too hot, and one too cool visitors. Let's order our Princess's birthday luncheon."

Selena, with her elbows on the table, and her big eyes almost crossed, was enjoying toying with a small piece of sponge, interrupted and beamed, "Sara how do you make these sponges? There were so many of them in all different sizes at that sponge market."

Sara smiled and explained aloud, "Those were once a living colony of sea creatures. After they die, the divers gather the sponges, which are really the squishy skeletons of those colonies."

Selena beamed, "Oh yeah, I remember now. I think we saw some sponge divers while we were diving in the Mediterranean off of Portofino, Italy last year. They had on big metal copper colored helmets but unlike our space helmets. They had a couple of bulky hoses attached to a noisy surface air pump down to their helmets."

Sara said, "That is right Selena. Before and during the war, many of those sponge divers came from the Italy as well as from the Dodecanese Islands in Greece. Their families were invited here, to Tarpon Springs, Florida, by the existing sponge diving industry that was located there. Some of those diver families re-settled right here in the Keys. Our country has always tried to welcome and help refugees." Sara then thought to Selena,

"So do you also, uh, snorkel and scuba dive?"

Glinda clicked softly and smiled as Selena answered, "Well, sort of, but we do not need such cumbersome hard hats nor scuba tanks. We just insert our nostril gills just like our tiny humidifier nose plugs and we can stay underwater for about 3 hours. Although whenever we need to dive to explore or salvage and work at depths below 60 feet (18 meters), we have special light duty or heavy duty diving suits and helmets with lights. We can use at the pressures of almost any depth that our Lifestar ship can descend to."

Sara grinned, clapped her hands and said, "Oh Selena that's fantastic. Please take me down with you someday."

Selena grinned as she beamed, "Ok girlfriend. No problema, it's a piece of cake."

Sara said, "I think I still have my blue dive mask out in California."

Selena beamed, "Oh yeah, but we don't need them. We have a special natural lens in our eyes that we can change the structure of for when we are underwater. Just like our dolphin cousins here."

Arthur, back at the little White House beamed," Yes Sara. This is why all of us male Delphins must wear eyeglasses in your earth's atmosphere. We have to make a very slight correction for the density and pressure of your atmosphere as opposed to the atmosphere and gas composition of our home planet as well as our ship's air. But of course we do not wear them in shallow underwater dives or while we enjoy swimming."

Sara placed her hand under her chin and as she touched her jaw she said, "Oh, now I see. But, why do your Delphin females not wear glasses too?"

Arthur looked upward, raised his glasses atop his head and clicked as he grinned and beamed, "Oh Sara you must ask the ladies about that."

Glinda squealed high to low, clicked, sighed and beamed, "Oh pooh Arthur! You know very well that the refractive index is so small that you guys really do not need your eyeglasses."

Selena squeaked, clicked and beamed, "Besides Sara, none of us females ever want to have to wear eyeglasses if we can help it. So we all wear uh, uh, squeak, uh, these contact lenses!" Selena grinned as she pointed to her left eye and by holding down her bottom eyelid she popped out a clear tiny lens. "These fit right over our eye lens and act just like glasses but no one can see we are using a visual aid. But just like our male podsters, we can not use these while we are swimming or diving underwater.

Glinda squeaked, clicked rapidly and proudly beamed, "We really don't want to wear glasses because, uh, well… we all look more attractive without any silly eyeglasses!"

Sara grinned, laughed and said, "Oh yes I agree! I wear glasses for reading but I hate using them. It's called female vanity here on earth dear amigas." Sara smiled in delight as she continued, "But, I am sure I can buy a dive mask in Charlotte Amelia." She then exclaimed, "Oh goodness! I can't wait to enjoy diving with you once we get to Water Island, I long to swim and dive in those warm waters. Whenever we went snorkeling off shore in Montecito or on voyages out to the Channel Islands; which are 22 miles out in the Santa Barbara Channel, we always had to wear uncomfortable wet suits and so uncomfortable weight belts but still, after an hour and a half or so, it got too darn cold to be enjoyable."

Selena squealed and beamed, "Oh Sara it will be so wonderful for us to be able to dive together. But you know, you will have to learn to speak dolphin though."

Sara wide eyed said, "Are you kidding me?"

Selena let out a series of clicks and squeals and beamed, "Yep I am!" Sara laughed and said, "Oh applesauce!"

Selena clicked slowly and looked questioningly at her earth amiga and beamed, "Applesauce." Isn't that what we had with our dinner the other night? I really liked it."

Sara grinned and said, "Applesauce is like horse feathers…."

Selena squawked and then started to beam, "What? I have never seen a horse with feathers. Birds are…"

Glinda reached out and took the forearms of her two happy girls and beamed "We are getting too noisy now with Delphin sounds and my earthly laughter. So cool it you two! You're beginning to attract far too much attention to us."

Selena then clicked softly and beamed, "I sure would love to ride a horse someday. The westerns we've read make riding seem to be such fun."

Sara thought, "My uncle has a horse ranch out in Goleta, it's west of Santa Barbara and we will go there right after your re-settlement orientations in Camp Roberts." She then thought, "Just being able to bunny (chat) just by thinking, is sure fantastic and easier and much less stressful than talking. To say nothing of the privacy it provides for us as we sit here in a very public restaurant."

Just then Glinda looked somewhat alarmed and as she touched Sara's arm she clicked softly and beamed, Sara I am reading the minds of those two men sitting at that table along the fence. They are FBI agents spying on us."

Sara looked and sure enough they were wearing grey open sports coats and this was typical hot and humid Florida day. Sara then stood and went over to her two secret services men and whispered in their ears.

The two then looked alarmedly at the the FBI agents, stood and the Secret Service lead agent then spoke to the two FBI guys. The two Federal agents then stood and almost started a fight but when the Secret Service lead showed his ID and badge.

The now furious and disgruntled agents turned and left. As they neared the rersteraunts rear entrance one of then exclaimed, Damm you.

Mr. Hoover is gonna get you two fired. You can bet on that". But unbeknownst to them. Delnoid 3F , a very attractive redhead was waiting to buy them a beer at Sloppy Joes and with in just 15 minutes of hugs and head touching she had totally erased the two bully agents minds .

Sara then sat and thought, "Gadzooks!. Is there no end to these FBI and Hearst spies…"

Arthur then beamed to Sara, Glinda and Selena. "Well ladies, so far we have been able to erase, as far as we know, all snoopers minds."

Sara said aloud, "Well, I sure hope that we never fail to spot any of them."

"Anyway, here comes our waitress with our menus. They will have a few pictures of the different foods and I will explain each item to you. They have excellent fish sandwiches and very good roast beef and also delicious cheeseburgers and hot dogs too."

Selena while excitedly scanning the menu whistled and beamed, "I think, for my birthday, I would like to try the cheeseburger you speak of Sara. I have never eaten beef but, as far as I know, it comes from cows."

Glinda reached over and touched her daughter's forearm and beamed, "Remember that delicious meat we had while we were visiting Punta del Este in Uruguay? Well my little fish eating girl, that was beef, honey."

Selena smiled, looked at her mother and beamed, "Honey? Why did you call me honey? That was something so yummy and sweet we had on our biscuits at the White House this morning."

Glinda squeezed her arm again and beamed, "Well, I call you that because you are so sweet dear princess daughter."

Selena made a disgusted face, frowned, squeaked and beamed, "Mom!

Sara told me that honey is bee poop!"

Sara laughed and said, "Ok Selena, cool it and I will show you some bees someday."

After Sara had explained the menu choices and also pointed them out on the menu images, she thought to Glinda, "So, what appeals to you Glinda?"

Glinda warily beamed, "Well Sara, I think I want to try a salad with tomatoes, onions, cucumbers and cilantro and a fish sandwich."

"We had no vegetables and lettuce aboard Lifestar."

Sara thought, "I want a good old American cheeseburger and fries. Selena, while she happily tapped her right flipper, beamed to Sara,

"What are fries Sara?"

Sara looked around and at a table near them and saw a man eating a cheeseburger and fries so she pointed to his plate and said, "That is a cheese burger and those very light yellow strips are the square sliced deep fried potatoes Selena."

Selena beamed, "What are potatoes Sara?"

Sara thought back to her alien sister, and Glinda, "Sister, you all have so much to enjoy discovering and trying to eat from our very diverse restaurants. Potatoes are a vegetable that was developed originally in Peru, 7000 years ago. It was a basic food for the Incas, the Moche and also for earlier west coast South American Indians. But, we now have foods from all over the world; Italy, China, Mexico and other countries which each have their own unique and tasty foods to share."

Meanwhile, back at the Little White House, Truman, Arthur and Del had taken a break from their negotiations with poker loving Truman. Harry was trying to introduce his alien amigos to his favorite card game. Harry was saying, "Truthfully fellas, my favorite form of paperwork is poker…"

Del, with his hand of cards was also tuning into Sara, Glinda and Selena at Peppe's restaurant. He, totally multi tasking and thinking, beamed to the three girls, "Potatoes as well as corn, tomato, cacao for chocolate, tobacco, pineapples, peanuts, squash, vanilla, quinine from the bark of the cinchona tree, avocado, pumpkin casaba and agave for fiber, for rope and cloths and tequila all originated in North America, Mexico, Central and South America… and…"

Glinda clicked strongly beamed, "Ok, ok Del! Enough already! Uh thanks." She then beamed, "What about food from England Sara?"

Sara grimaced and replied, "Boring, only meat and potatoes." As their waitress was returning, Sara thought to Selena and Glinda, "Do you want to try ordering your food with your notepads?"

Glinda and Selena looked a bit apprehensively at each other, clicked softly and Glinda beamed, "OK, let's give it a try. We do need to practice. I am so glad we both understand and can write fairly well in English."

Their waitress was standing there as Sara explained that her friends could not speak so they wanted to write down their orders. "Would that be ok?"

The Cuban waitress replied, "Siento senoras, yo no leer English. (Sorry ladies, I cannot read English).

Sara smiled and said, "That's ok. My amigas understand and can write in Spanish too."

Selena wrote on her pad, "Querro cheeseburger y papas fritas por favor."

Glinda scribbled, "Querro un ensalada y torta de pesca por favor." Each alien woman tore off their pages and proudly handed them to the waitress.

Sara read the waitress' name tag and she thought to Selena and Glinda, "Her name, as you can see," pointing to the name tag, "is Gloria."

Gloria smiled and asked, "Que querres beber?" (What would you like to drink). All three looked at each other and Sara nodded as she said, "Cokes all around please and 3 Hires root beer floats with three long ice tea spoons and three straws for us for desert."

Glinda and Selena squeaked and looked very anxiously at each other as Glinda cautiously touched Sara's arm and beamed, "Sara, I did not know that you drank beer?"

Sara grinned and said, "Root beer is a soda pop just like Coke. It's non alcoholic. A root beer float is delicious. You put vanilla ice cream in a large glass and then pour in root beer. You can drink the root beer and eat the ice cream with a spoon."

After the waitress left, Selena beamed, "What does all around mean Sara?"

Sara thought back, "Like if I said, ok, drinks all around. That would mean that I was going to buy cokes for every customer in the restaurant."

Glinda beamed, "Sara, why on Earth would you want to do that?"

Sara again realized that a complete social education would be needed before they could dare let their aliens loose on earth thought, "Dear amigas, there will be so much for you to understand and learn about our society for day to day living. But, I will be here for you every minute - no matter what!"

Glinda and Selena smiled as Glinda appreciatively beamed back, "OK, day by day we will learn your earthly food and social ways, dear Sara.

We are so glad that you are a part of our pod, uh family now. We could never make it here without you."

Sara caught Gloria's eye and when the waitress came over Sara stood and said, "Can you please excuse me for a moment? I have to talk briefly to Gloria."

Glinda and Selena nodded and beamed hesitatingly, "Uh, ok Sara…"

When Sara had Gloria out of the eyesight of her aliens, she reached into her purse and gave Gloria $ 40. She said to the astounded waitress, "Look Gloria, it's the young girl's 16th birthday today and I want you to please go to the nearby bakery and get a small but nicely decorated cake with 16 candles so once we have finished our luncheon, we can surprise Selena with a birthday cake. You can keep the change from this money, ok? But it is very important Gloria; there must not be any peanut products of any kind in or on the cake!"

Gloria nodded excitedly, said, "gracias senora". Taking off her apron she headed directly through the patio door. When she was in the bakery, she saw a nice yellow cake with chocolate icing and she said to the clerk in Spanish. "Oh, that will be perfecto!" And since she completely misunderstood Sara's warning about peanuts, she quickly asked, "Oh, could you please put some crumbled peanuts on top of it? Then, please deliver it through the side door to our kitchen at Peppe's, Gracias!"

Sara came back to the table and as she sat, she remembered that her aliens were totally telepathic and at the same time, Glinda was beaming privately to Selena to be sure to act totally surprised with whatever, click click click, squeak, a birthday cake turns out to be."

About 10 minutes later the food arrived and as Gloria placed each plate in front of them. Sara saw that Selena and Glinda looked confused so she thought, "Just, watch me for a minute." Sara picked up the yellow squeeze bottle of mustard and opened her burger and squeezed a little bit of mustard on her meat. She picked up and unscrewed the Hellmann's mayonnaise jar and using her knife, she spread a little bit of mayo on both insides of her buns. Glinda and Selena seemed to be mesmerized as they watched these earthly food preparation customs for the first time. After Sara replaced the bun on her meat, she used her fork to move her fries over a bit and she picked up the red ketchup squeeze bottle and proceeded to squeeze a small pool of thick ketchup alongside her fries.

As the red ketchup came out, Selena let out a rather loud squeak and beamed to Sara, "Is, is that blood?"

Sara trying to ignore the nearby diners reactions to the strange squeak, smiled and thought to Selena and Glinda "No, no, it's a tomato sauce called ketchup and we always put it on our french fries." She picked up a fry with her fingers and dipped one end of it into her pool of ketchup and popped it into her mouth. As she chewed, she thought to her aliens, "Hummmm this is so good. I have not really been able to sit and enjoy good fresh cooked fries for about three months now."

Selena and Glinda looked excitedly at each other and Selena then mimicked Sara's preparation of her burger and Glinda opened her fish sandwich but before she could squeeze anything on her fish, Sara looked at her and thought, "With fish, it's a little different. Please, just try a bite of your sandwich first then you can put a little bit of mayo or ketchup on it if you like. Also, try some of my fries to see how they taste and maybe put some ketchup on your plate like I have."

Glinda took a small bite of her fish sandwich and as she bit and chewed, she gave a small squeal of delight and beamed, "Sara, this is really terrific. It's so much unbelievably tastier than the processed fish pieces and pastes we get from our food synthesizers."

Sara grinned, looked at Glinda and thought, "See that yellow slice on your plate? Well, pick it up and lick it and see if you like it. If so, you can squeeze it to put some lemon juice on your fish.

Some people like it because it cuts some of the oils in fish, especially the extra oil on deep fried fish batter."

Glinda smiled and beamed, "Well, I think I will not try it on my fish because we love fish oils and the omega-3, as you call it, are very good for us." She picked up the lemon slice and licked it and immediately put it back on her plate, moaned softly and beamed, "I think that I shall never be keen on lemon."

Sara smiled and thought, "Well please don't give up on lemons just yet Glinda. After we get back home, I will make each of you some fresh lemonade to try because it's always sweetened and very refreshing, especially in this and other tropical climates."

Sara thought, "Aren't you going to try your salad your majesty?"

Glinda beamed, "Of course," as she reached for the ketchup and proceeded to squeeze a big squirt of ketchup on her salad…

Sara laughed and said, "We don't usually put ketchup on lettuce and tomatoes your majesty. Here, let me get another fresh salad for you and I will show you some of the sauces that we call salad dressing for you to try on your salad."

Sara raised her finger to signal Gloria and as she looked out for the waitress, she saw several restaurant customers including the two secret service agents were staring. Some of the other diners were pointing and grinning and giggling at the trio of strange women as well.

Sara stood up and harshly announced, "I know they seem funny to you, but my friends come from, well, another country where they eat only uh, fish, soups and, uh, breads." She then gave a sharp, boys am I going to talk to you two later, look at the secret service agents who immediately returned their stares and quickly fading grins back to their cheeseburgers.

When Gloria brought a fresh salad to Glinda, Sara smiled and vocalized, "Here let me show you Glinda."

Glinda smiled and beamed, "Thank you Sara, I'd like that very much." Sara realized that she may have offended the queen thought, "Is it ok if

I call you Glinda, your majesty?"

Glinda beamed, "I would love that and please stop calling me your majesty ok?"

Sara thought back, "Ok, thanks your, uh Glinda…" She placed a small serving tray of different salad dressings in front of Glinda and said aloud, "Ok, these two are olive oil and vinegar and you can sprinkle just a little oil and an even smaller amount of vinegar on your salad. These other creamier salad dressings, as we call them, are French dressing, Italian dressing and something uniquely North American, called Thousand Island dressing. Here let me fix a taster plate for you to try." Sara took a small saucer and put a little bit of each dressing on it and handed Glinda a spoon and said, "OK , please try these one at a time and see which one you like best."

Selena, munching and enjoying her cheeseburger and fries dipped in the blood red ketchup, squeaked and beamed, "Which one will be good on my burger and fries Sara?"

Sara looked at her and thought, "Well Selena, there is a restaurant in Glendale, California that when my dad and I would take the train down to his Burbank studio, we would always try to make time to go enjoy a Bob's Big Boy burger. They use red relish in their thousand island dressing on their burgers Selena and, it's really quite tasty."

Glinda tasted all of the salad dressing samples and while doing so, she had been reading the thoughts of the surrounding gawking patrons. She finally squeaked in annoyance, looked severely around at the rude onlookers took out her notepad and wrote, "I think that I like the oil and vinegar best."

She glanced again at the rude spectators as she proudly showed her note to Sarah. Then she got up and took the note to the gawking couple dining at the table right next to them and grinned as she proudly showed her note to them!

Sara became really alarmed, but after the woman at that table read the note, she said, "I am so sorry we were so rude dear lady. Uh, what is your name?"

Sara stood and joined Glinda at the table and said, "My visitors uh, have a genetic, uh, defect and they cannot speak; this is why they use these notepads to communicate."

The woman stood, held out her hand to Glinda and said, "Hi, My name is Betty, Betty Jones, and you are…?"

Glinda smiled and wrote on her pad, "Hi, my name is Glinda!" The two women shook hands and as Glinda returned to her lunch and the lesson on salad dressing, the other diners nearby became very understanding and sympathetic and they all started laughing softly and applauded politely for a few seconds.

Selena hearing this and recognizing the respectful applause, stood and before Sara could stop her, she stood up, grinned, clicked exuberantly, waved and gave out three short high pitched squeaks and two short, loud and clear happy thank you whistles.

Sara was really distressed at Selena's outburst, stood and said, "Uh, that is all that is left of their voice boxes from their, uh, tragic birth defects." Then almost everyone in the restaurant burst into polite applause again and for a moment some also enjoyed trying squeaking and whistling back with two fingers in their mouths then they all continued their lunches.

Selena looked really sheepishly at Sara, moaned and beamed, "Oh, Amador! I forgot Sara. I am so sorry…"

Glinda beamed, "Well it looks like this first encounter of the restaurant kind went ok amigas. Let's now enjoy our lunches, I am starving."

Sara thought, "Ok, but gosh, that was close to attracting too much attention to you. I can see now where we must start our earth customs and social classes as soon as possible when we are well isolated on Water Island."

Selena clicked softly and beamed to Sara, "Are you angry at me Sara?"

Sara smiled reassuringly and thought back, "No, not at all Selena.

I always worry about people seeing how very exceptional you are just now without your knowing and having practiced our day to day customs. It's just that I want to protect both of you always so that you will never suffer any ridicule, embarrassment or dangers as you re-settle on earth."

Selena and Glinda beamed to Sara, "We love and appreciate you so mucho dear earth guide."

After they finished their lunch, Glinda was beaming to Sara and Selena when Gloria and two other female waitresses paraded from around the counter with Selena's birthday cake as it blazed with 16 small white candles.

When they sang happy birthday in English and in Spanish all at the same time - most all of the other anglo and latino patrons joined in. As soon as Gloria put the birthday cake down on the table, Sara fortunately looked at it and saw the crumbled peanuts on it. She grabbed the cake up and roughly handed it to Gloria and said, "Dang it Gloria! Take this away! I said no peanuts on it! Oh, my God! Whatever were you thinking?" Gloria and the other patrons and especially Glinda and Selena were stunned at Sara's abrupt anger about the cake.

Sara looked around and stammered, "Oh, gosh, I am so sorry. Somehow this cake got peanuts on it and uh, my friends, are violently allergic to peanuts."

Glinda hearing this beamed to Selena, "Oh dear Amador! Now we know for sure we always need Sara with us. Maybe she will join our crew just like Amelia did!"

Selena burst into tears clicked super rapidly and beamed to almost everyone, "Oh squeak, squeak! I wanted my birthday cake."

Glinda beamed to her distraught daughter, "For Amador's sake! Be quiet! Stop beaming to everyone!"

Selena, still sniffling, instantly stopped beaming and looked fearfully around to the now astounded patrons but she could see in the hubbub that no one had paid any real attention to her thoughts echoing into their heads.

Selena looked at the two secret service agents and she read one of them thinking, "Dang, something is very very strange about the uh so called visitors that Sara and the President have received."

Glinda looked worriedly at the agent and beamed to Arthur and Selena, "Well, squeak, once again, we will have to perform more mind erasing before we leave Key West."

Sara took Gloria aside and admonished her, "I thought that I specifically told you, no peanuts." Gloria now in tears cried in Spanish, "Oh Miss I am so sorry! No he entendido bien y pensé que quería que agregara las cacahuates al pastel." "Yo soy así, lo siento señorita." Gloria reached in her apron pocket and said tearfully, "Oh lo siento mucho, Aquí tiene sus $ 20 señorita." ("I misunderstood and thought that you wanted the peanuts added on the cake. I am so, so sorry senorita. Oh I am so sorry. Here is your $20 back senorita.")

Sara gave a half smile and pushed the waitress's hand away saying, "It's ok now Gloria. I guess I probably over reacted. It's just that if my amigos had eaten any of that cake, they would have died."

"Now por favor Gloria. I want you to please do me another favor. Please go back to that bakery and buy a large rectangular yellow cake with chocolate icing on one half and uh, cherry icing on the other half and please have them decorate it saying. Happy Birthday Dear Selena."

She then handed Gloria $ 40 more dollars and said, "Then please have them be sure to deliver the cake to the Little White House guard shack before six o'clock this afternoon."

Gloria then realizing that Sara and her amigas were probably important presidential people said, " Aiiiii senorita, con mucho gusto y gracias por este extra propinas." (Aiiiiii miss. With much pleasure and thanks for this extra tip)

Sara, taking a lesson from this misunderstanding, resolved to always be sure anyone dealing with her and her aliens understood exactly what was needed and she also resolved to always double check everything from now on.

Just then, Glinda, Selena and Sara heard in their heads, "It's ok now." "Sara saved the day and fortunately you did not consume those deadly peanuts."

Sara with tears in her eyes, thought back to Arthur, "Oh your Majesty, I am so sorry this happened."

Arthur, Glinda and Selena beamed calming and loving energies to Sara. And as her upset subsided she thought, "I don't know what I would do it anything ever happened to you or any of you…"

Glinda and Selena put their arms around Sara's waist and beamed soothing and loving energies as they exited the now unforgettable first alien birthday luncheon at Peppe's Cafe.

After they had calmed down and re-assured each other, they walked abreast down Duval Street. Selena beamed, "Where are we going now Sara?" Sara thought to herself that she wished they could just go back to the White House and take a nap. Glinda and Selena beamed back agreement,

"Yes, let's go nap. It's way too hot Sara."

Sara said, "Ok, we can go enjoy the small Key West aquarium another

time."

Glinda beamed to Arthur and Delnoid back at the Whitehouse, but as

she probed for communication, she squealed a giggle, smiled and beamed to Selena and Sara… "Well, our hombres are all taking a siesta too."

CHAPTER 19 TOO DAMM SQUEAKEDY HOT

After the navy shore patrol at the gate saw that it was Sara with her VIP visitors, they immediately passed them through the White House gates. As they neared the Whitehouse west porch, Sara thought to Glinda and Selena, "Ok, you two go on upstairs and enjoy a nice nap. I have a couple of things I have to attend to down here first."

As soon as Selena and Glinda entered the White House porch door, Sara turned around and headed back to the guard shack and told the shore patrolman, "Please have John and Bill report to my downstairs office immediately." The sentry saluted, reached for the phone and saw that Lt. Commander Winchester looked really pissed off and meant business.

Sara returned to her office to soon find John and Bill knocking softly and nervously at her office door. She picked up an official Whitehouse report form and scribbled on it. She did not invite either secret service agent to sit down. Lieutenant Commander Winchester looked sternly up at the sweating aloha shirted pair of agents and said, "Ok you two! That restaurant scene was bad enough but you two did not help at all with your looking and sniggering at our official foreign visitors. In future, whenever we are out in Key West or elsewhere, you two will be seemingly disinterested tourists standing by to protect us and to instantly follow my orders. Is that NOW perfectly clear gentlemen?" The two now anxious agents replied in unison, "Yes Ma'am!"

Sara lowered her voice and said, "These meetings, as informal as they may seem, are critically important to the United States, is that unmistakably understood gentlemen?"

The two now chagrinned agents replied again in unison, "Yes ma'am!" Sara stood and said, "Dismissed."   After they left her office, Sara grinned and picked up her desk phone and dialed the

President's office extension but apparently he was still snoozing upstairs in the south Florida afternoon heat. She stood and walked up stairs to her and Selena's bedroom. When she got there she found Selena sitting glumly in a full tub of water. Sara asked, "Are you ok?"

Selena beamed that she was trying to rehydrate her skin. "Today was so special Sara. I really loved the cheeseburger and now I wonder what a fish burger with lemon and that Thousand Island dressing would taste like."

Sara saw that Selena was still in some kind of physiological distress, asked again, "Are you sure you're ok, my little Delphinian?"

Selena beamed that this earth visit was also a test of a new kind of nasal hydrator and a new powerful moisture retaining and sweat gland growing skin cream. But, she was finding the air in spite of its good 82% humidity to be just way too hot.

Sara thought to Selena, "Ok wait here in the tub. I'm going to check on Glinda."

Sure enough Sara found Glinda sitting in a filled tub of cool water and she too was apparently suffering from the heat too.. Sara asked, "How are you feeling your Maj… uh, Glinda?"

Glinda echoed the same complaint as had her daughter. Sara asked Glinda "How are Arthur and um, Delnoid doing?" Except she remembered that Delnoid was an android and that he probably never needed a nap nor would he be too much affected by the atmospheric temperature or humidity.

Glinda now seemed to be feeling somewhat better, beamed, "Arthur is ok since he did not accompany us on our walk about. But, it seems if we are going to walk about in this tropical heat, we will have to wear bathtubs full of cool water to keep cool."

Sara scrunched up her forehead in worry as she asked, "Does this mean you will have problems by remaining on Earth?"

Now awake Arthur beamed into the exchange from their sitting room and clarified, "No, not at all dear Sara. Our humidity needs, as you already know, are that we are used to a ship climate which is at 80% relative humidity but with an average air temperature just like you earthlings are comfortable in of, say, 68 to about 85 degrees Fahrenheit, (20c to 30 c). Our discomfort today is coming from the ceaseless daytime 94 degree air temperature and walking around under the beautiful Florida sunshine, combined with the nice for us, high humidity. Our humidifiers are working ok and actually… in these relative humidity levels we probably don't even need them. But, it's just that, with minimal sweat glands, we are not yet tolerant to these high skin temperatures that we are encountering here in South Florida."

President Truman had come into Arthur's room and hearing the openly beamed situation, asked Arthur, "So do you need to go back to your ship for now amigo?"

Arthur clearly sensed that President Truman was actually concerned and he beamed, "My family and I are thankful Mr. President that you and Sara are so concerned and attentive to our well being as well as treating my family, me and all Delphinians in such good caring friendship." He beamed, "Well Harry, let's see how we all feel tomorrow, ok?"

Truman nodded his head in agreement and said, "How about if all of you just continue taking more cooling time out and relax in your bedrooms, with a nice tubful of cool water in your bathrooms, and we can see and decide what we need to do tomorrow."

Sara then excused herself from Glinda's bathroom and headed back to Selena's bedroom. When she got there she found Selena apparently feeling much better was now relaxing on her bed, totally nude as usual and making soft clicks as she read one of the books from the bedroom's collection. Sara sat on her amiga's bed and thought, "Selena I am so sorry that I overdid your exposure to this distressing hot and humid south Florida atmosphere."

Selena clicked softly, smiled, held her Sara's hand and beamed, "It's ok Sara. If you were to come try to stay aboard our very humid starship for any length of time, you would suffer from the dankness and constant high humidity and it would take time for you to adjust." She squeaked and whistled and beamed, "Ha, sister! If you come to visit, we will have to make you a nostril or a face mask dehumidifier!"

Glinda beamed to Sara and the President, "Well, its too bad that we will have to postpone our birthday star and home star gazing picnic for another evening when that 16th birthday star, Altair will be visible."

Delnoid who was in the kitchen beamed to all, "Since I have a 24 hour star map in my programming and since I can also see stars thru blue skies if I want to. Well, I am gonna go out on the Navy dock and take a look at Selena's 16th birthday star as well as our home star….

 Glinda beamed, "Del, What are you doing in the kitchen?"

He replied, "Well I was just enjoying a Coke and a nice big slice of this excellent cherry and chocolate cake that someone left in here…

CHAPTER 20 COMMANDER SARA WINCHESTER, USN

As Harry and Sara were fixing the supper. Harry asked, Hummmmm… may I please have a slice of that birthday cake ?

Sara looked sad and sighed, "OK, sure. Go ahead. We will just have to reschedule a birthday star gazing picnic and get another cake for Selena." Sara, after cutting a thin slice for herself, and three more nice slices for her aliens then covered Selena's now munched birthday cake placed it in the walk in refrigerator.

Selena sleepily beamed to Sara and the President. Thank you. I love you…"

Sara then brought a simple cool supper to her alien family. After opening some Cokes she kissed each of them and bid them a good night. She then met with the President downstairs at the regular dining room where they ate the same simple tropical supper of a salad, cheese, fruit and bread and butter that Harry had finished fixing for them as Sara was taking supper to the aliens..

The President and his Navy anthropological specialist sat sipping their ice tea and lemonade. Truman handed Sara a piece of official Presidential stationary which read: 'For her ABCD - Above and Beyond the Call of Duty extraordinary services to the office of the president and our country; I hereby promote Navy Lieutenant Commander Sara Winchester to the rank of Commander and to the post of Extraordinary Special Liaison Officer.'

When taken aback Sara finished reading, the President said, "So, if you'll kindly hand me your gold oak leaf, I'll trade you for your new silver oak leaf."

Sara looked at the president with surprise and much pride and said, "Thank you Mr. President. Hummm, I don't know what to say. This is a top Presidential staff level position Mr. Truman. I am honored and also very thankful to be included in helping our refugees from out there re-settle down here on our, so appropriate for them, water world home."

Truman took Sara's hand, smiled proudly and pulled her close to him and said in a low voice, "Uh, well…as you can imagine Sara, I could not actually write, "Chief Extraterrestrial Alien Ambassador on your promotion letter, but now dear Sara that is who you are with my and the USA heartfelt thanks for your ABCD services."

Sara just sat there smiling for a few moments and after quickly regaining her composure said, "Mr. Truman, I so hope that we can successfully help our new family safely re-settle. They have been afloat between the stars for far, far too long now and it's time for them to come home." She then related to the president what Arthur had told her about their environmental needs and as Truman listened, he realized that their acclimatization to the atmosphere as well integration into the social realities of earth, was going to take a much longer time than he and Sara had anticipated.

He said to Sara, "You know that I am coming up for re-election very soon and I fervently hope to God that I will win so that we can maintain our plans and vital permanent homecoming continuity for these wonderful beings." And, using the term Arthur had taught him he smiled and continued, "By your having as good as is possible response ability for our alien amigos Sara. I will, almost immediately, have to focus most all of my time and efforts on campaigning for re-election. So, I must now depend almost completely on you my dear Commander Winchester for your continued leadership and response ability towards training and re-settling our alien friends." "So, accordingly, I have, this afternoon, after my meetings with Arthur, Delnoid and, uh, Glinda too, I have contacted all relevant government offices to advise them officially of your posting to full White House staff level as an extraordinary special liaison officer. I have also notified the GSA and federal payroll office to retro your new pay level up to 0-5 as of July 4, 1947, when that Roswell saucer crashed. That crash unfortunately hit the public awareness fan. Previously it had been mostly super secret alien encounter bullshit."

Sara again just sat there thinking… "Gosh, I never expected to become such a high level USA official. There is no way that I will ever let President Truman or our Delphinians down." She looked at the president and said, "Mr. President, I am totally devoted to this project and to our new allies. I will always and in all ways, to the best of my abilities, do all that I can to make their landing, social integration and our ongoing dealings with them safe and successful for the benefit of all mankind, sir."

Truman grinned as he said, "Commander, I could not have found nor picked a better brilliant and humane leader for this incredible and super critical alien situation and homecoming project. Sara, I am counting on you. So, also this afternoon, I ordered the development of your new special secure office in our deep underground Washington White House sub chambers. You will also have a small office upstairs near my oval office and also, Sara, any Federal and Armed Services personnel, equipment, planes, ships, helicopters, subs and whatever you require are at your disposal. All you have to do is pick up a phone and dial 25436 and say, Plato."

The president continued, "By the way Sara, now that you have top, top secret clearance and authority, you will also have full access to our top secret alien affairs files. And some of our, uh, secret special research bases like, our main alien technological and biological research facilities at the Wright Patterson Air Force base in Ohio and as well as the Ft. Huachuca Army Electronics Proving grounds near Sierra Vista, Arizona. All this can be done after our amigos have returned to Lifestar to prepare for their disembarkation next month aboard USS Midway.

"All of the earlier aspects of other incredible alien situations will be briefed to you in person from the secret pentagon Alien Properties Office by Col. Corso as soon as you get back to DC."

"Sara, In 1947, it was one of those little gray's hybrid alien ships that crashed near Roswell. Unfortunately it brought too much limelight to this extraordinary growing alien dilemma." "Gads Commander, what are we going to do if more aliens decide to come here? Will we have to establish you in a permanent Plato cabinet position?"

So, for the sake of all humanity and maintaining social order, it is imperative that we keep relentlessly applying and re-inventing all of the cover-up stories and maintain endless disinformation activities. And now on top of the growing cold war and probable future war in Korea, we have this amazing Delphinian homecoming to contend with along with all of the mind- boggling previous alien encounters."

The President continued briefing Sara, "By the way Sara, remember every time that I sent messages to our alien friends? Well, that special underground alien communications antenna is on base there at Ft. Huachuca, Arizona. It's design and it's sundial like construction and shape are based on the genius ideas of Tesla. It's also now being developed to use as a exceedingly low frequency laser pulse weapon as a defensive deterrent known as project Joshua to counter gray alien's craft and beam weapons."

Sara just sat stupefied as she asked the president, "Mr. Truman, I guess that there has been a lot going on about our, uh, those gray aliens sometime before 1947, huh?"

President Truman grimaced solemnly and said, "Dear Sara, I and some of my top secret MJ-12 staff like; Admiral Roscoe Hillenkoeter, Dr. Vannevar Bush who was a lead scientist on the Manhattan Project, Defense Secretary Forrestal and General Nathan Twining who is Corso's boss, have so much to brief you about. But nonetheless, I want you to try as best you can, to let them know little as possible about our wonderful Delphinians."

Sara thought to herself, "Oh yes I remember vaguely hearing something about the Aquarius alien history project from my special physics professor Tweed at the Naval Post Graduate School in Monterey, California two years ago. I sure hope that she wasn't letting some of this incredible alien cat out of a top secret bag."

Harry just harrumphed, grinned and continued, "We will do the best that we can Commander. That's about all we can do to muddle through these incredible events and visitations. But for now Sara, can you please get Howard Hughes on the phone for me?" Sara, stood to return to her small office said, "Why certainly Mr. President."

Later in her own room, since Selena had apparently crashed into a deep and needed sleep, Sara lay in her bed, fondly looking at her new silver oak leaf and her Naval Post Graduate School gold lapel pin thinking and trying to unwind from this, another unbelievable but extraordinary day.

She began to trust that she had become the chief extraterrestrial and alien affairs liaison for the United States as she giggled to herself. "Wow, as a Navy 0-5 pay grade. I'll now be earning about $5,400 each year! But dang, I can never ever tell anyone about my job or my accomplishments. I can never ever tell my parents in Santa Barbara nor any human husband, just to an alien, uh, mate that I may find."

Sara soon dropped into rem and then into deep level four sleep. Her deep sleep mind played out her new incredible life dreams back to the universe and the creators. Glinda and Selena had told her that all living beings in the universe do that each night, when their planets rotate into their night sides.

As the south Florida gentle morning sunlight brightened her room, Sara slowly awoke from a deep sleep and needful rest for her body, mind and spirit. After she showered and dressed, she went down the hall to Selena's room and there she found Selena, Arthur and Glinda all sitting on the bed holding hands. Sara was embarrassed because Selena was still nude. She thought to herself, "I will never get used to such open family nakedness." Sara spoke aloud, "Ahem, uh good morning, is everyone OK?"

Glinda smiled, clicked softly and beamed to Sara, "We are having our morning meditation and comparing opinions with everyone aboard Lifestar." Glinda sensed Sara's discomfort, beamed to Selena, "OK daughter, go into your bathroom and please hurry and get dressed for today." She then beamed to Sara, "Good morning dear earth daughter. How are you doing?"

Sara hugged her aliens and instead of speaking, she thought, "I am doing ok. How are all of you feeling?"

Selena beamed from the bathroom, "Fortunately, we are back to more or less our normal somewhat now moister skinned alien selves."

Arthur beamed, "We will be ok, but we have decided to rest here today and give our skin a bit more time to grow more sweat glands instead of going to Miami. Will that be OK Sara?"

Sara sat on the bed and thought, "Of course, and once we do go to Miami, we will stay at the nice air conditioned Biltmore Hotel in Coral Gables right near the coast and we'll also visit the Miami Seaquarium. But, I am now very concerned about your being able to successfully adapt to our atmosphere dear family."

Glinda took Sara's hand and beamed, "We realize now that once we land, we will have to just take it easy. With the help of our medicos, our body systems and our moisture needing skin can adapt to these warmer semi tropical temperatures. Your dolphin relatives, as you may know, have no sweat glands and we, as humanoids with uh, dolphin heritage, have only about 65 percent of your human sweat glands. Our medicos have developed a skin cream that will help keep our skin moisturized. We believe that within a fairly short time, the cream will cause our epidermis to grow many more sweat glands."

She continued, "I have communicated with our chief medical officer and she has calculated that we can eventually adapt to a coastal or island climate that has an average relative humidity of about 60% percent instead of the normal 80 percent on our ship. So you see Sara, it's just like our dolphin cousins here and back on our home world who have to keep their skin moist..."

Sara gently squeezed both Glinda's and Selena's hands and thought, "That is wonderful news. How long do your medicos think it might take for all of you to adapt so that you can be comfortable and normally active on earth?"

Glinda beamed to Sara, "We estimate that even with the new skin cream, it might take as long as six months Sara."

Sara thought back to her dear aliens, "Well, that's actually not too bad." She elaborated, "Before the war, I was still an undergrad in anthropology and in NROTC at the University of California in Santa Barbara. I volunteered to go on a cruise expedition to Peru and Chile. My professors were investigating the effects of climate and altitude changes on some of the high Andean villagers. The natives volunteered to come down to the coastal areas in quaint Trujillo in northern Peru and to the coastal Riviera of Chile in central Chile inVina del Mar." Sara kept thinking to her aliens, "So we discovered that it took these eager high Andean volunteers about six months to successfully adapt to a lower altitude and the much warmer climate. When about half of them returned to their mountain villages, it took another six months for them to re- acclimate back to the colder temperatures and higher altitudes."

Glinda beamed to Sara, "So why did only half of them return to the mountain tops Sara?"

Sara giggled as she thought, "They decided they loved the more lively warmer coastal life much better than their rugged cold and boring high mountaintop villages." Sara continued, "Oh, I so hope you can adapt but more importantly, that you will love your new earth home wherever you may be."

The women all hugged as Arthur beamed to Sara, "We can now assure you and the president that we will be able to adapt. And of course finally we will appreciate and enjoy our new home on your planet. We will be liberated at last from our seemingly endless generations aboard our floating, between the equally endless stars, in our composite macropourous collodial nano crystaline metal overgroan lifeboat of a star craft."

Sara teared up a bit as she thought, "I know, I know. It must be really frustrating and disheartening for all of you. All of you share racial memories of your entire history; and those memories of everyone in all of your generations who sacrificed their lives to make the brave exodus to come here. For me, a long too relaxing cruise or especially a long boring flight sometimes feels endless to me, so I can only imagine how a six generation journey must feel."

Glinda sat quietly and smiled, whistled softly and beamed, "Amen Sara, it will be so wonderful for us to get to our new earth home. Do you have any ideas about where we can settle my dear new Commander Alien Ambassador?"

Sara broke into a proud smile as she realized, of course, the Delphinians had read President Truman's and her mind. She said, "Thank you your majesty, uh Glinda…" Glinda squealed in delight and clicked in fun, regally extended her hand for her new ambassador to kiss. Then they all were able to loosen up as Sara laughed and her aliens clicked and squealed in merriment and satisfaction.

Sara thought to her aliens, "I am so glad that with your telepathy and common instant sharing of situations that you seem to always maintain your sense of humor and spirits of play. I sure wish more earth people could have your happy and playful demeanor dear family."

Sara asked aloud, "Is there anything I can get for you before I go down to meet with the President?" Glinda beamed to her, "Some breakfast up here in the second level sitting room would be wonderful. Can we help you get that Sara?"

Sara said, "Nope, part of the White House kitchen staff is on duty again." She picked up the desk phone and ordered breakfasts for four. She then remembered to tell the cook, "Remember, no peanut butter or peanuts ever for our visitors, ok?" She covered the mouthpiece and thought to her amigos. "So, what would you like to drink this morning?" Each of them beamed, Coke please.

Selena let out a laughter squeal as she clicked in mirth and beamed to Sara, "Sara since you are beaming to us, why are you covering the mouthpiece of the phone?" Sara looked, like duh and along with her aliens, they all broke again into more happy laughter and squeals. Sara, uncovered the mouthpiece, and thought to Selena, "I covered it so that the staff could not hear your joyful squealing!"

By then Del 1 had come into the room and as he grinned, smacked his lips he said, "I want another piece of that declious cake please Sara."

CHAPTER 21 WATER ISLAND PLANS

When Sara got downstairs for the traditional 8:00am White House breakfast, she found President Truman and another man, a Navy uniformed black man, sitting at the table. As she sat down, President Truman said, "Good morning dear Sara, this gentleman is one of my Naval attachés for the Caribbean. He has some good ideas about a secure home base for our, uh south American visitors. Lieutenant Commander Captain Peter Tamaryn, II, please meet Commander Sara Winchester, my Chief Liaison Officer in charge of this vital resettlement project."

The tall thin officer stood, smiled respectfully and cordially shook Sara's hand. The President went on to explain, "Sara is in charge of a special top secret project to find a safe place for 160, uh, South American refugees."

Sara, looked at Captain Tamaryn and felt that he seemed to be quite capable and trustworthy. She smiled as she remembered that she now had some powerful alien amigos who could read minds to find out if people were being ingenuous with her.

Just then, Arthur beamed to Sara, "So far, so good a nice fella Sara!" and Selena beamed, "He should be a first-rate eager beaver Sara!"

Sara grinned and said, "Mr. President, our visitors are still very, uh, tired from yesterday and they have opted to relax, sip Coke and rest up here for today."

President Truman smiled knowingly and said, "I think that is an excellent choice. Traveling over long distances is so exhausting. I know that after just sitting aboard my Air Force One, Independence over long flights, I usually find that I am totally pooped!"

Sara was tempted to quip about how one feels after flying for six generations but she kept that thought to herself. She heard Selena's voice beaming, in her head, "Oh Sara, go ahead say that!" And then came more beamed tittering, clicks and squeals of Delphin laughter.

Sara thought back to Selena, "Stop that! I am in an important meeting with someone who can find an appropriate initial base for you."

Arthur beamed in, "The Lt. Commander seems so far to be an entirely honest person. Go ahead Sara we will be tuned in…"

After the president, Sara and the Lt. Commander finished their breakfast. President Truman turned to Tamaryn and said, "Why don't you get out your Caribbean charts and tell us more about this island that you have found for our refugees."

Tamaryn stood, placed his large chart case on the now cleared table and spread out three maps. He said, "This map is a full chart of the entire Caribbean and this map is of the US Virgin Islands."

President Truman grinned and gave a quick wink to Sara as he said, "Oh yes Peter, I made a formal visit there on my yacht last February."

Lt. Commander Tamaryn grinned happily and said, "Oh yes sir Mr. President. Don't you remember shaking my hand when you disembarked in Charlotte Amile?"

The president blushed and said, "Oh, I am so sorry, of course I do remember you now. I shake so many hands as you may know."

Lt. Commander Tamaryn continued, "Anyway sir, this third map is of Water Island. It's now a restricted naval base in the US Virgin Islands. From what your intelligence office sent to me, this US controlled island may be, initially, at least, the best bet for your, uh refugees. You say they are from South America Mr. President. What country are they fleeing from?"

Sara looked at the President as the always quick thinking Truman, not missing a beat said, "Well sir, that is confidential. Let's keep to the task at hand, ok?"

The Lt. Commander stiffened and said, "Yes sir Mr. President." Truman relaxed and said, "Please, show us more about Water Island. It seems that I can now recall seeing it off of the starboard side of my yacht as we sailed into the magnificent Charlotte Amalie Bay."

Sara, sat there and thought to herself, "Wow, no wonder he is the excellent but wonderfully laid back, poker faced and astute politician that he is."

Arthur beamed to Sara, "He for sure is exactly that Sara." He beat the flippers off of me at lunch yesterday."

As the President and Sara looked at the map of Water Island, Sara suddenly exclaimed, "Look, there is a small beach called Tamaryn just in from Sand Bay." She asked, "Is, is that any connection with you sir?" Peter smiled as he said, "Yes, in fact I was raised there and my grandfather founded that little village. My great, great grandfather actually owned Water Island back in 1793."

Sara commented, "Gosh, that's an amazing coincidence!"

Tamaryn replied, "The Virgin Islands main naval office requested me because I know the island like the back of my hand."

Ever curious Selena beamed in, Sara, Why would we ever want to memorize the back of our hands?"

Sara grinned and thought back, "Its just another english idiom Selena."

Truman commented, "I think then, that you will indeed be our best expert about Water Island since you were raised there."

Peter gleamed and said, "Yes sir, Mr. Truman, you can count on me to get your refugees safely landed, billeted, oriented and re-settled sir. We still have 12 barracks buildings, a very large mess hall and the Flamingo Bay deep water dock.

Glinda then beamed in, "Oh that's perfecto Sara. That will mean that only 12 of us will be in each barrack. That means less crowding and more laid-back opportunities to practice our social skills on one another."

Peter continued, "There is also a recreation hall and even a small theatre on the 500 acre island. There is a general office and a small administration building. And, as you may know sir, there is also the Marine Bourne Airfield with its 4,800 foot runway just over on St. Thomas Island itself. The base also has a 60 bed dispensary."

The president asked, "How many sailors and marines are billeted on the island now?"

Tamarind paused as he consulted his wooden clip board and replied, "We currently have a compliment of 60 sailors, 12 marines and about 30 civilian workers who commute by boat from St Thomas every day."

Sara looked hastily at the president. Truman almost imperceptibly nodded his head and said, "Uh, you will have to immediately begin to reduce your crew and remove all civilian staff for at least uh…what do you think Sara?"

Sara thinking as fast as she could said, "Uh, Yes, all of those civilian workers will have to be re-assigned for at least three or four months just before our, uh refugees arrive. There must be only a skeleton military contingent sworn to total secrecy on Water Island."

Tamarynd, then nervously tapping his right index finger on the Water Island map, looked at Sara and the President said, "Uh, yes ma'am, of course I will arrange to reduce the crew and lay off all of the civilian staff as soon as possible."

The President looked momentarily at Sara, leaned closer to the Lt. Cmdr. quietly and seriously said, "We really appreciate your efforts for this uh, very unusual mission. Please remember that this particular situation is a top national secret security issue and your career and your personal autonomy depends on you completely respecting and keeping to the top security clearance you have now been issued by special order of my office."

Peter was almost tempted to stand and snap to attention but he just stiffened and said, "Yes sir Mr. President, you have my oath on this sir."

Sara noticed that the, more often than not, laid back Lt. Cmdr. was now actually sweating a bit. She heard Arthur beaming in her head, "It certainly sounds like a really good initial landing prospect for us. Please get all the information about that island for us to take to our planetary scientists, logistics dept and medicos."

Sara quickly thought, "OK, no problema amigos." She turned to Tamarynd and asked, "Can you please leave your charts and files here with us? I will call you after next week to begin our more exact planning."

He looked briefly quizzically at Sara and said, "Yes ma'am can do."

Sara asked, "Do your documents also have full historical and present day climatologically data about the island?"

Peter pulled out the legal size climate file and handed it to her, he said with kind a puzzled look on his face, "Here is all of the climatologically data we have about Water Island as well as all of the Virgin Islands. These records go back to the beginning of the Danish administration of the Virgins in 1666. Do you know that Water Island is only one of just a very few Caribbean Islands that have any fresh water? The thirsty pirates and others used to call there to refill their water barrels."

Sara smiled and said, "Ok … So that's why it's named Water Island." Sara took the file and thanked the Lt. Comander.

After Lt. Commander Tamaryn left, President Truman said to Sara, "Well, do you think Water Island will be an ok initial landing point for our, uh new members of our earthly family?"

Sara smiled as she said, "I think it will be perfectly ok for just a little while Mr. President, but just as an initial touchdown base to begin to let our Delphinians acclimate, grow sweat glands and adjust. But, I really think that we ought to get them all to Camp Roberts out in coastal California as soon as possible. It's larger and has more facilities and opportunities to travel to nearby central California communities for our newcomers to practice their evolving earthly social and practical day to day living skills.

Truman nodded his head and agreed, "In many ways I would prefer to take them all to Camp Roberts right off the bat. But first, I still have to win the 1948 election. Once we've cinched that, then we can make final plans to get them ASAP safely and happily to California."

Sara stood and said, "I agree completely Mr. Truman by their being in a safe area which we can, for the most part, control. They can begin to practice and realistically apply their social interactions and daily human routines initially with some restricted Camp Roberts personnel. They can then take guided trips to nearby Paso Robles and on down to San Luis Obispo and maybe even to my Santa Barbara hometown. And finally we can take them in small groups to their big graduation walk abouts and maybe even have them try living in government quarters at El Toro Marine Base for awhile to see how it goes for them in Los Angeles. Also, as soon as they are ready, I want to take them to visit the bizarre and fascinating Hearst Castle in nearby San Simion."

Truman chuckled and said, "Ok, great idea Sara. But you will have to count me out on the Hearst Castle visit. William Randolph Hearst would never allow me to set foot in his "Ranch" as he preposterously calls his baroque, renaissance make-believe faux concrete castle. But do feel free to contact William Randolph Hearst since it is well known that he is the only one who ever offers invites to his lavish play land. I have to fly as low as I can around him and his hawk newspaper publishing buddies for the sake of my re-election. William Randolph Hearst, the hawk, really hates my peace loving guts and he hates my policies and my liberal politics. The only thing we shared agreement on was the exposing and finally stopping the Holocaust and now the coming commie menace from North Korea and the cold war and Russian expansionist ambitions."

Sara grinned as she said, "Well sir, if I can't get an invite, my dad, who as you know, is a Hollywood producer, certainly can. Mr. Hearst, in past years, invited us to visit a few times and as out of place with Europe as his fairytale castle is, the other celebrity guests, music and food were really great. His large Neptune outdoor swimming pool overlooking the Pacific is a dreamscape to see and to swim in." "

By the way sir. My dad is good friends with Walt Disney and he says that Disney had long been dreaming of developing a Disneyland, uh, amusement park somewhere near LA with its own fairy tale castle."

Truman had never been to Hearst Castle grinned and said, "Well Sara, our Delphinians ought to really relish that pool."

Sara added, "Oh Mr. Truman, you really must come too."

Truman tried to grin and said, "Well thanks Sara, but not in this political minefield, and besides," He smiled for a moment but then slowly changed his face to disappointment as he recalled, "Besides Sara, my dear Bess would never come to visit such a wicked Hollywood extravaganza like Mr. Hearst's Castle. But I think that my wannabe singer daughter, Margaret, would love to hobnob with those celebrities and producers."

Glinda beamed into Sara's mind, "To heck with that stuffy country matron Bess. My older sister, Shiri would love to accompany Mr. Truman. She has, as you say here on earth, a crush on our president."

Sara grinned and thought back, "Ok, but remember no alien alienation of affection until after he wins the 1948 election Glinda."

Selena beamed in, "Sara does alienation's mean the countries where we might be going to live?"

Sara thought, "Selena, I will be upstairs in a few minutes and I will explain it all to you my dear little alienated alien sister… ok?"

Sara put her hand on Mr. Truman's shoulder and said, "Well you know best Mr. President. I know Mr. Hearst always loves to show off his estate at San Simion. He has a private airstrip below the Castle and I think a DC-3 could easily land there. There is also a pier at San Simion near Sebastion's quaint country store. I am sure I can get my dad to have Mr. Hearst invite you…"

Harry touched his assistant's hand, smiled sadly and said, "OK Sara, we shall see. You must respect that as the Delphinians have taught us, the ceaseless egos of alpha males is always relentless. Confidentially Sara, the FBI over the years has investigated the disappearances of at least two people whose last known place on earth was while working at or visiting Mr. Hearst's castle. And also, one major Hollywood producer fellow was supposedly accidentally shot by jealously outraged Mr. Hearst while visiting his yacht, Oneida, back in 1924. Hearst is really over protective and jealous of his lifelong mistress Marion Davis."

Sara straightened up and said, "Oh yes, I remember dad telling me about that hushed up case. "So, in that set of circumstances, I think since everything is better illuminated and considered now. We will just skip any visits by our aliens into the old publishing lion's lair."

Sara gave the Water Island maps and climate data sheets to Delnoid 1 to scan with his bionic eyes. She sat with her aliens and thought, "Well, it looks like we can now finally begin to get you and your pod landed Arthur."

Arthur smiled and beamed, "Thank you dear Sara. We are indeed beholden to you."

Glinda beamed, "Sara if you could only imagine what six confining generations aboard Lifestar has done to separate us, and even the Delnoid units, from our present time realities."

Sara said for all to hear, "Yes, I know it's been like being in a prison floating between the stars for all of you but now we are going to get you landed, oriented and living as free and happy as your dolphin cousins again." She hugged her aliens and cried, "Oh welcome home dear Delphinians. Welcome home to Earth and your new beautiful oceans!"

Sara then sat on the bed holding her yellow legal note pad and said, "I have a few questions for you."

Glinda beamed, "Certainly hija (daughter) go ahead."

Sara asked, "Ok, exactly how many Delphinians are aboard the Lifestar?"

Glinda beamed, "Sara there are 160 of us, 100 females aged from 6 to 125 and 20 males. We also have 30 female and 10 male children who are newborn to age 16. As soon as I get back to Lifestar, I will have radio send to you the complete list with all the names, gender and ages."

Sara replied, "But, Glinda, you told me that because all of you are telepathic and sonic for identifying each other that you don't use names."

Glinda smiled knowingly and proudly beamed, "Well, since we are going to be living on Earth soon, we all agreed to choose names. After the absurd Battle of Los Angeles back in 1942, Delnoid 8M visited your amazing Griffith Observatory in Los Angles. He went to the gift shop and bought for our library, a book titled Star Names – Their Lore and Meaning.

We each now have a bright as possible star name that you have given to the bright stars in your 88 constellations.

Sara sat in amazement and continued, "Oh Glinda, that is wonderful.

My dad and I always visited Griffith Observatory while we were in LA.

I can't wait to see the list and meet and get to really know each one of you on Water Island." Sara then paused a moment then looked matter of factually at her aliens and said, "Your star name choices are charming. But do you know what? Most of those old and even the new star names are very, very antiquated and uncommon now days. It might be better if we help you all choose some really more ordinary earth names. For you will soon have US Government security cards, passports and California drivers licenses made."

Glinda, Selena, Arthur and Delnoid 1 just looked - oh duh - at each other and squeaked and beamed… Delnoid 1 looked abashed at Sara and said, "Oh my gosh Sara, you are quite right about that. From now on, you can just call me Del One!"

Sara said, "I do not mean to put down your star names, but the less attraction you call to yourselves the better. But we can carefully look over your star names list and see if any of them would fit ok into our 1948 culture." She then mentally recalled her visits to the Westmont College Observatory in Montecito and chuckled as she remembered the name of Zubenelgenubi, a faint yellowish star 77 light years away in Libra, but with one of the longest star names. But she realized that Zuben could stem from that as an acceptable contemporary name.

Sara heard in her mind a sweet, "Hello Sara, I am Vicki, our astronomer and astro navigator. I am amazed that you can remember that long name and also the data about that star."

Del One then interjected, "So do I. Its located…" Glinda quickly beamed, Shut up Del, whoever you are!"

Sara grinned as she thought back to Vicki, "Well me too actually. I guess that it stuck with me because it is such an unusual and long star name." Sara smiled and continued thinking, "I am looking forward to meeting you soon. I have always loved astronomy and knowing about the stars and constellations. I imagine you have so much you can share with us about the universe. After you are acclimated and after your Camp Roberts orientations, I will be glad to introduce you to the leaders of Mt Wilson Observatory, and the new Palomar Observatory now being built by Cal-Tech in Pasadena. I will also introduce you to the astronomers at the Lick Observatory up on Mt. Hamilton east of San Jose. Actually, now that I think about it, the world's largest reflecting telescope, the 200 inch (5 meters) reflector, up on Mount Palomar should be dedicated next year."

Sara heard in her head a squeal of delight from Vicki as the Delphinian astronomer beamed, "Oh Sara that will be so wonderful to be able to share with other astronomers from your world."

Sara interjected, "Remember Vicki, it's now your world too."

Vicki sent loving thankful energies to Sara as she also beamed. "I am so looking forward to meeting you and other astronomers. Sara do you know that I am the leader of our astronomy research department? Isn't that what you would call it? Also everyone aboard Lifestar totally loves astronomy. We were all so thrilled when we were first able to clearly resolve the Earth and Moon through our digital telescopes."

Sara thought, "Well, we will introduce you to the astronomical communities here on earth as soon as we can. But remember, you have knowledge about the universe and the stars of our galaxy which is a thousand years ahead of what these earth star gazers know so you will have to fly low!"

Selena and Vicki chorused, "Fly low Sara, what does that mean?"

Sara smiled knowingly and answered, "It means not attracting too much attention. And, I sure know how much you love attention dear Selena, but you must always try to fly low here on earth, ok?"

Selena squealed and continued, "Ok, but I can't wait to learn how to fly a plane Sara. The idea just thrills me."

Sara raised her eyebrows as she thought, " Selena you are already a qualified flighter pilot. Why do you want to learn to fly an earth plane?"

Selena squealed, clicked and beamed, "So I can fly low and see all the places from above since my flying my… uh… one of our 30 foot flying saucers, as you call it, would just cause panics."

Sara thought to both of the exuberant Delphinians, "Whoa there soon to be earthlings. Patience, dear amigas. Patience, all in due time…"

Sara then realized that the aliens must have a serious imbalance in their birth genders and the significance of the Delphinian male / female ratios. She stammered, "There are only about 20 males?" Sara thought, "So why are there so few males Glinda "

Glinda looked worriedly at Arthur for a second and he nodded his head in consent. Glinda beamed, "This is how we reduce chances of having a domineering majority of alpha males."

Sara thought, "OK, now I am curious, why can't your genetic scientists control the proportion of non aggressive males and alpha males?

Glinda beamed, "Well they could, but we have found over the generations that it's best to simply keep the number of males at a minimum, while trying to maintain natural male vigor's."

Sara asked, "So, do you wind up with a lot of females who can't marry?

Glinda grimaced and nodded and looked at Selena to answer.

Selena beamed to Sara, "Remember that I told you how we have no qualms about uh, sleeping with different partners Sara?"

Sara looked a bit embarrassed, said, "Oh yeah, I forgot about that but now I appreciate a lot more about your loving and openly sharing social culture."

Glinda beamed, "Sara we are hoping eventually, as we integrate into your human societies, that our females will be able to produce viable true Delphinian human hybrids with the ability to speak and also not to need higher humidity levels, or sweat gland growing skin creams, or nasal humidifiers to be comfortable. And also males who are not too terribly alpha types…"

Sara paused talking as she scribbled a few notes on her pad and then said, "That actually makes good sense for you, us and peace on earth Glinda. Ok, now then, I need to ask that after you return to your ship, please get all of the clothing measurements and especially foot, uh flipper patterns for everyone so we can get a shoe factory to manufacture comfortable sturdy shoes, tennis shoes and other kinds of, uh special wide shoes for all of you."

Glinda beamed, "OK that will be great. Remember too, we have to also plan for earth shoes for our babies and on up ages to adult size flippers." Selena beamed, "I see we will have to open an exclusive shoe store workshop for ourselves after we really get settled in California."

Sara laughed as she thought, "Yes sister, I now know that all of you can go into almost any earth store to buy clothes, the exception is, you can not enjoy shopping in shoe stores…"

Selena looked at her idly wiggling flippers, squealed in delight and beamed, "Sara will you please teach me how to wear extra wide high heel earth shoes someday?"

Sara looked skeptically at her alien's wide flipper feet said, "Of course Selena, but we will have to somehow find a special cobbler to make them for you dear little flipper sister. You will have to practice learning how to walk on your tippy flips. It's not as easy as it looks princess…"

Selena beamed, "Alright Cool." And, she wiggled her flippers admiringly and let out a loud wheeeet whoooo !

Sara continued, "Speaking of shopping, the President asked me to tell you that he will arrange for under the official table funding for all of you to re-settle. You'll be able to get housing and schools and universities too. Now, fortunately, the post war California housing market is low but it will sky rocket in the next few years. We will also help you each find appropriate work or do your own businesses or also provide tuition, books and dorms for those of you who choose to attend universities or whatever you discover that you enjoy here on earth."

Delnoid and Arthur looked at Sara as Delnoid asked, "Sara what does under the table mean?"

Sara smiled cagily as she said, "It means unofficial money that there is no record of."

Arthur grinned, nodded his head knowingly and beamed, "Excuse me a moment, I have to get my backpack." When he returned, he put his pack on the table and like Selena, when he placed his palm on the top of his case a faint blue handprint appeared and the top simply popped open. He reached inside and took out a large, well worn tan leather bag, picked open its drawstrings and poured onto the table a fortune in diamonds, emeralds, rubies and other precious gems. He grinned as he craftily beamed, "Do these stones have any value on earth Sara?"

Sara was totally dumbfounded and awestruck as she stammered, "Where on earth did you get all of these jewels?"

Arthur started scooping the gems back into their bag and beamed to Sara, "We discovered them in your Atlantic Caribbean border in what you consider to be the Bermuda Triangle. It was actually rather close to where we first rendezvoused with you and Sea Cat Sara. They were all in a 1700's Spanish galleon that had sunk to a depth of about 16,500 feet. We had thought that perhaps we should have them to uh, buy us a safe place on Earth, rather like the great land purchases made by your United States back in 1626 when Peter Minuit bought Manhattan for only about 60 Dutch guilders or about $72 dollars.

Selena then piped in, "Oh yes and I remember reading in your United States history that in 1803 the Louisiana Purchase for $15 million got 888,000 square miles. In 1846, just over a hundred years ago, the whole northwestern USA Oregon territory was acquired by only a treaty with England."

Glinda then clicked and beamed, "Don't forget the Gaston purchase of the south western US in 1853 for only $10 million which bought over 30 million acres."

President Truman had come up to the alien's suite and stood quietly listening just inside the doorway, smiled in proud amazement. After he stopped chuckling a bit he interjected, "And then in 1867 we made the Alaska purchase from Russia acquiring 425 million acres for only $7.2 million."

Sara grinned and chipped in, "Back then it was called Stewards folly for buying all of that useless frozen and mountainous land just as a buffer against Russia. But then in 1896 gold was discovered near Juneau and the Yukon gold rush of 1897 was on!" Sara then exclaimed, "Gosh, you seem to know all of our history."

Truman looked Arthur straight in the eye and said, "You also have many super amazing technical as well as practical deep water recovery capabilities with your Lifestar ship your Majesty. But, If you all will kindly excuse me, I have to get back to my deskwork downstairs. Which reminds me, anyone up for a few hands of poker this evening? We could use your jewel bag for ante…"

After the laughter and squeaking and squealing and merry clicking died down, Truman harrumphed and said, "Ok, ok, just kidding…"

Arthur grinned, clicked again, nodded at Truman, raised his open palm and said, "Please Sara, try not call us your majesty." He grinned and squeaked in merriment, "Yes, it funtastic and true that we really enjoy our new royal pod dramatic personas from your King Arthur books but we are a true transparent democracy and family where we openly discuss all issues to make vital and all other decisions."

Sara thought to her aliens, "With your telepathy I imagine that you do achieve true, good and realistic agreements with each other."

Selena beamed, "Our complete openness, accord and unity is the only way we could have ever achieved our arduous six generation voyage through the endless stars in our stinky old ship to get here dear earth sister."

Sara said to everyone, "I am so glad that you, so bravely coming home to a place that you have never been before, actually made it here." Selena and Sara hugged as Glinda, Arthur and Delnoid all joined in as they touched.

Sara suddenly felt like she was floating among the stars and swimming and surfing just like a dolphin; on their powerful love energy filled waves as the whole group energy of the 160 Delphinians enveloped her mind and spirit and joined all their life hopes and dreams together for a few wonderfull moments.

Sara cried and whispered, "This is pure love energy my dear family and now I've really begun to understand your so precious children of the universe spirituality and connections to each other. I so love you."

The next morning after Sara and Selena had gotten up, showered and dressed, they went into Arthur and Glinda's room. Sara saw that they too had dressed and she asked, "So, how are you feeling today?"

Glinda beamed, "We are feeling great and ready to follow our earth sister tour guide anywhere you want to take us."

Sara thought, "Great, let's all go downstairs for breakfast with the President. I think he has some great official news for you."

They were seated around the table eating their breakfast. President Truman, dressed in his usual flowered Aloha shirt and white tropical trousers, said, "Well my dear alien friends, although you, through your incredible telepathic and mind reading abilities probably already know what I have arranged. But, none the less, I need to make an official Presidential announcement to you, ok?"

Arthur beamed back, "Of course Mr. President. We are looking forward to your official news."

After the table was cleared and again, all of the servants again banned from the White House for the day. Truman wiped his mouth with his napkin, cleared his throat and said, "We are happy to officially inform you that we have found a very secure island for you. It's just about half a mile from St. Thomas in the US Virgin Islands and it is all yours, for you weary space travelers, for as long as you need it to get acclimated to the climate here on earth. As soon as your medical officers feel you are physiologically ready, we will then transfer all of you to the middle of coastal California to our Army Camp Roberts for full social training and orientations. We will also finance your re-settling as you adapt and determine what further training and education you want and need for your studies, activities and work that you wish to do. The full backing of my office is at your disposal. The only daunting concern that I have right now is that if I lose the 1948 election, it may disrupt our plans for you. Please understand that since I cannot absolutely guarantee that the succeeding US President will follow through on our plans and verbal agreements. I therefore have drawn up this written treaty between us to make our, uh, understandably top, top secret agreements official. That way under our procedures and laws, the future presidents will be obligated to honor our, uh your treaty with the United States Government."

Arthur beamed to Truman, "Mr. President, we are glad to confirm our treaty with you based on the details that you and I and also, telepathically our whole crew agreed to in our extensive deliberations yesterday."

Truman smiled and said, "Let's all go into my little oval office and there, we can execute our historic agreement."

Arthur beamed, "Very well Mr. President. We shall meet you in your office in say, about15 minutes..."

CHAPTER 22 SEALED IN CRYSTALS

The aliens, President Truman and Sara stood around his desk. The President took a multi paged document from a large manila envelope. He opened his left-hand desk drawer and fumbled around in it for a few moments to find two official presidential signing pens. He finally drew them out and placed them on his desk next to the papers.

Arthur gave a low whistle and beamed, "Mr. President, why so many pens?"

Truman grinned and said, "Well, whenever we sign any historic document, uh, the President usually gives the signing pens as souvenirs to all of the signers. It's just a White House tradition"

Arthur smiled at Glinda as he pulled two transparent 3 inch octagonal flighter shaped crystals out of his small silver fabric bag. He beamed to Truman, "It is our custom to seal agreements with these quantum recording energy crystals Mr. President. They are encoded with what your physicists might someday call quantum nano entanglement. Encoded bits of information are entangled with pairs of light particles called photons. The photons, interestingly, can affect each other – almost instantly - even across the distance of our galaxy. Now sir, realize that none of us can ever alter the texts and agreements that will be sealed forever in these crystals. So you see that this quantum key's coding really protects you, Mr. President, so that your successors and or any of their mal intentioned subordinates or cohorts can never alter our treaty with us and the USA."

Harry Truman took to heart that he was dealing with an alien culture and that now his curiosity was thoroughly aroused as he reached for a crystal and asked, "How amazing, uh, how do we use and encode these two crystals to seal our agreements?"

Arthur, still hanging onto the stones, did not give one to the President, he then beamed, "You and I will now each hold a stone in both our hands and as we touch each other's hands, our agreement will be sealed.

Our agreement is recorded by quantum entanglement of the universal energy we use to live by. It is held forthwith and forever now in sacred trust of our un-alterable agreements. We will then exchange our crystals and the pact will be sealed. Call it kind of like you might say, it's a universal - set in crystals – official recorder's office."

Truman became a bit apprehensive for a moment as he asked Arthur. "Uh, does this mean that you will not be signing our documents Arthur uh, your Majesty?"

Arthur smiled and beamed to all, "Of course I, as leader of all of the remaining Delphinians, will also sign your official papers Mr. President."

As he and President Truman sat at the desk, Arthur reached into his pocket and pulled out his digital camera and handing it to Selena he asked her, "Princess, do you mind?"

As the two leaders sat at the desk signing the papers, Selena, along with android Delnoid 1M happily imaged away and recorded the historic human/alien treaty agreement.

Arthur then took each of the crystals and placed them in Delnoid's hands. After a minute, the now sweating Delnoid unit said, "It is done your Majesty and Mr. President. Our agreements are now unalterably recorded forever in these two quantum crystals. Arthur then held one of the now light blue glowing crystals and he handed the other equally glowing one to the President, he said, "We have to touch our foreheads together now for this Mr. President, do you mind sir?"

Truman hesitatingly offered his forehead and as Arthur touched his brow, the 33rd President was able to see, feel and hear the Delphinians all beaming in acknowledgment to the agreement.

Arthur continued, "We will now feel the universal energies being exchanged in the crystals to forever seal our agreement into the life dreams repository of this universe." Both of the leaders then became as one; united in the trust of universal love energies. Arthur slowly opened his palm and his crystal had become bright red and as the President opened his fingers, his crystal had also turned to a crimson red.

Arthur invited the President to again exchange crystals. After they had done so, Arthur put his crystal back into his pouch, smiled and extended his right hand to President Truman and beamed, "Well, as you earthlings say Mr. President, done deal. Be sure to always guard that crystal with your life Mr. President!"

Sara, Selena, Glinda and Delnoid 1 came to embrace the two leaders and as they smiled, they added their hands to the hands of both leaders and echoed, "Done deal."

Truman was completely flabbergasted but he maintained his composure as he said, "Dearest new allies, I, and the people of the United States, thank you and may our alliance endure throughout space and the times ahead." Truman was thinking, "Oh gosh, so where the heck can I safely hide this crystal?"

Glinda smiled and beamed, "The agreement is now recorded in the flow of life dreams that we each, all living things, flow back into the universe and our creators Mr. Truman. So please deposit the crystal in a very safe place where you can be sure to look at it occasionally. Because Mr. President, if our agreement is ever broken, the universe will know this via the nighttime brain waves which transmit the life dreams of the people involved. If our agreement is ever betrayed, both crystals will instantly change to what you call obsidian black."

(After LBJ,s betrayal of the aliens in 1965, the crystals turned black.)

The President said, "Ok, when shall we meet to do some more detailed planning for your transition to your beautiful tropical Water Island home?"

Glinda looked briefly at Arthur and beamed to the president, "Well Mr. Truman, Sara has promised us a trip to Miami, the first big city we will have tried to visit here on earth."

Harry Truman, being the true humane fellow that he was, said, "OK, I think that's a great idea for all of you to relax a bit today and tomorrow. As I work over the phone with my NSA staff, Navy department and Delnoid 5M here with me since he can talk your thoughts to me for us to plan and prepare more extensively for your homecoming to earth. Sara tells me that you will enjoy staying at the Miami Biltmore Hotel. It's an excellent world class resort and on Sunday, I shall try to get away from here in my helicopter to come visit and dine with you on Friday morning, er March 19th." Arthur do you, uh, that is, can you, play golf? I mean, would you like to learn our quaint relaxing putting game?"

Arthur smiled and beamed, "Harry that would be great."

Sara smiled and said, "Ok then, I will meet all of you in the foyer in half an hour. Please bring whatever clothes you may need and of course your extra humidifiers."

CHAPTER 23 THUMPA THUMPA THUMPA SIKORSKY H-34 CHOCTAW

The aliens re-gathered and each had their back packs filled with their needs. Sara said, "OK, please follow me." She led her alien family out onto the porch and there was a grey navy van waiting for them.

As they and two secret service agents piled in, Selena happily beamed to her new earth sister, "Are we going up to Miami in this?"

Sara smiled and said, "No of course not Selena, we are going to the Key West Navy airstrip where we have a helicopter waiting to take us directly to the Biltmore."

Arthur clicked rapidly, raised his eyebrows and thought, "Oh Amador! Are we actually going to have to fly in one of their primitive earthly mix master's?"

Glinda beamed to her husband, "Suush my love, be diplomatic."

Selena reading her parents private exchange, beamed to them, "It's the best they have for us, so at least, let's enjoy the ride with Sara."

Arthur grimaced, clicked agitatedly and privately beamed to the crew of their scout flighter stationed 125 miles overhead…"OK you two,, be ready to tractor beam and come and rescue us if I call." He received back thoughts from his crew beaming, "Of course Arthur." He quickly over read their added thoughts between each other, "Dear Amador! I would never try to fly in such a primitive contraption…" Arthur beamed back, "Ok you two, please be more, uh, confident – ok?"

After Sara and her three precious aliens were strapped into the Sikorsky H-34 Choctaw, the pilot radioed to the Key West Navy control tower and said. "OK, Marine Two is ready to depart. Have we been cleared through Miami airspace and cleared to land on the Biltmore golf course?"

The reply came back, "Affirmative, Marine Two is now cleared for takeoff for flight directly to the Biltmore golf course."

As the large Presidential whirlybird lifted and thumpa thumpa thumped off to the north, one of the navy control tower ratings turned to his duty partner and said, "Pancho boy, I sure wonder who the hell those VIP's are? It must be nice to just fly off for a few rounds of golf like that?" Pancho scowled to Roy, "A damn waste of my taxpayer money if you ask me amigo."

As the presidential chopper whirled it's way northward, Sara clicked the push to talk button on her headset's cord and said into her mike. "3,000 feet below us are the beautiful Florida Keys. Soon we will be approaching the south end of Miami and we will start to let down for our landing on the Biltmore Hotel golf course."

Unknown to Sara, the pilot, on his separate cockpit intercom said to his co pilot, "Hummmm that good looker Sara is some kind of high level stewardess ain't she?" The co-pilot looked over at the pilot and made a leering grin.

Arthur beamed to Sara, "What does golf mean?"

Sara, having learned its true acronym meaning on a trip to England when she was in high school, giggled as she carefully mentally spelled out the letters G-O-L-F. "It was started way back in 1475 in Scotland and in those days and even in some clubs up to now, women were not welcome at most gentlemen's clubs and activities. So, GOLF is an acronym meaning, "Gentlemen Only Ladies Forbidden.""

Glinda raised her eyebrows, clicked indignantly and beamed, "I simply cannot believe the absurd discrimination that you humans had and still have for separating your men and women."

Selena beamed, "Yeah, it's so disrespectful and unfair to your women."

Sara smiled and to avoid being overheard on the helicopters intercom system, she thought as diplomatically as she could, "Well dear Delphinian family, welcome to chauvinistic planet Earth – such as it was in 1475 and now apparently, still is in 1948."

CHAPTER 24 BLOW HOLES AND HOWARD HUGHES

The President's visitors settled into their two adjoining 12th floor rooms. Sara and Selena were standing looking out of their east side picture window. Selena took Sara's hand and beamed, "Sara, I am so glad you are with us for all of these fantastic but also kind of frightening new places, shopping and discoveries."

Sara squeezed her alien sister's hand and thought, "Hey that is what I am here for with my whole heart and spirit dear little sister."

Selena excitedly pointed out of the window to the northeast and beamed, "Sara, what is that place over the waterway with all of those big swimming pools?"

Sara grinned as she thought to Selena, "That is just one of the attractions that I want to take you to see my dear little sister. It's the Miami Seaquarium where they have dolphins that perform tricks."

Selena became very wide eyed and alarmed as she beamed, "Do you mean that those dolphins live there all the time in captivity?"

Sara looked sheepishly at her dolphin related alien sister and said, "Well, Selena it's, uh, the way some human business men make a

show place to show and teach all about the sea life, fish and sea mammals we all share our water world with."

Selena sadly moaned, clicked angrily and beamed, "Ok, but I do hope that my relatives were not kept there against their will Sara."

Sara thought, "Selena I really don't know if they are unhappy there. They get all the fish they could ever eat and also lots of loving attention, just like you always need my dearest Delphin girl."

Selena hugged Sara, squeaked and trilled as she beamed, "I can't wait to visit there."

Sara smiled and said, "Ok, but for now get your notepad and lets go meet your parents to get ready to go down for our late lunch."

Selena forgetting for the moment about her captive relatives smiled as she let out a small happy squeak.

After meeting Arthur and Glinda in their connected next-door suite, Sara picked up the bedside phone and said, "Hi, this is Sara Winchester, is our buffet lunch ready for us?" Sara then smiled as she thought... "Gosh this is meeee, Sara Winchester Hawks, California girl leading an alien Presidential VIP party."

Glinda beamed to Sara, "Be happy and proud dear human daughter. We are so glad and proud that it is you leading us. Sara, exactly what does VIP mean?"

Sara grinned and erected her head proudly as she said, "It means Very Important Persons."

Arthur clicked, grinned and beamed to all, "Well... I certainly pray to Amador that our status always stays that way..."

Sara, getting the drift of his concerns thought, "Dear Arthur, until I draw my last breath I will protect all of you because you are my second family now in my true heart."

Glinda was a little teary as she beamed, "Again dear Sara, we are so fortunate that you are at this place in space and time for us now. We love you too."

Sara had actually never felt so appreciated, respected and loved in her entire 26 years on Earth.

Glinda reading her feelings beamed, "Our deep emotional and spiritual connection is just normal for most all of us Delphinians dear earth daughter. Remember always dear Sara, there are no accidental meetings in the universe; just wonderful synchronicities for us to respect and join together in friendship, spirit, heart and response ability." She gathered her dear earth daughter of her true heart in her arms and beamed, "Again welcome to our pod, uh family, dear Sara."

They took the elevator down to the ground floor. The three hungry VIPs went into the poolside dining room where they found what was just a normal extravagant luncheon buffet for this world class hotel. Glinda and Selena saw the long table filled with every imaginable food. Glinda whistled and beamed to Sara, "Aiiiiiiiii Amadore. I cannot believe I'm seeing all of this incredible variety of food!"

Equally open mouthed Selena clicked slowly and beamed, "But, why is there so much? It's more than any of us can eat and I see that there are only 22 people here at the tables. What do they do with the leftover food Sara? Do they recycle it in their food synthesizers?"

Sara was embarrassed as she thought to her aliens, "Uh, well I guess that they just throw out the leftovers."

Glinda clicked indignantly and beamed, "Then, why on Earth do they prepare so much food?"

Sara, humbled, realized that this extravagant waste of food was just a ritzy show, or window dressing to impress and gratify their rich hotel guests.

She then thought to Glinda and Selena, "You know, you are absolutely right, this is a shameful waste of food. But as long as we are here, I think that it will be a wonderful chance for you to try a great variety of different earth foods. So let's enjoy our free lunch, ok?"

Glinda squeaked and beamed, "Ok, you're quite right Sara. Let us indulge in this opportunity to discover which earth foods we like. Sara, can you stay with us and, please explain the dishes to us?"

Sara smiled and thought, "Of course." Eight minutes later, after they had gone from hors d'oeuvres, soups, salads, cheese, breads, meats and fish to potatoes and veggies and onto desserts, Glinda beamed, "I am scandalized at this Sara. Is this how most earth people eat lunch?"

Sara thought, "Oh no Glinda, this is just a special display for guests here to enjoy. A lot of hotels and cruise ships have buffets like this for breakfast, lunch and for dinner sometimes so that people who are visiting can enjoy some special food and amenities. Usually Glinda, people just eat at home and fix their own small regular breakfasts, lunches and dinners. Kind of like how we fixed lunch day before yesterday back in the small White House kitchen."

Arthur grinned, clicked and beamed, "Hummmm, maybe we can open our own hotel someday and serve our fish based alien cuisine."

Sara looked at Arthur and thought, "So, where did you learn the cuisine word?"

Arthur grinned, clicked and beamed, as Glinda and Selena gave a small low squeak in laughter. "Remember dear Sara, we have in past, visited some small earth coastal towns and villages and we did have lunch at a delightful small dockside café in Cannes, France one time."

Selena beamed in, "Oh au Tant aimé que le pain et le beurre français

(I so loved that French bread and butter)."

Glinda smiled and beamed, "And, the cheese platter with Cambert, Brie de Meaux, Boursin, Munster, et Pont l'Eveque were absolutely, as you might say, divine. But… our waiter sure got insulted and indignant with us because we ordered Coke instead of wine!"

Arthur clicked, smiled and beamed, "Yeah, if only he knew who he was serving. I enjoyed the Roquefort and Chevre the best."

Sara looked at all of her aliens and thought, "Goodness, you are becoming quite the international gourmets, n'est-ce pas?"

Selena wrinkled up and pinched her supersensitive nose, clicked loudly and rapidly and beamed, "Except for that, 'squeakedy squeak,' stinky old Roquefort! It reminds me too much of our stinky old starship!"

After they finished lunch, and as they sat there, Selena kept looking excitedly out of the window and beamed, "That is such an awesome grand pool! Can we swim in it now Sara?"

Sara said, "Uh sure, but I must tell you that here on earth because we are now digesting our big lunch, it's recommend by most doctors that we do not swim until at least an hour after we eat."

Glinda clicked rapidly and beamed, "Well, dear over cautious earth girl. With our dolphin heritage, we can swim anytime we want. So let's go get our flippers wet!"

Sara said, "Well ok, let's go up to our rooms and change into our swimming suits."

By then Selena had her blouse totally unbuttoned and was groping behind her back to try to unhook her already detested, dratted bra, made a pouty face clicked impatiently, moaned and beamed, "Oh, that…"

After Sara, Selena and Glinda put on their swimsuits, Sara said, "Oh no, I forgot about your blowholes and with these scooped backed suits, your blowholes will be completely visible."

Glinda clicked, whistled and beamed, "I totally overlooked that."

Selena pouted, squeaked and beamed, "Oh, let's just go anyway. No one is really going to notice or care."

Sara reluctantly agreed as she thought to her amigas, "I sure hope not."

But she was thinking, "Ok, if it was just one of them, we could pass it off as some kind of unhealed wound but with three of them, it'll be obvious that their blowholes are some kind of weird not human characteristic on their backs."

Glinda reading Sara's worried thoughts beamed, "Sara, even if anyone sees us, they probably would not comment on our uh, Delphin characteristics."

Sara said to Selena and Glinda, "You are probably right. It's just that I am committed to protecting you at all costs." Glinda squeaked, clicked contentedly as she hugged her earthly daughter. As Glinda and Selena then headed over to their connected suite room to meet Arthur, Sara said, "Wait a minute." She went to the table and picked up the phone and asked for room 1225 - which was right across the hall from them.

The male voice answered, "Yes Miss Winchester?" Sara told her secret service agents, "We are going for a swim. So please get ready."

"Yes Ma'am" answered the agent. After he hung up the phone he leered and said to his partner, "Well, at least we get to see Sara and those two really gorgeous south American babes in swim suits today."

Sara went into the large walk-in closet, opened it and took the two terrycloth bathrobes off their hangers. She handed them to Glinda and Selena and thought, "We have to wear these whenever we go in hotel public places in our bathing suits.

Selena donning her robe beamed, "Sara, where is yours?" Sara grinned and said, "It's in Arthur's closet."

Glinda smiled as she concluded, "That makes sense that there would only be two robes in each suite." Glinda beamed to Sara, "Do all hotels have robes like these nice soft ones?"

Sara frowned and said, "Oh no, these nice terrycloth robes are only made available in very expensive hotels and aboard cruise ships.

Selena beamed in, "Cruise ships? What are they Sara?"

Sara smiled, recalling a romantic cruise she and a college boyfriend had taken from LA to Hawaii and back aboard Matson Line SS Lurline just before the war. She then said, "Well, they are really only giant floating deluxe hotels that passengers use to travel on the oceans to go like, for instance, from California to Hawaii or from New York City across the Atlantic Ocean to England or France. Since the voyage takes several days, the big ships are designed and built to be giant deluxe floating hotels."

Glinda became very curious about cruising and beamed, "Sara, do the passengers have to wear their robes before they jump overboard to swim in the sea?"

Sara laughed as she said, "Oh no, Glinda. There are fresh water and sea water swimming pools aboard the ships. The cruise ships never stop for the passengers to swim in the ocean."

Selena beamed, "If I had a cruise ship I would make many stops for people to enjoy swimming in the sea!"

When they came into their other suite they found Arthur clad in the Hawaiian blue and white flowered swim shorts that Sara had picked out for him. As he turned around, Sara thought, "Oh my gosh! What can we do about concealing your blowholes?"

Arthur clicked a short series and beamed, "Sara, I have thought about this." He opened his backpack on his bed and pulled out a white tube with an orange mark on it. As he did so, Glinda beamed, "Of course husband and fearless leader, you are a genius!"

Sara looking with total curiosity at Arthur asked, "Oh my gosh, what is that?"

Arthur smiled and beamed, "Well to make a long medical explanation short; Since we are so closely related in our DNA to you humans and our dolphins, we can, just like dolphins, heal wounds naturally and mostly painlessly and without any infections using our base stem cells in our own bodies. So this tube activates and really speeds up our super rapid regeneration's or just for temporary fill in cover for wounds."

Arthur commanded Selena to turn around. As he slowly passed the tube over her blow hole, it began to be covered with her exact flesh colored material. Arthur whistled happily and clicked rapidly as he finished concealing his daughter's blowhole, "OK Selena, remember that if you squeal, trill or whistle too hard, you might blow a hole in this emergency flesh patch."

back.

 Selena grinned as she pirouetted to show off her new perfect human "Ok" beamed Arthur, "Next!"

 Glinda, still trilling in merriment, presented her back to her husband to conceal her blowhole.

Sara said, "This is totally amazing. We have so much that we can learn from you."

Glinda took the tube and beamed, "Ok your Majesty turn around." As she was passing the tube over her husband's blowhole, she beamed, "Oh Amador!" squeak, "Its run out of flesh. Now what are we going to do? I did not think to pack my flesh aid tube. Selena did you bring yours?"

Selena shook her head and beamed, "I had not thought we would need it dad."

Arthur kind of scowled, clicked harshly and beamed to his daughter, "Dad? What is a dad?"

Selena squealed, pointed her finger at her king father clicked merrily and beamed, "Oh that's an earth word for you my dear daddy, father, poppa, Majestyo, Daddy-o!"

Sara still amazed at the alien first aid capabilities said, "I think I know what we can do. If anyone looks or says anything, we can simply say that it's just an old war wound our hero received during, uh, his services as a submarine captain."

Glinda beamed to Sara "You are so clever earth daughter." Selena pouted, squeaked and beamed, "Like me too!"

Sara asked Arthur, "So how long does your first aid, uh, flesh aid patch stay on?"

Arthur smiled and beamed, "As long as we live if necessary. It's not just a bandage, Sara, it becomes a living part of our skin."

Sara was fascinated as she asked. "OK, how do you remove it as the wound heals?

Glinda joined in and beamed, "Well, we do have another sonic laser device which can easily and painlessly remove these patches. We can use it to speed up to stop bleeding and infections just like our natural stem cells do if we are wounded. Our earth dolphin cousins do this same incredibly rapid healing naturally. Even a big shark bite is naturally healed with no pain or infections within only a month. Our Flesh aid works as an all porpoise uh, purpose catalyst in situations for wounds and also fortunately for cosmetics just like we need now."

Glinda, in fun, then puffed up her cheeks, crossed her eyes and tried to squeak and beamed, "We can never squeak and squeal again…" They all, with clicks and Sara's laughter, cracked up at Glinda's very funny face.

Suddenly, Sara became quiet and serious as she pointed to her aliens flip feet. She said, "Oh My God, in our worrying about your blowholes, we forgot all about your feet."

Glinda looked a bit perplexed. As she was trying to let out a blowhole moan she got an inspired look on her face and beamed, "Well, we could wear the special wide sneakers, as you call them that your navy cobbler modified for us."

Sara smiled and said, "OK then, let's go swimming."

They headed down the magnificent carpeted hallway towards the grand elevators. Sara looked over her shoulder and as expected there were the two secret service agents dutifully wearing aloha shirts, swim trunks, sandals, and terry cloth robes to hide their side arms. They also wore Rayex pilot type dark glasses. Sara looked at Selena who was obviously very down and as she took Selena's hand she thought, "What's wrong little sister?"

Selena beamed to all, "I, I… just really realize how long it's going to take us to change our habits and re-adjust to these new ways of having to constantly think, remember and worry if we are going to expose our alieness to you earthlings."

Sara, knew very well what complete free spirits her Delphinians were, thought to all, "I know it's very difficult to re-adjust and believe me, soon we will get you all acclimated on Water Island and for real life in California. I know life will become so much easier and freer for you." Sara hugged Selena who was then almost in tears.

Glinda beamed, "Come on Selena girl. Let's go enjoy a refreshing swim. You know playing in the water and sun always makes you a happy Delphin girl."

They exited the elevator and passed unnoticed through the lobby and passed through the arching glass portico doors. Sara was the first to notice a bunch of reporters with cameras and also a newsreel movie camera at the building side of the pool. Everyone was gathered around a really lovely looking dark haired young woman who was lounging on the flowered mattress of a pine wood sun chair. Sara thought to her aliens, "Hummmm I wonder who she is? She must be some famous movie star, model or a princess."

Selena after taking in the scene with so much attention being paid to the beautiful woman beamed, "Look at her uh, swim suit. It's kind of like the bra and panties you gave us to wear. Sara, can we please wear our bra and panties the next time we go swimming? This one piece swim suit feels like one of our spacesuit undergarments that's always squeezing and chafing me."

Sara then realized that of course, the Delphinians had spacesuits to go out to repair their spaceship. "Duh!" Sara had seen the bikini that the shapely young woman was wearing and she said to her alien girlfriends, "That is called a bikini swim suit. It's a new idea from France and it's a very tiny two piece swimsuit. It covers our uh, sexy parts but sure shows off our bodies at the beach or while we are swimming. I think I would be really embarrassed to wear one in public."

Selena beamed, "Oh no Sara, I think it's perfect for sun and swimming. Can I go ask her where I can get one?"

Sara realizing the risk from all the reporters and cameras thought, "No, Selena, there are too many reporters and cameras here." Sara thought to her family, "Uh, please excuse me for a moment." She went up to the two secret service agents and scolded, "Hey you guys! Keep your eyes on us and not on that gorgeous plaything, ok?" She added, "Be sure not to let any of those reporters near us. Tell them it's a visiting South American family and nothing else. If you have to show your holstered guns under your aloha shirts to mean business, do it!" The two agents looked directly into the eyes of their no nonsense, swim suited, gorgeous, Commander Sara and said, "Yes Ma'am!"

Selena pouted and beamed, "Ok, enough of this, squeak squeak, ever- present exposure to dangers. Let's go enjoy our swim!" She untied and dropped her terrycloth robe on one of the chaise lounges. From the side of the pool she made a perfect, unbelievable arching 6 foot swan dive into the pool, red sneakers and all. When she surfaced, Glinda telepathically read that her daughter was trying to let out a joyful squeal but of course her flesh patch stopped her. Selena quickly forgot about her patch and began swimming at an almost unbelievable speed down the length of the lovely pool that paralleled most of the south side of the hotel.

Glinda, in her blue sneakers, and Arthur in his white sneakers, disrobed and also made equally perfect 6 foot arching swan dives into the magnificent and cool pool.

Sara took off her robe, folded it neatly and placed it on the chaise lounge. Then, after pulling on her traditional white Playtex swim cap she tipi toed down the tiled pool stairs and began doing the traditional crawl stroke towards her aliens. As they swam past the crowd of reporters gawking and filming the starlet, Sara looked carefully at her and thought to her aliens, "Gosh, I think that is Jane

Russell who is the current starlet girlfriend of Howard Hughes. Maybe they are both staying here now."

Selena beamed to Sara, "Who is Howard Hughes?"

Sara recalling that she had just connected him to President Truman thought, "Uh, he is a famous pilot, airplane manufacturer and also a famous movie producer and that beautiful young woman is his uh, current girlfriend. I think that she is only about 25 and she stars in some motion pictures that he makes."

Glinda, relishing floating on her back beamed to Sara, "Star? Is that like one of the stars in space Sara?"

Sara smiled and continued thinking back to her aliens, "Oh, no, people who act in the movies are called stars because stars shine so brilliantly. It's probably like when you see acted out stories on your ship's view screens. Those people who play characters in your, uh digital movies are the main players or stars in the show."

Glinda looked downcast as she slowly clicked and beamed to Sara, "We only have technical, space nav, medical and other boring things to watch on our screens along with the ancient historic images that we showed you of our home world that is now probably long gone. Everyone aboard Lifestar is our emotional fulfillment and I guess also in some ways our entertainment as we share collective histories, personal stories and love energies with each other. It's kind of like if you humans, in your minds, could go back in time and share your whole collective histories; emotions of happiness and sadness with each other and all of your life dreams."

Sara thought back to Glinda, "Wow, but isn't that like not having any diversions and entertainment or... privacy?"

Glinda grinned and beamed to her heart's earth daughter, "Well in some ways you are quite right Sara. I hope we can learn more about your movies soon. They seem to be your vicarious replacement for emotional stimulation and sharing since you humans apparently lack our total empathic and telepathic abilities."

Sara thought back, "Well, I must take you to a movie as soon as possible. I will ask the concierge if there is a movie theatre close to our hotel and I will take you, Arthur and Selena on a date to see a movie."

Glinda clicked and beamed, "I think I ate some of those dates that you described for me at the buffet table."

Sara laughed as she thought to her alien mom, "A date is when two or more people go out to enjoy doing something together. If I had a boyfriend and he said, Ok, let's go out next uh, Friday night to a movie. He was setting a particular day and time for us to get together to enjoy going out. So a day on our calendars is also called a date, like today is, Thursday, the 18th of March, 1948."

Selena back near the shallow end of the long pool beamed, "OK, I wanna go on a date with my earth boy friend."

Glinda tried to squeal as she beamed to all, "Selena you don't have an earth boyfriend yet."

Selena beamed back to all, "I will after I can get myself one of those bikinis."

Everyone tried to laugh but the only one who could squeak was Arthur with his uncovered blowhole.

Glinda clicked with annoyance and beamed, "I will be so glad when we can remove these flesh patches."

Glinda was only about 35 feet (12 meters) away from Selena suddenly looked over towards her daughter. At almost the same instant, she was not swimming but seemed to be flying on the surface of the water towards Selena.

Sara and Arthur quickly followed and they got to where Glinda and Selena were now clicking excitedly in alarm while standing in the shallow waist deep water. Glinda was looking into Selena's now painfully contorted face and beaming, "What's the matter? Are you OK? You sent out such a desperate and surprised sonic wail to us. What happened?"

Sara was fortunately included in this vital telepathic conversation also reached out to hold Selena as she asked, "Selena, what's happened?"

Selena was recovering her composure and beamed to her mom, "Look at my eyes. They are hurting and really stinging." Sara and Glinda could see that Selena's eyes had become terribly inflamed and puffy to the point they were somewhat swollen shut."

Glinda holding her daughter's head in each palm probed again, "Selena ! Exactly what happened?"

Selena beamed that she had decided to swim the length of the 225 feet pool underwater and shortly after she opened her eyes underwater, they began really burning.

Sara realized that it must be the chlorine in the pool and she quickly said to her aliens. "It's the chlorine, a strong chemical we put into pools to kill bacteria because, well, many people simply pee in the pool instead of getting out to go use the toilet!"

Glinda looked astoundedly at Sara and then surprisingly, she, Arthur and even smarting Selena began smiling, clicking and trying to squeak in merriment the way Arthur was doing as quietly and carefully as he could, clicking and letting out short laughter squeals. Sara stood there in the water astounded and confused at their laughter over Selena getting her eyes badly irritated by the pool water.

Glinda beamed to Sara, "I'm sorry Sara. We laugh because of you humans putting chemicals in water to kill pee bacteria. How idiosyncratic. Just like you thinking you have to wait an hour after eating to swim."

Glinda placed her right hand over her daughter's eyes and Sara could see that she was really concentrating. In about 12 seconds Glinda removed her hand from Selena's eyes and beamed to all, "We are well."

Sara watched dumbfounded. She saw Selena open her now totally healed and clear beautiful blue eyes and beam, "Ahhhhh, thanks mom! I am ok now."

Sara looked at her friend's eye area and saw the extremely faint outline of a very light blue colored, promptly fading, hand imprint from Glinda's hand.

Sara thought to her alien family, "Wow, I am so glad that Selena is ok now. Here are the shallow end steps." She led the alien trio up the tiled exit stairs to walk back down the length of the pool to their chaises to get their robes. Sara noticed that the two secret service men had obeyed her orders to guard them and she smiled and nodded an approval to them as she looked over her left shoulder.

The trio of aliens was squishing along in their now wet and soggy wide tennies along with barefoot Sara. As they passed behind Jane's chaise lounge near the poolside crowd of reporters. Selena took a chance, reached out and gently touched Jane's shoulder and beamed to the lovely dark haired movie star, "Jane Russell, you are very lovely in your sexy tiny bikini, my star sister."

Jane receiving this in her head thought that someone must of said that to her. She quickly sat up. then stood up from her lounge and turned to the aliens and Sara and sweetly asked, "OK, who just said that to me?"

Selena clicked a few rapid alarm clicks and looked pleadingly at Glinda and then at Jane and, made like a grinning shrugging simpleton, pointed to her mouth and made a few un-intelligible noises as Sara stepped in and said, "Uh, hi Miss Russell, these are my friends from South America and they, um, because of a genetic defect, cannot talk."

Jane smiled and reached out her hand to Selena's arm and said, "Oh darling, I'm so sorry. Did you enjoy your swim?" Selena tying to mute her happy clicks and not being able to reply just made a big wide grin and enthusiastically nodded her head up and down.

Jane said, "Well as you know, I am Jane Russell and my boyfriend Howard and I flew down here from Hollywood yesterday for a few days to enjoy some Florida sun and sand. Howard is also supposed to have some kind of important meeting with some VIP government guy here tomorrow."

Sara, knew that her boss, the President, and Howard Hughes were golf nuts, So of course she immediately realized the reason for Truman's saying that he wanted to fly up to Miami to enjoy some golf at the Biltmore's magnificent golf course on Friday.

Sara extended her hand and right after she introduced herself as Sara Winchester she realized that she had no last names for her aliens. she, being the quick-witted female that she was, did not miss a beat as she introduced the aliens. "Miss Russell, this is Arthur Hernandez and his wife Glinda and their appreciative of your beauty, daughter, Selena."

Glinda smiled and glanced at Sara after she had shaken Jane's hand and beamed, "Good quick thinking Sara!"

After the cordial introductions, Jane asked Sara and her amigos from South America, "Would you like to join me for a drink inside and away from this sun and from all of these damn pesky drug store cowboy reporters?"

Sara glanced at the insatiable paparazzi's growing interest in her aliens and their soggy sneakers, winked at Jane and said, "We sure would Miss Russell. It is getting rather hot and really too crowded out here."

Sara noticed that some of the reporters were scribbling in their notepads. A few had raised their cameras and the cinematographer was filming her and her aliens with his Auricon 16mm, large 400 foot magazine newsreel camera, while his associate was holding up the short boom microphone in front of Sara and Jane and the aliens.

Jane knowing full well that they needed to get away from the reporters, reached for her robe and said to Sara, "Great! I'll see you." The reporters began to clamor to follow them, Sara looked at her secret service agents, raised her eyebrows and gave a curt nod. The agents moved in on the mob of reporters and barred their way from following their VIP's. Jane, Sara and her aliens walked and squished along towards the hotel lobby entrance.

Jane leaned over to Sara and said, "Honey, those are some formidable guard dogs your South American's have.

Sara smiled and said for all to hear, "All in the name of privacy and security." Sara knew how Howard Hughes always warily guarded his women leaned over to Jane and asked, "Uh, where are your guard dogs?"

Jane laughed and replied, "I finally persuaded Howard to leave them home for a welcome change over this nice long weekend."

Sara smiled and said, "Hummmm... we'll meet you at the bar in about an hour. Is that ok?"

Jane replied, "That would be nice, maybe I can get Howard to join us."

The aliens put on their terrycloth robes and were squishing back into the lobby towards the elevator. A bellboy in uniform came over to them and began fussily scolding and demanding that the trio remove their wet shoes. The self-important young upstart was sure shocked as two secret service agents grabbed him by each arm and roughly hauled him off to the side. Shortly after, the agents caught up with their charges waiting at the elevator. Sara grinned and asked, "Was he any trouble?" The lead agent smirked as he said, "No Miss Sara, that little twerp was no trouble at all."

After Selena and Sara left Arthur and Glinda in their suite to shower and change, Selena dropped her robe, peeled off her swimsuit, looked tiredly at Sara and beamed, "Would you mind helping me wash my back?"

Sara, by now was getting better accustomed to Selena's innocence and her almost total lack of inhibitions, dropped her robe and stripped off her swimsuit to join her alien sister in the impressive glass door and tile walled shower. After the girls showered and helped each other wash their hair, Selena said, "I am so glad to get that horrible chemical, what did you call it Sara? Chlorine washed off of my skin." Selena clicked rapidly and beamed, "I can still taste it in my mouth. I do hope that it's not done any permanent damage to me."

Sara smiled as she dried off and wrapped her hair in a towel turban said, "I guess your mom is also a medico for your ship."

Selena beamed, "Oh yes, mom and our ship doctors, nurses and nutritionists have been taking good care of us and what little is left of the fifth generation."

Selena was standing there wide eyed as she clicked and beamed, "That is amazing how you wrap your hair like that to soak up the water. Please show me how to do that Sara." Sara, again remembering where her little alien sister had come from, picked up a towel and was wrapping it turban style around Selena's semi curly, wet, dark brown hair she asked, "Selena, don't you have towels aboard Lifestar?"

Selena now thoroughly enjoying the attention she was getting, clicked excitedly and beamed, "Sara, we have only small towels. Primarily we have uh, what you might call infrared beams to stand under as we dry off with them and also a few uh, ceiling mounted warm air blowers in all of our shower areas. So I really love these nice big fluffy towels and especially now you showing me this, what do you call it?"

Sara smiled as she placed both hands on each side of Selena's wrapped hair and said, "It's called a turban, named after what a lot of middle eastern and some hindu men wear. Here Selena. Now you rub like this to dry your hair."

Selena was standing there vigorously rubbing her toweled head when Sara picked up the new fangled electric hair dryer and switched it on.

As Selena heard the fairly high pitched whirring of its electric blower motor, she would have let out a frightened squeal if her blowhole had not been stoppered up with the fleshaid. Sara grinned and began the ritual of drying her own hair as she also ran her very wide toothed comb gently through her hair. Sara thought instead of trying talk over the noise of the hair drier, "Selena, it's only a heated air blower to dry our hair. They are a fairly new invention and are usually available in high class hotels like this."

Selena was clicking softly and transfixed as she tentatively ran her fingers across the opening to the blower. Sara jerked the dryer away and said, "Oh be careful! It's really hot!" Sara finished towel blotting her neck and breasts and told Selena to sit on the bathroom seat. She began waving the hair drier over Selena's hair and handed the large comb to Selena and said, "OK, I'll blow dry as you comb through your hair. Remember Selena never use this in the shower, nor bathtub, nor in contact with any water because the electricity flows through water and a shock could kill you."

Selena looked curiously and cautiously at the hair dryer beamed, "Sara why then, do you humans allow the construction of such a deadly devise?"

Sara shrugged her shoulders and said, "I don't know my safety minded little Delphinian. I have read that sadly, many women and girls are killed each year from electric shock while simply drying their hair. Sometime just standing on a wet floor is enough to complete the circuit."

By the time everyone had showered and dressed it was almost 5pm. Sara asked her aliens, "Shall we go on down to meet Jane, have a drink and see if Howard Hughes is going to join us?"

Arthur and Glinda beamed, "OK, let's go." Selena took Sara's hand after they walked out of their door. They found one of their two secret service agents now dressed in slacks and his aloha shirt patiently sitting in a straight back chair right outside their doorway. Sara glanced at him and he nodded to her and made the ok sign with his thumb and index finger. Glinda noticed the exchange clicked and beamed to Sara, "Hummmm, good non verbal communication and I guess that the ok sign is very customary here on earth." She made the sign to Sara and to the now trailing agents.

After they exited the elevator, Sara noticed that the obnoxious bellboy had been replaced with a different guy. She thought to herself, "The empowerment of egocentric, petty people is the ruin of our society. I shudder to speculate what workers will be like in 50 years?"

Glinda had as usual picked up on Sara's thoughts beamed, "Sara we went through that thousands of years ago, thank Amador that we now have bred a mostly well behaved Delphs with no such absurd self important trivial alpha males."

After entering the foyer of the huge bar area, Sara saw Jane sitting with a black haired man wearing a casual linen beige jacket, white trousers and of all things, white tennis shoes. When Jane saw them, she stood and beckoned Sara to come over with her friends. As they approached, Howard Hughes painfully stood and extended his hand to Sara. He, as Sara introduced the alien trio, took in turn the hands of Glinda, Arthur and Selena and said in his soft Texan accent, "You have no idea how pleased I am to finally meet you. Jane has told me about your rude encounters with the paparazzi this afternoon. My office in Hollywood will be contacting their editors, and newsreel producers in no ambiguous terms."

Sara had reminded all of the aliens to bring their scribble notepads so that they could mock up having to write to Mr. Hughes. After everyone sat down, Howard further aroused Sara's suspicions when he said, "I am told that none of you drink. Well good then, neither do I. I only drink milk."

Sara glanced a little nervously at Mr. Hughes and at her alien trio and thought, "How did he know that? Don't let on that you know he knows more about us than we thought." But Sara knew almost for sure that, as brilliant and eccentric as Howard Hughes was that he most assuredly, had been sworn to secrecy by President Truman.

Howard then realized that he had let the alien cat out of the bag, glanced at Jane and said, "Jane honey, why don't you go see if you can round us up a waitress over there."

Jane realizing that he wanted her out of the way for a moment stood, bent over and kissed his head and said, "Of course darling. I'll be back in ten minutes. I'm going to the powder room." Jane looked at Glinda, Selena and Sara and asked, "Would you two latina ladies like to join me?" Glinda and Selena clicked and looked imploringly at Sara as Selena beamed, "Sara, what is a powder room?"

Sara smiled and thought, "Don't worry it's only a bathroom." Sara said, "I'm ok, but why don't you two go with Jane. Arthur and I will be right here."

As soon as the women left, Howard smiled and extended his hand to Arthur saying, "I am so thrilled to finally meet you your Majesty. I have so many questions I'd like to ask of you."

Arthur had been reading Howard's mind and beamed to the eccentric genius, "I am very glad to meet you too Mr. Hughes. Mr. Truman has told us that you are going to be our chief technological liaison and help us in our re- settleing on Earth."

Howard replied, "Yes, I am so glad to be included in your homecoming. You know Arthur I have one question that's been stuck in my mind ever since I was informed by President Truman of your presence on Earth. How in God's name, out of billions of stars, did you find Earth? I am supposing that you needed a water world like ours to come to."

Arthur smiled, clicked contentedly and nodded his head at the great intellect of Mr. Hughes. Arthur then beamed, "I am going to let our star ship chief astronomer Vicky beam that answer to you. It is certainly very astute of you to ask such a question since we are dealing with a distance of just over 97 light years."

Howard Hughes seemed momentarily taken aback as he heard a female voice in his head. "Hello Mr. Hughes. I am Vicky, the chief astronomer and astrogator for this sixth generation. I certainly look forward to meeting you in person someday soon. We used a unique and clever method, known as what you would probably call spectra polarimetry to examine your planet's light in distinct polarized light. As you may know Howard, planets shine in polarized light while stars do not. So in your weak earthshine, we found that bio signatures on Earth showed up fairly well in your reflected light. So we studied the color and degree of polarization of the light that was reflected from the Earth. We were able to distinguish details and changes on your planet's surface, and we also observed that Earth's atmosphere is partly cloudy. On the surface, we distinguished land surfaces and apparently very large ocean surfaces. We even saw signatures of your vegetation and we could essentially see the greenness of your oxygen providing vegetation canopies.

We knew that precise usage of spectro polarmetric techniques has excellent promise for studying exoplanets as a pathway toward finding primitive bio signatures on other distant planets because of how difficult it is to directly observe such faint light signatures from distant alien planets. This Mr Hughes, is because, the light from a distant exoplanet is so overwhelmed by the glare of its host star, it's very difficult to analyze. Its a bit like trying to study a grain of dust beside a 500 watt light bulb from miles, uh kilometers away. The light reflected by a planet is polarized, while the light from the host star is not. Our polarmetric techniques helped us to pick out and thoroughly analyze the faint reflected light of your beautiful water world from your G-2 V yellowish starlight."

But what cinched it for us was that as we drew nearer to your sol system The last generation science officers and astro navigators intercepted some incredibly powerful radio signals coming from, as we later learned, your now deceased Nikola Tesla's facility in the state you call Colorado.

We really hope that you can someday give us more information about that amazing genius who was so far ahead of his time. We sometimes speculate that he might have been a displaced future time traveler."

Howard Hughes now humbled and awed said, "Oh gosh, that is so logical and truly brilliant. I am so glad that you found us and chose to come here. But Vicki, I am now really curious. Did you do your polar metric analysis from one of your ground based observatories or did you accomplish it after you were in space?"

Vicki squeaked in delight at the astuteness of Howard Hughes and beamed, "Oh, Howard… we did all of our searching for our new home water world from our starship. Because, as you can imagine, any planet's atmosphere absorbs and distorts, you know twinkles, the starlight at most energy wavelengths and of course, once we were up in space, we could study the exact undistorted wavelengths and spectral energies that we needed."

Howard, speechless just looked at Arthur and Sara as he simply thought back to astronomer, Vicki, "I am totally impressed and amazed and believe you me, the President and I will do all that we can to help you safely re-settle here on your new home world. I have already deposited 25 million dollars into a special secret, interest earning, trust fund for all of you to get started here on our planet.”

Arthur as pod leader made a descending low whistle and beamed to Howard, “Oh my goodness Mr. Hughes that is really very generous of you and we thank you for your exceptional generosity and assistance.”

Arthur paused, smiled and thought only to Glinda and Selena who were still in the powder room with Jane “Oh my stars and dear Amador, that’s $156,250 for each of us.”

Glinda looked stealthily at Selena and beamed back to her husband, “Well, unfortunately for secrecy about our fortune. We must just add that to the billions we have aboard Lifestar now in jewels and gold that we have recovered from some of their sunken Spanish galleons. If we were to let Mr. Hughes or others know how wealthy we already are, we would probably lose their expectations for us and perhaps their helping us to land on Earth.” But my King Midas Delphinian, we must pay him back someday with interest in the future.

Arthur grinned like Midas, but repressing his squeals and clicks, as he thought back to Glinda and Selena, “I think that now we must be the richest aliens on earth.”

Selena grinned and beamed, “So just like Sara says, finders keepers, losers weepers! So, squeak, squeak, squeak, we could buy their Fort Knox and hardly miss any of our wealth.”

Sara, was sitting with Arthur and Howard and still mesmerized and awed as she tried to comprehend their incredible ahead of its time dialogue as Howard listened and then soon just gave up verbalizing as Vicki beamed as he, quickly adopted Sara’s simplicity in just thinking back to her aliens. She thought to herself, “Wow, that Howard is indeed some kind of genius. It’s almost like he was kind of an advanced alien himself. Maybe he crash landed here on earth in Texas back in 1905 and was like the Superman Clark Kent - an alien baby adopted by a kindly earth couple. But in Howard’s case, if he was an alien baby, he was fortunately adopted by some very, very rich Texas oil tool bit making parents.” Its sad. I remember my dad telling me that while Howard was a young student at the Thatcher School in Ojai. His poor mother died during what was supposed to be just routiene surgery in Houston.

So while Sara could not decipher the flow of the thoughts of Howard, Arthur and Vicki as they obviously ecstatically got into even way more ahead of the times subject matter, Sara stood and said, “Excuse me gentlemen and Vicki above, I think I shall join the girls in the powder room too.”

Howard stood and said, “By all means Commander, uh Miss Winchester, by all means. By the way, I had lunch with your father at the Paramount studio cafeteria last week.” Then he gave a big Texas grin.“I am finding this uh, mind talking er, telepathy completely bypasses my horrible deafness ! I now sure that wish I could communicate with everybody just like this…”

After Glinda, Selena, Sara and Jane returned from their chat in the powder room, a really cute latina waitress arrived at their table and asked, “What would you ladies and gentlemen like to drink before dinner?” Since none of them drank alcohol, Howard said, “Well, I guess they will all have Cokes and I will have a cold, unopened bottle of milk please.”

After the cokes and milk arrived, Arthur, for miss Russel's sake took out his note pad and scribbled, "We will toast Mr. Hughes and the lovely Jane from your south American amigos." He handed the note to Howard. Howard read the note aloud for Jane's benefit, raised his milk bottle and said, "Yes of course, a toast to happy landings."

Jane, sipping her Coke and knowing that Howard never drank smiled and thought to herself, "I sure miss my usual Hollywood social circles and being able to drink champagne and beer."

Glinda picked up on Jane's frustration at being in this non drinking circle and beamed to Sara, "It seems our Jane starlet quite understandably feels positively out of place with her Howard being so absorbed with us aliens."

Sara was quickly able to see that this evening was going to become a complete awkward calamity so she thought to her aliens, "Well, all here know about us except for Miss Russell."

She looked at Jane, smiled and encouragingly said, "So, maybe it's better that we girls all go to the movies and let Howard and Arthur enjoy their technical human uh, man talk."

Jane was totally relived from being stuck in this one-sided group, said, "That is a perfectly wonderful idea! I will meet you all in the lobby in about 10 minutes, ok?" Sara felt relieved and momentarily held Jane's hands and smiled as she said, "Perfecto amiga." Glinda and Selena just grinned and nodded their heads in agreement.

Glinda beamed to Arthur, "Would that be alright dear?"

Arthur smiled as he beamed, "I guess it would be best to save anymore of this awkwardness. But, be sure to beam to me all about the movie later."

Sara walked over to the two secret service agents and asked, "Do you guys have any more agents available?"

The lead agent said, "Sure Miss Sara." Picking up his walkie talkie radio he said, "I will call right now for a couple more to come from Miami. Why, what's up?"

Sara explained, "The gentlemen have business to talk about and we girls have decided to go to a movie."

The old and experienced agent smiled and simply said, "OK, got it. Two of us will keep everyone covered and protected here and I'll assign myself, Joe and one more agent as driver, for the movie Miss Sara. I'll call right now for your limo." As she returned to the group, Sara thought, "OK I got our car and security all arranged."

Arthur beamed privately to Glinda, "Alright. Now, I will try to find out what this remarkable earth genius has in mind. Please be careful out there in the real world and take care of you, Selena and Sara too."

Glinda bent over and briefly touched both sides of her husband's head and beamed all of her, Selena's and some of Sara's love energies now growing inside her true heart and spirit to him.

Mr. Hughes stood, smiled slightly embarrassed and said, "Thank you ladies. I simply could not accomplish our indispensable initial conversations if Jane had been here."

CHAPTER 25 MOVIES, CHESTERFIELDS AND DONUTS

When Sara and her aliens returned to the hotel lobby they found Jane standing at the concierge. As they stood beside her Sara said, "Did you find out if there is theatre near here?"

Jane answered, "Yes there is. I have stayed here a couple of times in the past and the Miracle Theatre is just about 2 miles from the hotel driveway entrance."

Sara turned to the concierge clerk and asked, "Do you know what is playing there tonight?"

The clerk, grinning from ear to ear, leered at Jane and said, "Young Widow is playing tonight and it stars this gorgeous actress standing right beside you." The clerk then asked Jane for her autograph.

As the ladies walked away from the concierge desk, Selena beamed to Sara, "Why did that man ask Jane to sign that piece of paper?"

Sara smiled and thought, "As soon as we get into our car I will explain."

Glinda beamed, "I trust so. Sara you humans have such different ways of doing things. I sometimes wonder if we will ever manage to master all of it."

Sara being the anthropologist that she was thought, "I know it's very confusing and overwhelming but, day by day, you will understand and learn our ways. I think these days of your first visit with me are the best realistic way to start to introduce you to some of our too unaccustomed ways. Then, after you and your people have been on Earth for only about one generation, all will have adapted almost totally to be proficient and really at home with our living and social customs here on your new planet."

Glinda clicked softly and beamed to Sara, "You appreciate that all of us are sub consciously streaming our experiences back to those aboard Lifestar. So at least our ongoing experiences and now, this realistic initial earth adventure is really vital and useful for all of us."

Sara thought, "Glinda it is fantastic that you all can link minds like you do." Sara looked over at Jane who was beckoning all of them to come to the taxi she had found. As soon as Sara and her aliens walked up to the cab, Sara told Jane, "Oh no, please join us. Our limo will be here in just a few minutes."

Jane looked kind of put off for a moment but she half grinned, groaned and said, "Oh… ok… uh, alright … but… I dread riding in limos. Every time I ride in one… I feel just like I am going to my own funeral!" In a few minutes, a four door, six passenger black Cadillac limo pulled in under the portico. When it stopped, the front passenger door opened and one of the secret service agents got out and opened the rear door for the ladies. Sara said, "You ladies go first. I will sit in the jump seat."

As Jane, who had been in countless limos had settled into her rear forward facing seat next to Glinda and Selena she saw that the agent in an aloha shirt and khaki slacks was sitting in the driver side rear facing jump seat next to rear facing Sara. She was also perplexed to discover that there were three telephones in the vehicle and that one of them was black and the other was yellow and the other one of was red. She exclaimed, "Oh my goodness Sara, this limo is some kind of ride! Is it yours?"

Sara laughed and said, "Oh no Miss Russell, it belongs to my, uh, employer."

Jane raised her eyebrow and just as she began to say something else, her eyes squinted as she looked at the engraved emblem on the small glass window separating the driver and passenger compartment. She exclaimed, "Say, isn't that… Why goodness, oh my gosh Sara!" isn't that the seal of the president!"

Sara could do nothing but grin and say, "Well, yes Miss Russell, uh Jane. This is an official government vehicle and your Mr. Hughes is now meeting with a very important, uh, South American leader. In fact, the president himself will be here tomorrow to enjoy a round of golf and further talks with your Mr. Hughes and Mr. Hernandez." Sara put her finger across her lips and said, "But please Jane, you have been with Howard at other important meetings and it's essential that this is kept top secret."

Jane nodded agreeing with Sara and subserviently said, "Of course Sara, mum's the word."

Selena not wanting to interrupt the conversation between the actress and her Sara, beamed to her mom, "I'm so confused and I have so many questions for Sara."

Glinda smiled back at her daughter, suppressed her nervous clicking and beamed, "I know, me too."

Selena beamed to her mother, "How are Arthur and that Mr. Hughes doing?"

Glinda frowned and beamed, "Selena, why aren't you beamed into them too?"

Selena beamed, "Mom, I am so tired of tuning into everyone and everything all the time. I just want to focus on experiencing this moment and enjoy our first movie."

Glinda hugged Selena and beamed, "I think for a nice change, I shall try to relax too princess."

Arthur, fully engrossed with Howard back at the Biltmore beamed in, "It's ok dear, do relax but be sure to at least keep your sonics on so I don't later have to re beam all of this to you and also so that I know you all are ok. Ok?"

Glinda grinned and sighed, "Yes your dear majesty of Earth and the Biltmore Hotel… I noticed that you said you all. That is sure something new from you…"

Arthur grinned and beamed back in the best southern drawl he could, "Yep you betcha and now you all be sure to enjoy yer picture show. You all hear… uh, dear." Selena then let out a soft descending whistle as she beamed, "Oh Amadore, now daddyo wants to be an actor in one of Mr Hughes movies…"

Growing ever more curious about these strange women, Jane, hearing Selena's strange whistle touched her shoulder and asked, "Why dear mute girl, what on earth was that whistle?"

Sara quickly said, "Why Jane that is just her, uh, err, remaining voice box whistle."

Sara to then try to change the subject asked, "So tell me Miss Russell, is the Young Widow your latest movie?"

Jane smiled and said, "Yes, it was released in January. It's ironic that Faith Domergue, Howard's former girlfriend is in it with me. We actually became good friends!"

Sara asked, "How about that western you made, The Outlaw. Has it come out yet?"

Jane winked sensually at Sara and while grinning at Selena and Glinda said, "Oh that one. Yes, that was my first movie and Howard is still fighting with the ridiculous Motion Picture Censor Board in Hollywood about my breasts."

Selena became wide eyed and quickly dug into her purse, pulled out her notepad and pencil and scribbled, "Miss Russell, you certainly have the biggest breasts I have ever seen." Selena was just trying to be a part of the conversation. She got a great big laugh from Jane as she patted Selena's arm and said, "Well honey, they are quite large and that absurd Hollywood movie board thinks Howard had me showing too much of my, uh natural endowments." As she said that the secret service agent was agape with his mouth open staring at Jane's alluring cleavage. Sara scowled, sharply elbowed him and said, "OK well, er, enough about breasts and chests for now, ok?"

Glinda grinning and suppressing her squeaks, beamed to her daughter, "Selena, maybe talking about breasts is not appropriate among humans."

Sara receiving that comment grinned, raised her eyebrows and thought, "At least, usually not in mixed male and female and particularly not in employee - employer company."

Fortunately the limo then pulled up in front of the theatre and Sara gratefully said, "Oh, good, here we are." Her door opened and the agent helped each woman out. The agent sitting in the back exited and as he was standing close to his fellow agent he gestured over his chest and whispered, "Wow, I was like, this close to Jane Russell's boobs!"

Glinda and Selena of course were reading his thoughts and Selena beamed to Sara, who was walking just ahead with Miss Russell, "Sara, what are boobs?"

Sara burst out laughing as she turned around and said, "Selena that's uh, gringo slang for breasts." Jane was no dummy, as endowed as she was, she thought, "Hummmm, Sara just answered a question from Selena that I did not hear."

Sara paid for their 60¢ tickets and they were standing in the lobby. Selena realized that she had better use her notepad, scribbled and tore off a sheet as she beamed to Sara, "What are all of these items for sale at this counter?"

Sara pretended to read Selena's note and said, "These are all candies, ice cream, popcorn and also your beloved Coke. "

Glinda beamed as she too scribbled and tore a sheet off of her notepad, "What is that wonderful odor Sara?"

Sara taking Glinda's note and pretending to read it said, "That is popcorn. Would you and Selena like to try some?"

Selena nodded her head and Glinda smiled. Sara turned to Jane and asked, "Shall we get some popcorn and cokes?"

Jane said, "Yeah that would be swell Sara." Jane was acutely interested in all of the apparent note writing between Sara and her so called mute South American amigas. She thought to herself, "From the way these two dames are acting, you would think that they had never been to a movie before."

Glinda beamed to Sara, "Oh, oh, this earth star is really wondering about us and our fake note writing Sara."

Sara thought back, "Yes, I have noticed her uneasy curiosity. This is a good lesson for us about how we must unfortunately, always be more careful about how we communicate with our notes and how you react to people. But Glinda, have patience and remember, it's going to take time and we have an expression here. Practice makes perfect. Try to relax. As long as no large crowds of people; especially people with cameras, reporter notebooks and newsreel movie cameras, don't notice us doing unusual things, we will be fine."

Glinda, to avoid arousing Miss Russell's curiosity any further, beamed to Sara and Selena, "OK, let's go enjoy the movie and try not to communicate too much.

Sara smiled and said, "Let's get the usherette to find us some good seats. Jane, do you like to sit up front or in the middle?" Jane replied, "Oh I like the middle but, anywhere that the usherette can find us seats together will be swell."

The usherette seated them in the center of the sparsely filled theatre and the house lights dimmed. Selena beamed to Sara, "That is the biggest screen I have ever seen."

Sara sitting just one seat over from Jane looked at Selena and smiled. As the newsreel started, Glinda beamed to Sara and Selena, "It's in black and white. Is there something wrong with their color digital system?"

Sara again looked at Glinda sitting to her right and thought as she squeezed her arm, "Remember I shouldn't answer unspoken questions with Jane sitting here with us."

Glinda gently squeezed Sara's arm and beamed, "OK…"

After the newsreel, the six minute cartoon started. It was a Technicolor cartoon titled Mickey's Delayed Date and as it played, Glinda clicked slowly as she beamed, "Hummmm, I guess this is kind of amusing, but I hope the movie is more interesting…"

Selena beamed back, "Oh look Mickey and his, I guess mouse girlfriend, are going to a theatre just like we are. I kind of like it."

Sara, by then had passed out the cokes, was struggling to hold her drink cup and also all four of the 10¢ popcorn bags. She passed two bags to Jane and asked, "Please give this one to Selena." She passed a bag to Glinda on her right and said, "OK, let's enjoy our popcorn. I have not had the time to enjoy a movie in several months."

As the cartoon was ending, Glinda clicked softly and beamed, "That was kind of cute but did you notice that when Minnie was yelling at Mickey, the telephone handset had no wire attached to it."

Selena squeaked inadvertently and beamed in, "Yeah and Mickey's cane top kept changing."

After the cartoon ended, the feature film started and after it had been running for a few minutes Glinda beamed to Sara, "Don't you have color movies Sara?"

Sara, knew they were safe to communicate by thinking in the dark theatre, thought, "There has been only a few Technicolor films since the war but now days more and more movies are being made in color." Knowing her movie producer and director father's work. Sara thought to Glinda. "The evolving Technicolor movie cameras are huge cumbersome things. They have to hold three different base emulsions to film. Later when they are printed onto a negative. They have to be exactly sandwitched together."

Selena beamed in, "Jane sure looks lovely on the screen. It's astounding to see such a giant picture of someone. You can clearly see every little mark on her face."

Sara chuckled and thought back to her sister, "That's why movie stars all wear so much makeup."

Selena beamed back to Sara, "What is makeup?"

Sara thought, "Have you noticed that bright red color on Miss Russell's lips? That's lipstick makeup. I will show you once we get back to the hotel."

The film had been running for about 15 minutes when a man came in and sat in the seat to Selena's left. He took out his pack of Chesterfields and flicked his Zippo lighter and lit up a cigarette.

Selena almost immediately started coughing and beamed a desperate sonic alert. As Glinda stood and turned to reach for her daughter, she accidentally caused Sara and Jane to spill their drinks and popcorn all over their dresses. Glinda caught a whiff of the cigarette smoke, she too began coughing and hacking and beamed to Sara, "We have to get away from this horrible smoke. It's stopping our breathing."

Sara immediately stood up and took Glinda and Selena's arms and led her aliens away through the aisle. Jane stood and quickly followed asked, "What's wrong Sara? Are they ill?"

Sara said to Jane, "I sure hope not. But, apparently they have some, uh, really severe allergies to that damm cigarette smoke."

The two secret service agents jumped out of their seats in the row behind the ladies and helped Sara guide her aliens up the main aisle and into the theatre lobby. Sara then got her two hacking, and gasping for air aliens, seated on a bench in the lobby and as she looked at Glinda and now really sick looking Selena, she was seriously thinking that maybe they should call an ambulance.

Glinda finally had begun to recover her breath and beamed urgently to Sara, "Is… is here one of those uh, powder rooms here Sara? I can heal myself and Selena but as you know, we must have total privacy."

Sara nodded towards the two on alert secret service agents and said, "Please help them into the ladies room and make sure no one except me enters."

The older agent respecting that these odd visitors of Sara and the president were really important said to Sara, "Ok will do. Do we need an ambulance Miss Sara?"

Sara said, "Noooo, I don't think so, at least so far, not yet. They should be better as soon as they can get some air and, uh, splash water on their faces." Glinda by then was feeling stronger, smiled at the agents and the astounded Jane and just nodded her head in affirmation of Sara's statement.

Sara then commanded the secret service agent to go in and clear the bathroom. He hesitated but he remembered his orders from President Truman to always do exactly and immediately as Commander Winchester asked. He marched bravely straight into the ladies restroom.

The female screams and angry, indignant shouts and curses died down pretty soon after his entrance then seven in a huff women were herded out of the restroom. Sara led Glinda and Selena into the ladies room and as Jane tried to follow, she found one of the burly secret service agents barring her way. She became cross and exclaimed, "Hey fella, those are my friends in there."

The agent shook his head and said, "Sorry Miss Russell but Commander, uh, Miss Winchester said that no one else is to enter."

As soon as Sara, Selena and Glinda entered the restroom, Sara saw several chairs and deco benches. She said, "Here Selena sit on this bench."

Glinda beamed, "Sara, I am feeling a bit better now but because Selena was closest to that, that fool smoker, I must help her first. Are you sure we are going to be alone in here?" Glinda then squealed in disgust as she beamed, "I can still smell the cigarette smoke from those women who were just in here." But as she sniffed the air, she noticed that fortunately the large overhead ceiling fan was dissipating the residual smoke.

Sara said to Glinda, "Yes go ahead. I have a secret service agent guarding the door."

Glinda placed both of her open palms on each side of her daughter's head and as she did so, a very faint blue white glow emanated from her fingers. Sara could see that Glinda was really concentrating and also had begun to perspire on her face as she directed her healing energies to her daughter. After about 30 seconds, Selena began to brighten up and stopped coughing and wheezing.

Sara took Selena's hand and asked, "Are, are you feeling better now?" Selena smiled and beamed to Sara, "I am Ok now. Let me help mom." Selena placed her open palms on the sides of her mother's head and again the strange faint blue white glow started as Selena concentrated and after about

30 seconds Glinda beamed, "We are well again."

Glinda, Selena and Sara all felt in their spirits the relieved happy energies of Arthur, Delnoid, and all the others back on Lifestar who apparently had been hooked into the Delphinian's mind circuits throughout the cigarette fiasco.

Glinda was smiling and beamed to Sara, "Why in the name of Amador do you humans so mistreat and disrespect your bodies Sara?"

Sara looked chagrined and thought, "Smoking is a stupid and foolish really bad habit. But, the tobacco industries that make the cigarettes know that the nicotine in their product is highly addictive and that once a human decides to try to quit smoking it's very difficult."

Sara continued, "I must confess that when I was a teenager I started smoking, because it was portrayed in the movies and other media such as magazines as a sophisticated and a socially cool thing to do. Once you have smoked only about five or six cigarettes you can become addicted to the nicotine and the toxins and poisons begin to build up more and more in your body. I fortunately, only through sheer will power and fear of contaminating my lungs and body, was finally able to quit when I was 19."

Glinda looked somewhat alarmed at Selena and beamed, "Help me Selena."

Selena and Glinda standing on each side of Sara, placed their open palms on Sara's chest and her back and began flowing powerful healing energies into her. After about a minute of the healing energies, Sara saw that Glinda and Selena were both sweating and they were obviously becoming exhausted. Then after removing their healing hands from Sara, Glinda clicked tiredly and stammered, "OK Sara, we have returned your body more or less to its original good condition as it was shortly after you were born earth daughter. So now, once again, "We are well!"

Sara felt re-empowered, fresher and more energetic than she had in years, hugged her alien mother and sister and cried as she said aloud, "Oh God, I feel, I feel just wonderful! Thank you! You have so much you can share with us about healing Glinda"

Just then, one of the secret service agents hesitatingly poked his head in the restroom door and asked, "Is everything Ok Command… uh, Miss Winchester?" Sara whirled around, glared and asked the agent, "How long have you been standing there agent?"

The startled agent stammered, "Uh, I just now looked in on all of you Miss." He said, "The limo is waiting out front and your lady friend seems very upset about all of this, uh, ma'am…"

Sara ordered the agent to leave and asked Glinda, "Are you ok now?" Glinda beamed to Sara, "Yes daughter we are fine now. Not to worry, ok?" Glinda added, "That agent was telling the truth about how long he had been standing there Sara."

Sara thought, "Oh God, I am so glad that he did not see us healing."

Glinda beamed, "Once we get settled on Water Island, I will try to teach you more about our universal natural healing energies Sara. You and most all humans have them too but they are not yet understood or developed or believed in by your people yet."

Sara thought to her alien mother figure, "You know, in ancient times many people recognized and used their innate natural self healing abilities on themselves and others. I think that since modern times, we have really, just like with our ancient innate telepathic abilities, we've forgotten who we were and what we can naturally could do, feel, heal and telepath."

Glinda hugged her earth daughter's waist, smiled and beamed, "Yes you have but we will help you remember and learn self healing and perhaps also more sensitivity for telepathy my dear Sara."

As Sara and her two aliens exited the restroom, Jane rushed up to them almost in tears and exclaimed, "Oh God, I was so worried. Are you alright now?"

Sara took Jane's hand and said, "Yes, they had a rare severe reaction to that cigarette smoke but, they are ok now."

Jane realized that she was with some really unusual women smiled and said, "Oh, I am so relieved that you are ok. Shall we go back to the Biltmore now?"

Sara holding Selena's hand said, "I think that is surely the best idea for now."

As they exited the theatre Selena noticed a shop to their left. She tugged on Sara's arm and beamed, "What kind of place is that Sara? Is it a restaurant? It smells so delightful and now, after my reaction to smoke and healing, my powers are really low and click, click, click and I am really really super hungry Sara."

Glinda beamed in, "Me too, using our energies for healing always drains us."

Sara looked at the shop and saw the familiar Krispy Kreme logo, grinned and said, "That is a donut bakery." Sara saw Selena's excited and interested expression and said to her little alien sister, "Would you like to try one?"

Selena clicked even more rapidly, squealed and bobbed her hungry head in anticipation.

Sara said, "Ok Krispy Kream, here we come!"

Jane looked at Sara and the aliens and said "Me toooo. Let's go have a donut and some java!" Jane touched Sara's arm and asked, "What the devil were those rapid clicks and I think I also heard a strange squeal?"

Sara looked earnestly at Jane and whispered, "Jane, please, please forget what you may see and hear with us tonight. Howard really needs you to respect this, uh, secret... ok?"

Jane smirked, squeezed Sara's arm winked and said, "Ok, ok again, mum's the word, uh Commander..." She then gave a smart three fingered Girl Scout salute.

Sara turned and asked the two agents behind them, "Would you guys like a donut and coffee break with us?"

The lead agent smiled and said, "Sure, that would be swell Miss Sara!" As they entered the Krispy Kream Donut shop, Sara guided the girls to a booth near the counter and the two agents sat themselves at a booth across the room of the, fortunately now, except for them, empty restaurant.

The waitress came over she smiled and said, "Hola, what would you like? Coffee?"

Glinda and Selena had both enjoyed coffee during one of their visit's to a small Colombian coastal town so both beamed to Sara to order café con leche.

Selena then proudly took out her notebook and wrote on it. "Which is the best donut?"

Sara winked at her and pointed to the standard sugar glazed Krispy Kreme wall mounted logo donut.

Selena wrote on her pad, "OK, I'll have three!"

Sara pretending to read the note smiled and said, "Selena, three is too many. They are almost pure sugar. Try just one and see how you feel, ok?"

The waitress, realizing that her guests could not speak, went back behind the counter and returned with a large 16x20 black and white photo poster of all their donuts and asked Selena and Glinda to point to the ones they thought that they might like.

Selena pointed to one with light toned icing and Glinda pointed to a darker one with coconut on it. Sara remembering the girls' allergy to peanuts asked, "Do any of these have peanuts?" The waitress became very sad looking as she pointed to the crumbled peanut donut image.

Sara said, "Just as long as they are not given anything with peanuts.

They are, uh, deathly allergic to peanuts."

The waitress started to tear up and she quavered in her intense spanish accent, "Aiiiiii senora. Last year, my little baby brother died from eating peanuts. It was his second birthday and mamma made him his first peanut butter and jelly sandwich and almost as soon as he had taken two bites, his little happy face became stricken and on the way to the hospital he died in the ambulance." By then the poor waitress was totally racking with sobs. Glinda stood up and took the stricken girl in her arms and as gently as she could, she transferred healing and calming energies to the girl. The girl feeling Glinda's soothing, soon stopped sobbing and look deeply into Glinda's eyes and said, "Tu eres un santa senora, gracias!" (You are a saint senora, thanks).

The waitress took the girls orders then turned to the agents table to take theirs. As she did so, Jane, being the playful spirit that she was, stood up and dramatically pointed to the agent that had stopped her from entering the restroom to be with Sara, said accusingly, "He's a bad cop, no donut for him!" At first Sara was shocked but she saw Jane was smiling and laughing, she said, "It's Ok! He can have a donut, he's a great, uh cop, guard dog…"

Selena and Glinda just sat there in perplexed silence since they realized that they could not let on that they had any idea why Jane had tried to forbid the agent from having a donut too. The two agents at first started to get pissed off but as they saw Sara and Jane were laughing, they joined in the laughter and that finally broke all of the tensions from the theatre fiasco. Sara thought, "It's lucky that we are the only ones here."

Glinda beamed to Sara, "Sara, why is everyone laughing?"

Astute Selena piped in, "Is it because that agent would not let Jane in the restroom?"

Sara smiled and verbalized to all. "Well, now that everyone has done his duty, let's enjoy our donuts and coffee."

Just as Selena was beaming to ask again what was happening and why the agent was a bad cop. The lead agent's radio crackled, "Pres. One, Pres. three calling."

The agent dug into his jacket's deep side pocket and hauled out the three pound walkie talkie. "Pres. one, go ahead."

"What are you guys doing in there? I want a donut and I could sure use a cuppa java too."

"Well, Pres. Three, you are a bad agent and so no donut for you now.

But, I'll bring one to you in the limo as soon as we come back out, ok?" "Uh, Pres. One, why am I a bad agent, uh, sir?"

The lead agent just smiled, chuckled and raised his eyebrows as he radioed back, "Uh, Pres. Three, disregard, I guess you are a good agent and deserve two donuts…"

There was a rather long pause and Pres. Three radioed back, "Uh, sir, uh, can I have a chocolate with crumbled peanuts?"

Pres. One remembered Sara's no peanuts rule pushed the talk switch and said, "Anything except peanuts. No peanuts around these people and remember that's you know who's orders agent."

"OK, then, just make it a glazed chocolate, ok?" The lead agent radioed, "Ok ten-four and out."

Sara, Jane, Glinda and Selena were engrossed in listening and as the agents' radio conversation ended, Sara announced, "OK, let's get two dozen to go back to the hotel." Sara turned to Jane and asked, "Uh, does Howard like donuts?"

Jane smiled and said, "He sure does but, uh, crumbled peanut is his favorite. Sara explained that they simply could not risk having any peanuts anywhere near the visitors.

Jane said, "OK, let's get a waitress choice but without peanuts."

Sara smiled, took a sip of her coffee and said, "OK, but, we will be swimming in donuts for the next three days."

Glinda, Selena and Sara heard Arthur beaming into their heads, "I want three lemon filled ok?"

Then to their surprise they heard from Delnoid who was still down in Key West, "Uh, great, I'll have two apple filled."

Then, Glinda, Selena and Sara could not help cracking up as they heard in their heads a cacophony of 157, beamed all at once, mixed ricocheting donut orders from everyone aboard the aliens' ship which was hovering about 125 miles over their heads…

Sara and her aliens finally stopped their squeals and laughter and Sara finally managed to stammer out to Jane, "Oh, we just remembered a great joke about donuts from uh, South America."

After leaning forward, the perplexed and skeptical Jane said, "OK, please do tell me the joke Sara…"

Glinda took out her notepad and carefully wrote, "Oh Jane, it just doesn't translate very well from Spanish into English…"

Jane looked intently intrigued and challenged, "OK… but try me."

Sara, realized she had to come up with something stammered, "Well its, uh, kind of about a donut delivery plane that crashed in, you know, the remote Amazon and the local headhunter Indians found it a week later with the dead pilots and about 3000 stale donuts, they, after sampling the uh, planes contents could not agree if the pilots or the stale donuts tasted better…"

Jane looked disgusted and said, "Oh God! That's a terrible joke and you are right, it probably doesn't translate at all."

Glinda, Selena and Sara heard, beamed from Arthur, "Uh, the pilots tasted better." Rather than crack up again, Sara and her two aliens tried, most unsuccessfully to concentrate on their coffees."

Sara looked at the Krispy Kreme logo wall clock and announced, "Well, its 10:45 already. I guess we best get our circus on the road back to the Biltmore." After leaving the waitress a $10 tip, which was a fortune in 1948, all left the donut shop and got into the Presidential limo.

They were just riding along with each engrossed in their own thoughts when Selena beamed to Sara, "What is a circus?" Just as Sara was thinking back to her alien protégé, "I will have to spend quality time with you and Glinda tomorrow to try to explain all of this." The yellow phone rang. Sara knew it was for her, picked it up and asked, "Yes Sir?" She heard the President chuckling as he asked for three coconut covered chocolate lemon filled donuts."

Sara grinned and said, "OK sir. We have at least that many chocolate coconuts in the two dozen we got to go. What time will you be landing tomorrow to enjoy your donuts and golf, sir?" As she listened, the President said, "All seems to be going rather well in spite of that near disaster from the smoking in the theatre Sara." Sara realized that Delnoid 5 had been filling him in on their evening's movie coughing and donut adventures. The President asked, "How do you think Mr. Hughes and Arthur are getting along?"

Sara said, "As far as I can tell sir, they are really hitting it off and when we left them they were completely immersed in technical, astronomical and, uh, aviation things."

The President sensing Sara's reluctance to speak openly said, "Uh Sara, is Jane Russell with you?"

Sara said, "Yes sir, she is right here." Sara held the phone out grinned at Jane and said, "Jane, the President wants to speak with you."

Jane dropped her jaw for a moment, brushed her hair back over her left ear and said, "Hi Mr. Truman… uh Mr. President that is."

Truman on the other end chuckled as he said, "I have been a fan of yours since I recently saw Young Widow at our Washington, DC White House theatre. It was great, but what I want to ask you is, when is your first film that, that, uh, cowboy outlaw story coming out?"

Jane cagily said, "You will have to ask Howard all about that tomorrow. He's still battling with the absurd moron motion picture board about my breasts."

Truman said, "Well wonderful, I will be looking forward to seeing them, uh, your film, that is, Miss Russell. See you tomorrow at brunch?"

Jane was grinning like a Cheshire cat as she purred, "Ok Mr.

President, sir, see you tomorrow at brunch."

Sara, at first hearing the President being so familiar and a bit flirty with Jane, frowned but recalled that the President had once quipped, "If I had not gone into politics, I might have made a good piano player in a whore house." She also remembered the photograph of Mr. Truman happily playing an upright piano and singing with Lauren Bacall coquettishly sitting on top of it swinging her beautiful gams. (legs)

After the aliens, Sara and Jane were dropped off at the hotel entrance, Sara said, "Well, what little we saw of your movie was nice Jane." Jane embraced Sara, Glinda and Selena, and said, "I better go see that Howard has hit the hay. See you all tomorrow at the breakfast buffet." As she walked off, Sara anticipating Selena's wonderful never-ending questions thought to her, "Just so you know, hitting the hay means to go to sleep."

Glinda beamed, "We have so much to absorb Sara. I hope we can soon understand all of your earthly slang and jargon."

Sara thought to Glinda and Selena, "Well, you and your entire pod will have all the time you need on Water Island and then at Camp Roberts in California."

Glinda wisely beamed, "But, it is unfortunate that on that island we will not have opportunities to interact with more diverse humans - except for the sailors, and marines - to better learn your ways and your weird and wonderful slang and other expressions and their actual intentions."

Sara and her aliens received Arthur echoing his wife's concerns as he beamed, "Glinda is right dear Sara. We will have to find ways to go out and interact with humans to practice our earthly social skills."

Glinda beamed to her husband, "So, how did the talks with Mr. Hughes go?"

Arthur beamed back, "Well he is definitely an extraordinary genius and he has many great ideas about how we can settle in and plan and work with him to share our technologies. It's wretchedly remarkable that he seems to have two sides as do most geniuses. He is super brilliant with a photographic memory just like us and also a technological expert but the other side of him is really paranoid and troubled. I think it's what those quack psychiatrists label as bi-polar. Also the drugs he is now addicted to from his last airplane crash injuries are really gravely affecting his mind and destroying his body. I feel that if you could meet with him sometime soon, you may be able to mind link with him and help him to release the needless fears which make him a desperate prisoner of his own mind and also heal his body from the painkillers that he is now so thoroughly addicted to."

Glinda beamed, "Arthur, I will gladly defiantly do that so he can become healthy again and more well-adjusted and also trustworthy for us!"

Sara was included in the beaming thought and said, "Dear Glinda that will be a needed miracle and I always feel that you and your people have so much that you can share with us. But, as you and Arthur of course realize, we, uh, you must be very limited and very selective about who you heal or mind link with."

Glinda smiled as she thought about Amelia Earhart now living happily married to Embry in Lifestar, then looked at her earth daughter and beamed, "I will always respect your guidance and opinions as we interact with others Sara."

Glinda continued, "I also sense that our dear Mr. Truman, even though he always proclaims that Bess is the love of his life; in reality though, it's almost totally a one sided, self destructive co-dependency illusion since narrow minded Mrs. Truman actually seems to resent and at times begrudge if not actually hate her husband. I wonder if we can offer to minister to our dear new confidant - even if he is the President of the USA."

Sara thought, "Confidentially I agree that our President does have a troubled, unhappy and dreadful one sided marriage. But please, for now, we must focus on getting all of you securely landed. Then we, uh, you can worry about saving some of us problematic humans that you are beginning to really identify."

Glinda beamed, "Sara my dear guide, you are of course totally right. It's just me being a natural empath. It's sometimes hard for me to not want to try and help others. It's my gift and at times, a curse as well as a blessing being a healer."

CHAPTER 26 WHACO GOLF AND SWIM SUITS

Arthur, Mr. Hughes, Sara, Selena and Glinda stood inside the temporary security barrier that the secret service agents had erected on the beautiful Biltmore golf course. They soon heard the thumpa, thumpa of the rotor blades of the powerful HMX-1 Marine One helicopter as it set down out of the clear blue south Florida sky. Right on schedule at 10 am Mr. Truman and his permanent aide Delnoid 5M exited from his chopper.

After saluting the Marine one crewman who had opened the door, the President walked up to Sara and her lady aliens and embraced them. He warmly shook the hands of Arthur and Mr. Hughes and said, "Well, how do you like this little country hotel my friends?"

Arthur beamed and looked hopelessly over at Delnoid 5 who had grinned as he too had saluted the chopper crewmen. "So good to see you again. We have been having quite a unique time uh, experiencing, learning and adjusting to your, excellent food, south Florida ways and movies." He grinned. "But we are fine and as you know, we each are sharing all that we experience and learn with our pod back aboard Lifestar." Del 5M then interuppted and said, "Today the President wants to invite you, Glinda and Selena if they and you would like to try a round of golf."

Sara immediately broke in saying, "Well sir, I have already arranged to take Glinda and Selena to the nearby Miami Seaquarium to see the dolphins and then enjoy the beach, a picnic and a swim."

Truman smiled and said, "Boy, I sure wish I could come enjoy the Seaquarium too, but, since Arthur, Howard and I still have to talk and then hopefully enjoy a round of golf, let's go enjoy brunch for now. I am starving. By the way Howard, where is your lovely Jane?"

Howard Hughes grinned and said, "She is anxiously waiting for you at the buffet Mr. President."

After a delicious brunch buffet, during which Sara had again enjoyed, by thought only, since Jane was with them, explaining to her aliens about the food choices. After eating on large slightly molded glass topped table, the president and his party were relaxing on the swimming pool veranda. Sara looked at her watch and said, "Please excuse me Mr. President. The limo will be here to pick us girls up in half an hour. So with your permission we will go get ready."

As Selena, Sara and Glinda were undressing, Sara thought, "I got you some new swim suits with higher backs that will hopefully cover your blowholes." Sara went to the dresser and extracted two one piece suits and as she held them up she asked, "OK, which one do you like Glinda?"

Glinda seeing the so radiant flower patterns reached for the red and yellow suit. As she did so, Selena formed a pout, squeaked impatiently and beamed, "I want a bikini just like Jane wears."

Sara smiled and said, "All in good time little sister, once we get to Water Island, I understand from Captain Tamarynd that there are a couple of French boutiques in Charlotte Amalie."

Selena scrunched up her brow and beamed, "What is a boutique Sara?"

Sara grinned, laughed and said, "Boutique is French, Selena and it's just a petite store with way over priced items."

Glinda squeaked a delighted laugh and beamed, "I am so glad that we do not have to cover our blowholes today. I always feel so stifled with a fleshaid plug."

Selena let out three very loud squeaks and agreed, "It's so good to be mostly natural again."

Sara said, "Let's put our swimsuits on under our clothes so right after our visit to the Sea Aquarium we can go enjoy the beach and you can finally swim in the ocean."

After they donned their suits, Glinda, saw that Selena's blue and white flowered suit back did not come up high enough to cover her blowhole, beamed, "Oh oh, I better get the new fleshaid tube that Delnoid 5 brought to us Selena. Your suit does not cover your blowhole."

Selena clicked agitatedly and let out a short loud moan as she beamed to her mother and Sara, "As a matter of fact I was hoping that we were out of fleshaid mom."

Sara thought to Selena, "Here, try my suit." They exchanged suits and Glinda beamed, "Turn around Selena, here let me see."

The phone suddenly jangled its two little clapper bells and Sara picked it up and said, "Ok, ok! We are still getting ready. We will be down in about, uh, 10 more minutes."

Glinda clicked in exasperation, looked at Sara and beamed, "Well, your suit rides even lower down than her suit.

Sara said, "OK you two turn back to back and I will try to see if Glinda's suit will work." As the alien mother and daughter were standing back to back, Sara said, "You two are so lovely resembling each other. I can't wait to see Selena when she turns 36 Glinda ."

Glinda and Selena still standing back to back looked apprehensively at their earthly guide and finally Selena beamed, "Well, should we change Sara?"

Sara shook her head no and said, "We will just have to take our chances at the beach. And once we are there, I am sure no one will even notice us."

They collected the terry cloth robes and four large fluffy napped beach towels and Sara said,

"OK, I can get my robe and towel from Arthur's bathroom on our way out." Sara grabbed her trusty large khaki backpack and stuffed the towels in it ans she then stuffed the bulky robes in a USN issue duffel bag. As she hoisted on her back pak, Selena beamed, "Sara, you are the only woman on earth that I have ever seen carrying a backpack."

Sara grinned and said, "Well, it's a habit I picked up while I was doing my anthropological travels in South America and a few of my former girlfriends at the University of California at Santa Barbara also used them. I guess it's a California thing to do."

Selena looked hopefully at Sara and before Selena could beam anything, Sara grinned and said, "Ok, Ok, we will get you a backpack as soon as we get to California"

Selena let out three more happy squeals as Glinda beamed, "Sara you are becoming a mind reader!"

CHAPTER 27 DOLPHIN ESCAPE AID

The Presidential limo with its agent driver and one other agent pulled up at the entrance to the Seaquarium. Sara noticed that there were two more agents in the usual secret service Hawaiian aloha shirts and black mid thigh length Bermuda shorts waiting for them at a specially reserved VIP parking space. She thought, "Great, at least we are prepared if anything happens."

Glinda clicked, moaned and beamed to Sara, "What on Earth could possibly happen here?" Both Sara and Glinda then turned in unison to look apprehensively at Selena.

Selena grinned; clicked happily and let out a loud whistle and as she did so. The two secret service agents sitting in the front seat suddenly looked around and jumped out of the vehicle with their pistols pulled. Then, the two other secret service agents outside the Presidential limo pulled their pistols out as they quickly moved to their standard protect the President at all costs positions around the limo. Before Sara could think or say anything, the large agent entered the rear passenger area and pulled the ladies to the floor and tried to flop his body over Sara and Selena to protect them.

Sara shrieked, "Get off of me damn it! Get off of me! It's Ok, It's ok. It's uh, just a, a, train whistle." After the pandemonium was over, Sara sternly thought, "Selena ! Ok kiddo, cool your blowhole pleaseeee…"

Selena starting to tear up mournfully and beamed to Sara, "I am so sorry Sara. I did not mean to upset our guards."

Sara took Selena into her arms and said, "It's ok dear little sister. You are only being you, but you must really practice being a non whistling earth girl."

Glinda beamed to Selena, Sara and Arthur, "I am so glad we have Sara guiding us, she's so patient."

Sara with her irrepressible good humor thought, "Oh Lord, please give me patience and… I want it right now!"

Glinda grinned, squeaked and beamed, "Why Sara, we say the same thing except we plead to Amador."

As the aliens and Sara recovered their composers and exited the car, one of the agents stepped up to her and said, "Uh, ma'am, here are your tickets to the Sea Show. And one of us will be sitting on each side of you and your, uh, visitors ma'am."

Sara smiled, accepted the tickets and said, "Ok let's go enjoy the show and remember… if anything else happens you are to help or rescue my two visitors no matter what. Got it?"

"Yes ma'am," said the agent as he promised, "No matter what happens…"

Sara and her Delphinians were seated in the front row center of the main aquarium tank. The recorded music started and the emcee stepped out onto the stage wearing a white black belted swim suit and a colorful red and yellow aloha shirt. Selena beamed, "Is he one of our guards Sara?"

Sara reached over and held Selena's hand and thought, "No he just happens to be wearing an Aloha shirt."

Selena beamed, "Where can I get one?"

Sara smiled and thought to her, like a kid being taken to the circus for the first time protégée, "Sweetie, we will go to the territory of Hawaii sometime after California and since that's where they are made, we will get as many as you like especially for you."

Selena squeezed her earth mentor's hand and beamed, "Oh Sara that will be wonderful. You know, I am just like a kid in a fish store as I discover everything about your home world." She let out a small squeal. Sara hearing the joyful expression just squeezed Selena's hand to remind her to try to be quiet as a human just for today.

Selena grinned, squeaked happily and beamed, "Ok Auntie Sara."

By then Selena noticed that there were several dolphins swimming rapidly around the large pool. So, she then, just as she had always done while swimming in the ocean from her spacecraft, beamed what was just a normal respectful hello to her cousins. Suddenly all of the dolphins turned and swam to the edge of the pool in front of her and all eight of them, began excitedly clicking loudly, squeaking, squealing and trilling whistles to this strange and exciting new visitor who could, so unlike all other humans, beam their language.

Glinda realized what was going to happen beamed to Selena and the dolphins…"Oh no, no, no! We must not talk now dear friends."

The dolphins then all looked excitedly at Glinda and beamed between themselves, "Oh click, click click, squeak, squeak, squeak! - Look! There's another human who can speak our language. This is a wonderful revelation, a miracle perhaps, from our Amadores?"

The dolphins started squealing and squeaking loudly as half of them started doing joyful back flips splashing and soaking most of the front row of humans. By then most all of the soaked humans were fleeing and Sara just sat there stupefied…

Glinda elbowed Sara and beamed between her squeals of Delphin laughter, "Well, Amador, what can we do Sara?"

Selena had completely forgotten all about her need to cool it. She stripped off her blouse, dress and shoes. Wearing bra and panties she did an impossible joyful 7 foot arch dive directly into the pool with her dolphin cousins.

The agent that had been sitting beside Selena looked dutifully at Sara as he stood; he kicked off his shoes and vaulted over the tank's edge into the pool following Sara's standing orders to rescue Selena. Two of the dolphins thinking that he wanted to play got him between them and started zooming him around the pool.

The flabbergasted Seaquarium emcee simply stood on the stage across the pool half heartedly blowing his whistle and hoarsely shouting unheeded commands through his megaphone to his dolphins…

Sara and Glinda just looked at each other and while being overwhelmed, Glinda squeaked and squealed and clicked as Sara laughed hysterically. Glinda stood and went to the pool's edge and beamed, "Selena you get back here this instant!"

Selena receiving her mom's sharp command, turned and swam begrudgingly back to the railing. As she reached it so did the four dolphins on each side of her splashing and squeaking and squealing their hearts out with pure joy and love in the dolphin tradition to Glinda and Selena.

Glinda beamed to all of them, "Ok, ok, we thank you for your love and greetings but please, we must not make such a commotion in front of these humans."

The pool pod leader became still and contrite and as his pod members also quieted down. He beamed to Glinda, "Of course your Majesty we are humbly apologetic for our commotion. But, we have never before met any humans who can beam our language."

Glinda beamed to all of the dolphins, "It's ok dear cousins, and maybe someday we can meet again at sea."

The lead dolphin beamed heartbreaking energies to Glinda as he explained that they all had been captives here for the last ten years since, one by one, they had been captured by the humans to perform in this absurd and cruel circus.

One of the female dolphins beamed, "Oh dear Amador, we are so unhappy here and we have been trying to figure out how to open that sea gate so we can escape and get back to our pods…We so miss our families…"

Selena by now was in total tears as she ran around the circular pool where it met the stage wall. She vaulted back in the tank and swam determinedly underwater towards the sea gate. As she reached it, she quickly unlatched the outward swinging solid steel barrier and beamed to her dolphin cousins, "Be free, swim home as fast as you can."

The dolphins came to her and with boundless joyful thanks beaming from their hearts, they scooped Selena upon the back of the alpha male and took her and themselves ecstatically through the sea gate to the open sea through the 500 feet drainage channel that was now flooded with rushing dolphin pool water.

Glinda stripped off her dress and blouse, kicked off her shoes and jumped in the pool to rescue Selena. As Glinda swam desperately towards the sea gate she beamed to Sara, "It's ok, we will be ok and we will meet you on the little beach just to the right of this damned dolphin prison."

Sara sat there dumbfounded but she quickly recovered her senses and mumbled to Glinda and Selena, "Uh, oK, ok, ok…I will go there immediately."

Sara was gathering up her amiga's soaked cloths and shoes when she happened to look up and there, hovering just 200 feet above the pool, was a 30 feet (10 meter) sky blue saucer shaped craft…. Sara looked exasperatedly at the open mouthed agents and screamed, "Well damn it Bill just don't sit there! Gerald, get out of the tank! You heard the lady! Let's get out of here and get to that small beach and by the way," she gasped… "This never happened! "Understand? Your jobs and probably your lives depend on your saying nothing!"

The agent Bill was still sitting there pointing up with his mouth agape as he pointed up with his right index finger he stammered to Sara, "Look ma'am, a flying saucer ma'am, it's a real blitzer flying saucer."

By the time Sara and her agents jumped back into the President's limo and pealed rubber racing to the nearby small beach. Sara started to pick up the yellow, or better yet maybe the red phone. "Damn, which one should I call the President on…" She suddenly heard Arthur beaming… "Sara, they will be ok. Just go to the beach and pick up Glinda and Selena…"

Sara looking totally why meeee upwards as if she was hearing God in heaven in her head, replaced the red phone and meekly thought, "Ok we will be at that beach in just 3 minutes." She thought to Arthur, "What about your saucer?"

Arthur beamed back to Sara. "It's ok; they rescued Selena and Glinda three miles offshore and super soniced to the dolphins to just go home…"

As the limo screeched to a skidding stop at the palm treed beachside roadway, Sara flew out of the door screaming to the agents to stay put and ran to Glinda and Selena who were standing on the beach in their bra and panties. As she approached them she could hear a mix of Delphin squealing laughter and crying squeals and moans coming from both of the alien women. Sara ran to them and wrapped her arms around them and she felt the powerful mixed energies coming from Glinda and her daughter. She pulled her head back in joy and amazement and asked, "What's so funny?"

Glinda looked at Sara with tears in her eyes and beamed, "Oh Sara we are so sorry about this fiasco. But as is said in your culture, blood runs deeper than water and in our case today in that unspeakable dolphin circus; our need for freedom in water ran way deeper than any human enterprise, laws or blood."

Sara smiled and slowly joined arm in arm in the laughter energies. After they entered the limo, the driver agent turned his head and asked Sara, "Uh, where to ma'am?"

Sara looked at him thinking about the upcoming meeting with the President, gritted her teeth and hopelessly said, "Oh, to the backside of the moon I guess…"

Selena and Glinda held their Sara and trilled as Glinda beamed, "It will be ok Sara. It was a needed and good lesson about the rights of all living creatures here or on other worlds. Arthur has already explained this to President Truman and I know he won't be angry with you…"

Sara entirely emotionally exhausted, laid her head on her alien mother's shoulder and cried, "I sure hope so Glinda. I think I would just die if I was to be taken away from you and Selena…" As she softly sobbed, Selena held her too and beamed loving, soothing energies to her dear soaked and dismayed earth sister.

Later, after the aliens had retreated to their suites, Sara and President Truman were sitting alone in his suite. Sara looked apprehensively at the President expecting to be scolded and warned if not fired and said, "Mr., Mr. Truman, what can I say, uh, sir."

The president took off his glasses and as he took out a hankie and wiped the lenses, he smiled and broke into roaring laughter as he whooped out, "By God Sara! That must have been some kind of a circus today." He reached for then crying again Sara and as he tenderly held her he said, "Dear Sara, don't worry. You did the best you could and this fiasco, as Arthur pointed out to me, was a valuable and needed lesson for all of us to take these amazing close encounters of the," he laughed and continued, "Dolphin – uh, Delphinian kind in smaller carefully thought out and planned steps."

Sara dried her eyes and smiled at Truman and said, "Gosh Mr President. I never used to be such a crybaby but I think our dear Delphinians are changing my sensitivity, heart and spirit…"

He, then holding her shoulders smiled as he said, "Maybe such sensitivity and response ability is indeed a needed change for us humans."

"But now I wonder if those agents will be able to keep their mouths shut? I hope so and I will meet with them shortly to make that perfectly clear."

Glinda then beamed in from 12 stories above, Send them right up here Mr. President and I will, as usual, erase their memories about this uh, er, funtastic… er… fiasco. She then totally cracked up squeaking and squealing and clicking helplessly in laughter.

As both the president and Sara recovered themselves after having also totally cracked up Truman wiped his eyes and said, "But again dear daughter, you did nothing wrong and you did the best that you could; just as I have always tried to do. And, by the way Sara, I have already ordered the, uh alien affairs disinformation division at Wright Patterson AFB to start the cover up of today's debacle."

Sara wiped her eyes, grinned and said, "They are sure going to have to put to good use their disinformation skills Mr. President."

He laughed and said, "That's for sure Sara. Were there any news people there?"

Sara replied, "I didn't see any Mr. President but of course a lot of those Seaquarium visitors had cameras and that blue saucer was sure in plain sight for awhile."

Truman said to Sara, "I am so glad that I have super capable, super observant and super response able you on my side." Sara grinned and gave a snappy three fingered Girl Scout salute and said, "Me too Mr. President, me too." She briefly hugged the president as she again wiped her tears with the hankie that the President had given her. She looked at him and said, "Mr. Truman, we now must realize and respect that our alien friends have some powerful mind and spirit healing abilities. Did Arthur talk to you about the possibility of Glinda helping Mr. Hughes to heal his bi-polar, obsessive compulsive, getting worse schizophrenic mind?"

Truman, starting to get the drift of his very astute assistant's thoughts, gave a half smirk and said, "Yes he did Sara and if you can think of some way to approach our mad genius Howard, as weird as he is. We must do that all we can to heal and protect the national treasure we have in Mr. Hughes's genius talent. I fear that the way he is going now, that in less than five years he will be stark raving mad and of no use to himself, his corporations or us."

Sara asked, "How long does he plan to stay here at the Biltmore?"

Harry replied, "I think he is planning to fly out on his Constellation with Jane tonight."

Sara thought a moment and asked, "So, can you, would you invite him to come down to Key West for a few more days of meetings?"

Harry smiled earnestly and said, "I will try Sara, I will try." He reached for the phone and asked for room 1207.

After the President finished asking Mr. Hughes if he would come down to Key West for more talks, he smiled as he replaced the phone and said, "Great, he will fly down to Key West tomorrow morning in the Cessna 140 that he keeps here in Miami."

Sara asked, "So, how did your golf game with Mr. Hughes and Arthur go this afternoon during our Seaquarium circus of the absurd?"

The President chuckled and said, "Well Sara it was, to say the least, very unusual, alien and kind of unfair."

Sara sensing that Arthur had probably used his alien powers said, "OK Mr. Golf Pro, please tell me what happened?"

Truman related, "Well, fortunately as it turned out Sara, we of course had three agents doubling as caddies to avoid any real caddies seeing Arthur in any weird actions."

Sara grinned, raised her eyebrows, and said, "Ok, do go on…" "Well… before we started I explained to Arthur that the object of the

game was to make the little white ball go into the cup at each green. So after I showed him several times how to place the ball on the wooden tee and how to swing the driver; I offered him a driver and placed a practice ball on a tee for him to take a swipe at. He did so and the ball flew off to the side of the fairway but then, it amazingly made an impossible forty five degree turn and flew 200 yards nonstop above the green and dropped directly down into the hole. After this defiance of the rules of golf, the laws of physics and gravity happened and I regained my composure; I turned to our astounded agent caddies and told them, you never saw that guys! They nodded their heads and muttered, 'Yes sir, Mr. President'."

Howard Hughes was still laughing hysterically, he whacked his golf club on the green and finally managed to croak, "Mr. Arthur that was mind- boggling but it's not the way we can yet openly defy the laws of gravity here on Earth."

The President continued, "Arthur of course beamed an apology and he then sonic beamed towards the agents and told me, "Ok, Mr. President, I just erased their memories of my, uh, unusual golf stroke."

Truman continued, "So we just went over to the putting and driving range so that Arthur could practice hitting a few balls earth style. We then went to the clubhouse where Howard had his ice cold milk and Arthur and I enjoyed a good laugh and some ice cold Coke."

Sara laughed and said, "Well, maybe the aliens can someday teach us one of their uh, Delphin games."

Truman grinned, harrumphed and said, "Oh by all means Sara, but I bet we would have to be able to swim like a dolphin underwater to play with them."

Sara went up to her room to change and as she walked in, Selena and Glinda were sitting on her bed waiting for her. They had dressed and were drying each other's hair. Sara embraced her two aliens and said, "Are you two ok?"

Glinda beamed back to Sara, "Yes we are fine now. How are you doing?"

Sara explained that she and the President had agreed that we need to be more careful about sightseeing until we can really help teach you more about our ways here on your new planet."

Selena teared up, moaned and beamed, "Oh Sara, I hope I did not get you into any trouble. I don't know what I would do if they took you away from us."

Sara hugged both of them and thought, "No, it's ok and the President totally understands." Sara grinned and said, "I am so glad that you were able to free those poor dolphins."

Glinda nodded her head and beamed, "They were in absolute emotional anguish Sara."

Selena beamed, "Remember that once I joked about becoming your dolphin ambassador? Well, I think now that is exactly what I want to do in future."

Sara looked proudly at her alien adopted sister and thought with total love and pride, "I think that after we get Mr. Truman re-elected and all of you settled; we must talk seriously about your doing just that Selena. After we finish up your orientations at Camp Roberts we can go down to La Jolla, near San Diego to the Birch Aquarium at the Scripts Institute of Oceanography."

Selena beamed, "I would love that Sara. I felt the hopelessness, heartbreak and desperation of my dolphin cousins, just like we always deeply, too deeply feel the discouraged emotions of each other in our stinky old starship."

Sara held Selena's hands and said, "Well soon, very soon we shall take all of you to Water Island for sunshine and frolicking with your dolphin cousins. You all have so much to offer us so troubled, fearful and angry humans. I can see that we are not fully emotionally connected as you are. We have no truly honest heart and soul links to enable us to totally communicate, understand, agree and live in peace. It's so regretful that we did not evolve from dolphins as you did."

Glinda smiled and beamed, "Its true Sara and your understanding of the evolutionary effects of planetary environments for molding our characters is now growing by light years and Delphin leaps dear daughter."

Sara looked earnest as she said, "Please take my hand and follow me as I follow you but remember always that we fear filled humans have always rejected and destroyed anyone who is even just a little bit different. We are still so damn tribal."

Glinda beamed, "I know dear Sara and it's so advantageous that we can read minds in order for us to foretell the true intentions and menace from others."

Sara thought back, "It's so wonderful that in your Delphin heritage you can always have true understanding of each other. I so wish we could develop that here in our troubled, self destructive, fear based human societies. Do you know that in South America and in many other ancient cultures; some people might have had such powers of mind and spirit, but once they were discovered by the other so-called normal humans, they were killed?"

Selena beamed, "Yes Sara, it is so fortunate that our podness, uh our tribalness comes from our ancestral social structures. With our telepathy we are always able to communicate entirely openly and honestly." Sara looked at her so cute young alien sister and was always amazed and impressed at her profound intellect and vision.

Sara said, "Selena, I hope after we get you settled, that you will think about attending my old university in Santa Barbara, California to study about human cultures as I did. People and why they do what they do has always fascinated me."

Selena smiled and beamed, "I would like that very much Sara. Are you planning to go back to California after you get us settled on Water Island or in California?"

Sara became sad and said, "I don't know. Remember that I serve at the pleasure of the President. If Mr. Truman does not win the 1948 election in November, I may have to leave the Navy and my government service. But please know I will always, one way or another, be with you till the end of my life on this world dear pod sisters."

As they were hugging and sharing love energies Arthur came into the room and beamed, "I am so thankful that the universe brought you to us and us to you dear Sara as we try to create and launch new life dreams here on your so beautiful world." He walked up to his family and joined their love energy hugs.

Being totally refreshed and rejuvenated by their sharing of love energies, Sara looked at her watch and said, "Well, we are supposed to meet Mr. Hughes, Jane and the President for an early dinner in half an hour. But before I go to get dressed, Glinda I need to ask you, what do you think we can do to help troubled Mr. Hughes?"

Glinda beamed, "If he sincerely in his true heart and spirit, wants to be helped and permit me to touch him, I can easily aid him to reclaim his life and vanquish the so fear filled and paranoid bi-polar personality he shares his mind with."

Sara smiled and said, "The President has talked him into staying longer and accompanying us back to the small Key West White House."

Glinda smiled and beamed, "Yes, I know he has and that's wonderful Sara."

Sara made a wry face as she said, "I guess that I will never get used to such complete mind reading."

Selena squeaked and put her index and center fingers to each side of her head and squealed four times.

Sara placed her thumbs on her temples and wiggled her fingers as she made a pinched lips face back to Selena and stuck her tongue out at her. As she did that, Glinda, Selena and Arthur's faces changed into shock and dismay.

Sara seeing that something had upset her aliens asked, "Oh oh, did I do something wrong?"

Glinda recovering her composure smiled and walked over to her earth daughter and beamed, "Oh Sara… sticking our tongues out through pursed lips is a really uh, how can I say this…Uh, it's a very crude gesture in our society."

Sara becoming very contrite stammered, "I, I had no idea. Here on earth that gesture is just a harmless and childish way of dramatizing, like what Selena meant when she touched her fingers to her head just now." Selena and Arthur came over and hugged Sara as Glinda beamed to all, "We really have so much to learn about each other."

Sara asked, "Is, uh, are there any other gestures I need to avoid?"

Selena squeaked and beamed to her sister, "Nope, that is really the only taboo gesture we have, except for some very rude sounds we can make with our blowholes like this…" Selena grinned and let out a very loud low pitched juicy raspberry.

Glinda looked at her daughter and beamed, "Selena please, enough noises and gestures for today – ok?"

Selena became slightly embarrassed and beamed to all, "Yes mom – majesty."

Arthur again hugged Sara and beamed, "It's Ok dear Sara, be light, all is ok now."

Glinda beamed to Arthur, "By the way dear husband, how did your first ever earthly golf game go today with Mr. Hughes and the President?"

Arthur grinned and beamed, "I won!"

Sara just cracked up as Selena beamed, "Ok let us in on the story." Arthur grinned proudly to his family, "It's just that I know more, ah,

about the meta physics of golf balls!"

Sara said, "OK, let's go down stairs to dinner and see what the plan is for us tonight and tomorrow."

Arthur beamed to Sara, "We will have to be getting back to our ship by Wednesday Sara. We will have to have our new super long lasting nostril humidifiers removed by then."

Sara said, "OK, I will tell the President as soon as we get downstairs."

Arthur looked kind of guilty as he beamed, "I, uh already beamed that to him earlier Sara and our ship will meet us on your sub at the same rendezvous point 45 miles north west of Havana, Cuba late on Tuesday night."

Sara leading her aliens out of their suite thought, "Ok, good, whatever…"

Selena exactly echoed, "Ok, whatever…" as she marched out to catch up with Sara. As they walked, Selena beamed to Sara, "I really like that whatever phrase. Where does it come from?

Sara smiled and thought back to her so inquisitive sister, "It's like, you know… like a California phrase Selena."

Selena looked puzzled and beamed, "Well, ok, like now, I guess I know cause you know… like, whatever you just told me."

After a needed and filling dinner in a private dining alcove of the magnificent Biltmore dining room, the President grinned and chuckled and said, "Well so ends a, uh, really fun day at the Sea Aquarium."

Jane supposedly had been feeling a bit down and stayed in her suite all day, quizzed, "Oh, did I miss something special at the Sea Aquarium?" Howard squeezed her arm under the table and she looked daggers at him and became sullenly quiet.

Sara smiled and told Jane, "Oh it's just that the dolphin show was really, really, er, uh really exciting."

Jane smiled at Sara and caustically said, "Oh, you don't say." Sara realized that Jane was not in a good mood just nodded, made a little smile slightly cocked her eyebrows and took her last bite of cherry pie.

Howard cleared his throat and intervened, "Well, I am having my co pilot fly Jane back to Hollywood tonight, on my Constellation." It has two bedrooms and she has to be on the movie set tomorrow morning." Sara and the President just nodded.

Jane tried to look debonair over her wrath at being sent home alone by Howard. She stood up and said, "Well everybody, Mr. President, I must excuse myself to go pack. Howard, are you coming up with me?"

Howard sighed deeply, raised his eyebrows in resignation and as he stood, he said in his always soft Texas voice, "Well Mr. President and everyone,

I too have to excuse myself to go help Jane prepare for her flight home." Howard grinned at Arthur and said, "I think after I see Jane off, I shall give my brains a needed rest after that uh, exhausting golf game."

Arthur and everyone at the table sniggered and Selena inadvertently let out a short low whistle.

Jane immediately stopped and demanded, "There, I heard it again.

What the hell is that?"

Howard holding her arm said, "It's just a train whistle Jane. It's just a little old way south Florida train whistle…" After Hughes and his very pissed off lady friend left, President Truman remarked, "Golly, you would need a chainsaw to cut that ice."

Selena immediately beamed, "What's a chainsaw?"

Sara squeezed her littler alien sister's arm and said, "Sis, I will explain later."

Selena turned and stuck her tongue out at Sara and as Arthur and Glinda clicked rapidly and beamed astonishment and admonishments to her.

Impishly grinning Selena squealed and beamed back, "Well here it's not a bad gesture at all. Just, you know, like uh, playful…"

Sara broke into laughter and President Truman asked, "Uh, did I miss something?"

Sara turned to the president and playfully stuck her tongue out at him with her saucy little girl face and seeing that, Truman grinned, laughed and returned the gesture… He sat chuckling too as all of the aliens were squeaking in laughter and he said, "OK whatever… I guess it's an alien joke thing…"

Sara said, "Mr. Truman, I will, uh explain later but be sure you never do that in front of any other Delphinians. Ok, sir?"

Harry, being the good natured mid western husband that he was, smiled and quipped, "Yes dear, I'll be double sure to always remember that." They all then agreed to meet in the lobby at 8am for breakfast. The president said, "I have ordered our helicopter to pick us up on the golf course at 9:30 am.

Selena squeaked, clicked nervously and beamed, "OK, I liked riding in your primitive contraption." President Truman just smiled and said, "Well, it beats walking or swimming."

Selena beamed, "Oh Mr. President, I can't wait to go swimming from the beaches at our Water Island, uh, sir.

Truman, being a father, put his arm around Selena and said, "You will soon have a whole island surrounded by lovely little beaches to swim in hija."

Sara asked the president, "Where did you learn Spanish Mr. President?"

Harry grinned and said, "Remember, I have made several trips down to Rio and Buenos Aires for meetings and I picked up a little of their lovely language."

The next morning in their private breakfast room; Howard Hughes walked in, and the first thing that everyone noticed was his very deep purple and black right eye.

Glinda immediately stood and walked over to him and beamed, "Oh dear Mr. Hughes, did Jane slap you?"

Howard was always reluctant to confront his personal life with others said, "Uh, no, I, uh, banged myself on the ah, the bathroom towel rack."

Glinda walked up to the billionaire and placed her left hand over his eye. She started radiating strong soothing energies and beamed, "Mr. Hughes, relax, let me heal you." Immediately a soft blue light shown from under her fingers.

Howard tried to jerk away, but Glinda had control of him. She continued beaming healing energies for about thirty seconds. She softly withdrew her hand and all could see that Howard's black eye was completely healed and that Howard, the reticent genius, was actually smiling and was totally calm and centered.

As he looked at Glinda, tears came to his eyes and he said, "Your dearest Majesty, I have never felt this well, centered and calm since I was, well like never before dear lady." He astonishingly pulled Glinda to him and hugged her and whispered his heartfelt thanks.

Glinda beamed to him something that she already knew, "Howard, while we are in Key West, I offer to help you completely release the fearful, compulsive, hypochondriac little boy inside you so you can finally be free from your genius affliction of bi-polar and be normal again. What do you think?"

Howard, having just experienced the incredible calming spirit and body healing energies from Glinda stammered, "I… I accept dear Glinda,

I promise that I desperately want to be able to function normally. The opiate pain drugs, that I have become addicted to since my July, 1947 plane crash in Beverly Hills, are ruining my mind." And my deafness which was always bad is now almost totally complete."

Glinda hugged the still astounded Howard Hughes and beamed, "Howard, you are a perfect child of the universe and if you will trust me and put your whole heart and spirit into self healing, together we will make you happy and free again to be the incredible creative genius that you are."

Howard became still, lifted his head from her shoulder and simply thought, "I trust and I believe you dear Glinda and I will be forever in your and Arthur's debit for your hopefully being truly able to free me from the bi- polar demons in my mind."

Sara and the President sat there taking in this unbelievable scene and finally the President leaned over and whispered to Sara, "We have just witnessed a miracle, an angel from the stars beginning to save one of our most needed and brilliant national treasure geniuses."

Sara impulsively took the President's hand and cried, "Yes, Yes, thank God and their Amador we have." Delnoid who was recording all of this sat there smiling as best he could as an android. Selena sitting to Sara's left held onto her earth sister's arm as she slowly clicked softly and whistled.

They then all enjoyed a nice breakfast together. Howard stood, wiped his mouth and said, "Well you all, I best be getting to the airport to get my Cessna." He turned to Glinda and asked, "Your dear Majesty, would you like to accompany me on my flight down to Key West?"

Glinda realized that she had some awfully significant things that she had found inside Howard's mind she needed to share with Sara said, "Mr. Hughes, I thank you but for our return to Key West, I best accompany my husband in the President's helicopter."

Selena reading this immediately piped up, "Mr. Hughes, I would love to fly with you in your plane!"

Sara glanced at Glinda and Arthur and thought, "I think it will be ok, but I'll warn Selena to keep her distance from Howard. He is an unbridled girl chaser and he especially chases young naive women."

Selena scrunched up her face in a petulant frown and squeaked as she beamed, "Mom! I can perfectly well take care of myself with our Mr. Hughes."

Glinda reluctantly beamed to Selena, "Well maybe it will be ok, but remember the warning Sara gave you about most earthmen."

Selena clicked fast to slow, looked haplessly at Sara and beamed, "Can, can you come too?"

Sara cleared her throat, stood up, looked Hughes in his now healed eye and asked, "Mr. Hughes, is there room for me on your small Cessna?"

Howard, who over the long years, was used to concerned mom and big sister types worrying about their dear daughters said, "Well no ma'am, unfortunately the little Cessna 140 I have is just a two place aircraft."

But, thinking on his feet he then acted as if he had just remembered that his PBY was docked nearby at the Miami pier. He looked Sara directly back in her eye and said, "Miss Sara, you are of course welcome to fly with me and Selena in my PBY seaplane. It carries six."

Sara thought to herself, Selena, Glinda and Arthur, "Can you also rid him of his seemingly incurable compulsive girl chasing?"

Glinda beamed to Sara, "That's not the only peculiarity we need to treat in him Sara."

Sara thought, "Why? What have you found out Glinda?" Glinda beamed, "I'll tell you later."

Mr. Truman was getting perturbed at the obvious Howard cat and young girl mouse game going on, stood and proclaimed, "Sorry Howard not this time. I have to keep our visitors protected with our secret service and my helicopter only holds eight."

Howard smiled, flipped his classic dark brown Fedora hat on and said, "Of course Mr. President… Ok then sir… whatever, I'll see you in Key West after lunch."

On the Marine One Presidential helicopter as it thumpa thumped southward from the Biltmore golf course, Selena distraughtly beamed, "Sara, are all earthmen like Howard?"

Sara frowned and took Selena's hand and asked, "Are your alpha males also like him?"

Selena puzzled for a few seconds about it but Glinda beamed in, "Sara we have our alpha males well trained and contained…"

Arthur sitting next to her, grinned and looked lovingly at his queen and beamed, "Yes dear."

Once they had re-settled into their upper level Key West White House suite, Glinda beamed to Sara, Selena, Arthur and Delnoid, "When I was healing Howard, I probed his neurotic paranoid mind and he is definitely bi- polar and also, uh, well how can I say this…

Sara interjected, "He's also bi-sexual. We have heard rumors about him and male Hollywood stars for years. It's also rumored he gets together with them aboard his yacht, Southern Cross out near Catalina Island."

Selena, half knowing anyway, beamed, "Bi-sexual, what does that mean Sara?"

Sara looked resignedly at her aliens and thought, "It means Selena that he, uh, likes to have sex with both women and men."

Selena made a face and some slow exasperated dolphin clicks and beamed, "Oh Amador, he must be a really self repressed person not being able to clearly define his gender role one way or the other."

Sara amazed at the insight of her so young alien sister thought, "Such uh mixed up personality and gender role choices and conflicts are very prevalent in our society. So for your safety dear little sister, Howard Hughes and anyone even remotely like maladjusted him is strictly off limits to you and all other Delphinian girls and women, ok?" She paused and continued, and I guess that goes for Delphin boys and men as well."

Glinda beamed, "That's now a royal pod decree Sara."

Sara asked, "In your Delphin based society, do you have bi-sexual and homosexual relationships?

Glinda smiled and beamed, "We are all naturally, as you now know, very loving and playful with each other, both male and female, just as your earth dolphins are Sara…"

The phone rang, Sara answered and the President said, "Lunch is served now. Come and get it before we throw it out."

As Sara and her aliens were walking out of their suite, Glinda caught Sara's arm and beamed, "Sara, something happened between Howard and Delnoid."

Sara's jaw dropped as she thought, "Oh God, What happened? Did, did Howard try to seduce him?"

Glinda smiled and beamed, "Well sort of Sara, Delnoid, as soon as he realized what Howard was trying to do, he simply zapped his mind with pure indignation to abolish Howard's inappropriate advances. I mean after all Sara, Delnoid is a gender neutral android…"

Sara thought, "When, when did this happen?"

Glinda beamed, "Last night after Jane had thrown Howard out of her bedroom. Frustrated and rejected Howard actually went to Del's room to supposedly talk about our plans for the alien research base at that Arizona fort, fort - what was it Sara?"

"Fort Huachuca," replied Sara. Catching her composure again thought to her alien queen, "Please tell Delnoid that we apologize for Mr. Hughes's totally unacceptable disrespect…"

Delnoid beamed in, "It's OK Sara, I am also one of our ships ethics officers and besides, I am not designed to be offended nor am I able to have sex."

Just after lunch one of the White House security agents came into the dining room and said, "Excuse me Mr. President. Mr. Hughes has arrived sir."

Sara looked at the President and as Truman stood, Sara stood and said, "Mr. President, I need to talk with you in private a moment before you meet with our Mr. Hughes."

Glinda clicked emphatically and beamed, "Be sure to tell him about Mr. Hughes advances on Delnoid Sara."

Sara thought, "That is exactly my intentions. While I am meeting with Mr. Truman, why don't you and Selena get ready for our walk about? I am going to take you to see the monument that marks the southernmost point of the continental United States. Then, we have been invited to have lunch with Mr. Ernest Hemingway at his cat house."

Selena beamed, "Sara why is it called a cat house?"

Sara following Truman out of the dining room thought, "Later Selena, I have to talk with our president."

As Sara and Mr. Truman stood privately facing each other in the hallway leading towards the White House front porch, Sara looked at Mr. Truman and as she did so, he being used to and actually liked and deeply appreciated Sara's directness asked, "OK Sara what's happened?"

Sara told him about Mr. Hughes' sexual advances towards Delnoid. As soon as she told him that, Harry Truman, being at times a bible toting, God fearing mid western Baptist steamed, "OK, that's it! We have, as you know, heard endless rumors about his homosexual escapades for years. That other queer weasel, Mr. Hoover of the FBI, came to me once to try to get me to use it against our national treasure. If Howard thinks all of his genius and wealth entitles him to be such a no account, he's got a lesson coming about that. I'm going to throw that queer out right now!"

Sara diplomatically listened and softly said, "Uh, please, Mr. Truman we desperately need his genius and besides, remember that he has agreed to let Glinda try to heal his bi polar mind."

As Harry cooled down he said, "Yeah, you are right Sara. We do need him. But right now I want you to go enjoy your outing with your aliens. I am going to meet Mr. Hughes in my private study and read him the riot act."

Sara grinned and softly said, "OK, but be sure not to piss him off too much, ok? Remember we need him and his Hughes Aircraft now more than ever."

Mr. Truman gently grasped Sara's arm and said, "Don't worry Sara. I am going to speak softly but carry a big Presidential Baptist stick! Please give my regards to Mr. Hemingway and tell him I really enjoyed his Men Without Women book."

Sara said, "I will be sure to do that Mr. Truman." She thought, "Oh if only Harry could be without his shrew Bess. He could be a truly contented man instead of always being preoccupied and frustrated trying loving someone who isn't lovable."

Sara went up to her room and got her backpack. When she got to Selena's room, Glinda was sitting on the divan and had both of her index and middle fingers on each side of her temples. As Sara approached, Glinda lowered her hands and opened her eyes.

Sara crouched down next to her alien queen and asked, "Is everything alright Glinda?"

Glinda smiled and beamed, "I think so, I was just reviewing and beaming all of my mental recordings to our ship's system since we soon have to diligently start our training for living on Earth."

Now getting more and more sensitive and empathetic Sara smiled and said, "Are you sure everything is ok Glinda?"

Glinda beamed to her earth daughter of her heart, "Well Sara, you are very astute, maybe you are better developing your sixth sense. I have been so sad that our dear President has such an unhappy, loveless co-dependent marriage to that really selfish, small minded and controlling mid-western, matriarch shrew wife of his. Remember all of us are genetically matched by our medicos. It's sad that such careful compatibility planning is not used on Earth. Sara, my sister Shiri seems to really like Mr. Truman. So I want to ask what you would think if we introduced her to Mr. Truman? As you can well imagine Sara, I have deeply perceived Mr. Truman's heartbreak which he conceals so valiantly. I know that Shiri would be an excellent companion and a supportive unconditional loving friend for Harry."

Sara said, "Wow, Glinda! I have been thinking the same things but, I don't know what to say except that I have on a few occasions been there while Bess was scolding and spiteful to our dear Mr. Truman. It really makes me sore to see her disrespect her husband that way and I would love to see our dear President be happier. He puts on such a good face, but I have many times seen him blinking back tears and felt his heartbreak and his hopeless self deluding co dependence with Bess. But, the problem is, if Harry and Shiri were to get together that would cause a bad publicity storm that right now could doubtless cost our President his re-election. So I really think we should wait until after this vital re-election is settled before we introduce anyone to Mr. Truman."

Glinda clicked softly, nodded and beamed, "You are quite right Sara and yes, we will have to wait until after this November election."

Sara thought, "After we return you to your ship tomorrow night, I will come back here on the sub. Late on Wednesday evening I'll fly to my new office in Washington. Once there, I can really fully concentrate on planning for your Delphinians' landing on Water Island."

Arthur walked into the suite beaming, "I wanted to ask you if you would like Delnoid 6F to accompany you to Washington to act as our communication link and planning coordinator?" Sara looked up and thought, "Arthur that will be so welcomed and would sure help us all remain on the same page."

Glinda clicked and beamed to Sara, "On the same page, I like that expression."

Selena realized that tomorrow she and her dear Sara would be separated, squealed, clicked rapidly and beamed, "Oh Sara… can I please come stay with you in Washington?"

Sara smiled and put her arm around her little alien sister and thought, "I am going to be too busy to also have to guard you from all of the unscrupulous people, men, circumstances and things you know nothing about in our hectic and too faced capital."

Selena moaned and looked crushed but she beamed, "OK Sara I understand and besides, I must help mother with landing plans and also join all of the earth landing training classes and preparations. Everything that has happened here during our initial visit has all been beamed up to our pod. I still want to take time to carefully teach and explain everything so that I am sure our pod really understands these initial earth social and cultural significances we are starting to try to learn.”

Glinda stood and hugged both Sara and Selena and beamed, “You two will be together again soon on our Water Island.”

Arthur beamed to Sara, “Did the President tell you about our plan to bring all of us to the island without arousing public curiosity?”

Sara thought back, “No, I guess he and I will have to schedule some quality time to talk and outline our plan once we get back to Washington. But, we will not have much time to plan together. Mr. Truman has to quickly board his special iron clad 285,000 pound railroad car ‘Magellan’ on his whistle-stop cross country campaign train - just a month after we get back to DC. Ha! I wish that we all had your telepathy abilities so that we could debate like you do and all agree about who we want for our leader. Then, that agreement could be registered with the universe in the red stones.”

Arthur gave a small approving squeak and beamed to Sara, “Well, just remember dear earth daughter, you humans still have a long way to go to reclaim and use you innate telepathic abilities.”

Glinda beamed, “Earth daughter, what you are saying is correct. Even though Arthur, Selena and I are the genetic royalty of our pod, every seven of your earth years we all mind link in a special conclave to re-confirm our leadership along with all the other department leaders.”

Sara then for the first time realized that Arthur might not be leader forever thought, “Arthur when, when is your next uh, re-election coming up?”

Glinda and Arthur looked at each other and at Sara as Glinda beamed, “We will need to re-select in uh, 1952 to decide our leadership.”

Sara thought, “That’s good. So you will be the leaders during this so vital transition to Earth, uh, your Majesties?”

Arthur beamed, “Yes we will Sara.” He continued, “Now, What I think is an excellent plan to get all of us and our meager but vital possessions and equipment to the island is to use one of your aircraft carriers. Initially the President thought about chartering a cruise ship, but there would be no way to keep all of those civilian crewmembers unaware and quiet about our, uh, uniqueness.

By using an aircraft carrier, the US Navy will use the secrecy act to silence crewmen, and if need be, we can erase crewmembers’ memories about us.”

Sara chuckled remembering what Glinda had done to erase the minds of Captain Jones, his treacherous dolphin shooting seaman and the nice submarine SONARman. She also remembered what Arthur had done to erase the secret service men’s memories of their incredible and hilarious Biltmore golf game.

“Sara, the plan for us now is to surface and meet the USS Midway aircraft carrier somewhere in the open Atlantic just east of the Virgin Islands. Then, the 6 remaining rotating crew aboard our Lifestar will take it to its hiding place, another ancient alien starship base, at Picada de Zancudo in Tierra del Fuego, Chile, that we have already prepared for it.”

Sara asked, “Why so far away from Water Island Arthur?”

Arthur gave a troubled smile as he beamed, "Well, we really debated about this among our command staff and above all else we must have a safe as possible place to hide our ship. Also, at this point in time, at least two thirds of our Delphs feel that eventually they probably want to go live in west and east coastal South America. From the extensive visits we have made along the Pacific, Caribbean and Atlantic South American coasts of Colombia, Ecuador, Peru, Chile, Argentina and Brazil, we have found the people there to be generally more friendly, warm and compassionate like we are. But, as we each become habituated to our new lifestyles starting in your California, quien savvy (who knows) if and where in your world everyone will scatter to."

Sara looked sad and asked, "But, don't you want to remain all together as a pod, uh family?"

Arthur clicked, looked at Glinda as she then continued to explain their plans. "Sara we need to marry humans to broadly diversify, to survive and prosper successfully here on your world after the six generations in our cloistered sardine can pod on Lifestar. But we all agree that for now, we will really become able to understand how to act correctly from your leadership and training on Water Island and at Camp Roberts in California if we are together. Later, the best thing for our long term survival and expansion is to of course stay telepathically and emotionally connected. We must diversify and integrate as fully as we can into the earth cultures that work best for our safety, happiness and prosperity. One major thing for us to learn is how to use money here."

Sara said, "Oh that's right, you don't use money in your society."

Glinda smiled and beamed, "Sara remember that we are a pod culture and over the centuries for our overall welfare, emotional and spiritual connections, we always made successful pro survival choices for the overall good of all of our planetary family without using money as exchange units. We use instead, I guess that you would say, we naturally use emotional love and spiritual exchanges for our pod agreements, happiness and safety."

Sara looked agreeable as she said, "Oh that would be such an ideal model for us humans. Right now without such respectful and loving family and social connections, we have what?"

Arthur beamed in, "Over 37 different religions and endless fear, abusive egos, greed and wars Sara. This is what you tragically have."

Sara smiled and took her alien's hands and continued, "Here without your powerful pod connections and abilities to really agree for the overall good; the main god worshiped on earth has become money driven by fear of the lack of it, and ego and greed. Have you seen the US Constitution and the Bill of Rights?" All the aliens clicked rapidly as Sara continued, "One of the rights is the right to life, liberty and the pursuit of happiness. I will get you 160 copies."

Glinda clicked softly, smiled and beamed, "Just one is all we really need Sara. We can have a Delnoid unit scan with his eyes into our computer system and everybody can absorb it into their minds and vision." Sara's jaw dropped as she thought, "Wow, that's cool. I always forget that most of you have photographic memories and how technologically advanced you are."

Glinda beamed to Ailema aboard Lifestar. "You recently told me that your dear friend, Eleanor Roosevelt is right now at your United Nations working to develop a Universal Declaration of Human Rights."

Embry beamed back to Glinda for his non telepathic human wife. "Yes Glinda that's right. And we do hope that the humans can and will learn, habituate, respect and apply all 30 articles of those so admirable fundamental planetary human rights, ideals and agreements."

Glinda beamed, "Sara, you share with us and we share with you. We have heard of your Universal Declaration of Human Rights that Eleanor Roosevelt is now working on at your fledgling United Nations in San Francisco."

Sara, always astonished by the amazing expanse of the Delphinians awareness, smiled and said, "Oh that's right Glinda, I do hope that we humans, especially the children, will be taught to respect each other and apply all 30 articles of the Universal Declaration of Human Rights each and every day. Selena sensing that Sara was becoming a bit overwhelmed beamed to her, "Earth sister! Remember I want to come live with you in California Sara…That is if you want me?"

Sara grasped her dear Selena and cried, "Of course, I want to be with you always my dear family from the stars." Anthropologist Sara thought, "You are totally right dear Arthur and Glinda. I guess this will be an invasion and assimilation of the friendly… umm… Delphin kind."

Glinda, Selena and Arthur just squealed in delight as Sara joined in the laughter.

Sara thought, "It's too bad that we do not have a really gigantic sub without windows that's big enough to hold all 160 of you." Sara smiled and dried her eyes and said, "Well for now though, let's go see the furthest south point of the USA. It is just 90 miles north of Cuba. And after we will enjoy a lunch with Mr. Ernest Hemingway, who is one of the most famous writers we have. He also loves cats and keeps a herd, uh, pod of sixteen lovely polydactyl cats."

Glinda beamed, "Poly… what?"

Sara laughed and said, "That means most of Mr. Hemingway's cats have six toes instead of five like the majority of felines normally have."

Selena brightened and beamed, "Oh, I have seen pictures of cats and some cute little animals that I thought were cats running around in some of the coastal villages that we have visited. Do you think Mr. Hemingway would let me touch one of his cats Sara?"

Sara looked earnestly at her and said, "Touch one of them? Touch one of his pussycats?"

Selena moaned and squealed high to low as her face despaired and then brightened with joy as Sara continued. "Mr. Hemingway would be broken hearted if you didn't pet his cats. You see, it seems that there are two kinds of people on this world. There are people who love dogs and there are people who love cats and just a few who love both."

Selena became anxious and let out a moaning squeal as she beamed, "Will he have dogs too Sara? I am really afraid of dogs."

Sara crinkled her brow, took Selena's hand and asked, "Why? What happened?"

Selena explained, "Well, three years ago, we enjoyed visiting the Braun Menendez Palace - Magallanes Museum down in far south Punta Arenas, Chile. Then we crossed into the central square and had just kissed the big toe of the Tehuelche Patagonian Indian at the base of the Ferdinand

Magellan statue in the nicely shade treed central park when a pack of stray dogs came up to us and surrounded us. They were all sniffing and barking and we saw that the hair on their backs was raised."

Sara interjected, "We call that raising their hackles. Dogs do that whenever they are afraid or defending themselves. Cats do it too.

Selena then scowled squeaked and beamed, "They kept barking and sniffing and one of them, a small one, came up and bit me on my leg and then another larger one was snarling with its teeth barred - attacked me and severely bit my hand."

Arthur clicked loudly as he recalled and beamed, "I had to uh, immobilize all of them. And we quickly got in one of those quaint collectivo taxis which took us back to the pier to our Peterson motor boat. It was moored at the dock down at the end of Independencia Avenue for us to get back out into the Malagenic channel. But, we had to wait three hours until nightfall so that Life star could safely surface and take us back on board. It was really freezing and windy out there in the straits even though we had a flighter hovering just 100 feet overhead. It was so far, the closest call we have had."

Sara asked, "Why didn't you just have the flighter pick you up?" Glinda clicked in loud agitation as she beamed, "Because my motor boat loving husband did not want to abandon his beautiful Peterson motor boat!"

Selena clicked in merriment and beamed, "Yes it is one of his proudest earth acquisitions!"

Arthur grinned and clicked excitedly as he beamed, "Well, uh, we had to somehow learn to understand and how to work on your primitive earthly gasoline motors."

Sara then placed her hand on Selena's shoulder and asked, "Why on Earth would you want to kiss the big toe of a giant bronze Indian statue?"

Glinda smiled and beamed in, "Oh the very nice staff at the Palace Museum told us that it was a tradition and everyone who kisses the toe of the Indian will be sure to return to Punta Arenas."

Sara raised her eyebrows and shrugged her shoulders and said, "Well, ok, seems like a nice folk tradition I suppose."

Ironically little did Sara and her Delphinians know that in 2009 after President G.W. Bush betrayed their treaty with Truman that they would all have to flee to far south Punta Arenas, Chile to live and be near their starship's secret hiding place in an ancient aliens 50,000 yr old cliff face hanger at Picada del Zancudo (52* 12' 13.86" S 71* 39' 48.20 W) elevation 1,455ft ASL

Sara smiled at her alien family and said, "I guess that pack of street dogs smelled your alieness because dogs and most other animals use their noises to sexually examine other animals and humans. I know if I am on my period and around dogs, they sometimes come up and try to sniff my crotch."

Glinda smiled and clicked softly as she said, "We too have a keen sense of smell, but we mainly use our telepathy and sonic beams to evaluate others."

Selena clicked rapidly, screwed up her face in non comprehension and beamed, "Sara, what do you mean having your period?"

Sara embarrassedly said, "Well you know… our regular monthly female cycle of ovulation and menstruation…"

Glinda and Selena looked at each other, clicked in mirth and then at Sara as Glinda beamed, "Nope… But I think I know what you are talking about Sara. You see, neither we, nor dolphins menstruate as you call it. We have an estrus cycle only once per year."

Selena squealed and clicked in delight, grinned lustily and beamed, "And oh boy do we ever get super passionate when our cervix opens for breeding!"

Sara grinned as she blushed and changed the subject said, "Well, I think Mr. Hemingway likes dogs for when he goes hunting. But, he is a true blue cat person and he generously shares his Key West home with I hear, with about 30 kitties. So I am sure that there won't be any dogs there this afternoon."

Glinda beamed, "Sara, does Mr. Hemingway have blue skin, like your Negro people have black skin?"

Sara realized that she had again used another undefined slang term laughed and said, "Oh no Glinda, true blue means that he is loyal, totally loyal to his dear cats."

Selena exclaimed, "Oh Sara I cannot wait to go see and touch his kitty cats. Can we go there right now and skip that south uh, monument?"

Sara smiled and continued, "No Selena, Mr. Hemingway has invited us to a late lunch at 3 pm. Don't worry dear little sister, we will only spend a few minutes at that orange, black and yellow southernmost USA point marker." Glinda beamed, "Arthur, do you think that you can please take a break from planning with the president to come and enjoy the cats with us?"

Arthur beamed, "Uh unfortunately, no dear ladies. The President, Mr. Hughes, Delnoid 1 and I still have much to talk about and plan. Besides Glinda, you will be tuned in – no?"

Glinda clicked softly and lovingly energized her husband and beamed, "Like always dear fearless leader, like always and in all ways."

Arthur grinned and let out a blowhole fairly authentic rurrrfffff and beamed, "I don't particularly like cats. I love dogs and monkeys."

Selena realized that her father was only kidding beamed, "Hummmm, no dad of mine can be a cat hater." She made a remarkable meow sound with her blowhole."

Arthur squealed a laugh and beamed, "Here kitty kitty, come to King Arthur and my doggie for dinner…"

Glinda, Selena and Sara grinned as Glinda beamed, "Sara do people eat cats?"

Sara frowned as she said, "Yes, unfortunately in some countries like China, and in northern Peru cats are considered to be a delicacy."

Selena beamed, "Do you love cats Sara?"

Sara smiled and said, "For the most part I really do prefer cats and as a matter of fact. My dear black cat, Haley that Mr. Hemingway gave me in 1946, is safely at home with my parents. They feed and water her and groom her and also empty the stinky kitty litter from her sandbox each day."

Selena, was totally engrossed about cats squeaked and beamed, "What is kitty litter and why do cats have uh, sand in a box Sara?"

Sara explained, "Selena cats are naturally very clean animals. They always, after pooping, need to bury it outdoors but indoors at night, when they are safely inside with their humans, they need to use their sandbox."

Selena clicked and trilled and interjected, "What is poop Sara?"

Sara laughed and thought, "I have so much to teach you young one. Like, when you go to the bathroom, two things come out of you; pee which is the liquid and the solid stuff is poop which we also call shit."

Selena and all other dolphin heritage creatures who only excrete semi solid and liquid thru one orffice - squeaked sharply and let out a rude juicy raspberry and beamed, "Ok, ok… I got it!"

CHAPTER 28 HEMINGWAY'S ALIEN CAT CAPERS

After driving in the Presidential 1939, Lincoln K, Sunshine Special limo to the southernmost point monument; dutifully walking around it taking some images of each other beside it with Selena's digital camera, they all piled back in the limo as Selena excitedly beamed, "Let's go see the kitties!"

As they drove up to 907 Whitehead Street, Selena looked impatiently out of her left window and beamed, "Oh Amador Sara, what is that artistic tall white tower with that black thing on top of it?"

Sara looked and replied, "Oh Selena that is the Key West Light House. I think it was built just before Mr. Hemingway's house was built back in 1848, over a hundred years ago."

Selena squealed again in delight and clicked rapidly in amazement as she beamed, "I really like it. I want to make a sketch of it."

Sara smiled and touched the arm of her young protégée as she was reaching into her purse for her notebook and mechanical pencil. "Later Selena, we have to greet Mr. Hemingway and his kitties now."

Selena frowned and sighed as she put her pad and pencil away and beamed, "It's ok Sara, I have now memorized it and I will make my sketch once we are back aboard Lifestar."

The secret service agent opened their right hand door; they then stood by the outside the gate of this lovely, typical two story, white, black balconied Key West home with pale green wooden window shutters. Selena squealed in delight and beamed, "Oh, listen, listen! I can hear the cats making a noise that sounds like meow…."

Sara remembering that her aliens all had incredible supersensitive hearing said, "Selena that's exactly what we call the cat sound. Meow…"

Selena amazingly squeaked out three pretty good high pitched meows in a row. Sara rang the gate bell.

She and her aliens noticed through the gate gaps that there were many cats milling and cavorting around just inside the gate and Mr. Hemingway's servant kept saying; "No kitties, no gatitos, get away! I have to open the gate for our special visitors. Get away! Vamoose! Scat, scat you damn cats!" Finally feeling secure enough that the cats would not swamp the visitors; the servant opened the gate, smiled and said, "Hola. Mr. Hemingway is expecting you please come in quickly so these piche cats will not go raid the fish market down the street."

The servant then quickly closed the gate and Selena found herself surrounded by all the kitties who were meowing and some standing up and gently pawing and scratching at the legs of these very out of the ordinary smelling new humans who had called to them in their own language.

Selena began to reach down to touch the cats and as she did so, one black cat jumped up into her arms. Selena tentatively touched and instinctually gently started stroking the cat. It started to purr and since Selena had connected to it telepathically and spiritually, she squeaked in delight, clicked softly in response to the similar purring and beamed, "Oh, it loves me, it loves me !"

Sara and Glinda were quickly surrounded by the other kitties demanding equal attention. Glinda picked up a tabby and copied Selena's petting of the cat and beamed, "Oh, listen it loves me too." Sara picked up a tuxedo cat and as she stroked it, it too began to purr.

Sara said, "I always thought that purring just meant a happy cat, but now with your amazing hearing and love energy sensitivities I know now that there is a lot more to a purr than just feline contentment.

They walked to the porch with cats in their arms and pursued by the rest of the cat pack. Sara walked up to Mr. Hemingway who by then was in stitches.

He finally recovered enough to say, "Dear Sara I have never ever seen my kitties take to strangers like this."

Sara smiled and thought, "Oh Mr. Hemingway, if only I could tell you the truth. You would be the first writer I would tell this unbelievable story to if I could."

Sara managed to get the now totally relaxed and happy cat into the crook of her left arm as she reached out to shake Mr. Hemingway's extended right hand. As she did so, two more cats did gravity defying leaps to try to get into their arms for more of this amazing attention like their cat kin were getting from these exceptional new visitors.

Sara and Mr. Hemingway suddenly found themselves with three loudly purring cats in their arms and then, two more leapt for their human's loving arms. Hemingway dropped his arms and exclaimed, "Ok, that does it! Scat you damn cats! Scat! Let us go enjoy our lunch now."

By then any little bashfulness between Sara, her aliens and Hemingway had evaporated as he, in typical latino custom, took the hands of Sara, Selena and Glinda, he kissed their right cheeks. He said, "Well, uh, a hardy welcome to my cat house dear ladies. It's so good to see you again Sara. What have you been doing? How are your mother and father and how is that little black kitten I gave you last year doing?"

Sara replied, "Oh Ernest, the kitten is doing great and mom and dad are ok and dad always remembers producing and directing your To Have and Have Not story back in 1944. It was Loren Bacall's first major film."

Sara and her aliens sat at his spacious dining room table and Sara said, "Mr. Hemingway, these are special visitors, hummmm… refuges that are from uh, South America. While they are visiting here the President is planning where to relocate them to."

Hemingway laughed as he admonished, "Sara, never end a sentence with a preposition…I remember visiting with you and your family in Montecito and I once tried to visit the observatory at Westmont College near your home. After I turned left onto the campus from Cold Springs Road, I became totally lost on those endless twisty small roads on their treed campus. I finally encountered a professorially looking fellow and asked him, "Excuse me sir, can you please tell me where the Observatory is at?"

That stuffed shirt, pompous professor became indignant and he said, "Here at Westmont my good man, we never end our sentences with a preposition sir."

"I grinned at him, dropped my stogie and ground it out in the grass and said, "Oh please do excuse me sir. I shall now rephrase my question. Dear sir, can you please tell me where the observatory is at, jackass!"

Sara had taken a couple of undergraduate anthropology classes at Westmont and knew very well how stuffed shirted and sanctimonious some of the professors were. Upon hearing the punch line, she cracked up. Hemingway quickly noticed that her friends were only smiling and that the younger one had dropped her arm and was eagerly trying to entice a black kitten to come to her.

Sara quickly recovered her glee said, "Oh Mr. Hemingway! Did you really say that?"

Hemingway grinned and said, "So help my cats I did just that Sara."

Sara quickly received beamed questions about prepositions and jackasses from both Glinda and Selena. She told Hemingway, "My, uh, our friends are mute from a family genetic mutation." Glinda and Selena took their cue from Sara, quickly reached into their purses and took out their notepads and mechanical pencils.

Hemingway said scratching his head, "Mute you say…" He then proceeded to speak rapidly in perfect Spanish to Glinda and Selena.

Glinda glanced anxiously at Sara and wrote on her note pad, "Oh dear Senor Hemingway, mucho gusto encontrelo." She continued amazingly scribbling more rapidly than Sara had ever seen in English. "I am sorry we cannot speak to you, but we do understand both English and Spanish."

Glinda ripped out her note page, grinned wryly and proudly handed it to Hemingway. He read it, smiled and said, "Oh dear ladies from so magnifico South America. I am so sorry that I was rattling so impolitely."

Selena stifled a mirthful squeak, looked at Mr. Hemingway and scribbled. "It's Ok, Esta bien Mr. Hemingway."

Glinda scribbled, "I would guess that you have spent a lot of time in Cuba from your so rapido espanol Senor but if we can just slow down, so that Selena and I can write, then we can all delight in sharing comfortably."

Hemingway, being the old and world wise hombre that he was said, "Of course dear ladies, I will slow down…It is so wonderful to see my Sara again. I used to work with her father when he was making some movies from my books. I spent many wonderful weekends with them up in their beachside Montecito home just south east of Santa Barbara."

Selena scribbled and tore, "I plan to attend Sara's university there someday."

Hemingway smiled and asked, "So, what do you plan to major in?"

Selena scowled and beamed to Sara, "Oh Amador, what does major mean?"

Sara thought back, "Study Selena, it means to study and learn." Selena scribbled, "Anthropology and dolphins."

Hemingway laughed quietly as he read. "So, you like dolphins?"

Selena, suppressing a squeal, smirked and just nodded her head enthusiastically.

Hemingway said, "I have always felt that dolphins are as intelligent as we are, if not more so."

Glinda grinned, suppressing her gleeful clicks and thought, "I could have told you that!" But instead, she scribbled, "I agree totally Mr. Hemingway…Te aquerdo todo."

Most all of the kitties had now invaded the dining room still meowing to be petted and cat beamed to by their wonderful new humans. As Hemingway noticed his cat mob twining around everyone's legs he said, "Well, let's eat before these dang cats eat us. I have had Lupe prepare a nice Cuban almuerzo for us. Fortunately it's mainly rice, beans and pancito (little bread rolls) to dip in olive oil mixed with finely granulated garlic and chopped cilantro with no fish, otherwise my dang cats would be todo loco by now with their starving kitty acts. So, before we begin our almuerzo, what would you ladies like to drink? Sara will you and your South American guests join me for a Daiquiri with Bacardi rum from Cuba?"

Sara recalling Hemingway's fondness for daiquiris smiled and said, "Oh gracias Ernesto, but we do not drink alcohol. My amigas simply cannot tolerate any spirits. So, Coke or juice will be fine thanks."

As they enjoyed their first Cuban meal, Glinda scribbled on her notebook, "This is muy bueno Senor Hemingway. We have had rice and beans and asada (BBQ) al the time in Argentina but this is really light, flavorful and delicious. It is especially refreshing in this so hot and humid south Florida climate."

After Hemingway read her note, he asked, "Do you like those little green leafy flakes?"

Glinda, still savoring a mouthful, picked up her notepad and scribbled, "Oh si, it's very nice, what is it?"

Hemingway smiled knowingly and responded by taking his new amazingly reliable, non smearing Rocket ball point pen out of his guyaberra shirt pocket and wrote, Cilantro. As he handed his note to Glinda he said, "It's strangely not really known or used in Argentina or in Spain. But it is used in most all other Latin American countries; especially in Mexico, Cuba and Chile. It's a mainstay for a flavorful seasoning and also used for making tomato, olive oil and lemon based salsa. People either love it or hate it, just like people either love or hate cats. Some people don't like it, they say it tastes like soap. But, I always tell them to just eat only the leaves and not the stems to avoid the soapy taste."

Sara, seeing for the first time one of the new fangled ball point pens asked, "Mr. Hemingway, may I please have a look at your pen? Where did you get it?"

Hemingway grinned as he absent mindedly clicked the pen in and out... "I got it for Christmas back in 1945. One of my publishers sent me a couple dozen from Gimbels in New York City." He stood and walked to the dining room sideboard, opened a lower drawer and said, "Ah, here they are!" He gave one to Sara, Selena and Glinda. When they started clicking their new pens Selena beamed to Sara and Glinda, "Hey it sounds kind of like our Delphin clicks, let's try to see if we can communicate using them." The aliens and giggling Sara were rapidly clicking away with their pens.

Hemingway amusedly sipped on his Daiquiri, chortled and said, "OK girls, are you having fun playing with your new pens?" Sara started laughing as Glinda and Selena speeded up their thumbs clicking the pens up to almost Delphin speed...

Selena beamed to Glinda and Sara, "Hey this works fairly well for sort of imitating a few of our lower frequency clicks..."

As the gleeful pen clicking died down, Hemingway noticed that Selena had enticed the still cautious little black kitten to her. The kitten mewed joyfully and used its claws to try to climb up her leg. Selena gave a short surprised squeak and scooped it up into her lap and as she started beaming love to it and was gently caressing it, the kitten purred like a happy little motor and went into total catnip ecstasy.

Selena noticed that Mr. Hemingway had a note he had scribbled in his hand for her. She took the note, squealed in delight, broke into tears and just nodded her head as happily as she could.

Sara was becoming alarmed at her alien's excited high pitched squeals and said, "Uh Mr. Hemingway that is one of the only sounds our friends can make."

Hemingway said, "It doesn't matter Sara. Look at the pure joy I have brought to our Selena and her new kitten." Selena handed the note to Glinda and it said, "This cat's for you hija. Always respect the wisdom of cats."

Glinda stood and walked over to the grizzly old author, hugged him and tearfully beamed silent loving and healing energies into him.

His writer's soul was now empty and his liver ravished after several months of depression and writers' block. He'd also consumed way too much rum and smoked countless stinky Cuban cigars.

After Glinda's healing energy filled embrace, Hemingway had tears in his eyes as he stammered, "I, I have never had such a loving hug ever before in my life." He stood and hugged Glinda and blubbered, "Gracias querida Senora, gracias. A sus ordenes siempre." (Thank you dear Mrs. I am at your service always). He hugged Sara and Selena and as even more Delphin love energies flowed into his body, mind and spirit he said, "Oh it's so great to see my Sara again and thank you for bringing these two, uh, so miraculous women into my cat house."

After lunch Hemingway said, "Come on, I'll give you the deluxe tour of my casa." As they followed him through his house Glinda beamed to Sara and Selena, "My this is a lovely home. Maybe someday we can build one just like it in Argentina."

Sara thought, "Or maybe purchase one like it in Santa Barbara. But, even though our Montecito beach sid house isn't, the architecture there along the south coast is a lot of Spanish colonia with red tile roofs."

When they entered Hemingway's upstairs main house study, library and writing office, Selena saw the Remington typewriter on his desk with a nice grey stripped kitten lying contentedly purring beside it. She stroked the grateful kitty as she sat and began typing, "Thank you dear Mr. Hemingway for my cute kitten. Her name is Gatita and I love her and you mucho." When she pulled the paper out of the typewriter and handed it to Hemingway, he read it, and broke into tears as he stood beside Selena clasping her shoulder. Selena stood and hugged the old softie author and beamed more pure love energies into him.

He stepped back from the embrace, and tearfully said, "I, I don't know what to say except, I love you too, dear ladies. Gracias, for sharing your so amazing wonderful and loving energies."

Glinda stepped up to Hemingway and hugged him and sweetly kissed his left cheek. As she did so, she beamed to Sara and Selena, "I do hope that we can visit him often in future. His left eye is bad from congenital diabetic retinopathy. His diabetes and hemochromatosis are now worsening, and heavy drinking is causing his depressions. He is also developing psychosis from the traumatic brain injuries he received in plane and auto crashes. These are the appalling reasons for his growing despondency, drinking, frustrations and fears over the past few years. Just like our Mr. Howard Hughes. If we can stay in direct contact with him, I can heal him. But to do so now at full force would be more than his troubled mind or he could understand."

She then wrestled her note pad out of her purse and scribbled. "We love you too Mr. Hemingway. You are a very rare creative and loving spirit. Please try to stop drinking and smoking those horrible Cuban cigars! Please respect your body and soul more."

Hemingway, clearly feeling the amazing, if not miraculous, healing energies said, "I believe you dear lady. And I believe you and now I tambien (also) believe in you senorita Selena."

Sara teared up and just thought, "Oh God there is so much good that these Delphinians can do in our world."

Glinda beamed to Sara. "Yes, but we must be very conscientious because you are still a culture of how do you call such fearful and overactive people Sara?"

Sara frowned as she thought, "Witch hunters Glinda. We call them witch hunters. A really significant example of such pathological false accusing and lying tactics is relentlessly heard from our current Senator Joseph McCarthy's communists hunting and tirades against our President Truman and other good people… particularly towards those in our motion picture businesses."

Selena beamed, "What are witches and what is a senator Sara?"

Sara smiled as she thought back, "Evil people like your mother just described Selena. Wait until Halloween and I will show you some."

Selena beamed in wide eyed astoundment, "What is Halloween Sara?"

Sara grinned mischievously and forgetting to think instead of saying… said, "Oh Selena witches come out on Halloween to ride their brooms with their black cats…"

Selena became bewildered as she started to beam a torrent of Halloween questions back to her earth sister.

Mr. Hemingway broke the spell and said, "Uh dear senoritas, shall we continue the tour of my casa?" But by then he was beginning to get an inkling of just how extraordinary Sara's charges were.

They exited out onto the balcony, through the arched glass double doors of his second floor study and library. Hemingway, holding hands with Glinda, led them around to the rear northeast corner of the wide balcony that completely surrounded the second floor. He then towed them across a three foot wide metal and wood trimmed walkway that led directly into the second floor of his cottage. They entered through the double portico ceiling to floor entrance. He said, "I had this bridge built so I can quickly get into my writing studio."

As they entered his writing sanctuary they saw that it was surprisingly almost empty. It had a round drop leaf writing table with a Royal typewriter, reference books, a notebook, a wooden box for his typing paper, three Rocket ballpoint pens and several #2 pencils with erasers in an empty Spam tin on the table. There were filled 4 level book shelves along the north wall between two more floor to ceiling wide windows which let plenty of natural light into his study.

Near the corner, from the white and blue trophy Tarpon, hung a clock, barometer, and a RH temperature instrument. At the round table he had only one straight back chair with a brown leather seat and a straight back Spanish style chair. There was also a rattan chaise for him if he wanted to relax and puff on a stogie or drink or think or take a snooze.

Selena entered and immediately squeaked and moaned as she beamed to her mother and Sara, "Oh dear Amador! What is that beautiful animal's head doing on the wall like that?"

Sara squeezed Selena's hand and said, "Mr. Hemingway is an ardent hunter and this is called a trophy head."

Hemingway noticed Selena's fearful and very concerned expression. He put his hand on her shoulder and said, "Dear Selena, this is the head of an African antelope I shot while I was on safari in Africa, uh, a few years ago…"

Selena was riveted, looking at the head she began to tear up and beamed to Sara, "What is a safari and why did this human who loves cats ever kill such a beautiful animal?"

Sara to be sure Hemingway got the drift said, "Well Selena you all capture, kill and eat fish right? Look at that nice big tarpon on the wall over there."

Hemingway pointed to the trophy tarpon and said, "I caught that last year while we were out fishing on my boat, Pilar. Would you like to come out fishing with me sometime ladies?"

Selena reluctantly nodded her head in agreement squealed and moaned and beamed to Sara and Glinda, "Well I guess this is the unavoidable way of this world."

Glinda hugged her daughter around her waist and beamed, "Selena there is good and bad, happy and sad and necessary realities on all worlds. Even our dolphin cousins feel such emotions but, they also have to hunt and kill for food."

Selena holding her notebook and pencil in hand wrote and handed it to Hemingway. "Mr. Hemingway, It sure was a beautiful animal but if you had to kill it for food, I guess that's alright…" She wiped a tear from her eye with the back of her right hand.

Hemingway then realized how the trophy head troubled her said, "Dear little Selena, Uh, why yes, of course we had to kill it to eat while we were camping out in the wilds of Africa." He really realized and began to respect for the first time in his years of hunting trophy heads, how that might make others feel. He put his arm around her shoulders and said, "Come on over here to this big window and see my 65 foot by 25 foot 9 foot deep saltwater swimming pool."

As soon as Selena saw his big swimming pool, she squealed, sonic beamed its depth, tore off her blouse and skirt and clad only in white bra and panties, bent over and pulled off her flipper cover sneakers. She then swept through the open double windows, leapt onto the porch roof and made an impossible 16 foot dolphin swan dive into the deep end of the pool. As she descended like a flying girl dolphin she squealed and clicked in delight and beamed to Glinda and Sara, "Oh Amador! Finally ! a pool without chlorine!" Sara just slapped her hand to her forehead and said, "Oh my gosh

Selena ! Now you have really done it…"

Glinda gathered up Selena's skirt, blouse and shoes as she started down to reclaim the impetuous Selena. She beamed directly into Hemingway's mind, "Oh dear Amador, Mr. Hemingway, I am so sorry about this. It's just that, uh that Selena is uh, squeakadee squeak, uh, a compulsive swimmer."

Hemmingway was cracking up and between laughs he said, "Yeah and that ain't all that she is or you either dear Glinda." Sara took Hem's hand and together they followed now running Glinda down to reclaim her joyously squealing Delphin swimmer girl."

After Glinda commanded Selena out of the pool, Hemingway shouted, "Lupe LUPE !!! Triar unas tollas. (bring some towels) Immediamente por favor!"

Hemingway looked at Sara, put his strong arms around her, chuckled and asked, "Ok kiddo, what's the true story here? Who are these wonderful dolphin sounding beings?"

Sara pleadingly looked at her old girlhood family friend and incredulously said, "Well, uh, Hem, can you please, please keep this a secret? It's a really big national security issue."

Hemingway looked at Glinda drying her daughter off and he could see that somehow mentally or telepathically she was really reading the riot act to shame faced Selena, it was probably at least about no more swimming while visiting people's homes…

In Glinda's serious dismay, she inadvertently let some thoughts slip out and both Sara and Hemingway heard in their heads mental sound bites like, "Oh Amadore Selena, how could you!" and "Danger for all of us. And, for Amador's sake daughter! He's a writer…. Why weren't you thinking?"

Nervous faced Selena just stood there crying, nodding her head and clicking rapidly - all the while quietly squeaking softly and moaning as she nervously tapped her righ flipper foot.

Hemmingway just grinned and put his arm around Sara and said, "OK, Sara, no problema. I know that you and Truman must have some really vital situation at stake here and because I utterly respect and trust the President and love you hija, I will seal my lips and typewriter about this. But, Sara If and when this is going to go public, I want the first scoop from you. Ok?"

Sara in tears hugged Hem and cried, "Ok! Oh thank you! It's a deal it's a deal…It's a done deal Hem."

Selena, still crying and with a yellow towel wrapped around her, ran up to Hemingway and hugged him and beamed directly to him, "Oh Mr. Hemingway, I am so sorry. I just saw your big deep pool and I felt so at home here that I just could not help diving in cause it had no chlorine to hurt my eyes again."

Hemingway hugging his now heart adopted, whatever the heck she was, said, "Corazon,(sweetheart) hija, no problema, mi casa y mi piscina es su casa siempre." (no problem, my house and pool are yours always). Glinda came over and joined the hug with Sara, Selena and Hem. Sara and Hem then collapsed into his wide trellised back solar yellow deck chairs and Glinda offered Selena her shoes.

As Hemingway looked down at Selena's feet he saw her wide flipper like feet without toes, he stroked his beard and raised his right eyebrow and laughed, "Well somehow your impossible dive to swim and now your uh, dolphin like flippers don't surprise me at all. I have so many questions now, but for your and Sara's sake, I will pretend that I saw and heard nothing." He pursed his lips, tightened his throat and tried to make a Selena like whistle and squeak.

Selena saw him and as she held his shoulder she grinned and beamed, "Oh no, Mr. Hemingway, it's like this…" Selena squeaked like a dolphin and meowed like a cat; as they then all released their tensions with laughter.

All the kitties heard Selena's enticing meow, rounded the corner of the studio cottage, meowing and twining around the feet of both the Delphinians. Gatita leapt straight into the arms and love energies of Selena as the other cats also sprang up into the arms of the humans and aliens they loved.

As they all sat there in the four trellised chairs petting the kitties, Hemingway roared, "Lupe! Lupe!" His amiable braided Cuban maid came out of the house and asked, "Si Senor?"

"Lupe do you remember where we put that little old wooden cat transport cage? Please try to find it and a half dozen each of small tins of tuna and sardines." Lupe, who was always amazed at the gatitos and Senor Hemingway's loving kindness to them, smiled and said, "Por su puesto Senor. OK, I will go find it for you."

Selena and Glinda watched in amazement as Lupe picked up Selena's Gatita and gently placed her little cat, meowing it's little head off, into the wooden cat carrier. Lupe handed the cage to Hemingway and he put his arm around Selena and said, "Well, hija, here is your gata and I guess it's going to be the first cat on earth going to wherever the heck it is that you are going to!" Sara laughed, grinned and pointed at Hem and exclaimed… "Uh, uh, Ernest…Remember… never end a sentence with a preposition!"

Selena took the precious cage and hugged Hem and proudly beamed, "I will take care of our gata always Mr. Hemingway. No Matter what!"

Hemmingway had written a little book titled The Wisdom of Cats, just grinned as he said, "Well my dear little Selena, life is always a cat after cat after cat. Take care of her and your mother and Sara - Ok?"

They hugged goodbye and Hem and Lupe scattered the kitties away from the gate. Sara, her aliens and now the meowing kitten, entered the president's limo. Sara told the agent driving, "OK guys back home to the cat house!" Glinda and Selena squeaked a snigger and the kitten meowed. The perplexed agent looked in his rear view mirror and said, "Uh, I beg your pardon Miss Sara, did you say that you want to go to a cat house?"

Sara sniggered and sternly said, "No, not that kind of cat house agent. Take us back to the White House." As they drove along Selena had her little finger stuck in the wire mesh and gently stroked and beamed calming love energies to her kitten. But the now freaked out kitten just ceaselessly mewed her head off.

Selena looked worriedly at Sara and beamed, "Oh Amador, Is something wrong with my kitten Sara?"

Sara, who had raised several kittens, put her arm around Selena and said, "No, remember, it's never been away from its mamma cat and brothers and sisters and right now it's just scared." Selena powered up her love energies and quickly the frightened little black kitten began to purr. But, the kitten did not close her eyes. Not even for an instant as she kept her Selena in view through the cage wires.

Sara gave Selena a little squeeze and thought, "That's brilliant little sister. Your kitten is so lucky to have your soothing energies. Tonight once kitty starts to freak out missing her family in her cat cage in our room, you will be able to sooth her so that we all can sleep."

Selena beamed, "Oh Sara, I shan't sleep at all. I will keep our kitten calm and secure."

The agents dropped off Sara, the aliens and the new feline resident at the White House under the entrance portico. Sara smiled craftily at the agent and said, "I need you to please go down to the beach and fill a large bucket with sand and bring it up stairs and put it in my room."

The surprised agent replied, "OK miss Sara, one bucket of beach sand coming up. But uh, ma'am, the oil absorbent used on garage floors is really lighter and works much better in absorbing poop odors and cat pee."

Sara grinned and said, "OK, wonderful agent Jones. Please get us some. Please pick up about 6 bags of it because we will need it for our uh visitors to take home with them."

The agent tipped his hat and replied, "Yes ma'am but, don't they have garages where they come from?"

Sara looked sternly at the agent and commanded, "Please just get the fancy kitty litter as I have asked you – ok!"

"Yes Miss Sara right away uh, Ma'am…"

CHAPTER 29 MOVIE NIGHT AT THE LITTLE WHITE HOUSE

At dinner Truman asked, "Sara, where is Selena? Is she not feeling well?"

Sara grinned and replied, "Mr. President, she is up in our room attending to our new White House kitten."

Truman smiled and said, "Oh wonderful! Did Ernest give her one of his precious cats?" Sara sniggered and said, "He sure did." Truman became sad and said, "Oh, I dearly love cats but my Bess hates them… so I have never been allowed to have a cat. Let's go see it."

Sara replied, "OK, let's go, but also I will have to fill you in later about our astute Mr. Hemingway now being just a little bit in our alien secret loop."

Truman looked alarmed for a few seconds and said, "Well above all other, uh outsiders, I know we can totally trust Ernest. He and I go back a long way and if we can ever authorize anyone to write about all of this, he will be my first choice."

Sara cocked up her eyebrows and said, "Oh good Mr. President, because that's the deal we made." Truman just nodded his head and said, "Hummmm…"

Sara asked the President, "So how did your meetings go today?"

Truman grinned and said, "Oh very well indeed. We got a lot of their landing preparation done and now we plan to use the aircraft carrier Midway. I have just ordered it to head out from Rome to return to Norfolk, Virginia. It will then be on standby for my orders to rendezvous with our alien's starship in the open Atlantic east of the Caribbean. That way, they can sail around out of sight for a few days for our alien's initial orientations before we drop them off at Water Island."

Sara worriedly asked, "What about its crew Mr. President?" "Doesn't an aircraft carrier have over 4000 crew members?"

Truman grinned as they entered the elevator, "Normally it does Sara, but its air wing has already been disembarked and half of its planes have already been flown to Davis Monthan AFB in southern Arizona for mothballing in their huge aircraft bone yard. So without her aviation contingent, we can dare to operate the carrier with only about 800 crew members."

Sara said, "Isn't that kind of risky to expose our aliens to so many crew members Mr. President?"

He sighed and said, "Well, Commander Joe Ciokon, assures me that the crew can be mostly sequestered in their engineering deck quarters and in officer's country and our aliens will be billeted in the junior officer's quarters. Its surely a rock and a hard place Sara, but it's the only thing big enough for us to have total government control over to get our 160 amigos off of their starship and secretly as possible and securely and safely to Water Island."

Sara nodded her head in agreement and said, "Ok we can only do the best that we can, Mr. President. I have been checking around for a post Water Island orientation and training place for the new members of our human family. And, I think that Army Camp Roberts in central coastal California will be a perfect final training and housing base for them before we turn them loose to pursue their life dreams on Earth." She went on, "Its right near Vandenberg AFB and there they would have a nearby top secret secure base for their uh, our technology work and development."

Truman whispered to Sara, "Well that will do for awhile. But the main alien research and development facility is deep down inside the Huachuca Mountains in south eastern Arizona." The President looked knowingly at Sara and continued, "Anyway, we can plan more later. I hear that kitten yelling its little head off."

When they entered the room, everyone was concerned to see Selena sitting on her bed fretfully petting the meowing kitten and beaming it love energies. As she saw Sara she beamed frantically, "Sara it won't stop crying."

Sara looked at the kitten and at the floor and said, "Did they put those bags of kitty litter in here yet?"

Selena clicked slowly and nodded toward the bags and beamed, "Do you mean those bags over there?"

Sara smiled, reached out and gave the kitten a quick caress and hugged her alien sister and said, "I'll be right back."

In a few minutes Sara returned carrying a shallow rectangular metal dishwashing pan, a small porcelain saucer and a pint bottle of milk. She set the saucer down on the bed and poured milk in it and said, "OK little cat owner sister, kitten lesson number one."

Selena released the kitten and she made a bee line for the milk. But she, never having tasted cow milk before, just tentatively sniffed at it. Sara picked up the perplexed but now starving kitten and held it firmly on her left arm, she dabbed her right index finger in the milk and touched the milk droplet onto the kitten's nose. It licked the milk off, squirmed free of Sara's arm using its tiny but sharp little claws and happily started lapping up her milk from the saucer…

Selena gently stroked her kitten with her fingertip and beamed, "Oh, it was hungry! Mom, do we have milk onboard our ship?" Glinda sitting next to the lapping kitten beamed, "No, but I'll bet our synthesizer can make some for Gatita."

Sara stood and walked over one of the 10 pound sacks, pulled the sewn bag sealing strings only a little bit across the top and placed the large rectangular dish pan on the floor and poured in about an inch of the light weight oil absorbing granules.

She turned to Selena and said, "OK princess of the cats, in just a few minutes, watch what your kitten will have to do in her sandbox!"

Selena squeaked with joy; the kitten hearing Selena's squeak with its cat supersensitive hearing, arched her little cat back, foomped up her back fur and made a tiny little hiss.

Selena seeing that, gave another high pitched squeak and the kitten jumped, re-arched her back, re-foomped her fur and hissed again looking frantically all around trying to find what the hell that squeak was.

Selena instinctually put two fingers behind each of the kitten's ears and as the scared little feline turned to bite her, Selena flowed soothing and loving energies to her kitten.

Sara said, "That's terrific Selena, you and that cat are bonding like no, uh, person, uh, delphin or cat has ever bonded before."

Selena beamed to Sara, "Why does the kitten arch its back and make its fur stand up like that Sara?"

Sara grinned as she explained, "Remember as I told you. Dogs as well as kittens and cats arch their backs and puff out their fur like that to make themselves appear bigger so that predators might think they are too big to attack."

Glinda, thinking about the great size of their room beamed, "I think for now we best put the kitten, its milk, food dish and its sandbox in the bathroom."

Sara agreed as she picked up the cat pan, entered the bathroom, closed the bathroom windows and said, "Ok now it's secure for tonight for our new bathroom resident." Sara, knowing kittens, also closed the toilet lid and said, "Be sure to always keep the lid down."

Selena beamed, "Sara don't cats know how to swim?" Sara laughed and said, "Yes they can swim Selena, but they generally really do not like to get wet."

She placed the sardine tin on the counter and used the can key to roll open the top which she then placed on the bathroom floor. Then, the now still hungry and curious kitten smelling the fish, leapt off the bed and headed into the bathroom for her delicious smelling solid cat food.

Sara, Glinda, Selena and Arthur noticed that Mr. Truman had small tears in his eyes. Selena sensing Mr. Truman's deep sadness at not being allowed a cat beamed, "Mr. Truman, should we get you a kitten from Mr. Hemingway to keep here?"

Truman reached out and touched Selena's arm as he sighed, "No my dear princess because I will soon be away to tour in my campaign train to try to get re-elected."

Selena held the President's shoulder and beamed, "It's Ok Mr. Truman. But someday we will get you a cat of your own and I don't care what your mean Bess thinks!" President Truman, his heart melting, just held Selena's hand as he continued to gaze at the kitten now in its bathroom cat heaven.

Selena looked over at her mother who was in deeply concentration and beamed, "Mom, that's a great idea." Sara too did not want to interrupt Glinda's obvious deep meditation waited with her hand on the President's shoulder. Arthur grinned and began to squeak some soft squeaks of laughter and the kitten did a quick hiss and arch but quickly returned to its sardine feast.

The President being kept out of Glinda 's thoughts asked, "Why, what's so funny Arthur?"

Arthur squealing and clicking with Delphin laughter beamed to the President, "Glinda is beaming to Mr. Hemingway asking for a sample of cat milk to give to our food synthesizer technicians."

Harry Truman roared with laughter and said, "Oh Lord in heaven!

What I would give to see Hem trying to milk a cat!"

Hemmingway had been peacefully sitting at his dining table enjoying a nice Cuban asada dinner with Lupe when suddenly his eyes widened and he twisted his head from side to side trying to figure out who in hell had come into the room. Lupe kept asking, "Heme, Heme que paso? Who are you talking to mi viejo?"

He tried concentrating and asked, "Hello is this really you Glinda? This is amazing I can hear you clearly in my head!" Glinda's unexpected and so strange long distance telepathic request for a cat milk sample came into his head. He dropped his fork and almost rolled off of his leather backed Cuban chair – and stamping his feet and roaring in confounded laughter said, "You have got to be kidding! It's impossible to milk a cat. Why, Natasha would scratch my eyes out and slice me to small pieces with her claws and her sharp teeth would make hamburger of my fingers for messing around with her little cat titties. She would never forgive me for such an indignation."

Glinda squealed in laughter and beamed back, "Ok, wonderful, we can communicate now Mr. Hemingway. Tomorrow I shall come over and get a cat milk sample, ok?"

Hemingway, still struggling to stay in his chair was pounding his left fist on the dining table and still howling with laughter said, "Ok great. Wonderful. I will look forward to seeing all of you again tomorrow for lunch at 11:30. Can Harry and your husband hopefully come along too?"

Glinda looked at the still amused chortling President and beamed, "Can you come have lunch with Mr. Hemingway tomorrow? Selena and I are going back over for a swim, lunch and hopefully, a cat milk sample."

Harry Truman needed a break from the White House and the last week's exhausting and intensive alien planning meetings, smiled and said, "Why sure. Why not, I do need and deserve a break and it'll be so great to see my old amigo Hemingway. How about you Sara, are you free to come too?"

Sara laughing had tried, mostly unsuccessfully, to vanquish the image of Hemingway tussling with a sharp clawed lady cat for a milk sample, giggled and said, "Great, I would love to see him again and also see how Glinda is going to get a cat milk sample!"

Truman laughed again and said, "I would not miss this for all the tea in China and all of the cats in the world!"

Selena beamed, "Can we take Gatita to see her mamacita cat?"

Sara smiled and explained, "Selena we best leave her here in her safe cat box because she is just now beginning to get over her fear and sadness at having to leave her mother, ok?"

Selena teared up and beamed, "Ok Sara, I guess you know best about cats. Will she be ok here alone?"

Sara smiled reassuringly and said, "She will be fine Selena, we will put some water in her open cat cage, leave the kitty litter pan on the bathroom floor and we will lock the bathroom door."

Selena, still petting her precious kitten smiled half heartedly and beamed, "Ok Sara but why can't we leave milk for her?"

President Truman chipped in, "You see Selena milk goes bad if it is left out too long or if it's not kept cold. Kitties must have fresh safe milk. And it's always way too hot here in the Florida Keys to ever leave milk out."

Selena looked lovingly and beamed to her kitten, "See Gatita, we will take care of you always and in all ways dear kitten." The little kitten stopped lapping looked up and started purring and twining around her alien's ankles.

Harry Truman looked at all of his dear aliens and thought, "Gosh, even that kitten understands about love energies. I am so glad that we are coming together and I will always do all that I can to help and protect all of you."

Sara and the aliens sensed that Harry was feeling very worried about what could happen to them if he were not re-elected in 1948.

Arthur put his hand on the President's shoulder sending encouraging energies and beamed, "Mr. President you are doing the best that you and Sara can do for us and we are blessed with your capable and caring response abilities. We will be ok no matter what happens. We still have our ship and plan A, B, C and D if we ever need it."

Harry smiled and so unlike the official President Truman, he hugged his alien compadre and said, "I am glad to be of all possible assistance for as long as I live dear amigos from the stars." He paused and looked thoughtfully for a moment and asked, "So Arthur tell me, what are your plans ABCD?"

Arthur grinned and beamed back, "It's a secret Mr. President - a deep dark alien secret that only we and now our six toed cat knows!"

With the kitten secured in the bathroom; everyone enjoyed a typical southern fried chicken, mashed potatoes, peas and carrots dinner. Arthur squeaked in happiness and beamed, "That bread that you call cornbread is really delicious."

Sara nodded and said, "I love it. My mother always made it for our Sunday picnics at Ledbetter Beach when we would go up to Santa Barbara for the Sunday Beach art fair."

Glinda beamed, "Oh Sara, I cannot wait to get settled and begin to learn all about earth cooking."

Sara grinned and said, "Oh gosh, that reminds me, I finally got the book that I ordered for you. Wait a moment and I'll be right back."

Sara returned from her office and proudly handed a package to Glinda. "Here," she said, concerned and remembering Selena's confusion about what to do with her gift wrapped framed photo present.

Glinda without a doubt knew what to do and quickly finished tearing open the present and pulled the wrapping away, she squealed twice and exclaimed, "Oh Sara. It's a book, a real earth book." Glinda stood and gleefully hugged Sara.

Sara quizzically asked, "Can you read it ok?"

Glinda read the cover and made an irrepressible smile and several squeaks as she beamed, "It's The Joy of Cooking. Oh Sara this is wonderful! I wish that I had a kitchen so I could try making every one of these 700 recipes." Glinda beamed warm loving thanks to Sara.

Sara took her alien mother of her heart hand and said, "Glinda, as soon as we get re-settled on Water Island we shall begin your cooking lessons in the navy mess hall. Do you think the other women and girls would want to join in?"

Glinda smiled and beamed, "Oh yes and I also think that a lot of our males would want to learn how to cook too."

Delnoid beamed in, "Hey what about us Delnoids, we need to know how to cook for ourselves and for you, too Majesties." Glinda hissed a shush to him and continued, "None of us have any experience in cooking. We have spent our generations all our lives depending on our food synthesizer. As you know it's able to mix a few basic chemicals and recycled Delphinian and food waste. That, since our splashdown on January 26th 1936, now combined with our automated fishing system since coming to earth, it still makes a mediocre and rather tasteless variety of food for us. But now, after trying and tasting your fantastic earth dishes; bread, fresh fish, meat, eggs, especially bacon, vegetables and fruit, I don't think I can ever again eat any of our synthesizer food!"

Selena nodded her head and made a frowning face along with a loud juicy Delphin raspberry sound. She beamed in, "I love the donuts. I want to learn how to make them for everyone!"

Sara was thoughtful and said, "Well unfortunately there will not be any markets on Water Island, but after we teach all of you how to act and shop; we can take the15 minute ferry ride over to St Thomas Island and go to the Safeway market and other stores. But as we start out, there will be a full navy kitchen with cooks for you and they will also have a gigantic store of foodstuff to cook good breakfasts, lunches, dinners and snacks for us including donuts for Selena and her kitten.

Selena beamed, "Sara, do kitties love donuts?"

Sara shrugged her shoulders and said, "I really don't know Selena. We will get one on our way back from Mr. Hemingway's tomorrow and offer a little bit of it to Gatita with some fresh milk."

Selena grinned, squealed and beamed, "That will be great because I can enjoy a donut and some milk with my kitten."

Sara was always awed by Selena's child like enchantment of her kitten and all of her other marvelous new discoveries on earth. She thought, "I am so happy to see our Selena be able to be such a joy filled teenager and at the same time apply and build her incredible earth understandings with her high intellect, fantastic photographic memory and learning abilities."

Forgetting that Glinda, Selena and Arthur were reading her mind Sara jumped a bit when Glinda and Arthur beamed, "That's our fantastic little big delphin girl Sara!"

Harry grinned with pride and said, "Well, now that dinner is over, how about we all go to this little old White House theatre and enjoy a movie with cokes and popcorn?"

Selena beamed, "That will be very nice. I never really got a chance to try my popcorn when we went to the Miracle theatre.

Harry chuckled, "Yes, that was quite a fiasco. We shall hope that tonight's Presidential theatre will make up for your trouble from that rude smoker."

Selena squeaked and beamed, "I thought I was going to die Mr. President but afterwards I did get to discover donuts at that Krispy Kream bakery."

When they entered the small 24 seat theatre they found a tray on a table with ice cold Cokes, glasses and an ice bowl. There was also, mounted on a large black wheeled carnival cart, a circus red and white stripped popcorn maker with deco clowns and a warmer that kept the butter melted. There were also two small bowls with tiny spoons to sprinkle salt or, as the visiting British loved, sugar on their popcorn.

Selena remembered how popcorn was served in the Miracle Theatre reached into the popcorn bin and used the scoop to fill her brown paper bag and then started to head for a seat.

President Truman touched her shoulder and asked, "Don't you want to try some melted butter and maybe a little salt or sugar on your popcorn? Here, let me show you." Harry scooped his bagful, dipped the small ladle into the hot butter and poured about half of it over his popcorn. He said, "I used to always put salt on my popcorn but after having so many British diplomats and VIPs here and at the Washington White House that loved sugar on popcorn, I have also come to prefer sugar on my popcorn. One time at Christmas I even put some brown sugar on my popcorn and it was superb."

Selena had already taken a couple of fingers worth of popcorn and as she munched she beamed, "Ok, it has a nice texture and crunch but it is kind of bland."

Harry poured the remaining half of his hot butter on her popcorn and asked, "Ok, would you prefer salt or sugar?"

Selena recalling her new fondness of sweet donuts beamed, "Oh sugar Mr. President. Sugar if you please sir!"

As the theatre lights dimmed, Sara said, "The Paleface is a new Technicolor comedy with Bob Hope and our friend Jane Russell. As it played Sara noticed that Arthur and Glinda were holding hands as they squeaked and squealed in laughter and shared a bag of butter popcorn with salt and sipped their Cokes.

Sara smiled and contemplated, "They are so like us. I hope that they can assimilate peacefully and happily into our complex earth society with all of the ruthless personalities, the interwoven and unspoken hidden social mores, expectations and agendas.

Glinda reached over and squeezed Sara's hand and beamed, "I hope so too dear Sara. I hope so too." Sara noticed that Arthur was squeaking and enjoying the Bob Hope semi slapstick gags movie, he seemed to also be concentrating.

Sara whispered to Glinda, "Isn't Arthur enjoying the show?"

Glinda grinned and beamed, "He sure is! In fact he likes it so much that he is beaming it back to everyone aboard Lifestar."

Hearing that, Sara had a flash of inspiration. She made a mental note to order three or four 16mm Bell and Howell sound projectors and extra bulbs from Gordon Enterprises in Hollywood and 16mm releases of all recent motion pictures to bring to Water Island so that her aliens could see and hear all possible human life dream and drama stories. She commented, "I really want to show you a wonderful and realistic film from 1946, about post World War II family life. It's called, The Best Years of Our Lives."

Arthur munching a mouthful of popcorn clicked in approval and beamed, "Sara you are the absolute perfect ambassador, teacher and movie mogul for us."

The President, Sara and the aliens stood at the elevator door. Truman still chuckling said, "That was a riot. I really enjoy Bob Hope. I have met him a few times and he is as funny in person as he is on screen. But, I still am undecided which was funnier this evening, Bob Hope or, the thought of Hemingway trying to milk a cat.

Arthur beamed to the President, "Harry, isn't a riot a group of people fighting?" Harry explained, "Oh, It's a word that can also be used to say that something was really fun or funny." Glinda grinned and squeaked, "Meow"

As they approached their bedrooms, they heard Gatita meowing her little cat head off. Selena ran into her bedroom, opened the bathroom door and there sitting on the toilet lid was her little black ball of fur licking her paw as if to say, "Ah, there you are! My meowing finally got my Selena back." Selena picked up her kitten and gently stroked and beamed love energies to her.

Sara said, "Ok, its bedtime and tomorrow will be a big day with our final meetings for your landing and having lunch with Hemingway." Sara grinned and chuckled, "Also to see Glinda try to get a cat milk sample. Then, after our lunch with Mr. Hemingway the navy van will pick us up back here at 5 pm to take us to the sub."

Selena holding her kitten, hugged Sara and cried, "Oh Sara, I surely don't want to leave you. I am so happy here with you and I hate the idea of having to return to our old stinky giant jalopy starship."

Sara thought, "Selena, I am always amazed at the rate that you are assimilating our language and slang." Selena just grinned and let out three delighted squeals. ...

Glinda held her daughter and Sara and beamed, "Selena, we will only be aboard our Lifestar for another month then we will all be reunited on Water Island, our island in the Caribbean sun. Also Selena, as you know, we will be constantly connected telepathically so you and Sara can always share as much as you like."

.

CHAPTER 30 THE BATTLE OF LOS ANGELES ITALIAN GIRLS AND LIFE DREAMS

The next morning after the White House breakfast, the President, Sara and the aliens all sat quietly sipping coffee andCoke. Each was rather isolated in their own thoughts. Glinda, Arthur, Selena and Delnoid One all shared telepathically and occasionally made soft delphin sounds.

Glinda finally broke the contemplative stillness by a short squeak and beamed, "Dear Mr. President, it is now time for us to thank you with our whole true hearts and love energies for your hospitality, for beginning the planning for our landing and introductions to earth people, and for your marvelous and so diverse life styles."

Harry looked up and said, "My dear Delphinians, words fail me as I consider the implications and magnitude of our species coming together now to choose living in peace and cooperation for our mutual security and benefits. I know that initially… life on post war empty Water Island will take some adjustment. But, as soon as Sara tells me that you have grown more sweat glands and accomplished adapting to our atmosphere in that tropical climate; we have arranged for all of you to be transported again aboard the USS Midway. The Midway will be standing by at sea to take you to Galveston, Texas to board a special military train to go west from Houston through New Mexico and Arizona to California. The train will then continue from Los Angeles north through Santa Barbara and along the magnificent Pacific coast past our Vandenberg Air Force Base. And on up to San Luis Obispo above Paso Robles just north of San Martin where we will accommodate you at our currently mostly vacant US Army Camp Roberts."

The President breathed and continued, "From Camp Roberts, after more orientations, training and social practice, you may together, or as you have told me; begin to step out individually or in families and groups to create your life dreams wherever you wish. Camp Roberts is 72 miles northwest of our Vandenberg Air Force Base and the camp is just 34 miles inland from the isolated Pacific Coast which is 20 miles north of Hearst Castle. I imagine at night you can bring Lifestar close to shore for whatever needs you wish."

Sara grinned and said to the President, "Don't forget to tell them about the cars Mr. President."

Harry smiled and said, "By the way, at Camp Roberts we will offer you driving lessons and California licenses and each of you will be given a new car."

Selena squealed and beamed, "A car! Gosh! That will be so grand to be able to drive and take my Gatita for a ride."

Arthur squeaked, clicked rapidly and beamed, "That will be terrific because Glinda and I can enjoy discovering California and the USA without using our flighters, uh, flying saucers as you call them."

Everyone broke into squeals and laughter. Harry, after recovering his composure chuckled, "If you go cruising and touring around California in one of your scout flighters, that would sure create a stir."

Glinda beamed, "Stir? Mr. President, what is stir?

Harry took off his glasses and was wiping them as he explained, "It means causing a lot of worry and excitement. Just after the start of the Japanese war, there was a big incident where our anti aircraft guns spent 2 hours firing over 2000 rounds at a large UFO hovering above Los Angeles. It was the early morning hours of February 25th 1942. The 37th Army Coastal Brigade kept their searchlights and blazing guns on a still unknown airship. Amazingly it wasn't harmed. We still have no idea if it was the Japanese or a UFO." As the president spoke, Sara noticed that Arthur looking rather alarmed at Glinda and Glinda looked nervously to Sara and the President. Sara picked up on their guilty looks asked, "Uh, do, do you know anything about this Arthur?"

Arthur let out a squeak and a low moan and beamed, "Well, Mr. President I must confess that it was us up there over Culver City and Los Angeles on that totally crazy night."

Truman slowly put down his Coke and asked, "Well then Arthur, please tell me what happened?"

Arthur looked somewhat resigned at Glinda, Sara and Mr. Truman as he squeaked and continued, "Well you see Mr. President, as you probably know, towards the end of the war from November, 1944 until April, 1945, the Japs launched at least 9000 crude balloon bombs aloft to drift eastward in the jet stream for 3 to 4 days in an effort to bomb along the west coast of the USA to ignite forest fires and to terrorize your people."

Harry stiffened and said, "Ah yes of course. Yes Arthur, those were the Fu-Go balloon bombs and they did cause some problems along our USA west coast. One of their damned terrorism devices did unfortunately kill a woman and her four children up in Oregon."

When Glinda heard this she hugged Sara and burst into tears. She beamed between squeaks and moans, "Oh dear Amador, Mr. President I am so sorry we let that one slip by our patrols."

Arthur interjected, "Yes, well you see, we discovered these strange balloon devices in your stratosphere drifting towards your west coast as early as January, 1942. Apparently the Japs had those horrible cruel bomb devices planned from the get go of the war. When we first encountered one, we took it aboard to our Marines, as you might call them. Took it apart and analyzed it and sure enough it was a small incendiary bomb. So Mr. President, we spent a good deal of your Pacific war finding and zapping these floating death traps for you. On that night of the 25th of February, we were patrolling at 80,000 feet off your Los Angeles area coast when we detected one of them slowly drifting downwards towards Los Angeles so we had to go down and retrieve it. But your ack ack guys opened fire and we had to remain hovering with our force shields full on until we could slowly drift towards the damn device to get it aboard through our hatch.

Then, we flew south towards Long Beach to check for further devices. We took the bomb way out over open water, deactivated it and dumped it in the Pacific."

Arthur looked worriedly at President Truman he beamed, "Harry I am sorry we caused so much UFO upset but if that had gone off it would have started a major fire and possibly killed and injured a lot of people."

Harry clasped Arthur's arm, pumped it and said, "Oh my God Arthur, you and your crew are brave heroes. We of course had no idea of the dangers of those balloon bombs that early on in the Japanese war."

So after a few minutes of hugs, thanks and squeals, Sara continued, "Well my dear hero amigos. "We certainly thank you for your bravery and patrols."

After everyone had sipped their cokes, Sara resumed relating her Water Island plans. "As you know we are going to rendezvous with you using the USS Midway aircraft carrier, it's south east of where we first met with you north of Puerto Rico. Then later when we dock at Water Island, we will use the USS Midway's cranes to unload all of your stuff on your first Earth home base. Once we get you all settled in the island's Quonset huts, we can begin to orient you and begin studies of the nuances of our language and social customs so you can more safely and better fit in when you start your lives in California."

Sara continued, "We will also supply you with dictionaries; plenty of US Government publications and the Britannica encyclopedia."

Delnoid 1 gave his usual know it all smile and interjected, "Well remember dear earthlings, we assimilate everything and always also beam it to our onboard pod and into our ship memory banks, which you call computers." Your first real electronic computing machine was developed and used secretly in England during WW II to try to decipher the German Enigma code machines. It was masterminded by an eccentric British mathematical genius who was a homosexual… Glinda looked sharply at Del and immediately he went silent.

President Truman turned to the sideboard and picked up a box with three books in it. And as he set it on the dining room table, he smiled almost reverently, cleared his throat and said, "My dear friends from the stars. I wish to present to you some bibles. This book is said to be the words of our Creator the uh, your, uh I mean of course, our God and your Amador who created the world and all of us.

We Christians use this to study to better guide our life choices and also enjoy the many stories in this ancient holy book."

As Glinda accepted her black leather bound, gold imprinted bible, she beamed, "Oh Mr. President, thank you and as you would say, bless you. This is wonderful to see and hold and I look forward to reading it again soon. We have several copies in our ship's library but this gift now is very special to me. We have also heard a lot about your God's book from some powerful AM radio transmissions that we intercepted from way out in space on our way SOLward. Del, from what station was that?"

Delnoid 1 speaking from his fathomless memory banks. "The term 'border radio' refers to the American radio broadcasting industry that sprang up along the US Mexican border in the early 1930s. High powered transmitters on Mexican soil, beyond the reach of U.S. regulators, blanketed North America with country western, religious and medical quack product ads and programming and various severe storm warnings for Tornado Alley."

Glinda moaned and clicked frustratedly, waved her left hand to silence the Delnoid as she beamed to Sara. "Oh my dear Sara there seems to be endless words, terms and significances we must learn before we will be able to fully duplicate and really understand your words, meanings, intentions and significances."

Sara took Glinda 's hand, smiled and said, "Oh dear Delphins, this is why I am here and I and others will teach, orient and guide you to more fully understand the lingo, jargon, nuances and slang of our so full of twists and turns ever changing culture."

Selena squealed, frowned and beamed, "What on earth is a quack?

Isn't that the sound a duck makes Sara?"

Sara chuckled as she explained, "A duck is a bird but quack, the noise a duck makes, means a person who tries without training or a license to practice medicine and sell cures and medicines that don't work and usually also harm buyers."

Glinda let out a stream of low clicks as she beamed, "Oh dear Amador!" Why would anyone want to harm others like that?"

President Truman replied, "Well, unfortunately dear Glinda it is greed and the desire of these snake oil doctors to try to make money in any way that they can." Unfortunately by some lawyers too !"

Glinda frowned in puzzlement and beamed, "Snake oil Mr. Truman?

Do they sell the oil from snakes?"

Truman chortled and said, "Oh no Glinda, snake oil salesman is slang for phony doctors and the useless homemade remedies and medicines that they try to sell."

Arthur raised his eyebrows and beamed, "Well it seems then that the actual main god on your planet is, sorry to say this. Its your money."

President Truman looked down, frowned, sighed and said, "I am afraid and mortified my dear aliens that this is sad but true. If only we humans had your total communicating sensitivities and spiritual capabilities comparable even to our own earthly dolphins..."

There was a pause while everyone was contemplating in silence. Delnoid 1 looked quizzically at everyone and rattled on again, "So, Mexico greedily accommodated these 'outlaw' radio operators, some of whom had been denied broadcasting licenses in the United States. Though the 'border

blaster' transmitters were always in Mexico, their studios were most of the time in the United States, and those stations were often identified by the American town just across the international border. Early on, hillbilly music proved to be one of the most effective means for pulling in listener mail and moving merchandise. But, in turn, those border stations sure played a significant role in popularizing country music during the genre's popularity growth years before and after world war two."

Harry hummed and said, "Oh that must have been XERF with its powerful transmitter in Cuidad Acuna, Mexico just across from Del Rio, Texas. Our Federal Communications Commission tried for years to dampen their 50,000 watt output. But, the darn Mexican government wouldn't help us at all. So, I reckon that Texas snake oil salesman fellow must have bribed the Mexican authorities very well. But you know, those stations also familiarized American listeners with Mexican and Mexican American artists. The highlight of those XERF programs, for me was the beautiful voice of the 'Mexican Nightingale', Rosa Domínguez, especially when she would sing Estrellita. (little star). This old Missouri farm boy thought for sure that must be how the angels would sound in heaven."

Sara said, "Well, none the less, it is still a weighty growing health problem here in the USA because unfortunately each year many people are gravely sickened or die from using, taking or drinking such toxic concoctions."

Glinda clicked in dismay and beamed, "Oh my, what is a concoction and Delnoid, have we registered this and all other quack products in our medical data banks as harmful substances?"

Delnoid 1 looked at his queen and said for the benefit of the President and Sara, "No your majesty, but we will research all of these hazardous concoctions and add them to our rapidly growing list of harmful earthly businesses, food, medicines and drinks." Delnoid 1 elaborated saying, "These toxins are indeed dangerous to this planet's seas and marine life. Especially for dolphins and whales because they add dangerous and destructive levels of mercury and organic toxins such as PCBs, Dioxins and PBDEs to the food chains of sea life and accordingly to humans who eat sea food. The organic chlorine actually mimic estrogen and other hormones. From our analyses since arrival on earth in 1936, we have found growing quantities of such toxins in all of earth's seas. We have especially noted the amounts of

pollutants are growing and spreading throughout this planets oceans even more rapidly since the end of World War II."

Arthur squealed scornfully as he beamed, "Aiiii Amador! I wonder now if we can ever learn to be safe from earth food, drink and chemicals getting into our pure body systems?"

Glinda who had just instructed Delnoid 1 to beam this toxic data and remarkable, critical, cultural, medical and food terms to their chief medical officer aboard Lifestar, patted her husband's arm and beamed, "Ojala (hopefully) dear."

Sara said, "I am so glad that you are able to keep on top of these deadly toxins because obviously we humans are not being response able for our own world. It's a shame that we aren't respecting this miraculous gift of planet and life the, uh our creators gave to us.

President Truman, who knew a few parts of the bible almost by heart, opened his bible and said to all, "Speaking of creation dear star friends please let me read this, uh, our story of creation by God, the ones you call Amadores. We call this part of the Bible, Genesis."

After reading the Genesis creation to the aliens, as President Truman put down his Bible, Arthur, Glinda and Selena became wide eyed as all whistled from high to low dolphin style and Glinda beamed, "Oh dear Amador Mr. President!" Your creation account is amazingly quite similar to ours stemming from so long ago on our home world. It, in so many almost miraculous and mind-boggling ways, parallels our own creation accounts."

Delnoid, drawing on his endless data banks then interjected, "Mr President, I must tell you that the climate in the Mediterranean with its insufficient growing degree days doesn't support the growing of apples and from the extensive research of our cultural climatologist, Ana Luisa, the apple that Eve ate in the er, Garden of Eden, must have actually been a pomegranate. But she is still trying to figure out the significance of all of the seeds a pomegranate has and about how, er, troublesome they are to eat."

Glinda beamed, "uh thanks again Del for un-asked for information as she then continued, "But your similar story, your Bible's account of creation does not surprise me since, we all are inside the mind of our prime creator and for you, the angels and for us, the Amadores, probably who you call archangels, are the prime creator's servants. Delnoid, please give me your porta vu screen."

Delnoid slipped off his ever present light blue back case and as he placed his hand on the lid. It swung open. He reached inside and pulled out an only one quarter thick white plastic encased 8" x 10" viewing screen. Glinda took it from him and after finding the images she wanted she said, "Look here Mr. President. We have many amazing computer derived images showing the whole aspect of what we both call the universe. As we pull back farther and farther away from the incredible awe-inspiring structures of streams of trillions of galaxies and great voids of our universe. We see a pattern that astoundingly, in actuality, resembles the micro structure of our brains with its neurons and synapses.

Our astro physicists and astro biologists have had plenty of time to derive this insight over our six generations of study about the incredible similarity between the universe's large scale structure and our brain micro structures. So that we now understand that we are all, and everything else in this and other universes, are inter connected. It's like it's designed for when all of our nightly life dreams are transmitted through H-alpha waves back into the galaxy, we all share and on out to the irregular galaxies associated with our, as you call it, Milky Way.

All life recordings stream back into our galaxy to enter black holes at the center of our and other galaxies. To then be transmitted just like a gigantic system of neurotransmitters of some indescribable genus back to the prime Creator of space and time from the trillions of galaxies, stars, planets and us." Glinda sighed and continued, "I have lain awake many restless nights wondering where the Prime Creator came from."

Selena beamed, "Well it makes perfect sense because, if a creator made us and everything, why would he and she not want to follow and enjoy the lives, adventures and misadventures of all creation?"

President Truman cleared his throat and as he wiped his glasses he said, "Dear God, it's true. We are all children of the universe and indeed we may all be inside God's mind. Incredible! You have today confirmed my lifelong belief of the infinity and magnificence of creation Glinda"

Arthur beamed, "It's so true Mr. Truman! It's like when we have a new thought, it comes into existence from almost nothingness to manifest our feelings, ideas, vision and creativity. Just like our universe bloomed to forever in a quantum instant from nothing. Perhaps we are indeed just a passing thought in the Prime Creator's mind."

Harry said nervously, "Well I hope to dear God, uh the Prime Creator always keeps thinking about us!"

As all of these overwhelming thoughts and profound ideas settled into the group of humans and aliens, everyone grew silent for awhile to let the awesome significance and realities of their universal beingness settle into each of their minds, spirits, vision and hearts.

Sara, on the other hand with all of these profound thoughts about creation was now wondering about child birth and the whole alien procedure and about the pain of it all when Selena looked with assurance at her and beamed, "Oh dear Earth sister, don't worry! Our maternity techniques are totally painless and even designed to be pleasurable in the warm salt waters of our birthing tank."

Glinda squeaked softly, clicked a few octaves, smiled reassuringly and beamed, "Of course, in our starship maternity ward, birthing will be totally painless for both of you."

As Sara heard this in her head she thought, "Oh my God, I really am going to be the mother of a Delphinian Human hybrid"

Selena was at the same time thinking, "Oh Amador, I will be a mother to a Human Delphin hybrid." Selena and Sara looked at each other and hugged with tears of new insight in their eyes.

President Truman noticed this exchange said, "Uh ladies, did I miss something? Did the Genesis snake in the bible upset you somehow?"

Sara impulsively hugged the old President and said, "Oh no Mr. Truman. Selena and I were just thinking about childbirth. You know… womanly things" Selena then stepped over to the President and as she hugged him she sent powerful loving energies into his heart and spirit.

Glinda turned to the president beamed, "Oh dear Mr. Truman, we were just uh… sort of… er… planning ahead…"

Harry just looked kindly at the Delphin pod queen and said, "Oh, I see. Well planning ahead is always a good idea." President Truman then turned to Arthur, cleared his throat and asked, "So, what will you do after you uh, park your Lifestar?"

Arthur smiled and beamed, "We will always have a rotating crew of 6 on it along with at least 2 Delnoids wherever we uh… park it Mr. President. As you know, it will be in a top secret location. This is for our security as well as for yours in keeping with our agreements, right?"

Harry Truman had to become the politician again as he stood offered his hand and said, "So sworn on our red crystals Mr. uh, your Majesty, er, Arthur."

As Mr. Truman held Arthur's hand he felt strong energies of sincere gratitude flowing into his mind and spirit. Glinda and Selena stood and together took his left hand and added to the loving and grateful energies flowing into the President of the United States...

Sara stood and clasped Selena and Glinda's hand and felt and knew in her whole heart and spirit that they were, at least for now, united in peace, love, trust and vision...

As Harry sat down he cleared his throat of deep emotions and mumbled, "Amen dear friends, amen." The three aliens beamed to all. "Peace to us always dear Amador..."

Mr. Truman brightened and said, "If only your Delphin loving societies could combine more fully with humankind. I realize now that worldwide humane education is probably the only way we can choose and try to end war and create true peace.

Glinda looked directly at the President through her amazing azure eyes and beamed, "Let us begin then, after all, such initial assimilation would only take about four Delphinian and six to eight human generations Mr. President."

Harry appreciated that perhaps this unparalleled meeting was the Amador's plan to guide and change humans to be loving, trusting, respectful of each other and the planet. After about 8 million untold years of perpetual, relentless and merciless tribal fear, greed, fighting and war for food, territory, ego and gold; it would be a welcomed change.

Glinda, Arthur, Selena and Delnoid 1 nodded their heads in agreement. Sara broke the silence and asked, "Well, Everyone, are you all packed yet?"

Glinda beamed, "Almost finished Miss Sara. What time are we going to go to Mr. Hemingway's house?" Sara said, "Well, we best leave here about 11am to be on time for our lunch with Ernest and his cats."

Selena squeaked and clicked rapidly in alarm as she beamed, "What about Gatita Sara? You said we shouldn't take her with us to Mr. Hemingway's."

Sara said, "Oh that's right Selena, we will stop back here to pick up your kitten and all six of the 25 lb bags of the oil absorbent... the kitty litter."

Delnoid 1 beamed, "Sara, Please not to worry about the kitty litter.

I can arrange for a scout flighter to come pick up the heavy stuff next dark moonless night on one of the empty keys just offshore of Key West. The next new moon should be on April 9th."

Harry thought for a moment and said, Delnoid that seems to be a good idea. I can have a navy launch drop off whatever you want or need, perhaps on Crawfish Key, or Mule Key or even Barracuda Key since its farthest away from Key West."

Sara was very puzzled and said, "But Delnoid,I thought that you are coming up to Washington to help me."

Delnoid laughed and said, "I will Sara but that will be my clone, Delnoid 3. And… I might as well let you know that my other clone, Delnoid 5, will be with you on Water Island and you see Commander, the remaining Delnoids can all function separately or as one as we need them. If it gets too eventful we can activate more Delnoids in just six weeks in our clone incubation pods."

Mr. Truman said, "It's truly amazing isn't it? I will have Delnoid 4 with me from now on. We will pass him off as a special secret service agent answerable only and directly to me at all times."

Sara smiled and said "Ok….So I suppose we will be picking up all these Delnoids as we drop off the royal family?"

Truman grinned and said, "Only two of them Sara. Delnoid 2 and Delnoid 4 will come back to Key West with you. That's the doppelganger plan Sara."

The Delnoids all had been exquisitely bio engineered and programmed as all purpose diplomatic staff, audio and video recorders, pilots, and security agents, seemed to also have Delphinian traits along with their astounding abilities to understand, evaluate and act faultlessly in situations with their super computer, cyborg minds.

Delnoid 1 grinned and said, "Mr. President, Sara, did I ever tell you about the time Delnoid 6 almost got run through by a fisherman's pike during our brief but amorous and harrowing visit to Portofino, Italy back in 1945, just after the end of the war?"

From his grin, Sara rightly suspected that maybe there was an alien joke coming… So Sara bit and said, "No, but why don't you tell us about Delnoid 6… uh Delnoid 1…"

Arthur, Glinda and Selena all looked exasperatedly at Delnoid 1, raised their eyebrows and clicked tisk, tisk, tisk and moaned softly.

Delnoid continued, "Well, Delnoid 6, who spoke Italian, was carefully meeting with some of the locals in that lovely and picture post card perfect tiny Italian Riviera port village. Delnoid 6 had Arthur send ashore the Delnoid 7 unit. Since it looked exactly like Delnoid 6, the locals understandably became alarmed and suspicious. Delnoid 6 told them it was his twin brother Mario. This took place awhile after the fall of the Nazis. So the locals were understandably still jittery and very apprehensive about any Nazis and all other strangers. But Delnoid 6 and Delnoid 7 always kept beaming caring and loving energies to the villagers.

The war weary fisher folk soon came to trust the Da Vinci twins and soon some of the lovely village girls began to try to attract these two handsome strangers.

Well, as you know Sara, Delnoids are not designed to breed. So, the satirical part of this story is that the girls and villagers decided that these handsome strangers but obviously not interested in girls were omosessuales (queers). Nonetheless – because of the war loss of almost all of the young men in the village - some of the fisher wives and their daughters approached Delnoid 6 and Delnoid 7 to plead if they could please possibly make love to some of the village girls - even if they were fascina.(gay) The two quick thinking Delnoid units explained that they were honored by the request but during chemical warfare they were both unfortunately sterile. But, they told the disappointed women that they had some shipmates who were normal males and they would send them to Portofino to help make babies.

Glinda smiled cunningly and beamed, "When we met with some of our eligible bachelor males and explained the breeding mission, every hand shot up with passionate squeals and squeaks of pleasure during the call for two volunteers." Glinda squeaked in mirth and beamed, "So, we flesh aided their blowholes and sent ashore two of our males because we wanted to see if we could breed with the human girls and also try to help repopulate the village.

Some of the girls quickly and enthusiastically got down to basics with Jorge and Marco… Everything was going fine to help impregnate some of the girls and our guys were never happier. But, the enamored girls soon began wondering why their lovers never took their strange square toed shoes off. One night after deeply snoring Marco had pleasured Maria, his current amiga, she quietly got up and took off his shoe. When she saw his flipper instead of toes, she ran screaming out of the room to her mamma. In a few minutes her papa and mamma and several villagers came into the bedroom and rudely awakened the nude except for one flipper cover, Marco. They demanded that he explain his strange feet and also bluntly demanded if his babies would have such deformed feet. Mario by then had beamed to Jorge and to us to get them out of there before they were skewered on the fishing pikes some of the growing village mob was carrying."

Selena grinned and beamed in, "Jorge and Marco fled to their small motorboat, jumped in it just a pike ahead of the angry villagers and roared out of the harbor zigzagging between the many small boats and fishing boats. We launched a rescue scout flighter and picked them up a mile offshore."

Glinda beamed, "As we debriefed these two first Delphinians to have sex with human females, they each related that they were so blissful that they wanted to return to Portofino to finish their noble work helping repopulate the village."

Arthur squeaked, grinned and beamed in, "I had to order them to forget It until we could devise some lasting blowhole and flipper, uh, what you call plastic surgery for them. So I know exactly where these two Romeo's will want to go just as soon as we can doctor them up and orient them fully to life on earth…"

Sara asked, "So what did those Italian Delphinian babies look like?"

Glinda looked down and quietly said, "As far as we know, none of those village girls became pregnant…Remember what I told you about our nurturing love energies from both parents being so vital to successful childbirth." Well the turmoil caused by their lover's feet nixed any loving fetal bonding."

As Sara was imagining what her future Delphinian lover, husband and father of her future hybrid babies might look like, she thought, "Well then, the Portofino escapade was no joke, it was a really, uh, rousing story."

Glinda beamed, "All in good time Sara. You can maybe meet one of our available bachelor Delphs while we are on Water Island." Glinda hugged Sara and beamed loving energies to her.

Selena beamed, "What about meeee? When will I meet my earth husband?"

Sara thought, "After Camp Roberts in California Selena you will have your pick of over 50 million men and of that respect that unfortunately only one or two of them will be really trustworthy and good enough to understand and truly love you and keep the secret of an alien Delphin girl."

At this, alarmed Selena squeaked and beamed, "Only one or two Sara?"

Sara thought, "Good men are really hard to find and you don't want to marry the wrong one."

Delnoid then interrupted, unasked, and from his endless data said, "Uh, Sara, there are now in 1948, precisely 146,631,302 people in the USA after your horrible war. That leaves only 73,315,651 males and of those, only 29,326,260.4 may be eligible males for Selena. But that depends of course on how many of them are already married."

Everyone then looked at Delnoid and chorused, "So who asked you anyway?"

Sara after stopping giggling with the others and continued, "Dear alien sister, I know it's better to be alone than to be alone with the wrong person. Remember also dear little sister, earth men are not like your Delphinian total loving and sharing and communicating males."

Glinda privately beamed to Selena, "You must sit down sometime and mind meld with Amelia about the horrible relationship she sufferd for 6 years under her George Putman ex husband…"

Selena agreed and then hugged her Earth sister and beamed, "You must be my cupid dear Sara." Please try to help me identify and find a good human – ok?" The two young women laughed and hugged as Sara said, "OK little alien sister the same goes for me for finding a good Delphinian husband."

CHAPTER 31 MAMMA CAT'S MILK AND HASTA LA VISTA

The Presidential limo dropped everyone off at Hemingway's cat house all the kitties meowed their happy greeting and twined around their legs. Hemingway came out and he and Harry Truman hugged and patted each other's backs. Glinda beamed to Sara, "Why do earthmen hug in such a standoff way?"

Sara grinned and said, "Well, here on earth it's considered not appropriate for men to affectionately hug. But, they do it whole heartedly in France, Italy and South America. Here, the old 1692 Salem witch trials and over sanctimonious absurd moralistic persecutions of the Puritan's beliefs, gender rules and taboos still prevail."

Glinda clicked softly and beamed, "Hummmm" as she reminded herself to later ask Sara more about the Puritans. She, Selena and Arthur then wrapped their loving arms around the, grinning from ear to ear, President and the grizzly old author.

Hemingway then hugged Sara and said, "Well, How's their uh, visit going?"

Sara with her arm around her adopted uncle Hem smiled and said, "Well, we are getting organized and tonight our friends will return to their, uh, base."

Hemingway being the wise seasoned reporter that he was said, "Gosh I guess that means they are going to return to their ship." Hemingway turned to Harry and Arthur and said, "Do you mind if I come along?" Harry frowned and said, "Come on Hem, that as you very well know, is off limits and totally out of the question my inquisitive reporter amigo."

Ernest shrugged his shoulders and looked his old friend Harry in the eye and said, "Ok, ok, you can't blame me for trying amigo. I will respect your need for total secrecy. But remember, if this incredible alien contact story is ever to be released, I get dibs on the scoop."

Harry smiled his best political smile and said, "Ok Hem it's a deal."

If either man could have read each other's minds they would have found each thinking, "Oh God what it I/you lose the election."

Arthur, reading their realistic election fears beamed to both men, "I choose to remain positive about the election and our Delnoid 4 will be there to uh, vector our help, uh, ideas during Harry's campaign."

Selena squeaked and beamed, "I'll vote for Mr. Truman." With that everyone laughed as Sara exclaimed… "So will I, so will I!"

Then they all, except for Hemingway, heard ringing in their heads, So will we! So will we from all the Delphinians aboard Lifestar.

Hemingway extended his arm and said, "Ok, let's stop worrying about the election and go enjoy the Cubano almuerzo (lunch) Lupe has prepared for us."

After lunch, with Lupe sitting at the table, Hemingway looked at her and said, "Lupe por favor triar la gata Natasha and also please bring the cat towel and those leather gloves. I think I last saw them in the swimming pool pump shelter a few months ago."

Harry whose wife had never let him have a cat, looked at Hem and asked, "What are the towel and gloves for Hem?"

Hemingway grinned and chortled, "Well, the towel is to wrap kitty up in and the gloves are to keep Glinda from being clawed and bitten as she tries to get a cat milk sample."

Sara, Arthur and Harry started to chuckled and Harry said, "Oh damn, I forgot my camera. This will be front page headlines of you trying to get a cat milk sample Hem. It will even exceed all of the ferocious lions and tigers that you have bagged."

Hemingway looked at the President and gestured towards now jovial Glinda and said, "Hey I am not about to tackle getting a milk sample from that mama cat. Its gonna be Glinda's fate to get her arms shredded."

Selena beamed to Hem. "Why do you wrap the poor kitty up in a towel Mr. Hemingway?"

Sara interjected, "Whenever we have to give a cat a pill or an injection we wrap it tightly up in a towel. It usually can't claw or bite us. Kitties do not ever accept being forcefully held while being given pills or being milked and will always fight, scratch and bite in order not be subjected to such terrifying indignities."

Hem grinned and asked, "OK Glinda, how the hell are you going to milk the cat if she's all wrapped up in the towel?"

Glinda, smiling knowingly beamed, "Ok here, let me take Natasha over to this table." She took the alarmed pussy in her arms and almost immediately the wide eyed cat, who had been flicking her tail, relaxed as she was carried over to the side table. Glinda then laid the now peacefully sleeping cat on the table reached down to pick up her back pack, took out a small clear suction vial and as she milked each little tit she soon collected a few ounces of cat milk. She held the vial out towards the now chagrinned Hemingway and beamed, "OK, any more doubts gentlemen?"

The mama cat soon awakened and after licking her paw she looked around and jumped off the table and ran over to Selena, jumped up in her lap and started meowing and meowing and meowing… Selena stroking the obviously perturbed mama cat smiled and beamed, "Oh dear, she is worried and is asking me if her kitten is ok and she is asking me to be sure to give her love to Gatita."

Hemingway and Truman were both astounded as Harry asked, "Oh my gosh, are there no limits to your powers?"

Glinda smiled, made some scolding clicks, walked over to both men and as she put her arms around each man's neck she grinned and beamed softly. "Nope!"

Hemingway looked skeptically at Selena and asked, "Selena, can you, are you really able to talk with that cat?"

Selena still petting the now purring mom cat, squealed with glee, clicked in mirth, grinned and beamed, "Nope!"

Arthur, his family, Sara, the President and Hemingway and Lupe all broke into roars of laughter.

Harry commented, "You know, I have not laughed so much in too long of a time." Hemingway added, "Me neither dear amigos - ni yo tampoco."

Lupe recovering her glee asked Hemingway, "Algo mas querido loco mastero del los gatos?" (Anything else dear crazy cat master?)

Hemingway still chuckling said, "Lupe, gracias para este bonita almuerzo." (Thank you for this nice lunch.) He turned to everyone and said, "Well, I am sure glad that I did not make a bet with you Harry about Glinda being able to milk a cat. Would anyone like coffee or coke?" Everyone chorused, "Si, Coke please."

After everyone enjoyed their cokes and coffee, Hemingway turned to Lupe and asked, "Lupe, do you think you can find that long haired grey cat you and I talked about?"

Lupe suppressed a smirk as she giggled, "Oh si senor Hem. I will go get him now." She returned to the table with a green eyed long haired cat. Hemingway who was sitting next to Harry took the cat in his arms and looked mischievously at Harry and said, "Say old amigo, how would you like a special cat for the White House?"

Harry reached out and as he stroked the now contentedly purring cat said, "Oh I would love it, but as you know, I must soon depart of my campaign trail on my Magellan train and try to get re-elected so we can be sure to help our uh, new amigos."

Hemingway smiled and said, "Ok amigo I will keep him here for you and anytime you are ready. He is all yours."

Harry still contentedly petting the cat asked, "Say Ernest, what is his name?"

Hemingway grinned and chuckled as he said, "Hairy Truman of course!" At that everyone cracked up and the now startled kitty leapt off Hemingway's lap and sashayed indignantly out of the dining room.

The group shared tearful but cheerful goodbyes and hasta prontos (see you soon) and vaya con Dios (go with God). When they were back in the Presidential limo Sara turned to Glinda and asked aloud, "Glinda, why do all of you love Coke so much?"

Glinda explained, "We first tried it during our first coastal towns walkabouts back in 1936. There were Coca Cola signs almost everywhere we went." Then soon, we all got kind of addicted to it because it's just the perfect mix of caffeine and sugar that we like and also need to boost our high metabolisms. It's somewhat like you all drinking coffee all the time. The Argentineans drink Mate but we soon noticed that they always put heaps of sugar in their bombillas." (ornate silver decorated drinking gourds with a 6 inch silver combination stir straw).

Sara realizing just how extensively her Delphinians had explored and walked about on our planet asked, "Why don't you just get your food and drink synthesizer to make Coke for you?"

Selena squeaked and beamed, "Oh Sara, we tried that but, it was just not… the real thing…"

Glinda clicked sternly, raised her eyebrows, squeaked a laugh and beamed, "Oh come on Selena, you know perfectly well that is from the Coke radio jingle we have heard ever since we passed Jupiter and came within stronger AM radio range of Earth!

CHAPTER 32 HASTA LA VISTA… TQM

They returned to the Key West White House and collected their backpacks, Selena's kitten, Gatita, and several bags of things they had purchased while shopping until they dropped in Key West with Sara. They met the President in the dining room. As they sat there sipping their cokes under the softly whirling ceiling fan, each realized that this marked the conclusion for awhile of a fantastic and funtastic meeting between their alien, yet so similar, cultures, hopes and life dreams.

President Truman was the first to break the contemplative reverie as Arthur had done when they first met on Lifestar back in February. He held up his glass and toasted, "May we live together in peace and, er, with Coke always dear amigos from the stars and now soon to be residents of Earth. We are happy that you are here and we welcome you home and we will help you in any way that we can."

Arthur stood, smiled and beamed, "Mr. President, Sara, family and now Gatita too. We sixth generation Delphinians have indeed traveled far and now we anticipate the landing for our 160 pod, uh family on our new home on this so magnificent Earth. We too appreciate you and all that you are doing to give us, at last, a home that we can walk upon and also swim in your magnificent life-force filling seas. We in turn will share with you our technologies and medical sciences. But, it is our resolute expectation, as we wrote in our covenant now sealed in the red stones, that what we share with you is to be used for the good of all mankind and uh, Delphinian kind and not for warfare, heartless and irresponsible ego, or cruel selfish greed." All then stood and raised their Coke filled glasses and Glinda beamed blessings and loving energies to everyone as Gatita mewed happily in her little wooden cat box.

The Delphinians had tearfully, yet brave heartedly hugged Sara goodbye on the gently rolling deck of the USS Sea Cat submarine. They stepped onto their blue beam walkway and when they were in the middle, they all turned and raised their hands in the universal peace sign. Aboard the sub, a tearful Sara in turn raised her hand with the V peace sign.

Selena clicked sadly and moaned as she beamed to Sara, "Ok…See you in April, aboard USS Midway dear Earth Sister. I love you Sara."

Sara thought back to Selena, Arthur and Glinda "Te querro mucho mi querido familia de las estrellas. (I love you very much my dear family from the stars) TQM = Te Querro Mucho

After Sara's alien family entered their starship, Delnoid 4 and 6, each wearing rather large dark blue backpacks and another alien, pushing what seemed to be a big wheelless floating shopping cart came across the amazing light gangway and reached the sub's deck. He smiled and said, "I am Delnoid

8. He picked up all of the aliens Florida shopping bags and as soon as he had placed them in the amazing anti gravity cart, he gave the peace sign and said, "Good bye for now Sara. I shall see you soon on Water Island."

Entering the sub's wardroom with Sara, Delnoid 4 and Delnoid 6 each grinned and asked, "Do you have any Coke on board?"

Sara smiled halfheartedly and said, "Sure, I'll get it." She placed the chilled bottles and an opener on the mess table and hastily excused herself. After she slid the dark blue curtain across the doorway, she softly cried herself to sleep on the unfolded lower bunk for the short voyage back to Key West.

CHAPTER 33 CAPT. CIOKON UNDERWAY TO HOMECOMING

USS Midway aircraft carrier CVB-41 Docked at berth 7 In the R&R port of Civitavecchia, Italy, 38 miles (61km) northeast of Rome.

09:00 Central European Time - 10 March 1948.

The Executive Officer on the bridge, Commander Frank Stryker, had just finished reading the top secret sealed envelope marked eyes only and super urgent for Captain Joe Ciokon. He turned to the senior chief petty duty officer and said, "is the captain still in Rome?"

"Yes sir", answered the SCPO. He is still sightseeing with his wife who flew into Rome yesterday on MATS from Norfolk sir."

"Well please get an SP and get down to dockside and commandeer a jeep. We have to get him back to Midway ASAP."

SCPO Spillman just grinned and said, "Uh sir, can't we just radio him?"

XO Stryker gritted his teeth as he growled, "No chief, our topmast antenna array cannot connect with the captain's short range walkie talkie that far away and besides, I know that he left his radio in his cabin so he could finally spend some quality time with his wife. So as far as I know they are staying at the Hotel Columbus right next to Vatican City. Check with the SP office. They will have a map of Rome and the address of that hotel. When you get there, hopefully the concierge will know where the captain and his wife went for sightseeing today. "I would guess that since he and his wife are Catholics, I imagine they went to Vatican City to see St. Peters Basilica or maybe to the nearby Vatican Museum.

Meanwhile I will try to telephone the hotel to see where they went. If we are able to get that information, we will radio you as you get underway to Rome in the jeep.”

Stryker then poured himself a cup of good navy coffee, sat down in the captain's bridge chair, rolled his eyes and thought, “Oh jeeeze luiseee, I sure wish I was authorized to open this message.”

About an hour later, the throngs of visitors in St Peters Square were both surprised and alarmed to hear a siren. Then they saw a grey navy shore patrol jeep with a white helmeted driver beeping his horn and slowly ploughing its way through the St. Peters Square visitors. There was a white uniformed CPO Spillman standing up in the passenger seat with a bullhorn repeatedly shouting, “Captain Ciokon! Captain Ciokon! Come to this jeep immediately.”

Inside the hushed and serene ancient basilica, Joe and his wife Mary were standing admiring Michelangelo's, La Pieta sculpture of Mary holding the dead Jesus. Mary whispered to Joe, “Oh Joe, this is just magnificent. Thank God for you finally getting a break from Midway and for the new MATS flying me here so we can finally enjoy the Vatican.”

Joe put his arm around his wife's waist and whispered, “I am so glad that we at last have a chance to make this special pilgrimage Mary.”

Mary looking lovingly at Joe started to say thanks husband, but she stopped looked around and said, “Shushhhh! Joe… do you hear that?”

Joe, after taking a reflected light meter reading was aiming his Bell and Howell 16mm movie camera with its 25mm lens to compose the scene he wanted, was then totally engrossed framing the La Pieta, smiled and whispered, “Hear what Mary?”

She shushed him again and whispered, “Oh Jesus, Joseph and Mary. I hear someone calling for Captain Ciokon! Can't you hear it?”

As he listened, Joe lowered his camera and looked back towards the nave and mixed in with the mummer of other voices and countless footsteps echoing on the polished marble he faintly heard. “Captain Ciokon. Please come to this jeep…” He looked at Mary and snarled under his breath, “Oh Jesus Christ! Damn it all anyway! Now what in blazes do they want?”

Taking Mary's hand, they exited through the Door of the Sacrament, turned right and out the portico where two orange and blue stripped uniformed Swiss Vatican guards stood. They went down the stairs and sure enough, there was a grey navy jeep surrounded by four very concerned Swiss Guards with eager beaver SCPO Spillman standing up calling again for him through the bullhorn.

Thursday 11 March – 07:30 - USS Midway underway from Civitavecchia steaming at flank speed of 32 knots westward toward the Pillars of Hercules 1,186 miles ahead towards the 14 mile wide Mediterranean exit between Jebel Musa, Morocco, Gibraltar and Spain into the Atlantic.

Captain Joe Ciokon stood on the portside captain's bridge catwalk known as vultures row because at times, off duty crew were allowed there to watch the aircraft take off and land. As he stood there above the Admiral's bridge with his executive officer Frank Stryker, the chief navigation officer, Lt. Commander Fred Wells and Lt. JG, Fernando Rojas, the chief radio and communications officer.

He looked around to be sure there were no seamen in earshot and said, "Well gentlemen, now that my second honeymoon in Rome was scuttled, here is what we have to do and it's a really unbelievable Presidential top, top secret mind-boggling order."

Thursday 11 March – 19:30 – USS Midway Captains Conference Room

"Good evening gentlemen. There is plenty of coffee, cokes, donuts, munchies, fresh sandwiches, and cheese and crackers along the sideboard and believe me; we'll probably need it all to get this vital meeting, agenda and planning accomplished. We are probably going to be here until the wee hours. I have asked all 21 of you Lt. Commander Department heads here. And you, Chief Boatswain Vidal with your completel crew rosters to ask you to begin to ASAP think, decide and carefully choose the maximum of officers and crew from all departments that we can temporarily leave in Norfolk when we are to depart there on Saturday, April third.

We must minimize to the absolute minimum - officers and crew onboard for a very ah… unique and special, fairly short – probably uh, so far, a three week mission we have been directed to accomplish by the President himself. I know we are now at full complement of about 3800 hands. But we must somehow whittle that down to 1000 and if possible, even less.

So guys, you need to carefully evaluate and decide what the absolute bare bones minimum crew can be kept aboard to adequately and safely run your departments. We must also completely shut down any unnecessary departments and there will be only a minimum of medical, flight ops and pilots needed. CAG Campbell and Air Boss Vidal, we will need only two HUP-1 Retriever and five Sikorsky H-19 Chickasaw helicopters and aircrews.

"We will need no other than those aircraft maintenance crews or other pilots aboard for this upcoming top secret mission. Other than those, the entire remaining air wing must be launched and temporarily based ashore. CAG, you will try to discover if there are enough tarmac spaces available at Chambers Field in Norfolk and other shore side Naval Aviation bases along the east coast. We will meet here tomorrow again at 19:30 and we can then finalize and approve your crew plans for this weird mission. Also, after you select your departing crews, please tell no one until after I ok it and… only after March 17th when we have been docked in Norfolk. So, that is all gentlemen."

USS Midway aircraft carrier CV-41 berthed at Pier 12 south Norfolk Naval Base 18:10 hours 31 March 1948.

As Captain Ciokon sat in his office, XO Stryker came in and said, "Excuse me Joe, here's another top secret urgent dispatch for you." Joe took and opened the manila envelope and as he read, his eye widened and he said, "Oh Mother Mary! Frank, please get me a jeep and driver. I have to get over to Chambers Naval Air Field by 20:00 to meet President Truman. He's helicoptering down from Washington in Marine One."

Frank's eyes also expanded as he stiffened his posture at hearing that the President was coming. "Oh jeeezzze Joe, what do you suppose he wants?"

Joe sighed, "Well, he is apparently coming to personally brief me on this secret mission and he will also be dropping off a Commander, er, uh, Sara Winchester who will be leading this mission to our, uh, final destination."

XO Frank pushed his cap back on his head and whistled, "So do we know where this final destination is at?"

Joe, grinning, waved his hand and quipped, "Come on Frank, never end your sentences with a preposition!" Joe still reading, then just shook his head and said, "But I guess that I'm, sure as shooting, going to find out during this meeting."

As Captain Joe Ciokon sat edgily in the passenger side of the jeep, he said, "Sailor, park right here on this grassy area then you walk on back over to the NNB ID center over there and wait there for me until I honk 3 times for you. I reckon it'll be about an hour or so."

While Joe watched the sailor walking eastward towards the building, he began to hear a faint but growing louder, unmistakable thumpa thumpa of a Sikorsky H-34 helicopter. As the President's Marine One settled on the grassy patch just north east of the east end of runway 28, Joe held onto his hat as the downwash settled. He then brushed the blown grass and small leaves off his uniform as best he could. Once the door of the copter slid open, he saw a Marine guard beckoning him. As he approached the helicopter, all of the crew, both pilots, as well as the second Marine guard exited and headed towards him. As the guard approached he saluted and asked, "Excuse me Sir. Where can we wait until the President wants to take off again?" Joe pointed to the ID building where his sailor driver had gone and said, "I guess over there."

He then saw a lovely, young, brown haired woman in her khaki Commanders uniform beckoning from the door of the helicopter. As he approached, she came down the steps, saluted and shook his hand and said, "Hello Captain Ciokon. I am Sara Winchester, please come aboard. The President and I have a lot of vital briefing and planning to carry out with you."

About an hour later, after helping Sara and her two stuffed blue B-43 NAVY flight bags and another giant shopping bag full of gift wrapped presents down the steps of the Presidential helicopter, Joe could still not believe the magnitude and critical and utterly extraordinary importance of his mission.

As they walked towards the nearby jeep, the almost totally incredulous Joe recalled the President's momentous words to him: "You sir, are sworn to total secrecy about this incredible mission. It's upon pain of your career and possibly imprisonment that, after your officer's and crew's memories have been erased by our, uh, guests, this mission's actual purpose is to be known only to you. You are to work with and consult with Sara exclusively and you are to also unhesitatingly follow her exact orders."

Joe honked the jeep's horn three times and as soon as he did, the President's crew and his own driver came running on the double. As soon as his driver got to them, Captain Ciokon jerked his thumb towards all the luggage and bags to be piled in the back of the jeep. He and Sara helped arrange the bags while the President's crew re-entered the Sikorsky H-34 and soon its giant rotors began whirling faster and faster until they had enough rotary wing lift. The chopper rotated and Joe and Sara stood there watching the noisy thumping bird wing away on its northwest heading of 344 degrees to return 146 miles to the White House south lawn.

USS Midway aircraft carrier CVB-41 berthed at Pier 12 south, Norfolk Naval Base 07:30 April 1st 1948.

As Sara entered the captain's private office adjacent to his cabin, she saluted and he returned her salute. He stood and said, "Good morning Ms., uh, Commander Winchester. Did you sleep well?"

Sara, anticipating lots of hands on work and supervising, was now dressed in her navy dungarees and chambray blouse, sleepily ran her fingers through her tousled hair, yawned and said, "Yes, thank you captain. I actually slept very well. I have been working almost 16 hours a day since I returned to my office in Washington from Key West back on March 25th.

Now all we have to do is prepare the mess and junior officer's bunk areas for our, uh, guests. Also today, get all of the supply crates loaded aboard. Have the delivery trucks shown up yet Captain?"

"Yes ma'am. All 12 of them arrived on the 22nd, just as scheduled and all of your last minute supplies and equipment will be loaded aboard and stowed by 22:00 tonight. It's sure a lot of supplies Miss Winchester."

Just then there was a knock at the door and a black seaman appeared with a tray full of toast, scrambled eggs, bacon, ham, sausage, pancakes, butter and maple syrup. Sara smiled as the steward set the tray down and said, "Oh thank you seaman. That coffee smells wonderful and I am famished."

The seaman grinned and said, "Yes ma'am, you are quite welcome. There is more hot coffee and fresh ice cold orange, pineapple and apple juice. There are nice fresh donuts and a jar of Skippy peanut butter on the side board and lots more food where that came from just around the corner in my Captain's galley."

Sara gasped as she remembered her Delphinian's allergies to peanuts, looked worriedly at the captain and said, "Oh gosh! I just remembered thank God, our, uh visitors, uh, because of a family genetic trait, they are all severely allergic to all peanut products and all alcoholic beverages too. We must brief all cooking staff and stewards about this as soon as we can Captain."

Ciokon looked at the steward and said, "James, please arrange a 19:00 meeting in B-205-22, the main galley so we can brief everyone about this. I have heard of people with allergies to peanuts actually dying from even the smallest trace of peanuts.

Please order the chief supply officer and head cook to begin to remove all peanut based products as well as all of the peanut butter from our main stores. Have Boson Twain be double sure that the crew stows it in locked store room A-202-A forward.

Sara looked a bit more relieved said, "Oh thank you Captain. It is so important that none of our visitors get sick. Say, how the heck can you remember all of those carrier location designators?"

Captain Ciokon smiled and said, "Well, Miss Winchester, it's actually a very logical layout plan."

Sara looked quizzically and asked, "Oh, how so?"

The Captain continued, "Each area is divided up according to bulkhead deck frame number and compartment number. So over the years I have gotten at least a fairly good mind map of where each location is at."

Sara grinned and giggled as she waggled her left index finger at the Captain, he laughed and chorused with her, "Never end a sentence with a preposition!"

Sara said, "Hummmm, so will our visitors have to memorize all of that?"

The Captain grinned and said, "Oh no Ms. Winchester, er, Commander. We will orient them and show them the basics like fire safety drills, mustering, and of course head use. Say, uh, er, do these aliens use the head like we do?"

Sara sipped her coffee, grinned as she affirmatively nodded her head and said, Please call me Sara. She then asked, "Captain, why is it called a head of all things?"

Ciokon chortled and said, "Well Sara, back in the days of sailing ships, the toilets were placed in the bow or the head of the ship for two reasons. First of all since most vessels of that era could not sail directly into the wind and fortunately the winds mostly, came across the rear of the ship which placed the head essentially downwind. Secondly, if placed somewhat above the water line, vents or slots cut near the floor level would allow normal wave action to wash out the facility. And, the men would simply go astern or forward to the masthead to pee off the side and that's where the term head came from."

Sara smiled and said, "Ok, thanks Captain. Now I know. I have wondered about that ever since being on the USS Sea Cat submarine." Sara, buttering her pancake smiled and said, "Thank you for your kind offer of more food seaman. I can't even begin to eat a bit more of this terrific chow.

Say Captain, have you eaten yet? If not, please sit and help me polish off more of this yummy food. Do you always eat so extravagantly?"

Joe Ciokon smiled as he said, "No ma'am, uh Sara, I ate at 05:30 and this is just a special welcome aboard breakfast for you, and it's a sample preview uh, of our visitors' food."

Soon the steward left and the Captain closed and locked the door. Sara, took a deep final swig of her coffee sighed and said, "Captain, arranging for all of their supplies, clothes and special flipper covers; uh, custom made shoes for 160 Delphinians aged infant to 125. I've also collected books, encyclopedias, AV equipment, films, music, song records and cokes. That is what has almost worn me totally out over this last hectic week."

Captain Ciokon scratched his head and said, "Yeah, I noticed that we took on board a whole truckload of bottled Coke. " He then looked around his cabin to be sure that they were alone and asked, "I am of course very curious about these 160 Delphinians. Uh, do they, well, do they look…"

Sara smiled as she put down her empty coffee cup and said, "Yes Captain, they look as human as you and me except they have almost toeless wide flipper like feet and all of the men almost always wear eyeglasses.

This is why once they get settled aboard and we are cruising zig zags in the Atlantic - as planned - to give us plenty of extra time to get them comfortably clothed and issue their custom made shoes before landing them at Water Island." Sara remembering said, "By the way Captain, did the 6 navy cobblers and the 12 navy tailors and all of their sewing machines, cloth, materials and shoe making supplies report to Midway yet?"

Ciokon nodded his head and said, "Yes Sara. They and their crates arrived on the 19th."

Sara nodded smiled and said, "Good. Getting our arrivals clothed is so essential for their acclimatization and comfort and not being conspicuous in society."

"But one other important thing Captain, they are completely telepathic and cannot talk. And for lack of a simpler way to putting it, they can also read our minds. However also like our earthly dolphins, they also squeak, squeal and click amazingly rapidly at times. And they have sonic echo location just like our earthly dolphins."

Just then, Sara and the startled Captain heard in their heads, "Squeak squeak! Hi Sara! How is everything coming along for our rendezvous? It will be so, click click click, click, click wonderful to see you again!"

Hello Captain Ciokon, it's me, Glinda our pod co-leader. How are you today sir?"

The flabbergasted Captain looked frantically around the room then stared wide eyed at Sara and stammered, "Oh my God! You weren't kidding about them being completely telepathic. Where on earth are they?" Sara, laughing, grinned as she looked up and pointed her right index finger upwards.

Sara and Captain Ciokon then heard some joyful squeaks as Arthur beamed, "Well sir, right now, we are stationed about 260 miles above your ship."

At this point the Captain, almost freaking out, just slumped in his chair and looked helplessly at Sara as he asked, "What, just what should I say to them Sara?"

Sara giggled and said, "Well sir, just welcome them and as you hear them in your head, all of us can either by thinking or speaking, just carry on an ordinary conversation with our Delphs."

He heard a male voice his head, saying, "Hello Captain Ciokon. I am Arthur our other pod co-leader. I am certainly looking forward to meeting you and touring your Midway aircraft carrier sir."

Ciokon tentatively stammered, "Oh, uh, Arthur, how nice to uh… uh… hear you sir. I will be glad and proud to show you our USS Midway. We have been busy making many preparations for your arrival."

Arthur beamed, "Good, I shall look forward to seeing your ship sir." Joe then heard a delighted squeal and a younger female voice saying,

"Hi Captain! It's me, Selena, squeak squeak, the dolphin ambassador to Earth!"

Joe felt a bit foolish, looked again around his private office and said, "Gosh, uh… Hello, uh, your Majesties and uh, is it Princess Selena? Uh, I am so glad to encounter you, uh that is hear you, and I am looking forward to meeting with all of you in person in about a week."

Selena giggled and beamed, "Captain, may I bring my Gatita cat aboard with me?"

Ciokon finally smiled as he said, "Oh, of course little girl, er, person uh Delphinian. Uh, what does you kitty like to eat?"

Selena squeaked, clicked and said, "Oh, she only eats fish dear Captain. Fish and her mother's cat milk which we now produce here in our food synthesizer."

Ciokon then began to receive some really happy and calming love energies in his mind and as he calmed down he said, "Oh Peter, Paul and Mary. Gosh, I can really feel your, er good energies in my mind and spirit."

Sara just grinned and said, "See Captain, you are having your first close encounter of the super friendly Delphinian kind. It's really overwhelming at first of course, but you will soon meet my Delphins in person and we all will have much to share. Of course such one to one encounters will be restricted as much as possible and remembered only by you and me and the Delphins."

Joe finally realized that this was really happening sighed and said, "Well dang! In all my living days at sea or ashore, I never imagined such an encounter as this." He then heard some merry squeaks in his head as Arthur and Glinda trilled in perfect unison, "Us too dear Earth captain, us to. See you soon!"

Joe just sat there quietly and finally said, "Sara, please just kick or pinch me to be sure I am awake, ok?"

Sara grinned as she reached forward and gently stroked the captains hand and said, "This will become one of the most amazing and also a beautiful life changing spiritual experience in your life Captain Ciokon…"

The Captain nodded his head and quietly said, "It's almost like a miracle Sara. My whole universe has changed forever since our meeting yesterday with President Truman."

Sara again squeezed his hand and said, "Yeah, me too, since last February when we first went aboard their starship Lifestar."

After a minute or so, Ciokon straightened up in his chair and harrumphed, "Uh, well, I suppose we ought to get on with our planning huh?"

Sara withdrawing her hand said, "Yes sir, I guess we better."

Joe cleared his throat and said, "So, uh, what was it we were talking about?" Oh, I remember, I was a bit concerned about their clothing."

Sara gave a little giggle as she said, "Oh captain, not to worry. They usually wear something like silver flight suits and some special wide black flipper, uh foot covers. But please always respect their privacy in the forward Junior Officer billeting areas that you have isolated for them. They are mostly accustomed to sleeping in the nude."

The captain's eyes widened as he let out a whooooeeee and said, "Oh Jeeeeeze! OK … I shall post those areas to be totally off limits. We better put up some privacy screens around the chow line."

Sara smiled as she said, "Its ok Captain. We will have everyone up and dressed by 08:00 or out of sight of the galley area. And, my alien friends have been instructed to try to not squeal, squeal, click or moan nor send any telepathic thoughts to any humans who are aboard. Nor run around nude in front of any sailors."

The captain, lacing his fingers together, looked seriously at Sara and said, "Sara the mess crew starts at zero dark hundred each day. So I really do suppose I ought to put some screen stands up around the galley area anyway. In fact, if you wish, we could simply pass trays out to them sight unseen by the galley crew.”

Sara thought for a moment and said, “Well Captain, I have mixed feelings about that. On the one hand our new comers could get to see, smell and choose which foods they find they like and prefer and also begin to get used to earth foods, or… if the security of isolating our Delphs outweighs the assimilation…We could…”

Just then Glinda broke in and beamed, “Sara and Captain! We are all excited to see, smell and taste all of your galley foods. Sara told me that the Navy had the best, uh, how do you say it Sara?” Sara laughed and said, “It's called chow Glinda. It’s different from ciao in Italy.”

Glinda continued, “We would not miss this first earth ship’s galley eating experience for the world. Besides, we can just erase the memories of any of your crew members who see or interact with us Captain. In fact, we will have designated Delphinian crew members and all four Delnoid units constantly monitoring and erasing memories accordingly.”

The astonished captain sat there shaking his head in amazement and said, “Well ladies…It seems that our security and secrecy problems are now mostly solved, especially if you really can erase such memories. Thank you dear uh lady, uh pod leader…” He turned to Sara and asked, “What should I call her, uh them?”

Sara smiled and said, “Captain they will all soon have normal earth names.”

Glinda beamed in, “Captain Joe, may I call you Joe? Then please dear earth sir, just call me Glinda and call Arthur - Arthur and call Selena, Selena, ok? No problema at all Captain Joe.”

The captain broke into a smile and said, “Uh, yes ma am, ummm Glinda that is.”

Glinda beamed, “Well, back to my endless preparation efforts here for our rendezvous next week. Thank you, dear Captain Joe. See you in a week and we can all share a Coke aboard Midway soon.”

Sara voiced, “Ok Glinda and thanks, we’ll see you soon.”

Selena beamed to Sara, “Oh Sara, I have been missing you so mucho.” Sara smiled and thought, “Meeee too Selena, meeee toooo, muchoooo!”

Arthur beamed in, “Captain Ciokon, do you like to play golf sir? We have, since our visit to the Biltmore in Miami developed an amazing Delphin golf game. Maybe we can enjoy putting a 6 hole, par 6 course of it topside on your flat top sir?”

Joe grinned in amazement and said, “Of course Arthur. I really love golf and am now sure curious to see what 6 par game you have come up with. But on our flat top wouldn’t the golf balls always fly overboard, Your Majest… uh, Arthur?”

Arthur squeaked and beamed back, “Nope Captain, we have modified the golf balls to obey our gravity mind commands and boundaries.”

Joe exclaimed, “Do you mean that you can play golf with your mind sir?” Arthur remembering his mind control golf ball while beating President Truman back in Miami, squeaked and beamed, “Well, uh, something like that Joe.”

Joe just shook his head in utter amazement and said, "Well Arthur I'll have you know I average a par below 72. How about you, what's your average par?"

Arthur grinned and beamed, "I always hit only holes in one!"

Captain Joe said, "Gosh, you are invincible…Well ok. I am looking forward to you showing me your uh, alien golf game soon."

Arthur beamed deep friendship energies to the now almost overwhelmed Captain and further beamed, "Ok amigo, see you soon."

Selena then beamed privately to Sara, " Do you know what my daddyo did while we were at our backside Moon base Sara ? He and a coupla Delnoids as caddies and even Amelia and some crew members put on their spacesuits and went to the 6 hole golf course we made on top of the crater rim and whacked a few bucketfuls of yellow golf balls into eternity !"

Sara was about to think back, when Selena then squeaked in alarm to her mother, Oh dear Amadore. I hope I did not let the Amelia cat out of the secret bag mom…"

Glinda squealed and clicked in alarm and immediately powerfully beamed to Sara, "Oh gosh Sara, Ailema and Embry certainly enjoyed the one sixth gravity vacuum putting practice. She then beamed sharply to Selena, "Aiiii princess you just gotta try to be more careful what you beam !"

"But anyway not to worry sweetie. We will introduce Ailema to Sara as the true Amelia that she is once we are aboard the Midway."

Sara, who did not register Selina's slip of her beaming, sat there for a moment giggling about alien lunar golf games said, "Well…Where was I Captain? Oh yes…I understand that at least 800 crew members will need to be aboard to run the ship. So in case any of the mind erasing fails, what have they been instructed about never ever disclosing anything that they might see during this mission?"

Captain Joe looked very authoritative as he said, "Commander Winchester, we have briefed each of them as a group and individually by their department Commanders. Each has now signed a specially drawn up for this mission, extra Uniform Code of Military Justice form swearing them to total secrecy."

Sara looking worried said, "Yes Captain, but can they really be counted on to keep quiet and also not write home or take Kodak Brownie snapshots about some of the uh, unusual things and actions by our aliens that they undoubtedly might see?"

Ciokon stood and walked to his bookcase and took down his dog eared copy of the Uniform Code of Military Justice. He opened it on the table in front of Sara, and said, "We have verified that they all had sworn to the whole UCMJ that they signed back when they enlisted; but now we have reiterated their respecting secrecy by having them sign and swear to honor these specially selected UCMJ applicable articles. We have, as you can see here, had them confirm their understanding, respect and serious consequences of articles, 88, 90, 92 and 94. We will also search, seize and burn any letters or diaries, drawings, film and notebooks after you have taken your, uh, our aliens ashore on Water Island."

Sara looked at the book and saw that several articles had been underlined in red by the captain and the Judge Advocate General (JAG) liaison officer aboard. As she read them she gasped and said, "But Captain, this Article 94 about mutiny is punishable by death."

Captain Ciokon gravely nodded and said, "That's right Commander. We have really tried to put the fear of God, Davie Jones and the UCMJ into these remaining 800 crewmen and as far as we can estimate, perhaps hopefully only… maybe 100 of them will ever likely see or interact with our uh, visitors Sara. You know like the mess boys, medicos and longboat and helicopter pilots and the air crews and crane operators as we transfer them ashore at Water Island."

Sara sighed and said, "Yes Captain it's any crew who might be directly interacting with our Delphinians. Especially like the mess boys, cooks and other lower ratings that we are worried about. Because Captain right now, our new comers do not know at all how to cook or as far as that goes clean." As Sara then recalled the food synthesizer and the incredible stink in the ancient starship."

Captain Ciokon nodded in agreement and said, "When do you plan for us to disembark them and all of these tons of supplies?"

Sara looking sort of perplexed sighed and said, "Well, as soon as we can get them processed, clothed, shod and also give them their basic island kits. I imagine that this should take at least 6 or maybe even 8 extra days sailing around out in western the Atlantic before we can head back to the Virgin Islands for their Water Island disembarkation."

Captain Ciokon sighed and said, "Gosh Sara, you have really had your plate full arranging all the details for this uh, landing."

Sara smiled and said, "Well Captain, you don't know the half of it. But it's all been completely worth it. These super intelligent beings are so exceptional and so advanced beyond us and also totally caring, healing and loving. They have so much wisdom and peaceful ways to offer our troubled and constantly warring society."

Ciokon chuckled as he said, "I totally agree Sara, but I then would be out of a job."

Sara laughed too and said, "Well maybe we could convert Midway into a cruise ship or a hospital ship or maybe even into a valiant naval carrier museum docked somewhere in southern California." Maybe in San Diego near those other Navy facilities."

The captain took another swig of coffee, cocked his eyebrows up, smiled and said, "All right Sara…Just so long as I can still have this deck under my feet. He then chuckled as he got an absurd, yet in some ways an attractive idea and picture in his mind. He grinned at Sara, laughed and said, "You know what Sara? Maybe we could turn the flight deck into a unique and exclusive golf course and dock it in San Diego."

Sara laughed and said, "Oh Captain, my dad and I and uh, Bob Hope like to play golf so I hope you and I can tee off someday at the exclusive 5 acre flat top Midway golf resort!" Sara gave a laugh and then said, "Or, we could build the biggest miniature golf course in the world topside !"

After the Captain and Sara finished laughing, he continued, "Well, I guess that the real potential freak out will be when we rendezvous with their… what is it called Sara?" Sara replied, "Lifestar Captain. Their incredible, undersea and flying between the stars ship is called Lifestar."

"Well anyway Sara, the main concern I have is when that ship rises up out of the sea to hover over our forward deck near the number one elevator and these 160 creatures disembark their craft to step on Midway. Just before their ship rises, I will issue orders that all of the portholes and windows on the primary flight control tower, my bridge and the hatch between navigation and my bridge and all other portholes be closed until well after they have all gotten below and after their amazing ship has departed. By the way, how big is their star craft?"

Sara fondly recalling her still unbelievable visit to Lifestar, sighed and said, "She's about 300 feet in diameter Captain and she's just about 100 feet from bottom to top."

The captain picked up his clipboard with a yellow legal pad on it and withdrew his pen from his left shirt pocket and as he sat down, said, "Please let's now list any other tasks you need from me."

"Well, about their Coke captain, they totally love it and a lot of them apparently drink almost half a liter each day. It, in a good way, makes them feel more centered and more relaxed at the same time. It's like Coke is a tiny stimulant for most of us. But, it always seems to make them feel more calm, happier, centered, aware and on task. Which reminds me, can you please radio Captain Tamarynd on Water Island to see if they have any ice machines? They prefer ice cold Coke. I know I ordered four Coke machines for the chow and rec hall but now that I think about it, we'll probably need a couple more."

The Captain noted that and said, "I hate warm Coke. " He commented, "You know Sara. We get it onboard to keep in our food lockers and in our Coke machines which keeps it cool to sell to crew for only 5 cents. But only because Coke gladly distributes its beverage to all serving military personnel at the least possible cost."

Sara nodded her head in agreement as she finished eating and said, "Thank you again Captain. I was famished and now we must continue meeting to do all the planning to land our 160 aliens at their first home, on their beautiful new water world. Also, can you please send a seaman ashore to get one more 10 pound bag of that uh granular stuff that garages use to absorb oil on their floors? What I ordered is now packed in crates to be opened only after we get our, uh, visitors landed."

Captain Ciokon looked incredulously at Sara, wrote down the request and replied, "Sure Commander. Is it for some weird alien purpose or grinning he mocked, for an alien er… cat box?"

Sara also grinned as she said, "Well you are astute Captain. It's actually for Delphinian Princess Selena's little kitty cat. Her name is Gatita. But, if the oil absorbent is not readily available, we shall have to get a few large buckets of beach sand and a large rectangular baking tray or two from the mess kitchen."

The captain dutifully noted the request as he looked at Sara and exclaimed, "Jeeezeeee. So are some of them really alien royalty Sara? I am still flabbergasted just realizing that we are not alone in this Galaxy."

Sara finishing her final sip of her third cup of coffee said, "Well yes sort of Captain. Their leader, Arthur, and his queen, Glinda, and Selena are what we would probably classify as royalty but they just see their echelon only as pod leaders."

The captain still not believing all this was real, said, "Incredible, just like our earthly dolphins!"

Sara smiled as she said, "That's exactly right Captain. The Delphinians are a totally communicating and loving society and we are lucky to have them coming to Earth. They have changed my life and vision completely. We must always and in all ways, from here on out, do all that we can to guide, help and protect them."

CHAPTER 34 HOMECOMING

USS Midway aircraft carrier CV-41 Latitude: 20 degrees 00 minutes 18.02 seconds north. Longitude: 66 degrees 00 minutes 12.78 seconds west. Tuesday 6 April 1948.

It was almost 22:00 and the Midway had slowed to a stable headway crawl. The sea was a little bit choppy with a 6-12 mph head wind coming from the north. Captain Ciokon had maneuvered his ship to stay into the wind to provide maximum stability for the ship which was now cleared of all masts and antennas from the island and the forward flight deck to the bow.

As the now 15 day old just a bit past full moon bathed the sea and ship, various yellow and white tinted floodlights filled the flight deck and the salty misty air with miniscule billowing and glowing sea water particles.

Aside from the headway breeze and the sound of the ships prow rhythmically slicing thru the sea, it was quiet under the faint stars. The moonlight washed out the Milky Way trying to arch across the tropical sky as Midway awaited the arrival of the alien starship.

Sara was up in the navigation bridge with the Captain. She was really keyed up as she stood next to him at his plotting table. The bridge and maps were bathed in red battle light to maintain everybody's dark adaptation.

Sara and the Captain then heard Arthur in their heads, "Hi Sara, hello Captain Joe. Are you ready for us to surface, hover to drain seawater and begin our disembarkation?"

Sara smiled as she gripped the edge of the chart table and replied, "Yes Arthur, we are ready. Remember the number one forward deck elevator can only hold about 60 people. Which is about the weight of one of our

F-4 Corsairs. So, each group will have to wait aboard Lifestar until their turn. So we figure that it will take about three or four groups for each elevator trip down to the hanger deck.

There will be several officers and enlisted there to guide all of you to your quarters below and forward on the second deck and third deck. Please remember to beam to everybody not to squeal, squeak or click and not to telepath to any of us humans and your alien secret should hopefully be safer." Sara grinned as she then heard in her head from all 160 Delphinians, "Ok, we promise Sara!" followed by squeals and squeaks of laughter.

Glinda beamed to Sara and the Captain, "We are so excited to finally be coming aboard your ship. I know everyone will be on their best behavior and that we will soon be on Water Island."

Selena beamed in, "Sara I will be so happy to see you and I can't wait for us to go swimming at Limestone Bay beach. Have you found a ship's cabin for me and Gatita?"

Sara smiled as she thought, "Yes Selena. We will be putting you in a bunk right next to mine in my office and bunk area. And we can safely keep Gatita right there in my office. I even had the ships carpenter make a larger cat cage with feeding ports and a secure latching door for your kitty."

Selena squealed and beamed, "Oh Sara, Gatita and I will be so glad to see you again."

Sara thought, "Meeee tooo Selena. See you in about half an hour."

Captain Ciokon and Sara heard in their heads from Arthur, "Well, if you are ready….We will ascend and once we've broken surface, we will hover for awhile to drain the seawater from our hull and then move ahead to hover over the forward deck next to your number one forward elevator."

The captain then looked at his minimal bridge crew of 3 officers and four enlisted and said, "Ok men. Maintain this exact heading as steady as she goes and cover all portholes and windows with blackout panels and you are to remain here in navigation in red light until further orders from only me."

"Aye aye sir" chorused the crew as they quickly began to cover the viewports.

Captain Joe took Sara's hand and towed her out to the port side bridge wing and as they both looked forward they gripped the rail. Ciokon said, "OK the elevator crew is in place and if our boarders do not make any strange noises or in head thoughts, we are as ready as we ever will be. So what should I do now Sara? Just think to Arthur?"

Captain Ciokon heard in his head Arthur beaming, "OK Captain, here we come." In about a minute Sara and the captain heard a low pitched hum and began to sense a weak vibration. The Delphinian star ship began rising from the sea about 150 feet (45 meters) off the port side and grew bigger and wider. It was completely unlit except for a blue light along the bottom of the craft.

As Captain Ciokon looked, he could see a tiny figure waving to him from one of the wide Inca imperial style trapezoidal windows just above the centerline of the craft. Joe in all his years at sea breathed, "Oh Jesus, Joseph and Mary… I cannot believe this is happening." He then heard in his head from Glinda "Ok Captain Joe. One, two, three, ready or not… here we come!"

Sara said to Captain Joe, "OK! We better get down to the flight deck asap."

Sara and Joe got down the ladders and through the island forward hatch of the flight deck control with its two big 2 inch thick glass windows, onto the flight deck. The giant star craft was then exactly keeping the carriers cruise speed and heading and hovering accurately one meter just forward of the elevator.

As Sara breathlessly ran up to the forward portside edge of the closed elevator, she took Joe's hand and said, "OK, now watch this amazing blue light gangway come on." They then saw a 24 foot wide by 12 foot high rectangular drop down port opening on the farside bottom of the gently hovering star craft. And then a 20 foot wide but only 6 inch thick shimmering blue light beam ramp flashed out maintaining exact positioned just about one half inch above the slowly rising and settling flight deck. After Joe took all of this in he said, "My gosh Sara. It's exactly compensating and holding its height just an inch above our pitching deck."

Sara tugged his sleeve and excitedly said, "Look Joe." As they both looked they saw a young dark haired girl wearing a blue flowered skirt and a white long sleeved blouse. She carried a small wooden and wire cage and ran down the light ramp in her wide black tennis shoes. Before Joe could say cat's meow, Selena was in Sara's arms crying and squealing and squeaking and as they hugged.

Joe then heard the insistent meows of a little yellow eyed black ball of fur inside the cage. Joe harrumphed as he said, "I'll bet you must be Princess Selena but remember, no more uh, Delphin uh, dolphin noises."

Selena took the captains hand and as she shook it, she grinned haughtily and beamed, "Oh Captain Joe, no one can hear me on this windy flight deck."

Joe nodded his head towards some open mouthed gawking sailors and said, "Uh, well your uh, princess… Those guys sure saw you."

Captain Joe looked back at the ramp and saw a stunningly beautiful woman carrying a large white bag and dressed similarly to Selena in a lovely red flowered skirt and a flowered blue top. He noticed that she was also was wearing her very wide red tennis shoes below her astoundingly lovely legs. He heard a squeak of delight and in his head, "Hi Captain. It's me, Glinda and remember we will erase all these memories of us for your men constantly and just after we get landed on Water Island." Glinda walked hurriedly to Sara and took her into her arms, cried and beamed, "Oh Sara, por fin, at last… we are coming home!"

Joe stepped over to the edge of the 125 feet by 130 feet elevator and said to the crew, "Well just don't stand there gawking men! Help the ladies with their bags."

"Aye Aye sir" chorused the sailors as they hesitatingly approached Glinda, Sara and Selena to collect all their bags.

They began moving the bags onto the elevator as one sailor nudged his mate and whispered loudly, "Gosh that young one is sure a dilly." The other, a bit older sailor let out a loud rude wolf whistle and said, "Dang, that older dame is also a real looker. Did ya see her gams?"

Glinda reading his mind, looked wide eyed at him and beamed to Sara, "What are gams and on your planet whatever does that whistle mean Sara?"

Sara grinned and thought back, "That wolf whistle is the way some earthmen and most sailors show their appreciation of beautiful women. And gams are your lovely long legs."

Glinda flounced and put her right hand on her hip and beamed, "Well, those sailors must be related to our ancient alpha males." She moaned and clicked rapidly in delighted mock indignation.

Selena looked dreamily at the group of about a dozen sailors as she loudly echoed the seaman's wolf whistle through her blowhole and beamed to Sara and her mother, "Maybe my earth husband is here!"

Sara, Selena and Glinda received Arthur beaming, "Oh no you don't, miss Princess! You for sure ain't ready for an earth husband. Not just yet."

Glinda beamed to Sara, "What does ain't mean?" Sara thought, "Its it's a contraction which means, are not." And she turned and hugged a warm welcome to Arthur.

Arthur, wearing tan khaki slacks and a brown yellow flowered aloha shirt and his wide black earth sneakers, reached out and warmly shook Captain Ciokon's hand as all three aliens beamed caring and peaceful loving energies into Joe.

Joe taken aback could not help grinning in enchantment as he felt the Delphinians kind and loving energies and stammered, "Uh gosh, so glad to finally meet you in person uh, Your Majesties, uh Delphinians…"

Arthur still holding the Captain's hand pleasantly beamed, "Please Joe…just call me Arthur."

Captain Ciokon then noticed a nice looking tall fellow with medium length slicked back dark hair dressed in khaki slacks, wide black tennis shoes and a beige three button sports jacket over a dark blue, white flowered aloha shirt, standing there with his hand stuck out for shaking. He startlingly said, "Hello Captain Ciokon. I am Delnoid 1M and I am an android and I can speak. I am Arthur's personal adjunct, XO in your terms, and I and six other male and female Delnoid units will be at your service during our voyage and orientations to Water Island."

Captain Ciokon was overwhelmed with all of these unbelievable aliens and he quizzed, "Now ah…What did he call himself?"

Arthur grinned as he beamed, "An android Captain. We made him."

Joe sighed as he shrugged his shoulders and said, "Ok. Please pinch me! This is all just too mind-boggling." So, just as he'd asked, Delnoid 1 shrugged his shoulders too, grinned mischievously, reached over and soundly pinched Captain Joe on his left arm. As Joe pulled his arm away in surprise at the pinch, he got defensive for just a second - but by rubbing his pinch spot he relaxed and started laughing along with Sara and the Delphinians who were now squealing in merriment. As now grinning Joe looked up from the pinch, he was shocked to see a a small group of 21 elderly male and female Delphinians each sitting in some kind of amazing floating solid back with solid sides white chairs. Maybe it was like a wheelchair and as Joe and Sara looked - the 21 floating chairs were each being guided by what Sara quickly recognized as the starship's medical staff.

Glinda clicked softly as she and Selena and Arthur became solemn and then tearfully each took Sara's and Joe's hands as she clicked softly and sadly and beamed, "Oh dear Amadore. Thank you, these are the only surviving fifth generation Delphinians to make it here to this homecoming touchdown tonight."

As soon as the surviving elderly Delphins were all parked on the forward elevator deck seven of them, feebly in the unaccustomed earth gravity, valiantly tried to stand to put their flippers on the deck to feel their homecoming. Four of them, three crying and clicking females and one gritting his teeth male pitifully collapsed to their knees as their medicos rushed to help them back into their float chairs."

Then, Arthur, Glinda, Selena then heard in their heads, "Oh Amadore, we have sacrificed so many to come home to this magnificent water world. We bless and thank you and all our self sacrificing brave fore mothers and fore fathers for this safe landing from our endless life journeys between the stars.

Tear streaming Glinda, Selena, Arthur, Delnoid, Sara and even then weepy Capt. Coikon ran over to the elders and one by one Glinda hugged and kissed and gave thanks and love energies to each one.

Then one very elderly male Delph feebly stood in front of his queen, shakily grasped her hands, and as he looked into the heart and soul of Glinda he moaned softly and collapsed... Glinda rushed to kneel beside and hold him as he softly beamed, "Thank you Arthur and Glinda, as least I made it to this deck. But, I so wanted to set my flippers on the Earth and the beach sands of our island. Please, please don't bury me at sea your majesties. Bury me in this good Earth on Water Island your majesty... He then closed his eyes with a soft moan and a few soft clicks he passed into the eternity of the stars.

Glinda softly and sadly moaning and clicking in tears then gently removed his eyeglasses and as she put them in her dress pocket she softly beamed, "Oh dear fellow star mariner, rest now in eternal peace in the mind and spirit of our Universal Creator.

Every Delphinian both outside and inside the starship then began moaning and slowly clicking and beaming powerful sad energies and all then in unison, except for Sara and the Captain, beamed the soul rendering Delphinian funeral final prayer.

"Beloved Amadores, creators of space, time, and precious light, life and awareness, we bless and release the body our fellow being as all of his 123 space and now Earth years of life dream mind recordings have now forever returned to you."

After the Delphinian medicos had replaced the dead Delphin in his chair and respectfully covered him with a gold cloth. All of the elderly float chair Delphs were taken below on the elevator to be birthed in the ships forward hospital which had been given over to the alien medicos.

As the giant elevator returned topside. A large group of Delphinians with all the males wearing eyeglasses and all dressed alike in semi shiny silver, like flight suits began to decent to finally set flipper on deck along with all of the really lovely females were also all dressed in the same semi shiny flight suits and the same wide black tennis shoes as the males were wearing.

As they were all uncertainly descending the blue shimmering ramp. Each was towing a large dark blue suitcase with an extended sturdy luggage pull handle and clever small rollers on the back edge.

Still wet eyed Joe remarked, "Say, that's an amazing and simple idea. Here on earth we always have to lug our suitcases around with just one grip handle."

Arthur looked at Joe grinned, winked, squeaked and cheerlessly beamed, "Oh, we always will now have to use our roller suitcases instead of our antigravity suitcases because they would cause too much of a hullabaloo here on your planet. It's so much easier you know."

Joe then noticed that each alien also had on a light blue backpack. Joe broke into a wide smile with a little laugh, when he saw that the children also had their own little light blue backpacks and each also was towing a cute little blue roller T handled suitcase of their own.

As the first group of the Delphinians had all gathered around Arthur, Glinda, Sara and Selena with the Captain in the center of the elevator. Joe was then astounded to see more aliens clad in blue jumpsuits coming down the ramp and each pushed what looked like extraordinarily large grocery shopping carts filled with what looked like large blue duffel bags. Each wheel less cart was just floating about 2 inches above the ramp and deck.

Joe squeezed his own right arm to make sure that he wasn't dreaming and exclaimed, "Oh gosh, also antigravity shopping carts! I wonder what else these amazing beings have with them?" Joe's jaw dropped even further as two groups of four Delphinians also wearing blue jump suits came down the ramp and each foursome easily pushed and guided a enormous cargotainer by hand.

The rectangular corrugated wall containers were remarkable. Each about 7 feet high, 18 feet long by 6 feet wide and they too simply floated above the amazing blue light beam ramp onto the deck - just as the antigravity shopping carts had effortlessly floated. Each container had a set of red, yellow and green small round lights located horizontally just above what Joe supposed was the large sliding side door of the container.

Seaman Malcon Mc Lean was also gawking and dumbfounded and totally impressed with the incredible huge cargotainers. Captain Joe noticing his absorption for the containers said, "Sailor ! Look sharply there and lend a helping hand!"

Mc Lean then shook his head and came to present time and glanced still amazed at the Capt and said, Uh, sure, uh, aye, aye, Sir…" He would later in 1957 develop and manufacture cargotainers for ships and also for railroad cars and so… he sort of became one of the first humans to put into actual operation the incredible alien practical industrial technologies and equipment. But because of the Delphin end of cruise brainwashing. It took Malcon until 1955 for him to understand the strange fragmented dreams he was, almost every night, having about floating cargotainers.

Arthur still grieving the death of the elderly Delphin tugged on the Captain's sleeve and quietly beamed, "Captain Ciokon, If you don't mind, we will just keep these containers aboard until Midway takes us to, where is that Sara?"

Sara also still sad at the elders death, just said, "Remember Captain, after their climate acclimatization at Water Island, we will hopefully, within only a month or two, take them all to Galveston, Texas to load everything on a special army train of passenger carts, boxcars and some flat cars which will take us to Camp Roberts in central coastal California."

Captain Ciokon, just said, "I am impressed Arthur. Those containers look like they should fit perfectly - one each - on our navy railway flatcars.

Arthur soberly beamed, "We noticed that from our early aerial reconnaissance of your rail systems and laser measurements of your rail cars."

Arthur looked Ciokon directly in his eye and beamed, "These containers are very important and I will be assigning a security contingent of two extra Delnoid units aboard to watch over them."

Captain Ciokon straight faced said, "Of course Arthur, no problem at all. Hummmm…Don't you need more of your Delnoid units to adequately guard these two containers?"

Arthur beamed directly to Ciokon, "No Captain. Our Delnoid units when required can go with almost no sleep, very little food and water, but they too, like us, are now addicted to your superb Coca Cola."

Glinda squeezed Joe's hand and beamed, "Oh Joe we have many more useful things but please don't forget that you must always keep our secrets." Joe blushed and nodded as he looked at Glinda's mesmerizing beautiful pure azure blue eyes and said, "Oh yes Ma'am to be sure. Uh, we can lash these two containers right back there on our aft flight deck."

Arthur beamed, " If you please Capt. Stoner, we will have to take them below to store on your hanger deck. I am apologetic captain. But keeping them topside I fear will interfere with your flight operations until you return to pick us up at Water Island."

Joe shoved his hat up a bit from his forehead and sighed as he said, "Well whatever you need Arthur. We have just today been ordered by President Truman to simply cruise the Caribbean to keep our crew isolated from shore and family and other social contacts. Until we get Sara's call to come back and pick all of you up and take you and your possessions to Galveston, Texas for your train to California."

Arthur then beamed, Oh in that case Captain. We should stow these cargotainers topside until we off load em at Galveston. Will that be ok sir?"

Captain Ciokon looked directly in to his alien counterparts eyes and said, OK, no problema shipmate !

Sara thought privately to Arthur, Glinda and Selena, "Well that's a load off my mind about keeping any crew isolated with residual memories; so that now they absolutely cannot get ashore to phone home…"

Just then a shore patrolman came over to the Captain, saluted and begged his pardon. The captain said, "Yes, what is it?" The shore patrolman, wearing white leggings, wide white pistol belt and a blue armband with a yellow SP on it, pointed sternward and there, up on the port wing of one of the dark blue Corsair F-4 were two aliens, each wearing light blue one piece flight suits.

Glinda glancing at the pair, let out a short whistle and beamed to Ailema and Embry, "Oh oh, one of their guards has spotted you."

Arthur beamed in, "Ok you two, what are you doing up on their crude propeller driven airplane?" Receiving this, the pair jumped down to the deck and promptly trotted back to Arthur, Glinda and

Captain Ciokon. As they approached, the male extended his hand and beamed, "Hello Captain Ciokon. I am Embry and this is my life mate Ailema. We are heads of our, uh flighter squadron and we just could not resist going to see your ancient, er, great F4UB Corsairs."

As Embry explained, Captain Ciokon, amazed by their so accurate knowledge of their fighters, was also doing a big double take as he thought, "Ailema somehow sure looks familiar."

Glinda picked up the Captain's thoughts got a serious face and beamed, "Say captain, don't you think we ought to get on with our disembarkation."

Ailema grinned impishly and looked the captain right in the eye and said, "Oh Captain Ciokon, I sure would love to try flying one of your Corsairs someday. Its gull wings are really beautiful to me!"

Captain Ciokon stammered, "Uh sure, uh miss Ailema. But, uh, pardon me, how is it that you can talk? Are you an asteroid like uh, I mean, like that Delnoid 1 fellow, er, I mean android?"

Amelia, not flinching a bit, raised her eyebrows knowingly and said, "Oh come now, Captain, let's just say that I was an experiment to see if we could be given uh, vocal chords."

Captain Ciokon thought, "Oh yeah, sure lady…", and he said, "OK… well, uh, very nice to meet both of you. We will go flying together someday, er, in the uh, future."

Glinda then beamed sharply to Amelia, " Why did you choose to actually speak to the captain ? Aren't you afraid of revealing your secret ?

Alemia just sighed, frowned and thought, "Well… I'm sorry Glinda but I just got carried away with the, er, aviation of all of this. I'll be more careful in the future."

Glinda smiled, clicked a few tisk tisk tisks and beamed to her dear Earth aviator. Its OK Amelia. I too would have felt the same during any homecoming to think the least.

Arthur then hugged Ailema and beamed, "Well, welcome home dear aviatrix after your 11 years, er, away. At least we have made it this far and so far so good and ok…"

After the first group of 60 aliens, Ailema and Embry along with the now unloaded forklift pallets and the contents of just a few of the 30 antigravity carts were gathered on the elevator; Captain Ciokon nodded and waved to the yeoman to lower away the elevator.

As it descended, Arthur beamed to Captain Joe, "Well, I hope you will have extra space on this hanger deck to stow all of our gear since we dare not show our antigravity carts to any more of your crew."

Joe still looking amazed, nodded his head and said, "Of course your Majesty, uh, Arthur. We have plenty of heavy duty hydraulic loaders, forklifts and hand trucks here on the hanger deck and we will gladly store all of those boxes and bags for you. Uh, are there any things you all might be needing from those boxes Arthur?"

Glinda looked at the Captain and beamed, "Oh no Joe, we have everything we will need for everyone in our backpacks and suitcases until we all get landed on Water Island. We certainly are homecoming with just the flightsuits on our backs…"

CHAPTER 35 WELCOME ABOARD

THWARTSHIPS AND DEADLY DONUTS

USS Midway aircraft carrier CV-41: Saturday, 7 April, 1948. Overnight on the 6th the USS Midway made a heading of 120.96 at 26 knots per hour in the Atlantic towards the British Commonwealth island of Barbados.

After enjoying their first earthly breakfast, the Delphins all assembled in the second deck forward all crew galley with its large checkered blue and white linoleum floor and bench mess tables.. The breakfast was really chaotic. Sara, Glinda, Selena spent the whole time trying to guide their refugees through the food line; all the while explaining about the traditional food of eggs, toast and jam, bacon, ham, pancakes, cereals, oatmeal and all of the many different juices, tea and coffee to the Delphinian newcomers.

Most of the Delphinians seemed to prefer tea and Coke. The Delphinians quickly cleaned out all 6 of the donut trays. Selena was beaming to them, "These are real earth donuts, just like the ones we had at the Krispy Kreme shop while we were in Coral Gables. Aren't they yummy?"

After All of the crew, except Captain Ciokon and XO Stryker, had been cleared from the mess area and everyone had been seated. Captain Ciokon stood, cleared his throat while still holding his cup of good strong navy coffee in his hand said, "Well, my dear friends from above, and uh, below. Welcome aboard the USS Midway. It will be your home for the next week or so as Sara…"

As soon as he said Sara, there arose many gleeful Delphin whistles, squeaks, squeals and lots of happy rapid clicking as the Delphinians beamed love energies to the earth woman that they now loved.

"How nice…," said Captain Ciokon, "Ah, as I was saying, we proudly welcome you to your new home planet and we will do all that we can to see to your safety and orientations while being aboard our navy ship and as you know Sara, er, Commander Winchester will also be here to guide and help all of you. There are several things to be aware of while living aboard our ship. It's a floating city, uh, I guess just like your starship was. But soon, you will be landed at Water Island and there you can begin to be truly free to enjoy the sunshine, beaches and ocean in our US Virgin Islands. But, right now I have asked Delnoid, uh, 2 or is it 4? I can never keep your look alike Delnoids straight. Anyway, last night, after your box lunch dinners and Cokes, as you know Sara had passed out to each of you our USS Midway Personal Information Booklet. It will tell you all that you need to know."

Delnoid 1, holding his copy of the booklet, cleared his throat and beamed to all while at the same time saying for the benefit of the earthlings, "I will beam to all of you the contents of this little booklet and as you read it, it will also give you more practice in reading English."

All 160 of the Delphins beamed back, "Delnoid!" click click click, "What the heck are you talking about? You know perfectly well that because of our total telepathic group connection and generational pod memories, we can all read, understand, and memorize English and several other earth languages from our studies since we were 60 light years out from Earth." Then there followed a few rude raspberry noises from a few blowholes along with merry squeak, squeals and a lot of sharp Delphin whistles.

Delnoid 1 stiffened as he said, "Well, none the less, this is vital information for living aboard that Captain Ciokon wants you to know.

Right now I will turn this over to the Executive Officer, Commander Stryker, for him to outline some of the major points for you. Remember everyone; safety is most important aboard any US Navy ship." He was then almost bowled over by strongly beamed choruses of "Weeee know Delnooooid. Aboard starships tooo…"

Delnoid beamed to all, "Well just so you will be safe and not get lost." "But, click click click yourselves. Please let me continue. I studied this little booklet all last night. There are 235 frames in the ship, numbered from bow to stern. A frame is a thwartship rib extending…" Delnoid looked hopelessly at now chuckling XO Stryker and asked, "What in Amador is a thwartship?"

XO Stryker just easily smiled as he replied… "Delnoid, why don't you just let your people, uh beings, read it for themselves in the little booklet that they are getting? If any of you need me, my office door is always open at C- 221-IL-3 at frames 194-198. You can also ask for anything you need from what we call our hotel department at 2-213-3. There is also our uh, religious chapel which will seat about 50 people at C-214-IL."

Glinda beamed to all, "Since we are now away from our Lifestar chapel, each of you please be sure to go there to thank Amadores for our safe landing."

Sara looked at her two Delphin leaders and gave a half smile of hope as she held up her crossed two right fingers. Glinda and Arthur knowing now the earthly custom clicked softly, smiled and raised their right hands with fingers crossed. Glinda beamed to Arthur and Sara, "Yes, so far so good and with Amador's grace, all will be well."

The XO continued, "The main thing that we always must be aware of aboard any navy or other ship is safety and what to do if there is a fire."

He quickly heard many moans and alarmed squeaks and then in his head… "Oh Amador, remember that time two generations ago, when that terrible fire broke out in our main engine room and 20 of our crew were killed…"

Captain Ciokon was also deeply moved as he felt waves of sadness from the 160 Delphins' pod memories, he also saw tears in their eyes as several moments of Delphin moaning followed. After the emotions had settled, as most of the male Delphs were wiping their glasses, he said, "I am so sad and sorry that you lost ship mates on your brave voyage between the stars…." He then, to his surprise, found himself wondering how they buried beings in space. He turned in reprieve to Glinda as she reached and held his left hand and beamed, "Dear Captain Ciokon, we too have our burial ceremonies before we release the bodies to the vacuum of space, stars and eternity."

The captain instinctively squeezed her hand and said, "Oh, I never doubted that and I, I am so glad we are connecting spiritually like this. It shows us how universal we are."

Glinda held his hand and beamed, "Yes dear Captain, it's true that we are all precious children of the universe."

As the Captain reluctantly turned his gaze away from the so compelling queen, he saw that most everyone was grinning with some slow impatient clicks here and there among the Delphs as they good-naturedly were waiting for him to continue. So he blushed a bit, harrumphed, cleared his throat and said, "Uh, XO, can you now please outline the amenities we had the yeomen mark in red in our little Navships booklet."

XO Stryker stood after his first time experiencing the powerful emotional waves and telepathy when all the Delphinians shared their emotions with full sound, vision and feelings into his head. He wiped his eyes, cleared his throat and said, "Uh, of course sir. Thank you Captain.

So, remember that for your secrecy and security you must always stay forward of thwarthead, uh frame 75 which runs from the bow sternward. You are also restricted to the second and third decks while you are accomplishing your clothing issuance, fittings, other orientations and classes here aboard Midway for the next week or so before we land you on lovely Water Island." He immediately felt powerful cognition energies as the alien group began to realize and share their rising excitement that their sixth generation was really finally at homecoming. He then got choked up himself as he felt their happy energies. "Uh, please, If I can please have your attention, uh, folks. We will assemble here every morning at 08:00 for your breakfast. And then, Sara and lovely, uh Glinda, er… will take over to assign you to various classes. They will also send you to your special ships stores to be fitted for your, uh island clothes kits and also for your post island USA traveling clothes. The fitted and altered traveling clothes will be stowed with your other supplies for your return sail to Galveston, uh, Texas to be put on your special secure US army train to California.

Glinda, Arthur and Selena looked shrewdly at each other as Glinda beamed, "I am awed with the uh, power women can have over some of these earthmen."

"Uh, so, here are some services and important shipboard places and how to get to them for you to use and enjoy while you are aboard. This is of course all fully outlined in your little tan Midway booklet.

There is an officer's barber shop in compartment C-227-IL3, it's on the third deck, starboard. We have set up your own clothing and small stores issue room forward on this deck and Sara will take you on a tour this afternoon after lunch to help better orient you to your new temporary home at sea. There is also a crew store for candy and uh, your sundries and other things that you may need. The store also sells chewing gum and bubble gum. We call our ship stores the Geedunk, which is Chinese for… place of idleness."

Glinda clicked rapidly and looked perplexedly at Sara and beamed, "But, I just realized that none of us have any money." Sara smiled and thought back, "It's ok Glinda, all items will be free for all Delphinians."

Glinda clicked impatiently, frowned, shook her head and beamed, "Sara, its always very important to always put in an exchange for all things in this universe. So, we must begin learning about using your money as soon as we can."

Sara remembered the high response ability levels of her aliens thought back, "You are quite right and I shall go to the purser in admin services after this meeting and get paper money and coins to issue to you for all of your people."

Arthur squeaked a laugh as he beamed, "Yeah ok Sara, but, first we have to get some earth cloths like those chambray shirts and dungarees with pockets to hold our money!" The whole pod squeaked and squealed and clicked in delight as Sara, Captain Ciokon and XO Stryker laughed heartily.

Captain Ciokon then stood and said, "Ok thank you XO. My office is also always open to you. It's at frames 178-181; compartment C-213-L. That's on the hanger deck starboard side. We also have a small chaplain's office at 219-IL, but he is not aboard for this, uh… extraordinary mission. There is also a small library at frames 164-175 in compartment C-322-L. Just go to frame 170 on the port side. We also have an excellent dental office with 5 dental chairs and a good dental lab. Sara informs me that all of your health and dental care will be attended to by your own medicos. So we have, for this voyage, opened the forward infirmary and dental clinic to your doctors and nurses for your health needs and care. Sick Bay is located at frames 171-175 in compartment C-320-1L and C-320-5L. It's on the third deck. Just walk inboard to the crew's mess, which is where you are now and then down the hatch at frame 172 to the third deck, turn right and walk athwart ships…"

Selena who was sitting by her best friend whose earth adopted name was Maria, raised her eyebrows, moaned and beamed, "Maria I hope this ho- hum talk will end soon. I really have no idea what he is talking about."

Maria let out a squeaking snigger and beamed, "Meeee toooo Selena, but that sailor we saw at breakfast with that curious red hair was sure cute…I have never seen red hair on anyone. It's like a beautiful orange flame flowing from his head."

Selena squealed and clicked in agreement and said, "I wonder what bubble gum is."

Maria squeaked and beamed, "I think that it is a sweet tasting gum that we can chew and blow bubbles with it." Like that er, cook fella over there is doing.

Selena squeaked and beamed, "Is that like when we blow bubble rings when we are playing while we are swimming underwater?"

Maria just shrugged her shoulders and beamed, "I guess so Selena, we must get some and try it." Maria grinned provocatively and beamed, "Yeah, maybe we can get that cute red headed sailor to show us how to chew it!"

The XO's voice then impinged again on the two teenaged Delphinians as he said, "And finally the tailor shop is a service you will all be using everyday to get your nice new earth clothes fitted and tailored for each of you. In fact we have established six more tailoring shops and four cobblers, er, shoe shops onboard especially for your fittings. Apparently your Delnoid units, just before we land on Water Island, will collect all of your, uh, alien clothing to be returned to your star ship for safekeeping."

Several of the boys and also a few young adult male and female Delphs stood, clicked loudly, whistled and interrupted by beaming to all, "Hey we like our comfortable silver flighter suits."

Glinda stood and as she sternly looked straight back at the juvenile outbursters, they sat meekly and each let out a soft Delphin moan through their blowholes.

Captain Ciokon stood and said, "OK thank you XO. Now I want to tell everyone about a very special ship's service we have at frames 60-67 on the second deck portside. It's the soda fountain where you can, anytime you want, from 13:00 until 21:00 go and enjoy ice cream and cokes." He was then deluged with happy squeals of mirth, excitement and waves of questions about, "What in Amador's name is ice cream?"

Sara, laughing, stood and said to all, "You will love ice-cream and it comes in three different flavors; chocolate, vanilla and strawberry."

With her arms agreeably across her chest Sara grinned and chuckled as she looked over at a gleeful, rather pudgy Delphin boy who had a donut in each hand. She noticed that he had taken a big bite out of one of them and Dear God, it was a peanut crumble donut! She instantly reached over to him and slapped the donut out of his hand and as she did, he squealed and clicked in alarm while looking terrified with wide fearful eyes at her.

Then, his blue eyes rolled up into his head as he squeaked, moaned pitifully clasped at his chest and collapsed. His Delphinian glasses fell off and clattered across the linoleum blue and white checkerd deck and he started convulsing and making whimpering sounds mixed with fading rapid fearful clicking… By then Glinda had joined Sara kneeling beside the stricken youngster and Sara screamed, "Corpsman! Dear God, Jesus! Get us a corpsman!"

After a few minutes, Glinda who had been giving loving and powerful healing energies to the boy's chest put her other hand on Sara's shoulder, moaned, sighed sadly and tearfully beamed, "Oh dear Amador, it's too late Sara. We've lost our little Lonnie…" His mother and father had now run over to their now lifeless son. They dropped to their knees, held him and began rocking him back and forth and letting out pitiful moans and slowly diminishing tears filled clicks. The entire telepathic pod of aliens also had begun muted grief moans and slow clicks. Quickly the intensity of this needless tragedy settled into the telepathic minds of the entire pod as the grief crescendo grew.

Glinda tearfully holding Lonnie's weeping parents in each arm, tearfully and powerfully beamed, "Beloved Delphinians, this loss is terrible, but as you know there will be losses as we bravely re-settle on our new home world. That peanut donut was, I am sure, an accident. So please release any resentment you may have towards this air craft carrier's crew."

Arthur stood, moaned with tears and beamed, "Yes, it was an unfortunate accident but we must, none the less, continue on our brave homecoming."

The Delphin medics carried Lonnie on a Stokes litter down to the infirmary just one deck below. Sara turned to the Captain and cried, "Oh my God Captain! Lonnie just died from eating a peanut donut. Why? How? How in Amador's name did it get into those donut trays? My God Captain, he was only eleven."

Captain Ciokon took the sobbing Sara into his arms and said, "Oh sweet Jesus dear Sara, I am so sorry. Some idiot cook or mess boy screwed up about our absolutely no peanuts orders. We will investigate." He turned toward XO Stryker and said, "Absolutely no more damn donuts in their mess. And I want you to personally oversee that order as well as have the head chef thoroughly and completely search all of their Delphin mess areas. He's to include our officer's mess and the CPO mess at C-301 to remove any and all peanut or peanut based products and alcohol. Then make it crystal clear to all crew, without exception, that our uh, visitors can not be exposed to any peanut products or alcohol of any sort." He, still holding the shaken Sara asked, "Was there only one peanut donut Sara?"

She sobbed, "Yes Captain, I sure hope that was all of them. But, Selena, Delnoid 2F and I will personally search all round and under all of the tables and in all of the donut trays and ovens."

Captain Ciokon still holding the shaken Sara said, "None the less XO, I still want that kitchen thoroughly searched by two different mess crews and also meticulously cleaned from stem to stern. Any and all peanut products and alcohol on board the whole carrier are to be weighted and sealed in 55 gallon water filled drums and dropped overboard ASAP!"

CHAPTER 36 TAPS

That evening at sea the sun serenely sank into the Caribbean with the Atlantic on Midway's port side. All of the Delphins, Captain Ciokon and XO Stryker, Sara and a lone bugler gathered at the sternward edge on the port aircraft elevator at hanger deck level.

As Arthur beamed, Delnoid 1M recited aloud their Delphin life dreams burial prayer: "Beloved Amadores, Creators of space, time and light, precious life and awareness; we bless and release Lonnie as all of his 11 years of life dream mind recordings and his young spirit have now returned to you."

As taps was played by the seaman, Arthur tearfully tilted the burial board and the shrouded weighted body of little Lonnie slipped downward to the waves and eternity on his new but final earth home.

All of the Delphins, shipwide, cried out with heart wrenching moans and slow clicks… Glinda had her arms around Sara, tear-filled Selena and Lonnie's parents. Six Delphinians, three male and three female, sang their own slowly moaning and sadly squealing and low slow clicking haunting Delphin funeral dirge.

Later, after most of the Delphins had left the port aircraft elevator, Sara, Selena, Glinda, Arthur and Lonnie's devastated parents stood at the small and more private starboard side forward of the fantail sponson. As they were sadly looking south westward a darkening twilight settled over the now wavelet capped sea. They quickly began to see a large pod of earthly dolphins swimming and jumping in the phosphorescent wake of Midway's four churning 200,000 HP propellers. And as the earthly dolphins sonic beamed their sadness to the Delphinians on the ship, Glinda just hugged Lonnie's parents as she beamed, "Oh Amador we are all completely connected to these timeless oceans on all life holding planets. We bless and thank you for our homecoming on this magnificent water world."

Glinda squeaked and clicked loudly in alarm as she quickly tried to grab Marina's arms as she wailed and leapt over the small sponson deck safety chain and fell shrieking into the sea 30 feet below. Her husband Kree had been holding her hand, started to follow his life mate overboard.

Arthur gripped him by his arm and passionately beamed, "No! No Kree! No…You must not try to join your little Lonnie in eternity! Some of us over the generations insanely took that final air lock pod family walk into eternity. But Kree, please!" Arthur squeaked and clicked loudly – "Now that we have finally made it here to Earth, on this wonderful water world, we need each and every one of you here as we all must try to come home and survive and multiply in this place we've never been before. Kree, please try to respect that no one is expendable!"

As Arthur beamed that, Sara shouted, "Look" and pointed as one of Lifestar's flighters quickly descended to the darkening sea. The pilot, Ailema switched on her craft's bottom flood lights which instantly turned the night sea surface into day. They then all saw a pod of dolphins and felt their worried sonic beams from the score of anxious dolphins now surrounding Marina and were holding her up.

Arthur, Glinda, Selena, Kree and Sara could see as the 3 person flighter crew quickly put a swimmer into the now more turbulent sea and rescued Marina from a watery grave.

Seeing that his life mate was safe, Kree released his thoughts about jumping and he collapsed into Arthur's arms moaning and clicking. As Glinda looked at Arthur, she nodded, they each took his arms and gently escorted the anguished husband away from the cable barrier of the sponson deck on thru hatch # 2 at 214-2 and up topside onto the giant hanger deck.

Sara, fully in on the telepathic loop from this near tragedy understood completely what almost happened. Selena beckoned Sara to join her as they walked warily hand in hand together behind the anguished Kree.

As the UFO rescue drama unfolded, The XO quickly summoned Captain Ciokon and just after he was summoned, he entered the bridge.

All hands jaws dropped as the 30 feet (10 meter) dark blue Delphinian rescue flighter rose above the port side of the flight deck, hovered and then gently touched down amidship abeam the aircraft carriers island and bridge.

Captain Ciokon and his XO and bridge crew watched, smiled and applauded as they saw the rescued Delphinian woman wrapped in a silver space blanket being led gently down the blue ramp beam from the flighter and into her waiting life mate's arms.

Almost as smoothly as the flighter had landed, it's blue ramp beam flicked off. As the hatch snapped closed, it rapidly twinkled its yellow, red, green blue and white running lights and soared swiftly upward. In next to no time, it became just another faint shooting star against the moon light faded Milky Way arching through the tropical moon and star filled skies overhead.

The captain turned to his bridge watch crew and said, "OK you guys, you never saw that. Remember the articles of the UCMJ you signed and re- signed for this uh, special mission." The four sailors and two ensigns with wide anxious eyes tautly saluted as they incredulously chorused, "Aye, aye sir. Aye, aye."

After Glinda had taken the anguished couple to their Jr. Officers cabin, she deeply sedated Marina and Kree with her powerful mind waves. She, Selena, Sara and Arthur then sat in Sara's office. After they had stopped weeping and moaning again for little Lonnie, Arthur wiped his eyes, put his glasses back on and beamed, "Thank Amador that we were there with them. If not, today would have been a triple tragedy for all of us and an irreplaceable loss for all since our whole pod experienced Marina's frightening plunge and Kree's anguish equally. Tomorrow night we must have a mourning and healing meditation with our whole pod. But for now, we all need and deserve a relaxing coke!"

Sara hugged her dear alien family and said, "I so love each of you and we will do all that we can to prevent any more tragic accidents."

Glinda sighed as she clicked softly and beamed, "Oh my dear Sara, in any brave transitions there will always be casualties. I just pray to Amadores that we can minimize any more losses of the dear and irreplaceable hopes and life dreams of our pod..."

CHAPTER 37 HERE KITTY, KITTY. GATITAAAAAAAA

USS Midway aircraft carrier CVB-41: Wednesday 14 April 1948.

WATER ISLAND landing day. 06:00. 200feet (100 meters) off Flamingo Bay dock with only selected hands preparing for docking.

The specifically selected crew of crane operators and helicopter crews were busy preparing to disembark their Delphinians. At exactly 06:14 - ten minutes after sunrise – suddenly everyone aboard: sailors, officers and Delphinians alike heard in their heads a piercing, panic filled, loud, anguished scream. "Gatitaaaaaaaaa, Oh dear Amador! Where is my Gatita kitty? She's gone! Squeak, squeak, squeak, moan, oh moan, click click click, moan, "She's gone. My little kitty cat, she's gone…"

Glinda, who had just been finishing her early breakfast of toast, coffee and oatmeal with a little bit of butter and orange marmalade stirred in it, dropped her spoon and raced to her daughter's cabin. When she got there Sara was trying to restrain the freaking out Selena in her arms saying, "Oh Selena, I am sure that Gatita has not gone too far. Please don't panic like this. We will find her as soon as we can."

Glinda looked at her anguished daughter and beamed, "When was the last time you saw her?"

Selena trying mostly unsuccessfully to recover her composure squeaked, clicked and worriedly beamed, "Oh mother, I gave her some milk in her cat cage last night just before lights out and now she is gone! She's vanished." Selena squealed and moaned and clicked wildly as she freaked out again and resumed beaming openly to the whole ship, Gatitaaaa! Gatitaaaa, here kitty, kitty. Oh Gatita please come here…"

The panicked Selena was still beaming openly to everyone, and the whole ship's compliment knew without a doubt among any of them that she had lost her cat. Glinda realized that Selena had totally lost control of her selective beaming. She grabbed her anguished daughter, looked her directly in the eyes and beamed, "If you cannot control your selective beaming, I will have to put you into a deep sleep! So stop beaming to Amador and everyone aboard. Please! You have to control yourself!"

Selena looking fearfully at her mother, sobbed, nodded and beamed, "But, squeal, moan, click, click, click, click, click, My Gatita is gone…"

Glinda placed her palms on each side of Selena's head and powerfully beamed, "One…Two….Three…Selena stop it!"

Selena looked anxiously at her mother beamed, "Ok, ok… ok mother, I will try to limit my cat calls…" She, with her mother's strong and caring but absolutely commanding love energies, was able to finally focus her frantic beaming to just her pod and Sara and hopefully to Gatita too.

After the shrill bosom's pipe sounded from the bridge through the entire ship's PA system, announced, "Now hear this! Now hear this. Apparently the little kitten of one of our, uh guests has run off. All crew please keep a sharp look out for a little black kitten with green eyes as you continue your duties. That is all!"

As usual, whenever the bosom's pipe sounded, its shrill notes always caused all the Delphinians to frantically cover their ears with their hands. Somehow the frequency of that traditional navy pipe utterly throbbed their supersensitive ears and brains.

As Arthur, Glinda and Selena judiciously lowered their hands from their ears, Arthur moaned, squeaked, clicked in sufferance and beamed, "Dang… that little pipe sure shatters my whole melon and brain!"

Glinda still holding her hands over her ears, moaned and nodded in agreement as Sara said, "Me too… It's so shrill, but I guess it had to be in order to get sailors attention back in the old days at sea." As she removed her index fingers from each ear, Sara exclaimed, "And these days it's even louder through the ship's modern PA speakers."

Selena dressed and as she rushed out of her cabin door she beamed, "Oh beloved Amador, I have got to go look for Gatita! Mr. Hemingway's cat means so much to me and he would just die if he knew that I lost his kitten."

Sara looked frenziedly at Glinda and Arthur and as she rushed after Selena said, "Please continue with the disembarkation. I will help Selena hopefully find her dear kitten as soon as we can…We will get a Marine corpsman to guide us through these endless maze of corridors and hatches."

As Selena and Sara were searching and calling for Gatita for about an half an hour up and down the endless corridors of B deck; all the while Selena was beaming out her special love energies to call her kitty.

The ships PA system then announced, "Will Commander Winchester please report to the bridge immediately." Sara put her hand on Selena's shoulder and said, "As you can hear, the captain wants me topside pronto. Will you be ok to continue searching with corporal Russo for now?"

Selena took her earth mentors hand and beamed forlornly, "Oh yes Sara, I will be ok and I can reach you or mom telepathically if I need you."

Fifteen minutes later Selena beamed to her mother, "Mom, I feel Gatita's energies, but she must be so scared and lost or trapped somewhere. If only we could somehow use our echolocation to find her."

Arthur beamed in, "Princess you are quite right. That is exactly what we must do. Mom and I will join you now. Where exactly in this endless maze of bulkheads, corridors and hatchways are you?"

Selena looked at her handsome marine escort and tapped his arm and half raised her arms and eyebrows in a questioning gesture…. She pointed to the black letter location sign on the wall and the Marine smiled and said, "Oh, You want to know where we are on the ship do you? Well, miss we are now in the corridor C-0100L on portside, near the hanger portside C104C # 3 aircraft fire control booth."

As he said that, the marine tentatively touched Selena's shoulder to reassure her and as soon as he did, she burst into tears and thought to him, "Oh thank you, thank you. I need my parents here to help us locate my kitty." Lance Corporal Russo was totally taken aback by receiving the lovely princesses' thoughts being beamed into him. He also then felt her fear and sadness, put his arm around her to comfort her. Selena read his caring thoughts and intentions put her right arm around him as she clicked softly, squeaked and sniveled some more.

As soon as Glinda and Arthur received Selena's location beams they also read her exchanges with her marine escort. Glinda started running as she beamed, "Oh Amador Arthur, she is so upset that she is revealing our telepathy to her marine escort."

Arthur now running beamed, " Glinda, Glinda…Calm down! As soon as we get to her, I can erase all of his memories about this uh too close for comfort contact of the Delphinian Princess kind in an aircraft carrier maze."

After Glinda and Arthur arrived at passage C-0100L, they found Selena hugging the young handsome marine as she tried to comfort her homesick escort.

As soon as Glinda sensed what was going on she gently but firmly pushed the marine towering over her daughter away and nodded to Arthur who simply placed his palm on the left side of the marine's face and wiped out his memories for the last half an hour. He looked shaken but was totally happy and relaxed as he said, "Oh gosh dear visitors, I hope we can find your kitty cat." Arthur just waved his hand and indicated for the marine to leave them alone.

Selena wiped her eyes and beamed, "Oh mother what am I going to do? I simply cannot leave this aircraft carrier unless I find Gatita!"

Arthur turned to Selena and Glinda and beamed, "OK, if we spread out a bit and each use our sonic echo location we can perhaps triangulate on Gatita's location as she responds to Selena's love energy probes."

After about five minutes of the three aliens echoing with their sonics for location, Selena beamed, "Oh Amador, she is right near here." As the alien trio breathlessly exited the hanger deck door they sensed that Gatita was in of all places, the fire control observation station number 3 half way up the port side of the hanger deck.

Arthur and Glinda with Selena joyfully sprinting well ahead of them quickly found the hatch to the narrow stairs which ran up to the thick windowed fire control station. When Glinda and Arthur finally got there, they found Selena grabbing a young red haired sailor's sleeve as she openly beamed to him, "That's my kitty and you can't keep her."

The young sailor was in tears as he cried, "Oh, but I found this kitten when I came on duty two hours ago and I love this cat. She so reminds me of my kitty Pyeracat back home in Iowa. I miss her so."

Just then SCPO Spillama and XO Stryker entered the crowded fire control center and as soon as Stryker realized what was going on, he snapped, "Seaman Jones, give the kitten back." He picked up the wall phone and called for the SP's to come and arrest Jones. "Mr., that cat belongs to a very important, uh visitor aboard and why young sir, did you not call and advise us that you had found the kitten?"

The obviously distraught and totally homesick sailor wailed, "Oh Sir, I am so sorry. When that little kitten came out from under the FSP console here and jumped up in my lap, I started petting her. I felt almost like…"

"Like what sailor?" demanded the XO. "Well sir, it was like this kitten was sending out some kind of love energies and I just could not help loving her." He turned to Selena tearfully holding her kitten and said, "Oh miss, I am so sorry I overreacted about your kitten. I think it must be a very special kind of kitten indeed." When the SP reached to cuff the boy, Glinda put her hand on the XO's arm and beamed privately to him and her family, "Frank, please let him go. I think it's understandable that such almost uncontrollable homesickness might have been stimulated by Luna's, uh, special kitten."

XO Stryker stiffened and said, "But uh your Majesty, this sailor disobeyed a ship wide command to look for the kitten and he should of course called us as soon as he found your kitten."

Arthur touched the XO's arm and with Glinda, both beamed loving and forgiving energies into him. The XO smiled as he said, "Well, I imagine lots of galley and deck work duties will remind this sailor to follow orders in future."

Glinda smiled and reached over and hugged the now totally frustrated and bewildered boy. As she hugged him, she beamed loving and caring motherly love energies and as she did so, Arthur touched the right side of his head with his palm and erased his memories of the event.

As the lad then stood there, he blinked twice and stammered, "Say, who are you? What are you doing in this hanger fire control center? No one except duty staff is allowed up here."

The XO said, "At ease lad. It's ok now sailor, at ease and as you were."

The erased sailor then noticed the black kitten that still tearful Selena had in her arms and said, "Oh my goodness sir." "She looks just like my Pyeracat back home in Iowa…"

Selena, Gatita, Arthur and Glinda followed CPO Spillman back to their quarters deck. Glinda privately beamed to Selena, Sara and Arthur. "Hummmm, it looks like all of the petting and love energies that Selena has been beaming to Gatita since March may actually be changing her little cat's brain waves and love energy output."

At 18:36 the sun was sinking into the sea after the long 12 hour and 32 minute tropical day. All of the Delphinians stood on the dock with their suitcases and blue backpacks as the gangway and the heavy mooring hawsers were slipped up from the dock's bollards and hauled up by their capstans back aboard the carrier.

Captain Ciokon blasted three times on the one octave ship's horn. The Delphinians all waved good bye as Selena kept her petting finger in Gatita's cage to calm the sensitive kitten as the ship's horn sounded for sail away.

CHAPTER 38 DELPHIN DOLPHIN REUNION

In just a very short time the Delphinians had comfortably settled on Water Island. They enjoyed swimming and frollicing each morning before their social classes and orientation practices, with a few of their dolphin cousins in the warm azure, west facing Limestone Bay and its Honeymoon Beach which was 536 feet long with pure white sand. Sometimes in the late afternoons, near sunset at 7pm, they would again enjoy their friendships and sharing their life dreams with their earthly dolphin cousins.

Soon, more and more dolphins, got the news about these marvelous humanoids who shared their spirituality and could converse with them, would come to visit the Delphinians each day. And, of course, just like humans would understandably gather to galk at any alien visitor, there were, by the end of April, 1948, hundreds of the aliens' dolphin earth cousins swimming, squeaking, squealing, clicking and sonic beaming while visiting and frolicking with the Delphinianians. The earth dolphins would also bring fish and squid to their alien cousins.

Early, at about 6am, Sunday May 16th 1948, Sara and Selena were awakened by the sound of gunfire coming from the small 65 feet beach facing Limestone Bay. Alarmed, they pulled on their shorts and ran down to find four sailors and two marines using their rifles to shoot at the dolphins nearby in the bay. Soon Arthur and Glinda ran up next to Sara who was shouting, " Stop shooting, Those are dolphins !" Selena was franticaly squeaking moaning and clicking as she beamed the same to the rifelmen. Arthur immediately sent a powerfull sonic beam to the sailors 60 yards away. As he did so, the six shooters instantly dropped unconscious to the ground.

Sara was flabbergasted as she saw this first demonstration of Arthur's incredible sonic alien powers. She desperatly asked, "What are you going to do Arthur?" By then Delnoid 1 had arrived and he beamed to Arthur.

Arthur nodded his head towards the sailors. Sara screamed, "Oh no Arthur, please don't kill them!"

Delnoid picked up their rifles and in wrath threw them one by one, an astounding 10 yards (8 meters) out into the bay. Then, before each sailor woke up, Delnoid, under the command of Arthur, completely erased the memories of the incident and the shooting from the minds of these heartless humans who had killed so many dolphins.

Selena and Glinda had stripped off their flipper covers and ran into the water. Sara then saw them swimming near a small pod of dolphin leaders - as if by magic - most all of the dolphins began swimming hastily away from the bay and back out to sea.

Selena and Glinda returned to the beach and sat breathlessly down next to Sara. Selena and Glinda were in tears and moaning from their blowholes and Selena finally managed, between her cries of anguish, to beam to Sara, "They horribly wounded 12 of our kind Sara and killed 7. They heartlessly just shot them dead…"

The dolphin leaders had beamed about the horrible hunting and fishing of their species and now, since WWII, he also raged about all of the deadly toxic chemicals now spreading throughout all of the oceans of earth that were, each year, killing thousands of newborn, young and older dolphins.

One of the dolphin alpha male leaders had beamed, "If we could walk and make guns or weapons like the mines the navy has strapped on some of our drafted dolphins; we would declare war on these ignorant humans who are destroying us and vast numbers of other marine life and polluting our oceans!"

Sara, then fully grasping the dolphin and planetary harm and destruction, looked at Selena and said, "I shall call President Truman immediately and have him stop all military experiments on dolphins and have him also make the navy free all impressed dolphins and … Selena, as you study in California… if you wish, I definatly will try to see to it that you become our dolphin ambassador!"

Selena beamed through her moans of grief and outrage, "Yes Sara, I want to be just that to try to stop this lunacy of ignorant humans destroying dolphin life dreams along with the oceans and the ecological enviroments on their own world!"

Sara then suggested that perhaps only 25 or 30 dolphin visitors a day would better keep from arousing more local curiosities and suspicions….

Delnoid glowered and beamed, "Sara, tell their Captain Tamarynd that they must never again shoot at our people, uh that is our dolphins."

Arthur and Glinda put their arms around Selena and Sara with soothing love energies and then Arthur beamed, "Maybe the Amadores also brought us to this magnificient world to also try to stop your ignorance and disrespect of the interconnectivness of all things Sara."

Sara cried as she said, "Oh Arthur… I am so ashamed for this destruction today and I will do all I can with President Truman to begin to stop this insanity and disrespect and destruction of other intelligent specie's life dreams."

CHAPTER 39 SAIL AWAY
NOVEMBER 25TH 1948 THANKSGIVING DAY

After a hectic day of reloading their supplies and Water Island equipment and precious life dreams back aboard the USS Midway. And after the magnificent aircraft carrier had let go its lines. Capt Joe Ciokon sounded his horn as Midway manuvred away from the Flamingo Bay dock to take his Delphinians to the Naval port at Galveston Texas to board their special Army train for their new base at Army Camp Roberts in Central coastal California.

After a welcome back aboard special Thanks Giving day banquette in the forward mess hall. The newly oriented and trained Delphins and Capt. Ciokon and XO Stryker sat just relexing and sipping Cokes. Glinda beamed to her delphs, Sara and the Capt and XO. Well… As we sail away this early evening towards our new life and dreams in California. It is indeed appropriate that we give thanks to all of you for your help and training. Amadore and God willing we shall soon arrive at Camp Roberts to really fully learn how to live on Earth. So let us all now give thanks to Amadore and to whoever or what ever you precieve the Creator to be. Her thanks was greeted with squeaks, clicks and claps from the humans present. As all of the Delphs saw the clapping they too joined in and everybody clapped for eachother.

Later that tropical evening, Arthur, Glinda, Selena and Sara were just relaxing and sitting on the fantail watching the ever dimming sky swallow the horizon and wake behind them.

Delnoid 1 then decided it was time to again show off his knowledge as he said to all "We are now on a more or less direct heading of 297.74 deg towards Galveston Texas. We now have 2,168.7 miles to go at our current cruising speed of 35 miles per hour…

Arthur waved his hand and Del looking crushed as usual when cut off just stood beside his leaders as they began sharing their hopes, dreams and fears about the coming chapters and books ahead.

Glinda moaned, clicked softly and beamed, "Let us now remember those we have lost so far on this homecoming saga. The fifth generation elder, Little Lonnie and back on Water island tragically last September 22nd. Four of our precious Delphinians were killed, hacked with machetes as evil devils by some Voodoo worshipers at Sandy Beach on the north west side of St. Thomas." Our unfortunate poodsters forgot about concealing their feet. When the already frenzied and hallucinating tribe making a Miami Wata voodoo ceremony on the beach that night saw their feet. They thought that they were evil spirits and the two pregnant females and their husbands were hacked with machetes before their security contingent of two SP's and Delnoid 3 or even their protective scout flighter 125 miles overhead could get to them…

Delnoid 3, who was along for their security and to record local activities and events, had to put up a force field to then stop the Navy shore patrol sailors from shooting all of the insane voodoo's. As it was. The sailors had wounded three of the Voodoos. Later that night our Delphinian scout flighter descended and retrieved the bodies.

So, at least let us now give thanks to Amadores with prayers for our safety and survival now that we are only 153 remaining after six generations across endless space and time to accomplish our homecoming. Amadore only knows how many more will perish in our quest to sustain our race and life dreams in California.

Arthur, Selena and Sara then just hugged Glinda as the stars of space and time twinkled across the Milky Way and uncaringly shone on forever.

CHAPTER 40 CLICKETY CLACK - DON'T LOOK BACK DEL 5M SWEATS IT

Aboard the Presidential railway car, Ferdinand Magellan: 11:59 pm September 19, 1948

In the rear lounge car of the amazing 285,000 pound (129,274 kg) 142 ton car with rail steel reinforced bomb proof concrete undercarriage and one inch steel armor plate and 3 inch thick bullet proof windows, sat President Truman, his daughter Margaret and Delnoid 5. Truman's wife Bess had retired to the First Ladies bedroom B right after their short stumping whistle stop in Junction City, Kansas. The train was flying westward, zinging and clicking almost as rapidly as a dolphin, on the full moon lit steel rails. Harry Truman just sat there fully concentrating on his speech notes for the next campaign stop scheduled in Denver, Colorado at noon on the 20th.

Delnoid 5M uncharacteristically nervously glanced over at Margaret who was sitting, reading, mouthing and humming some of her singing music sheets. He then stood and anxiously tapped the President on his shoulder and beamed so as not to alarm Margaret, "Mr. Truman, I think that you should look at the speedometer above Margaret's chair sir!"

When Harry looked up, his jaw dropped at the indicated 105 mph (169 kph) velocity that they were now dashing through the night over the seemingly endless moon lit Kansas plains. He then looked astoundedly back at Delnoid and said, "Why my goodness gracious Del yes, you are quite right that we are going way too fast." He quickly picked up the phone he said, "I shall have the train Captain tell the engineer to slow down to no more than 80 miles per hour."

Before the president had agreed to slow down, Delnoid 5 who could no longer stand the apprehension was thinking and beaming to Lifestar. "Oh my dear Amador, I have traveled in our starship at point three of the speed of light and also without any concern in our flighters which these earthlings call flying saucers and also somewhat fretfully in their primitive helicopter contraptions with President Truman; and never in my 106 years of awareness and life have I ever been this terrified."

His female counterpart Delnoid F5 in Lifestar 200 miles overhead beamed back to her beloved. "Oh Del, please make them slow down my droid. If something happened, your heavily armored Presidential car would simply crush all sixteen of the cars ahead between you and the steam engine."

Del continued, "Yes, and there are about 100 people on board plus the train crew, military guards, reporters and other, uh security personnel like me!"

After Harry had put down the phone, the train began to slow and as the President looked at Delnoid, he actually saw him sweating and still looking really worried. Harry reached out and laid his hand on his android helper's arm and said, "Well I am glad that you alerted me to the excessive speed Del. We certainly don't want to get in a train wreck before I am re-elected." Truman then grinned as he said, "But none the less my dear Droid, it's really great to see that your sweat gland growth salve is working successfully!"

They averaged eight whistle stops day and night at villages, small, medium, and big city stumping stops. As Harry Truman instinctually and politically knew, his only chance of winning re-election lay in the common folk and vets who fought in the war and now farmed and worked across the USA. He relentlessly admonished the do nothing 80th congress and asked people to vote to re-elect him; he criss crossed the USA from Washington, DC for two months going through 30 states and covering 30,000 miles.

There were two 24 hour diner cars and three lounge cars as well as a press car equipped with a radio telephone and teletypes. The deluxe Presidential Ferdinand Magellan car was one of six other deluxe private cars owned by the Pullman Co. They were all named after famous explorers. In 1942, the car had been completely remodeled for President Franklin Roosevelt.

The remodeled Presidential car had four bedrooms, a dining room and the rear observation lounge where the President could step out through the armored rear door onto the rear platform to address voters during whistle stops. Without it and the Delphinians, President Harry Truman, the 33rd President of the United States could not have won re-election in 1948.

CHAPTER 41 INAUGURATION DAY

Thursday, January 20th 1949

South Portico, United States Capitol

Very cold 32 degrees F (0c) with a stiff freezing wind out of the north 100 % blue skies and cold sunshine.

The newly re-elected 33rd President, 64 year old Harry Truman stood on the inaugural platform outside the US Capitol building. He had been receiving the Delphinian's caring, supportive, empowering and loving energies since March, 1948. He was an almost completely changed, new, confident, positive, dynamic energy and happy man.

He removed his top hat, scarf and overcoat and raised his right hand as Chief Justice Vinson administered the forty-three word oath of office. Harry laid his left hand on top of two bibles. One had been used during his traumatic swearing in a lifetime of four years ago on April 12th, 1945, just six hours after President Roosevelt had died and the other bible, a large facsimile of the Gutenberg bible which was a gift from the people in his hometown of Independence, Missouri.

It was 1:29 pm after the swearing in and the now again President Truman passionately and gratefully faced the Washington record breaking crowd who had gladly braved the cold - estimated to be more than one million people.

There were also more than 10 million coast to coast TV viewers of this, the first Presidential Inauguration to be broadcast on national TV. There were also an estimated 100 million radio listeners.

"I accept with humility the honor which the American people have conferred on me. I accept it with resolve to do all I can for the welfare of this nation and for the peace of the world."

He then paused, turned and smiled knowingly and proudly at Sara looking fantastically smart in her Navy Commanders uniform. He thought upward to Arthur, Glinda and Selena. "And also with heartfelt thanks and blessings now for your priceless spirit, light and healings for all mankind."

He, Sara and Delnoid 5 heard in their heads, "Mr. President we thank you for your true and ceaseless efforts to bring us to Earth. And we are so relieved and happy now that you have been re-elected for the next four years. We can now securely and confidently continue our orientations, training and re-settlement in California. By the way Harry, each and every one of us has now agreed to try to remain in the USA so that we may always help you in all ways that we can."

Arthur then squealed and sniggered, "Also just as we have helped you to get re-elected."

Hearing this, Harry cracked an irrepressible smile and thought back to his aliens. "Ok, ok, but uh, all that you and my Delnoid did was, er, to read the voters' minds, er, that is intentions. And thanks to you, after all, I got 49% of the popular vote and a landslide of 303 electoral votes." He grinned, chuckled and thought, "But, from now on this will be our uh, alien top secret! And, Selena's ingenious idea for my Presidential campaign comic book was brilliant. We distributed 3 million of them to all possible working folk voters."

As the newly renewed in office and in spirit, Harry Truman, neared the end of his carefully written and practiced inauguration speech, he said, "The future of mankind is at stake and democracy is the vitalizing force in our world. The American people have stood firm in the faith that has inspired the nation from its beginning in 1776. Americans are united in the belief that all men have a right to equal justice under the law and equal opportunities to share in the common good."

Harry then thought to his aliens, "And you too, as long as I have anything to say about it, you too shall always enjoy these earthly human rights."

He turned to the crowd, the TV cameras and radio microphones and went on to conclude by saying, "The old imperialism – exploitation for national and foreign profit has no place in our future. More than half the people in our world are living in misery and life dream killing, poverty."

As he again briefly looked skyward visioning the Delphinian starship stationed 125 miles overhead, he smiled and confidently said, "For the first time in earth history; the knowledge, skills and technology are becoming available for us to educate and help us better understand how to relieve suffering and poverty."

He again glanced briefly skyward, looked back at the crowd and concluded, "The future emphasis must be on knowledge, and technologies with humane motives rather than on ego and greed based blood money profits."

Then, the roar of 200 military planes crossed the clear blue Washington skies along with 5 gigantic six engine B-36 bombers that had flown 2000 miles from their Texas base. As the trailing B-36's passed overhead, Harry and Sara perceived Embry beaming, "Ailema says those new piston jet bombers are sure remarkable… but now… watch this."

Ailema then lowered their flighter to an altitude of 26,000 feet in the 40F temperature and released a 100 feet (30 meters) wide streaming red white and blue, contrail which stretched 600 miles (960km), almost from horizon to horizon above the frosty capitol.

As the astonished crowd looked up and saw the spectacular red white and blue rainbow display, the lookit's and the oooohs and the ahhhh's and the oh my goshes were echoing everywhere and the applause was thunderous and relentless.

One of the perplexed and awed navy admirals turned to Sara and asked, "Commander, now what the heck do you suppose that was?"

Sara sniggered and replied, "Well sir, it must of been one of our new high altitude navy jets or just maybe… one of those dang UFO's we've been seeing and hearing so much about ever since Roswell.

WWW.DELPHINHOMECOMING.COM

289